About the Authors

Rebecca Winters lives in Salt Lake City, Utah. With canyons and high alpine meadows full of wildflowers, she never runs out of places to explore. They, plus her favourite holiday spots in Europe, often end up as backgrounds for her romance novels because writing is her passion, along with her family and church. Rebecca loves to hear from readers. If you wish to e-mail her, please visit her website at: www.cleanromances.net

Marion Lennox is a country girl, born on an Australian dairy farm. She moved on, because the cows just weren't interested in her stories! Married to a 'very special doctor', she has also written under the name Trisha David. She's now stepped back from her 'other' career teaching statistics. Finally, she's figured what's important and discovered the joys of baths, romance and chocolate. Preferably all at the same time! Marion an international award winning author.

Raye Morgan has been a nursery-school teacher, a travel agent, a clerk and a business editor, but her best job ever has been writing romances – and fostering romance in her own family at the same time. Current score: two boys married, two more to go. Raye has published more than seventy romances, and claims to have many more waiting in the wings. She lives on the Central California Coast with her husband.

D0682808

The Princes

COLLECTION

An Heir for the Prince

REBECCA WINTERS

MARION LENNOX

RAYE MORGAN

MIX
Paper from
responsible sources
FSC
FSC C007454

This book is produced from independently certified FSC™ paper
to ensure responsible forest management.

For more information visit www.harpercollins.co.uk/green

Printed and bound in Spain
by CPI, Barcelona

MILLS & BOON

All rights reserved including the right of reproduction in whole or
in part in any form. This edition is published by arrangement with
Harlequin Books S.A.

This is a work of fiction. Names, characters, places, locations and
incidents are purely fictional and bear no relationship to any real
life individuals, living or dead, or to any actual places, business
establishments, locations, events or incidents. Any resemblance is
entirely coincidental.

This book is sold subject to the condition that it shall not, by
way of trade or otherwise, be lent, resold, hired out or otherwise
circulated without the prior consent of the publisher in any form
of binding or cover other than that in which it is published and
without a similar condition including this condition being imposed
on the subsequent purchaser.

® and TM are trademarks owned and used by the trademark owner
and/or its licensee. Trademarks marked with ® are registered
with the United Kingdom Patent Office and/or the Office for
Harmonisation in the Internal Market and in other countries.

First Published in Great Britain 2020
By Mills & Boon, an imprint of HarperCollins*Publishers*
1 London Bridge Street, London, SE1 9GF

AN HEIR FOR THE PRINCE © 2020 Harlequin Books S.A.

A Bride for the Island Prince © 2012 Rebecca Winters
Betrothed: To the People's Prince © 2009 Marion Lennox
Crown Prince, Pregnant Bride! © 2011 Helen Conrad

ISBN: 978-0-263-28078-4

0220

**DUDLEY
LIBRARIES**

000003037591	
Askews & Holts	23-Jan-2020
AF ROM	£7.99
2DU	

A BRIDE FOR THE ISLAND PRINCE

REBECCA WINTERS

I'd like to dedicate this book to JULIE the speech therapist at the elementary school. With her sunny smile and dedication, she helped my children work through a difficult period for them and I'll always be grateful.

CHAPTER ONE

PRINCE Alexius Kristof Rudolph Stefano Valleder Constantinides, Duke of Aurum and second in line to the throne of Hellenica, had been working in his office all morning when he heard a rap on the door. "Yes?" he called out.

"Your Highness? If I might have a word with you?"

"What is it, Hector?" The devoted assistant to the crown poked his head in the door. Hector, who'd been the right hand to Alex's father and grandfather, had been part of the palace administrative staff for over fifty years. He knew better than to disturb Alex unless it was urgent. "I'm reading through some important contracts. Can't this wait until after lunch?"

"The national head of the hospital association is here and most eager to thank you for the unprecedented help you've given them to build four new hospitals our country has needed so badly. Would it be possible for you to give him a little of your time?"

Alex didn't have to think about it. Those facilities should have been built long before now. Better health care for everyone was something he felt strongly about. "Yes. Of course. Show him to the dining room and I'll be there shortly."

"He'll be very pleased. And now, one other matter, Your Highness."

"Then come all the way in, Hector."

The substantial-looking man whose salt-and-pepper hair was thinning on top did Alex's bidding. "The queen instructed me to tell you that Princess Zoe has had another of her moments this morning." In other words, a temper tantrum.

He lifted his dark head. His four-year-old daughter meant more to him than life itself. For this reason he was alarmed by the change in her behavior that was making her more and more difficult to deal with.

Unfortunately the queen wasn't well, and Alex had to shoulder his elder brother Stasio's royal responsibilities while he was out of the country. He knew none of this was helping his daughter.

For the past four months her meltdowns had been growing worse. He'd been through three nannies in that period. At the moment Alex was without one for her. In desperation he'd turned to Queen Desma, his autocratic grandmother, who, since the death of his grandfather, King Kristof, was the titular head of Hellenica, a country made up of a cluster of islands in the Aegean and Thracian seas.

She had a soft spot for her great-granddaughter and had asked one of her personal maids, Sofia, to look after her until a new nanny could be found. What his grandmother really wanted was for Alex to take a new wife. Since by royal decree he could only marry another princess, rather than being able to choose a bride from any background, Alex had made the decision never to marry again. One arranged marriage had been enough.

Lately Zoe had been spending most of her time in the

quarters of her great-grandmother, who'd been trying in her unsubtle way to prepare Zoe for a new mother. The queen had been behind the match between Alex and his deceased wife, Teresa. Both women were from the House of Valleder.

Now, with Teresa gone, his grandmother had been negotiating with the House of Helvetia for a marriage between her grandson and the princess Genevieve, but her machinations were wasted on Alex.

"I had breakfast with her earlier this morning and she seemed all right. What happened to set her off with Sofia?"

"Not Sofia," he clarified. "But two new situations *have* arisen. If I may speak frankly."

Only two? Alex ground his teeth in worry and frustration. He'd had hopes this was a phase that would pass, but the situation was growing worse. "You always do."

"Her new American tutor, Dr. Wyman, just handed in his notice, and her Greek tutor, Kyrie Costas, is threatening to resign. As you know, the two have been at odds with each other over the proper curriculum for the princess. Dr. Wyman is out in the hall. Before he leaves the palace, he requests a brief audience with you."

Alex got to his feet. Two weeks ago he'd been forced to withdraw her from the preschool classes she went to three times a week because her teacher couldn't get her to participate. Fearing something was physically wrong with Zoe, he'd asked his personal physician to give her a thorough examination. But the doctor had found nothing wrong.

Now her English tutor had resigned? Alex's wife, who'd spent a portion of her teenage years in America, had died of a serious heart condition. Before passing away she'd made him promise Zoe would grow up to be fluent in English. He'd done everything in his power to honor her wishes, even hiring an American tutor. Alex himself made an effort to speak English with her every day.

He took a fortifying breath. "Show him in."

The forty-year-old American teacher had come highly recommended after leaving the employ of Alex's second cousin, King Alexandre Philippe of Valleder, a principality bordering the Romanche-speaking canton of Switzerland. No longer needing a tutor for his son, the king, who was best friends with Alex's brother, had recommended Dr. Wyman to come to Hellenica and teach Zoe.

"Your Highness." He bowed.

"Dr. Wyman? Hector tells me you've resigned. Is my daughter truly too difficult for you to handle any longer?"

"Lately it's a case of her running away when she sees me," he answered honestly. "It's my opinion she's frightened about something and hardly speaks at all. What comes out I don't understand. Mr. Costas says it's my method, but I disagree. Something's wrong, but I'm only a teacher."

Since Zoe's medical exam, Alex had considered calling in a child psychiatrist for a consultation. Dr. Wyman said she was frightened. Alex agreed. This behavior wasn't normal. So far he'd thought it was a case of arrested development because Zoe had been born premature. But maybe not having a mother had brought on psychological problems that hadn't been recognizable until now.

"If she were your child, what would you do?"

"Well, I think before I took her to a child psychologist, I'd find out if there's a physiological problem that is preventing her from talking as much as she should. If so, maybe that's what is frightening her."

"Where could I go for that kind of expertise?"

"The Stillman Institute in New York City. Their clinic has some of the best speech therapists in the United States. I'd take my child there for an evaluation."

"I'll look into it. Thank you for your suggestion and your help with Princess Zoe, Dr. Wyman. I appreciate your honesty. You leave the palace with my highest recommendation."

"Thank you, Your Highness. I hope you get answers soon. I'm very fond of her."

So am I.

After Dr. Wyman left, Alex checked his watch. By the time he'd had lunch with the head of the hospital association, the clinic in New York would be open. Alex would call and speak to the director.

Dottie Richards had never ridden in a helicopter before. After her jet had touched down in Athens, Greece, she was told it was just a short journey to Hellenica.

The head of the Stillman Speech Institute had picked her to handle an emergency that had arisen. Apparently there was an important little four-year-old girl who needed diagnostic testing done ASAP. A temporary visa had been issued for Dottie to leave the country without having to wait the normal time for a passport.

For security reasons, she hadn't learned the identity of the little girl until she was met at the helicopter pad in Athens by a palace spokesman named Hector. Apparently the child was Princess Zoe, the only daugh-

ter of Prince Alexius Constantinides, a widower who
was acting ruler of Hellenica.

"Acting ruler, you say?"

"Yes, madame. The heir apparent to the throne,
Crown Prince Stasio, is out of the country on busi-
ness. When he returns, he will be marrying Princess
Beatriz. Their wedding is scheduled for July the fifth.
At that time the dowager queen Desma, Princess Zoe's
great-grandmother, will relinquish the crown and Prince
Stasio will become king of Hellenica.

"In the meantime Prince Alexius is handling the
daily affairs of state. He has provided his private helicopter so you can be given a sightseeing trip to the palace, located on the biggest island, also called Hellenica."

Dottie realized this was a privilege not many people
were granted. "That's very kind of him." She climbed
aboard and the helicopter took off, but the second it
left the ground she grew dizzy and tried to fight it off.
"Could you tell me what exactly is wrong with Princess
Zoe?"

"That's a subject for you to discuss with the prince
himself."

Uh-oh. "Of course."

Dottie was entering a royal world where silence was
the better part of discretion. No doubt that was why
Hector had been chosen for this duty. She wouldn't
guess the older man was the type to leave the royal
household and write a book revealing the dark secrets of
the centuries-old Constantinides family. Dottie admired
his loyalty and would have told him so, but by then she
was starting to experience motion sickness from the
helicopter and was too nauseated to talk any more.

Several years earlier, Dottie had seen pictures of

the Constantinides brothers on various television news broadcasts. Both had playboy reputations, like so many royal sons. They'd been dark and attractive enough, but seen in the inside of a limo or aboard a royal yacht, it was difficult to get a real sense of their looks.

Dottie had never been anywhere near a royal and knew nothing about their world except for their exposure in the media, which didn't always reflect positively. But for an accident of birth, she could have been born a princess. Anyone could be. Royals were human beings after all. They entered the world, ate, slept, married and died like the rest of humanity. It was what they did, where they did it and how they did it that separated them from the masses.

Raised by a single aunt, now deceased, who'd never married and had been a practical thinker, Dottie's world hadn't included many fairy tales. Though there'd been moments growing up when Dottie had been curious about being a queen or a princess. Now an unprecedented opportunity had arisen for her to find out what that was like.

Dottie had seen and heard enough about royals involved in escapades and scandals to feel sorry for them. The trials of being an open target to the world had to be worse than those of a celebrity, whose popularity waxed strong for a time in the eyes of public adulation and curiosity, then waned out of sight.

A royal stayed a royal forever and was scrutinized ad nauseum. A prince or princess couldn't even be born or die without a crowd in attendance. But as Dottie had learned during an early period in her life, the trials of an ordinary human were sometimes so bad they drew unwanted attention from the public, too. Like with King

George VI of England, her own severe stuttering problem had been an agony to endure. However, to be human and a royal at the same time placed one in double jeopardy.

At the age of twenty-nine and long since free of her former speech problem, Dottie loved her anonymity. In that sense she felt compassion for the little princess she hadn't even met yet. The poor thing was already under a microscope and would remain there for all the days of life she was granted. Whether she had a speech problem or something that went deeper, word would get out.

One day when the motherless princess was old enough to understand, she'd learn the world was talking about her and would never leave her alone. If she had a physical or a noticeable psychological problem, the press would be merciless. Dottie vowed in her heart she'd do whatever possible to help the little girl, *if* it were in her power.

But at the moment the helicopter trip was playing havoc with her stomach and the lovely sightseeing trip had been wasted on her. The second they landed and she was shown to her quarters in the glistening white royal palace, she lost any food she'd eaten and went straight to bed.

It was embarrassing, but when she was green around the gills and unable to rally, nothing except a good night's sleep would help her to recover. When her business was finished here and she left the country to go back to the States, she would take a flight from Hellenica's airport to Athens before boarding a flight to New York. No more helicopter rides.

* * *

Alex eyed his ailing, widowed grandmother, whose silvery hair was still thick at eighty-five. She tired more easily these days and kept to her apartment. Alex knew she was more than ready for Stasio to come home and officially take the worries of the monarchy from her shoulders.

No one awaited Stasio's return with more eagerness than Alex. When his brother had left on the first of April, he'd promised to be home by mid-May, yet it was already the thirtieth with his wedding only five weeks away. Alex needed out of his temporary responsibilities to spend more time with Zoe. He'd built up his hopes that this speech therapist could give him definitive answers. It would be a step in the right direction; his daughter was growing unhappier with each passing day.

"Thank you for breakfast," he said in Greek. "If you two will excuse me, I have some business, but I'll be back." He kissed his petite daughter, who was playing with her roll instead of eating it. "Be good for *Yiayia*."

Zoe nodded.

After bowing to his grandmother, he left her suite and hurried downstairs to his office in the other part of the palace. He'd wanted to meet this Mrs. Richards last evening, but Hector had told him she'd never ridden in a helicopter before and had become ill during the flight. There'd been nothing he could do but wait until this morning and wonder if her getting sick was already a bad omen.

He knew better than to ask Hector what she was like. His assistant would simply answer, "That's not for me to say, Your Highness." His tendency not to gossip was a sterling quality Alex admired, but at times it drove Stasio insane.

For years his elder brother had barked at Hector that he wasn't quite human. Alex had a theory that the reason why Hector irked Stasio was because Stasio had grown up knowing that one day he'd have to be king. Hector was a permanent reminder that Stasio's greatest duty was to his country, to marry Princess Beatriz and produce heirs to the throne.

Like the queen, who wanted more great-grandchildren for the glory of Hellenica, Alex looked forward to his brother producing some cousins for Zoe. His little girl would love a baby around. She'd asked Alex for a sister, but all he could say was that her uncle Stasi would produce a new heir to the throne before long.

After reaching his office, he scowled when he read the fax sent from Stasio, who was still in Valleder. *Sorry, little brother, but banking business will keep me here another week. Tell Yiayia I'll be home soon. Give Zoe a hug from her uncle. Hang in there. You do great work. Stasi.*

"Your Highness? May I present Mrs. Richards."

He threw his head back. Hector had come in the office without him being aware of it and was now clearing his throat. A very American-looking woman—down to the way she carried herself—had entered with him, taller than average, with her light brown hair swept up in a loose knot. Alex was so disappointed, even angered by his brother's news, he'd forgotten for a moment that Hector was on his way down. Stasio had taken advantage of their bargain.

"One month, little brother," he'd said when he'd left.

"That's all I need to carry out some lucrative banking negotiations. Philippe is helping me." But Stasio had been gone much longer and Alex wasn't happy about it. Neither was the queen, the prime minister or the archbishop, who were getting anxious to confer with him about the coronation and royal nuptials coming up soon.

Pushing his feelings aside, Alex got to his feet. "Welcome to Hellenica, Mrs. Richards."

"Thank you, Your Highness."

She gave an awkward curtsey, no doubt coached by Hector. He hated to admit she looked fresh, appealing even, as she stood there in a pale blue blouse and skirt that tied at her slender waist, drawing his attention to the feminine curves revealed above and below. He hadn't meant to stare, but his eyes seemed to have a will of their own as they took in her long, shapely legs.

Alex quickly shifted his gaze to her face and was caught off guard again by the wide, sculpted mouth and the cornflower-blue of her eyes. They reminded him of the cornflowers growing wild alongside larkspurs on Aurum Island where he normally lived.

He missed his private palace there where he conducted the mining interests for the monarchy, away from Hellenica. The big island drew the tourists in hordes, Aurum not quite so much. He shouldn't mind tourists since they were one of his country's greatest financial resources, but with his daughter in such distress, everything bothered him these days. Especially the woman standing in front of him.

A speech therapist could come in any size and shape. He just hadn't expected *this* woman, period. For one thing, she looked too young for the task ahead of her. No wonder Hector hadn't dropped a clue about her.

"I've been told you suffered on your helicopter ride. I hope you're feeling better."

"Much better, thank you. The view was spectacular."

One dark brow dipped. "What little you saw of it in your condition."

"Little is right," she acknowledged in a forthright manner. "I'm sorry your generous attempt to show me the sights in your helicopter didn't have the desired outcome." Her blunt way of speaking came as a surprise. "Will I be meeting your daughter this morning?"

"Yes." He flicked his glance to Hector. "Would you ask Sofia to bring Zoe to us?"

The older man gave a brief bow and slipped out of the office, leaving the two of them alone. Alex moved closer and invited her to sit down on the love seat. "Would you care for tea or coffee?"

"Nothing for me. I just had some tea. It's settling my stomach, but please have some yourself if you want it."

If *he* wanted it? She was more of a surprise than ever and seemed at ease, which wasn't always the case with strangers meeting him.

"My boss, Dr. Rice, told me your daughter is having trouble communicating, but he didn't give me any details. How long since your wife passed away?"

"Two years ago."

"And now Zoe is four. That means she wouldn't have any memory of her mother except what you've told her, and of course pictures. Did your wife carry Zoe full term?"

"No. She came six weeks early and was in the hospital almost a month. I feared we might lose her, but she finally rallied. I thought that could be the reason why she's been a little slower to make herself understood."

"Was her speech behind from infancy?"

"I don't really know what's normal. Not having been around children before, I had no way to compare her progress. All I know is her speech is difficult to understand. The queen and I are used to her, but over the past few months her behaviour's become so challenging, we've lost her art, English and dance teachers and three nannies. Her Greek tutor has all but given up and she's too much for the teacher to handle at her preschool."

"It's usually the caregiver who first notices if there's a problem. Would that have been your wife?"

"Yes, but a lot of the time she was ill with a bad heart and the nanny had to take over. I took charge in the evenings after my work, but I hadn't been truly alarmed about Zoe until two weeks ago when I had to withdraw her from preschool. As I told you earlier, I'd assumed that being a premature baby, she simply hadn't caught up yet."

"Has she had her normal checkup with the pediatrician?"

"Yes."

"No heart problem with her."

He shook his dark head. "I even took her to my own internist for a second opinion. Neither doctor found anything physically wrong with her, but they gave me the name of a child psychiatrist to find out if something else is going on to make her behind in her speech. Before I did that, I decided to take Dr. Wyman's advice. He recommended I take her to the Stillman Institute for a diagnosis before doing anything else."

"I see. What kind of behavior does she manifest?"

"When it comes time for her lessons lately, Zoe has tantrums and cries hysterically. All she wants to do is hide in her bed or run to her great-grandmother's suite for comfort."

"What about her appetite?"

This morning Zoe had taken only a few nibbles of her breakfast, another thing that had alarmed him. "Not what it should be."

She studied his features as if she were trying to see inside him. "You must be frantic."

Frantic? "Yes," he murmured. That was the perfect word to describe his state of mind. Mrs. Richards was very astute, but unlike everyone else in his presence except the queen and Stasio, she spoke her mind.

"Imagine your daughter feeling that same kind of emotion and then times it by a hundred."

Alex blinked. This woman's observation brought it home that she might just know what she was talking about. While he was deep in contemplation, his daughter appeared, clinging to Sofia's hand. Hector slipped in behind them.

"Zoe?" Alex said in English. "Come forward." She took a tentative step. "This is Mrs. Richards. She's come all the way from New York to see you. Can you say hello to her?"

His daughter took one look at their guest and her face crumpled in pain. He knew that look. She was ready for flight. With his stomach muscles clenched, he switched to Greek and asked her the same question. This time Zoe's response was to say she wanted her *yiayia*, then she burst into tears and ran out of the room. Sofia darted after her.

Alex called her back and started for the door, but Mrs. Richards unexpectedly said, "Let her go."

Her countermand surprised him. Except for his own

deceased father, no one had ever challenged him like that, let alone about his own daughter. It was as if their positions had been reversed and she was giving the orders. The strange irony set his teeth on edge.

"She probably assumes I'm her new nanny," she added in a gentler tone. "I don't blame her for running away. I can see she's at her wit's end. The first thing I'd like you to do is get her in to an ear, nose and throat specialist followed up by an audiologist."

He frowned, having to tamp down his temper. "As I told you a minute ago, Zoe has already been given two checkups."

"Not that kind of exam," she came back, always keeping her voice controlled. "A child or an adult with speech problems could have extra wax buildup not noticeable with a normal check-up because it's deep inside. It's not either doctor's fault. They're not specialists in this area. If there's nothing wrong with her ears and I can't help her, then your daughter needs to see a child psychiatrist to find out why she's regressing.

"For now let's find out if more wax than normal has accumulated recently. If so, it must be cleaned out to help improve her hearing. Otherwise sounds could be blocked or distorted, preventing her from mimicking them."

"Why would there be an abnormal amount of wax?"

"Does she get earaches very often?"

"A few every year."

"It's possible her ear canals are no longer draining as they should."

That made sense. His hands formed fists. Why hadn't he thought of it?

Her well-shaped brows lifted. "Not even a prince

can know everything." She'd read his mind and her comment sent his blood pressure soaring. "Will you arrange it? Sooner would be better than later because I can't get started on my testing until the procedure has been done. That child needs help in a hurry."

As if Alex didn't know… Why else had he sent for *her*?

He didn't like feeling guilty because he'd let the problem go on too long without exploring every avenue. Alex also didn't like being second-guessed or told what to do. But since it was Zoe they were talking about, he decided to let it go for now. "I'll see that a specialist fits her in today."

"Good. Let me know the results and we'll go from there." She turned to leave.

"I haven't excused you yet, Mrs. Richards."

She wheeled back around. "Forgive me, and please call me Dottie." Through the fringe of her dark, silky lashes, her innocent blue gaze eyed him frankly. "I've never worked with a parent who's a monarch. This is a new experience."

Indeed, it was. It appeared Alex was an acquired taste, something he hadn't known could happen. He wasn't a conceited man, but it begged the question whether she had an instant dislike of him.

"Monarch or not, do you always walk away from a conversation before it's over?"

"I thought it was." She stood firm. "I deal with preschoolers all the time and your little girl is so adorable, I'm hoping to get to the bottom of her problem right away. I'm afraid I'm too focused on my job. Your Highness," she tacked on, as if she weren't sure whether to say it or not.

She was different from anyone he'd ever met. Not rude exactly, yet definitely the opposite of obsequious. He didn't know what to think of her. But just now she'd sounded sincere enough where his daughter was concerned. Alex needed to take the advice his mother had given him as a boy. Never react on a first impression or you could live to regret it.

"I'm glad you're focused," he said and meant it. "She's the light of my life."

The briefest glint of pain entered her eyes. "You're a lucky man to have her, even if you *are* a prince."

His brows furrowed. "Even if I'm a prince?"

She shook her head. "I'm sorry. I meant— Well, I meant that one assumes a prince has been given everything in life and is very lucky. But to be the father of a darling daughter, too, makes you that much luckier."

Though she smiled, he heard a sadness in her words. Long after he'd excused her and had arranged for the doctor's appointment, the shadow he'd seen in those deep blue eyes stayed with him.

CHAPTER TWO

DOTTIE stayed in her room for part of the day, fussing and fuming over a situation she could do little about. *I haven't excused you yet, Mrs. Richards.*

The mild rebuke had fallen from the lips of a prince who was outrageously handsome. Tall and built like the statue of a Greek god, he possessed the inky-black hair and eyes of his Hellenican ancestry. Everything—his chiseled jaw, his strong male features—set him apart from other men.

Even if he weren't royal, he looked like any woman's idea of a prince. He'd stood there in front of his country's flag, effortlessly masculine and regal in a silky blue shirt and white trousers that molded to his powerful thighs.

He'd smelled good, too. Dottie noticed things like that and wished she hadn't because it reminded her that beneath the royal mantle, he was human.

Already she feared she might not be the right person for this job. Dr. Rice, the head of her department at the Stillman clinic, had said he'd handpicked her for this assignment because of her own personal experiences that gave her more understanding. Fine, but in order to give herself time to get used to the idea, she should have been told she was coming to a royal household before she boarded the jet in New York.

The atmosphere here was different from anything Dottie had known and she needed time to adjust. There was so much to deal with—the stiffness, the protocol, the maids and nannies, the teachers, the tutors, a prince for a father who'd been forced to obey a rigid schedule his whole life, a princess without a mother....

A normal child would have run into the room and hugged her daddy without thinking about it, but royal etiquette had held Zoe back from doing what came naturally. She'd appeared in the doorway and stood at attention like a good soldier.

The whole thing had to be too much for a little girl who just wanted to be a little girl. In the end she'd broken those rules and had taken off down the hall, her dark brown curls bouncing. Despite his calling her name, she'd kept going. The precious child couldn't handle any more.

Dottie's heart ached for Zoe who'd ignored her father's wishes and had run out of his office with tears flowing from those golden-brown eyes. She must have gotten her coloring from her mother, who'd probably been petite. His daughter had inherited her beauty and olive skin from her father, no doubt from her mother, too.

The vague images Dottie had retained of him and his brother through the media had been taken when they were much younger, playboy princes setting hearts afire throughout Europe. In the intervening years, Zoe's father had become a married man who'd lost his wife too soon in life. Tragic for him, and more tragic for a child to lose a parent. Unfortunately it had happened.

Dottie was the enemy of the moment where Zoe was concerned, and she'd would have to be careful how she approached her to do the testing. Soon enough she would discover how much of Zoe's problem was emotional or physical. Probably both.

With a deep sigh she ate the lunch a maid had brought her on a tray. Later another maid offered to unpack for her, but Dottie thanked her before dismissing her. She could do it herself. In fact she didn't want to get completely unpacked in case she'd be leaving the palace right away. If the little princess had a problem outside of Dottie's expertise, then Dottie would soon be flown back to New York from the island.

At five o'clock the phone rang at the side of her queen-size bed. It was Hector. The prince wished to speak to her in his office. He was sending a maid to escort her. It was on the tip of Dottie's tongue to tell him she didn't need help finding the prince's inner sanctum, but she had to remember that when in Rome… Already she'd made a bad impression. It wouldn't do to alienate him further, not when he was so anxious about his daughter.

She thanked Hector and freshened up. In a minute, one of the maids arrived and accompanied her down a different staircase outside her private guest suite to the main floor. The prince was waiting for her.

Out of deference to him, she waited until he spoke first. He stood there with his hands on his hips. By the aura of energy he was giving out with those jet-black eyes playing over her, she sensed he had something of significance to tell her.

"Sit down, please."

She did his bidding, anxious to hear about the result of the examination.

"Once we could get Zoe to cooperate, the doctor found an inordinate amount of wax adhering to her eardrums from residual fluid. She hated every second of it, but after they were cleaned out, she actually smiled when he asked her if she could hear better. The audiologist did tests afterwards and said her hearing is fine."

"Oh, that's wonderful news!" Dottie cried out happily.

"Yes. On the way back to the palace, I could tell she did understand more words being spoken to her. There was understanding in her eyes."

Beneath that formal reserve of his, she knew he was relieved for that much good news. A prince could move mountains and that's what he'd done today by getting her into an ear specialist so fast. In fact, he'd made it possible for Dottie to come to Hellenica instead of the other way around. What greater proof that the man loved his daughter?

"This is an excellent start, Your Highness."

"When do you want to begin testing her?"

"Tomorrow morning. She needs to have a good night's sleep first. After what she's been through today, she doesn't need any more trauma."

"Agreed." She heard a wealth of emotion in that one word. Dottie could imagine the struggle his daughter had put up. "Where would you like to test her?"

Since the prince was still standing, Dottie got to her feet to be on par with him, but she still needed to look up. "If you asked her where her favorite place is to play, what would she tell you?"

After a moment he said, "The patio off my bedroom."

That didn't surprise Dottie. His little girl wanted to be near him without anyone else around. "Does she play there often?"

She heard his sharp intake of breath. "No. It's not allowed unless I'm there, too." Of course not. "My work normally goes past her bedtime."

"And mornings?"

"While we've been at the palace, I've always had breakfast with her in the queen's suite. Zoe's the most comfortable there."

"I'm talking before breakfast."

"That's when I work out and she takes a swimming lesson."

Dottie fought to remain quiet, but her impulse was to cry out in dismay over the strict regimen. "So what times does she get to play with you on your patio?"

He pursed his lips. "Sunday afternoons after chapel and lunch. Why all these questions?"

She needed to be careful she didn't offend him again. "I'm trying to get a sense of her day and her relationship with you. When is her Greek lesson?"

"Before her dinner."

"You don't eat dinner with her, then?"

"No."

Oh. Poor Zoe. "You say she was attending a pre-school until two weeks ago?"

"Yes. The sessions went in two-hour segments, three times a week. Monday, Wednesday and Friday. But lately I haven't insisted for the obvious reasons."

"When does she play with friends?"

"You mean outside her school?"

"Yes. Does she have friends here at the palace?"

"No, but we normally live on Aurum where she has several."

"I see. Thank you for giving me that information. Would it be all right with you if I test her out on your patio? I believe she'll be more responsive in a place where she's truly happy and at ease. If you're there, too, it will make her more comfortable. But with your full schedule I don't suppose that's poss—"

"I'll make time for it," he declared, cutting her off.

No matter how she said things, she seemed to be in the wrong. It wasn't her intention to push his buttons, but she was doing a good job of it anyway. "That would be ideal. It's important I watch her interaction with you. Before you come, I'd like to set up out there with a few things I've brought."

His brows lifted. "How much time do you need?"

"A few minutes."

He nodded. "I'll send a maid to escort you at eight. Zoe and I will join you at eight-twenty. Does that meet with your approval?"

Eight-twenty? Not eight-twenty-one? *Stop it, Dottie. You're in a different world now.* "Only if it meets with yours, Your Highness."

This close to him, she could see a tiny nerve throbbing at the corner of his compelling mouth. His lips had grown taut. "If I haven't made it clear before, let me say this again. My daughter is my life. That makes her my top priority." She believed him.

"I know," Dottie murmured. "While I'm here, she's mine, too."

A long silence ensued before he stepped away. "I've instructed Hector to make certain you're comfortable while you're here. Your dinner can be served in the small guest dining room on the second floor, or he'll have it brought to your room. Whatever you prefer. Anything you want or need, you have only to pick up the phone and ask him and he'll see to it."

"Thank you. He's been so perfect, I can hardly believe he's real."

"My brother and I have been saying the same thing about him for years." The first glimmer of an unexpected smile reached his black eyes. He did have his human moments. The proof of it set off waves of sensation through her body she hadn't expected or wanted to feel.

"If you'll eat your eggs, I have a surprise for you." Zoe jerked her head around and eyed Alex in excitement. "I'm going to spend time with you this morning and thought we'd play out on my patio. That's why I told Sofia to let you wear pants."

She made a sound of delight and promptly took several bites. The queen sent him a private glance that said she hoped this testing session with the new speech therapist wasn't going to be a waste of time. Alex hoped not, too. No one wanted constructive feedback more than he did.

After Zoe finished off her juice, she wiggled down from the chair and started to dart away. Alex called her back. "You must ask to be excused."

She turned to her grandmother. "Can I go with daddy, *Yiayia*?"

The queen nodded. "Have a good time."

Alex groaned in silence, remembering the way his daughter had flown out of his office yesterday after one look at Dottie.

Zoe slipped her hand into his and they left for his suite. She skipped along part of the way. When he saw how thrilled she was to be with him, he found himself even more put out with Stasio.

As soon as his brother got back from Vallader, Alex planned to take more time off to be with his daughter. While he'd had to be here at the palace doing his brother's work plus his own, he'd hardly had a minute to spend time with her. Maybe they'd go on a mini vacation together.

The curtains to the patio had been opened. Zoe ran through the bedroom ahead of him, then suddenly stopped at the sight of the woman sitting on the patio tiles in jeans and a pale orange, short-sleeved cotton top.

"Hi, Zoe," she spoke in English with a smile. Dottie had put on sneakers and her hair was loose in a kind of disheveled bob that revealed the light honey tones among the darker swaths. "Do you think your daddy can catch this?" She threw a Ping-Pong ball at him.

When he caught it with his right hand, Zoe cried out in surprise. He threw it back to Dottie who caught it in her left. Their first volley of the day. For no particular reason his pulse rate picked up at the thought of what else awaited him in her presence.

"Good catch. Come on, Daddy." Her dancing blue gaze shot to his. "You and Zoe sit down and spread your legs apart like this and we'll roll some balls to each other." She pulled a larger multicolored plastic ball from a big bag and opened those long, fabulous legs of hers.

Alex could tell his daughter was so shocked by what was going on, she forgot to be scared and sat down to

imitate Dottie once he'd complied. Dottie rolled the ball
to Zoe, who rolled it back to her. Then it was his turn.
They went in a round, drawing Zoe in. Pretty soon their
guest pulled out a rubber ball and rolled it to his daughter right after she'd sent her the plastic ball.

Zoe laughed as she hurried to keep both balls going.
His clever little girl used her right and left hand at the
same time and sent one ball to Dottie and one to him.
"Good thinking!" she praised her. "Shall we try three
balls?"

"Yes," his daughter said excitedly. Their guest produced the Ping-Pong ball and fired all three balls at
both of them, one after the other, until Zoe was giggling hysterically.

"You're so good at this, I think we'll try something else. Shall we see who's better at jumping?" She
whipped out a jump rope with red handles and got to
her feet. "Come on, Zoe. You take this end and I'll hold
on to the other. Your daddy's going to jump first. You'll
have to make big circles like I'm doing or the rope will
hit him in the head."

"Oh, no—" Zoe cried.

"Don't worry," Dottie inserted. "Your daddy is a big
boy. It won't hurt him."

So their visitor *had* noticed. Was that a negative in
her eyes, too?

Zoe scrutinized him. "You're a boy?"

"Yes. He's a very big one," Dottie answered for him
and his daughter laughed. Soon Zoe was using all her
powers of concentration to turn the rope correctly and
was doing an amazing job of it. After four times to get it
right he heard, "You can jump in anytime now, Daddy."

Alex crouched down and managed to do two jumps

before getting caught around the shoulders. He was actually disappointed when their leader said, "Okay, now it's Zoe's turn. How many can you do?"

She cocked her dark brown head. "Five—"

"Well, that's something I want to see. Watch while we turn the rope. Whenever you think you're ready, jump in. It's okay if it takes you a whole bunch of times to do it, Zoe. Your daddy isn't going anywhere, right?"

She didn't look at him as she said it. He had a feeling it was on purpose.

"We're both in your hands for as long as it takes, Dorothy." He'd read the background information on her and knew it was her legal name.

"I never go by my given name," she said to Zoe without missing a beat while she continued to rotate the rope. "You can call me Dottie."

"That means crazy, doesn't it?" he threw out, curious to see how she'd respond.

"Your English vocabulary is remarkable, Your Highness."

"Is she crazy?" Zoe asked while she stood there, hesitant to try jumping.

"Be careful how you answer that," Dottie warned him. "Little royal pitchers have big ears and hers seem to be working just fine."

Alex couldn't help chuckling. He smiled at his daughter. "She's funny-crazy. Don't you think?"

"Yes." Zoe giggled again.

"Come on and jump." After eight attempts accompanied by a few tears, she finally managed a perfect jump. Dottie clapped her hands. "Good job, Zoe. Next time you'll do more."

She put the rope aside and reached into her bag of

tricks. His daughter wasn't the only one interested to see what she would pull out next. "For this game we have to get on our tummies."

The speech therapist might as well have been a magician. At this point his daughter was entranced and did what was suggested without waiting for Alex. In another minute Dottie had laid twenty-four cards facedown on the floor in four rows. She turned one card over. "Do you know what this is, Zoe?"

His daughter nodded. "Pig."

"Yes, and there's another card just like it. You have to remember where this card is, and then find the other one. When you do, then you make a book of them and put the pile to the side. You get one turn. Go ahead."

Zoe turned over another card.

"What is it?"

"Whale."

"Yes, but it's not a pig. So you have to put the card back. Okay, Daddy. It's your turn."

Alex turned over a card in the corner.

"Tiger, Daddy."

Before he could say anything, he saw their eyes look to the doorway. Alex turned around in frustration to see who had interrupted them.

"Hector?"

"Forgive me, Your Highness. There's a call for you from Argentum on an urgent matter that needs your attention."

Much as Alex hated to admit it, this had to be an emergency, otherwise Bari would have sent him an email. Barisou Jouflas was the head mining engineer on the island of Argentum and Alex's closest friend since college. He always enjoyed talking to him and got to his feet, expecting an outburst from Zoe. To his astonishment, Dottie had her completely engrossed in the matching game.

"I'll be back as soon as I can."

Dottie nodded without looking at him.

"Bye, Daddy," his daughter said, too busy looking for a matching card to turn her head.

Bye, Daddy— Since when? No tantrum because he was leaving?

Out of the corner of her eye Dottie watched the prince disappear and felt a twinge of disappointment for his daughter. They'd all been having fun and it was one time when he hadn't wanted to leave, she felt sure of it. But there were times when the affairs of the kingdom did have to take priority. Dottie understood that and forgave him.

He might be gone some time. Dottie still had other tests to do that she preferred to take place outside the palace. Now would be a good time to carry them out while Zoe was still amenable. Her speech was close to unintelligible, but she was bright as a button and Dottie understood most of what she was trying to say because of her years of training and personal experience.

Once they'd concluded the matching game she said, "Zoe? Do you want to come down to the beach with me?" The little girl clapped her hands in excitement.

"All right, then. Let's do it." Dottie got up and pulled a bag of items out of the bigger bag. "Shall we go down from here?"

"Yes!" Zoe stood up and started down the stairs at the far end of the patio. Dottie followed. The long stairway covering two stories led to the dazzling blue water below.

It was a warm, beautiful day. When they reached the beach, she pulled out a tube of sunscreen and covered both of them. Next she drew floppy sun hats from the bag for them to put on.

"Here's a shovel. Will you show me how you build a castle?"

Zoe got to work and made a large mound.

"That's wonderful. Now where do you think this flag should go?" She handed her a little one.

"Here!" She placed it on the very top.

"Perfect. Make a hole where the front door of the castle is located."

She made a big dent with her finger at the bottom. Dottie rummaged in the bag for a tiny sailboat and gave it to her. "This is your daddy's boat. Where do you think it goes?"

"Here." Zoe placed it at the bottom around the side.

"Good." Again Dottie reached in the bag and pulled out a plastic figure about one inch high. "Let's pretend this is your daddy. Where does he live in the castle?"

Zoe thought about it for a minute, then stuck him in the upper portion of the mound.

"And where do you sleep?" Dottie gave her a little female figure.

"Here." Zoe crawled around and pushed the figure into the mound at approximately the same level as the other.

"Do you sleep by your *Yiayia*?"

"No."

"Can you show me where she sleeps?" Dottie handed her another figure. Zoe moved around a little more and put it in at the same height. Everyone slept on the second floor.

"I like your castle. Let's take off our shoes and walk over to the water. Maybe we can find some pretty stones to decorate the walls. Here's a bucket to carry everything."

They spent the next ten minutes picking up tiny, multicolored stones. When they returned to the mound Dottie said, "Can you pour them on the sand and pick out the different colors? We'll put them in piles."

Zoe nodded, eager to sort everything. She was meticulous.

"Okay. Why don't you start with the pink stones and put them around the middle of the castle." Her little charge got the point in a hurry and did a masterful job. "Now place the orange stones near the top and the brown stones at the bottom."

While Zoe was finishing her masterpiece, Dottie took several pictures at different angles with her phone. "You'll have to show these pictures to your daddy. Now I think it's time to put our shoes on and go back to the palace. I'm hungry and thirsty and I bet you are, too. Here—let me brush the sand off your little piggies."

Zoe looked at her. "What?"

"These." She tugged on Zoe's toes. "These are your little pigs. Piggies. They go *wee wee wee*." She made a squealing sound.

When recognition dawned, laughter poured out of Zoe like tinkling bells. For just a moment it sounded like her little boy's laughter. Emotion caught Dottie by the throat.

"Mrs. Richards?" a male voice spoke out of the blue, startling her.

She jumped to her feet, fighting the tears pricking her eyelids, and looked around. A patrol boat had pulled up on the shore and she hadn't even heard it. Two men had converged on them, obviously guards protecting the palace grounds. "Yes?" She put her arm around Zoe's shoulders. "Is something wrong?"

"Prince Alexius has been looking for you. Stay here. He'll be joining you in a moment."

She'd done something wrong. Again.

No sooner had he said the words than she glimpsed the prince racing down the steps to the beach with the speed of a black panther in pursuit of its prey. The image sent a chill up her spine that raised the hairs on the back of her neck.

When he caught up to them, he gave a grim nod of dismissal to the guards, who got back in the patrol boat and took off.

"Look what I made, Daddy—" His daughter was totally unaware of the byplay.

Dottie could hear his labored breathing and knew it came from fright, not because he was out of shape. Anything but. While Zoe gave him a running commentary of their beach adventure in her inimitable way, Dottie put the bucket and shovel in the bag. When she turned around, she discovered him hunkered down, examining his daughter's work of art.

After listening to her intently, he lifted his dark head and shot Dottie a piercing black glance. Sotto voce, he said, "There are pirates in these waters who wait for an opportunity like this to—"

"I understand," she cut him off, feeling sick to her stomach. She'd figured it out before he'd said anything. "Forgive me. I swear it won't happen again."

"You're right about that."

His words froze the air in her lungs before he gripped his daughter's hand and started for the stairs.

"Come on," Zoe called to her.

Dottie followed, keeping her eyes on his hard-muscled physique clothed in a white polo shirt and dark blue trousers. Halfway up the stairs on those long, powerful legs, he gathered Zoe in his arms and carried her the rest of the way to the patio.

"The queen is waiting for Zoe to have lunch with her," he said when she caught up to him. "A maid is waiting outside my suite to conduct you back to your room. I've asked for a tray to be sent to you. We'll talk later."

Dottie heard Zoe's protests as he walked away. She gathered up the other bag and met the maid who accompanied her back to her own quarters. Once alone, she fled into the en suite bathroom and took a shower to wash off the sand and try to get her emotions under control.

No matter how unwittingly, she'd endangered the life of the princess. What if his little daughter had been kidnapped? It would have been Dottie's fault. All of it. The thought was so horrific, she couldn't bear it. The prince had every right to tell her she was leaving on the next flight to Athens.

This was one problem she didn't know how to fix. Being sorry wasn't enough. She'd wanted to make a difference in Zoe's life. The princess had passed every test with flying colors. Dottie was the one who'd never made the grade.

After drying off, she put on a white linen dress and sandals, prepared to be driven to the airport once the prince had told her he no longer required her services.

As she walked back into the bedroom, there was a knock on the door.

Dottie opened it to a maid who brought her a lunch tray and set it on the table in the alcove. She had no appetite but quenched her thirst with the flask of iced tea provided while she answered some emails from home. As she drained her second glass, there was another knock on the door.

"Hector?" she said after opening it. Somehow she wasn't surprised. He'd met her at the airport in Athens for her helicopter ride, and would deposit her at Hellenica's airport.

"Mrs. Richards. If you've finished your lunch, His Highness has asked me to take you to his office."

She deserved this. "I'm ready now."

By the time they reached it, she'd decided to leave today and would make it easy for the prince. But the room was empty. "Please be seated. His Highness will be with you shortly."

"Thank you." After he left, she sat on the love seat and waited. When the prince walked in, she jumped right back up again. "I'm so sorry for what happened today."

He seemed to have calmed down. "It's my fault for not having warned you earlier. There was a kidnapping attempt on Zoe at her preschool last fall."

"Oh, no—" Dottie cried out, aghast.

"Fortunately it failed. Since then I've tripled the security. It never occurred to me you would take Zoe down that long flight of stairs, even if it is our private beach. We can be grateful the patrol boats were watching you the entire time. You're as much a target as Zoe and you're my responsibility while you're here in Hellenica."

"I understand."

"Please be seated, Mrs. Richards."

"I—I can't," she stammered. Dottie bemoaned the fact that earlier during the testing, he'd called her Dorothy and had shown a teasing side to his nature. It had been unexpected and welcome. Right now those human moments out on the patio might never have been.

He eyed her up and down. "Have you injured yourself in some way?"

"You know I haven't," she murmured. "I wanted to tell you that you don't need to dismiss me because I'm leaving as soon as someone can drive me to the airport."

His black brows knit together in a fierce frown. "Whatever gave you the idea that your services are no longer required?"

She blinked in confusion. "*You* did, on the beach."

"Explain that to me," he demanded.

"When I swore to you that nothing like this would ever happen again, you said I was right about that."

His inky-black eyes had a laserlike quality. "So you jumped to the conclusion that I no longer trusted you with my daughter? Are you always this insecure?"

Dottie swallowed hard. "Only around monarchs who have to worry about pirates and kidnappers. I didn't know about those incidents and can't imagine how terrifying it must have been for you. When you couldn't find us today, it had to have been like déjà vu. I can't bear to think I caused you even a second's worry."

He took a deep breath. "From now on, whether with Zoe or alone, don't do anything without informing me of your intentions first. Then there won't be a problem."

"I agree." He was being much more decent about this than she had any right to expect. A feeling of admiration for his willingness to give her a second chance welled up inside her. When their eyes met again, she felt something almost tangible pass between them she couldn't explain, but it sent a sudden rush of warmth through her body, and she found herself unable to look away.

CHAPTER THREE

THE prince cleared his throat, breaking the spell. "After spending the day with my daughter, tell me what you've learned about her."

Dottie pulled herself together. The fear that she'd alienated the prince beyond salvaging almost made her forget why she'd come to Hellenica in the first place.

"I'll give you the bad news first. She has trouble articulating. Research tells us there are several reasons for it, but none of it matters. The fact is, she struggles with this problem.

"Now for the good news. Zoe is exceptionally intelligent with above-average motor and cognitive skills. Her vocabulary is remarkable. She understands prepositions and uses the right process to solve problems, such as in matching. Playing with her demonstrates her amazing dexterity. You saw her handling the balls and jumping rope. She has excellent coordination and balance.

"She follows directions the first time without problem. If you took a good look at that castle, it proves she sees things spatially. Her little mound had a first floor and a second floor, just like the palace. She understands her physical world and understands what she hears. Zoe only has one problem, as I said, but it's a big one since for the most part she can't make herself understood to anyone but you and the queen and, I presume to some extent, Sofia."

Alex nodded. "So that's why she's withdrawing from other people."

"Yes. You've told me she's been more difficult over the past few months. She's getting older and is losing her confidence around those who don't have her problem. She's smart enough to know she's different and not like everyone else. She wants to avoid situations that illuminate the difference, so she runs away and hides. It's the most natural instinct in the world.

"Zoe wants to make herself understood. The more she can't do it, the angrier she becomes, thus the tantrums. There's nothing wrong with her psychologically that wouldn't clear up immediately once she's free to express herself like everyone else does. She pushes people away and clings to you because you love her without qualification. But she knows the rest of the world doesn't love her, and she's feeling like a misfit."

The prince's sober expression masked a deep fear. She saw it in his eyes. "Can she overcome this?"

"Of course. She needs help saying all her sounds, but particularly the consonants. *H*'s and *T*'s are impossible for her. Few of her words come out right. Her frustration level has to be off the charts. But with constant work, she'll talk as well as I do."

He rubbed the back of his neck absently. "Are you saying you used to have the same problem?"

"I had a worse one. I stuttered so severely, I was the laughingstock of my classes in elementary school.

Children are cruel to other children. I used to pretend to be sick so I wouldn't have to go to school."

"How did you get through it?" He sounded pained for her.

"My aunt raised me. She was a stickler for discipline and sent me to a speech therapist every weekday, who taught me how to breathe, how to pace myself when I talked. After a few years I stuttered less and less. By high school it only showed up once in a while.

"Zoe has a different problem and needs to work on her sounds every day. If you could be the one encouraging her like a coach, she would articulate correct sounds faster. The more creativity, the better. I've brought toys and games you can play with her. While she's interacting with you, she'll learn to model her speech after you. Slowly but surely it will come."

"But you'll be here, too."

"Of course. You and I will work with her one on one, and sometimes the three of us will play together. I can't emphasize enough how much progress she'll make if you're available on a regular basis."

He shifted his weight. "How long do you think this will take?"

"Months to possibly several years. It's a gradual process and requires patience on everyone's part. When you feel confident, then another therapist can come in my place and—"

"I hired *you*," he interrupted her, underlining as never before that she was speaking to a prince.

"Yes, for the initial phase, but I'm a diagnostician and am needed other places."

His eyes narrowed on her face. "Is there a man in New York waiting for you to get back to him?"

No. That was a long time ago, she thought sorrowfully. Since then she'd devoted her time to her career. "Why does my personal life have to enter into this discussion?"

"I thought the point was obvious. You're young and attractive."

"Thank you. For that matter so are you, Your Highness, but you have more serious matters on your mind. So do I."

There she went again, speaking her thoughts out loud, offending him right and left. He studied her for a long time. "If it's money…"

"It's not. The Institute pays me well."

"Then?" He left the word hanging in the air.

"There is no *then*. You have your country to rule over. I have a career. The people with speech problems are *my* country. But for the time I'm here, I'll do everything in my power to get this program going for Zoe."

An odd tension had sprung between them. "Zoe only agreed to stop crying and eat lunch with the queen as long as she could return to the patio to play with you this afternoon," he said. "She had a better time with you this morning than I think she's ever had with anyone else."

Dottie smiled. "You mean besides you. That's because she was given the nonstop attention every child craves without being negatively judged. Would it be all right with you if she comes to my room for her lessons?"

"After the grilling you gave me, will I be welcome, too?" he countered in a silky voice that sent darts of awareness through her body. The prince was asking *her* permission after the outspoken way she'd just addressed him?

"I doubt Zoe will stay if you don't join us. Hopefully in a few days she'll come to my room, even when you can't be there. The alcove with the table makes it especially convenient for the games I've brought. If you'll make out a schedule and rules for me to follow, then there won't have to be so many misunderstandings on my part."

"Anything else?" She had a feeling he was teasing her now. This side of him revealed his charm and added to the depth of the man.

"Where does her Greek tutor teach her?"

"In the library, but she's developed an aversion to it and stays in her bedroom."

"That's what I used to do. It's where you can sleep and have no worries. In that room you can pretend you're normal like everyone else." Maybe it was a trick of light, but she thought she saw a glimmer of compassion radiate from those black depths. "As for your patio, I think it ought to remain your special treat for her."

"So do I. Why don't you go on up to your room. I'll bring Zoe in a few minutes. Later this evening you'll join me in the guest dining room near your suite and we'll discuss how you want to spend your time while you're in Hellenica when you're not with my daughter."

"That's very kind of you," Dottie murmured, but she didn't move because she didn't know if she'd been dismissed or not. When he didn't speak, she said, "Do I need to wait for a maid to escort me back to my room?"

His lips twitched, causing her breath to catch at the sight of such a beautiful man whose human side was doing things to her equilibrium without her consent. "Only if you're afraid you can't find it."

She stared into his eyes. "Thank you for trusting me. With work, Zoe's speech *will* improve."

On that note she left his office, feeling his all-seeing gaze on her retreating back. She hurried along the corridor on trembling legs and found the staircase back to the guest suite. Now that she'd discovered she was still employed by him, she was ravenous and ate the lunch she'd left on the tray.

Before he came with Zoe, she set things up to resemble a mini schoolroom; crayons, scissors, paper, building blocks, beads to string, hide-and-seek games, puzzles, sorting games. Flash cards. She'd brought several sets so he could keep a pack on him. All of it served as a device while she helped his daughter with her sounds.

That's why you're here, Dottie. It's the only reason. Don't ever forget it.

Alex found Dottie already seated in the guest dining room when he joined her that evening. She looked summery in a soft blue crochet top and white skirt that followed the lines and curves of her alluring figure.

He smiled. "May I join you?"

"Of course."

"You're sure?"

"I came from New York to try to be of help."

It wasn't the answer he'd wanted. In truth, he wasn't exactly sure what he wanted, but he felt her reserve around him when she wasn't with Zoe and was determined to get to the bottom of it. He sat down opposite her and within a minute their dinner was served.

Once they were alone again he said, "Whenever you wish to leave the palace, a car and driver will be at your disposal. Hector will arrange it. A bodyguard will always be with you. Hopefully you won't find my security people obtrusive."

"I'm sure I won't. Thank you." She began eating, but the silence stretched between them. Finally she said, "Could I ask you something without you thinking I'm criticizing you or stepping over the line?"

"Because I'm a prince?"

"Because you're a prince, a man and a father." She lifted her fabulous blue eyes to him. "I don't know which of those three people will be irked and maybe even angered."

Alex tried to keep a straight face. "I guess we won't know until I hear your question."

A sigh came out of her. "When did you stop eating dinner with Zoe as part of your natural routine?"

He hadn't seen that question coming. "After my wife died, I had to make up for a lot of missed work in my capacity as overseer of the mining industry of our country. Hellenica couldn't have the high quality of life it enjoys without the revenue paid by other countries needing our resources. It requires constant work and surveillance.

"I spent my weekends with Zoe, but weekdays my hours were long, so she ate dinner with her nannies and my grandmother, who could get around then and spent a lot of her time on Aurum with us. However, I never missed kissing my daughter good-night and putting her to bed. That routine has gradually become the norm.

"With Stasio gone the past six weeks, I've had to be here and have been stretched to the max with monarchy business plus my own work."

"Do you mind if I ask what it is you do for your

brother? I've often wondered what a crown prince's daily routine is really like."

"Let me put it this way. On top of working with the ministers while he runs the complex affairs of our country on a daily basis, Stasio has at least four hundred events to attend or oversee during a year's time. That's more than one a day where he either gives a speech, entertains international dignitaries, attends openings or christens institutions, all while promoting the general welfare of Hellenica."

"It's very clear his life isn't his own. Neither is yours, obviously. Where did you go today after our session with Zoe?"

Alex was surprised and pleased she'd given him that much thought. "I had to fly to one of the islands in the north to witness the installation of the new president of the Thracian college and say a few words in Stasio's place. I should have stayed for the dinner, but I told them I had another engagement I couldn't miss." Alex had wanted to eat dinner with her. He enjoyed her company.

"Do you like your work? I know that probably sounds like an absurd question, but I'm curious."

"Like all work, it has its good and bad moments, but if I were honest I'd have to say that for the most part I enjoy it—very much, in fact, when something good happens that benefits the citizenry. After a lot of work and negotiations, four new hospitals will be under construction shortly. One of them will be a children's hospital. Nothing could please me more."

"Does Zoe know about this hospital? Do you share some of the wonderful things you do when you're with her?"

Her question surprised him. "Probably not as much as I should," he answered honestly.

"The reason I asked is because if she understood what kinds of things take up your time when you're away from her, she'd be so proud of you and might not feel as much separation anxiety when you're apart."

He looked at her through shuttered eyes. "If I didn't know better, I'd think you were a psychiatrist."

She let out a gentle laugh. "Hardly. You appear to have an incredible capacity to carry your brother's load as well as your own and still see to your daughter's needs. I'm so impressed."

"But?"

"I didn't say anything."

"You didn't have to. It's there in your expression. If I ate dinner with my daughter every evening, her speech would come faster."

"Maybe a little, but I can see you're already burning the candle at both ends out of concern for your country and necessity. It would be asking too much of you when you're already making time for her teaching sessions." She sat back. "I'm so sorry you lost your wife, who must have been such a help to you. It must have been a terrible time for you."

"It was, but I had Zoe. Her smiling face made me want to get up in the morning when I didn't think I could."

Moisture filmed her eyes. "I admire you for the wonderful life you're giving her."

"She's worth everything to me. You do what you have to do. Don't forget I've had a lot of help from family and the staff."

"Even so, your little Zoe adores you. It means whatever you're doing is working." She pushed herself away from the table and got to her feet. "Good night, Your Highness. No, no. Don't get up. Enjoy that second cup of coffee in peace.

"What with worrying about your grandmother, too, you deserve a little pampering. From my vantage point, no one seems to be taking care of you. In all the fairy tales I read as a child, they went to the castle and lived happily ever after. Until now I never thought about the prince's welfare."

Her comment stunned him before she walked out of the dining room.

Two nights later, while Alex was going over a new schedule he'd been working out with his internal affairs minister, a maid came into his office with a message. He wasn't surprised when he heard what was wrong. In fact he'd half been expecting it.

"If you'll excuse me."

"Of course, Your Highness."

Pleased that he'd been able to arrange his affairs so he could eat dinner with Zoe and Dottie from now on, he got up from the desk and headed for Zoe's bedroom. He heard crying before he opened the door. Poor Sofia was trying to calm his blotchy-faced daughter, who took one look at him and flung herself against his body.

Alex gathered her in his arms. "What's the matter?" he asked, knowing full well what was wrong. She'd been having the time of her life since Dottie had come to the palace and she didn't want the fun to stop.

Sofia shook her head. "She was asleep, and then suddenly she woke up with a nightmare. I haven't been able to quiet her down, Your Highness. She doesn't want me to help her anymore."

"I understand. It's all right. You can retire now. Thank you."

After she went into the next room, where she'd been sleeping lately, Zoe cried, "I want my mommy."

She'd never asked for her mother before. From time to time they'd talked about Teresa. He'd put pictures around so she would always know what her mother looked like, but this was different. He pulled one of them off the dresser and put it in her hand. To his shock, she pushed the photo away. "I want Dot. She's my mommy."

Alex was aghast. His daughter had shortened Dottie's name, but the sound that came out would make no sense to anyone except Alex, who understood it perfectly. "No, Zoe. Dottie's your teacher."

She had that hysterical look in her eyes. "No—she's my mommy. Where did she go?"

"Your mommy's in heaven."

"No—" She flung her arms around his neck. "Get my mommy!"

"I can't, Zoe."

"Has she gone?" The fright in her voice stunned him.

Alex grabbed the photograph. "This is your mommy. She went to heaven, remember?"

"Is Dot in heaven?"

Obviously his daughter's dreaming had caused her to awaken confused. "Dottie is your teacher and she went to her room, but she's not your mommy."

"Yes, she is." She nodded. "She's my new mommy!" she insisted before breaking down in sobs.

New?

"I want her! Get her, Daddy! Get her!" she begged him hysterically.

Feeling his panic growing, he pulled out his cell phone to call Hector.

"Your Highness?"

"Finds Mrs. Richards and tell her to come to Zoe's suite immediately."

"I'll take care of it now."

Alex could be thankful there was no one more efficient than Hector in an emergency.

When Dottie walked into the room a few minutes later with a book in her hand, his daughter had calmed down somewhat, but was still shuddering in his arms.

"Dot—" Zoe blurted with such joy, Alex was speechless.

"Hi, Zoe. Did you want to say good-night?"

"Yes."

"She thought you were gone," Alex whispered in an aside.

Dottie nodded. "Why don't you get in bed and I'll read you a story. Then *I* have to go to bed, too, because you and I have a big day planned for tomorrow, don't we?"

Zoe's lips turned up in a smile. "Yes."

Like magic, his daughter crawled under the covers. Dottie pulled up a chair next to the bed. "This is the good-night book. See the moon on the cover? When he's up there, everyone goes to sleep. Freddie the frog stops going *ribbbbbit* and says good-night." Zoe laughed.

Dottie turned the page. "Benny the bee stops *buzzzz-ing* and says good-night." She showed each page to his daughter who was enchanted. "Charlie the cricket stops *chirrrping* and says good-night. Guess who's on the last page?" Zoe didn't know. Dottie showed it to her. There was a mirror. "It's *you!* Now *you* have to say good-night."

Zoe said it.

"Let's say the *g* again. Mr. G is a grumpy letter." Zoe thought that was hilarious. "He gets mad." She made a face. "Let's see if we can get as mad as he does. We have to grit our teeth like this. Watch my mouth and say *grrr.*"

Alex was watching it. To his chagrin he'd been watching it on and off for several days. After half a dozen tries Zoe actually made the *grrr* sound. He couldn't believe it. In his astonishment his gaze darted to Dottie, but she was focused on his daughter.

"You sounded exactly like Mr. G, Zoe. That was perfect. Tomorrow night your father will read it to you again. Now Dot has to go to sleep. I'll leave the book with you." She slipped out of the room, leaving the two of them alone.

Zoe clasped it to her chest as if it were her greatest treasure. Alex's eyes smarted because lying before him was *his* greatest treasure. She fell asleep within min-utes. As soon as she was out, he left the room knowing Sofia was sleeping in the adjacent room and would hear her if she woke up.

He strode through the palace, intending to talk to Dottie before she went to bed. Hector met him as he was passing his grandmother's suite on his way to the other wing.

"The queen wants to see you before she retires."

His brows lifted. "You wouldn't by any chance be spying on me for her, would you, Hector?"

"I have never spied on you, Your Highness."

"You've been spying for her since the day Stasi and I were born, but I forgive you. However, Stasi might not be so forgiving once he's crowned, so remember you've been warned. Tell the queen I'll be with her in ten minutes."

He continued on his way to Dottie's apartment. After he knocked, she called out, "Yes?"

"It's Alex."

The silence that followed was understandable. He'd never used his given name with her before, or given his permission for her to use it. But considering the amount of time they'd been spending together since her arrival at the palace, it seemed absurd to say anything else now that they were alone. "Would you be more willing to answer me if I'd said it's Zoe's father, or it's your Royal Highness?"

He thought he heard her chuckle before she opened the door a couple of inches. "I was on the verge of crawling into bed."

Alex could see that. She'd thrown on a pink toweling robe and was clutching the lapels beneath her chin. "I need to talk frankly with you. Zoe has decided you're her new mommy. She got hysterical tonight when I tried to tell her otherwise."

"I know. She's told me on several occasions she wishes I were her mother. This happens with some of my youngest students who don't have one. It's very normal. I just keep telling them I'm their teacher. You need to go on telling her in a matter-of-fact way that Princess Teresa was her mommy."

"I did that."

"I know. I saw the photograph and see a lot of the princess's beauty in Zoe. What's important here is that if you don't fight her on it, she'll finally get the point and the phase will pass after a while."

"That's very wise counsel." He exhaled the breath he'd been holding. "You made a breakthrough with her tonight."

"Yes. I've wanted her to feel confident about one sound and now it has happened."

"How did you know she would do it?"

"I didn't, but I hoped. Every success creates more success."

Talking through the crack in the door added a certain intimacy to their conversation, exciting him. "Her success is going to help me sleep tonight."

"I'm glad. Just remember a total change isn't going to happen overnight. Her vowels are coming, but *G* is only one consonant out of twenty-one. Putting that sound with the rest of a word is the tricky part."

"Tricky or not, she mimicked you perfectly and the way you read that book had her spellbound."

"There was only one thing wrong with it."

"What's that?" He found himself hanging on her every word, just like his daughter.

"It didn't have a page that said the prince stopped *rrrrruling* and said good-night."

Alex broke into full-bodied laughter.

Her eyes smiled. "If you'll forgive me, you should do that more often in front of Zoe, Your Highness."

"What happened to Alex? That is my name."

"I realize that."

"Before I leave, I wanted you to know that I've worked things out with my internal affairs minister so I can eat dinner with my daughter every night. From now on he'll take care of the less important matters for me during that time period."

"Zoe's going to be ecstatic!" she blurted, displaying the bubbly side of her nature that didn't emerge as often as he would have liked to see.

"I hope that means you're happy about it, too, since you'll be joining us for our meals. Good night, Dottie."

"Good night, Alex."

She shut the door on him before he was ready to leave. After being with her, he wasn't in the mood to face his grandmother. As he made his way back to her suite, he thought about his choice of words. The only time he'd ever *faced* the queen was when he'd been a boy and had a reason to feel guilty about something.

Tonight he had a strong hunch what she wanted to discuss with him. After Zoe's nightmare, now he knew why. If she'd told *Yiayia* that Dottie was her new mommy, nothing would have enraged his grandmother more. She would have told Zoe never to speak of it again, but that wouldn't prevent his daughter from thinking it in her heart.

Until the phase passed, Dottie had said.

What if it didn't? That's what disturbed Alex.

Zoe's insistence that Dottie was her new mommy only exacerbated his inner conflict where the speech therapist was concerned. Since he'd peered into a pair of eyes as blue as the flowers fluttering in the breeze around the palace in Aurum, he couldn't get her out of his mind.

In truth he had no business getting physically involved with someone he'd hired. He certainly didn't need the queen reminding him of what he'd already been telling himself—keep the relationship with Mrs.

Richards professional and enjoy the other women he met when he left the country for business or pleasure.

Too bad for his grandmother that he saw through her machinations and had done so from an early age. She always had another agenda going. Since Teresa's funeral, she'd been busy preparing the ground with the House of Helvetia. But until Stasi married, she was biding her time before she insisted Alex take Princess Genevieve of Helvetia to wife for the growth and prosperity of the kingdom.

Lines darkened his face. The queen would have to bide away forever because Stasi would be the only one doing the growing for the Constantinides dynasty. He was the firstborn, Heaven had picked him to rule Hellenica. Ring out the bells.

Alex had a different destiny and a new priority that superseded all else. He wanted to help his daughter feel normal, and that meant coaching her. With Dottie's help, it was already happening. She understood what was going on inside Zoe. Her story about her own stuttering problem had touched him. He admired her strength in overcoming a huge challenge.

His first order of business was to talk to Stasio tonight. His brother needed to come home now! With Alex's work schedule altered, he could spend the maximum amount of time with Zoe and Dottie throughout the day. It was going to work, even though it meant dealing with his ministers in the early morning hours and late at night when necessary.

Once Stasio was home, Alex would move back to the island of Aurum, where he could divide his attention between helping Zoe and doing the work he'd been overseeing for the country since university. With Dottie installed and a palace staff and security waiting on them, Zoe couldn't help but make great strides with her speech and he'd convince Dottie she couldn't leave yet.

CHAPTER FOUR

LIKE pizza dough being tossed in the air, Dottie's heart did its own version of a flip when the prince entered her schoolroom a few days later with Zoe. They must have just come from breakfast with the queen. Zoe was dressed in pink play clothes and sneakers.

Dottie hardly recognized Alex. Rather than hand-tooled leather shoes, he'd worn sneakers, too. She was dazzled by his casual attire of jeans and a yellow, open-necked sport shirt. In the vernacular, he was a hunk. When she looked up and saw the smattering of dark hair on his well-defined chest, her mouth went dry and she averted her eyes. Zoe's daddy was much more man than prince this morning, bringing out longings in her she hadn't experienced in years.

He'd been coming to their teaching sessions and had cleared his calendar to eat dinner with Zoe. Dottie was moved by his love and concern for his daughter, but she feared for him, too. The prince had the greatest expectations for his child, but he might want too much too soon. That worry had kept her tossing and turning during the night because she wanted to be up to the challenge and help Zoe triumph.

But it wasn't just that worry. When she'd told Alex

she'd had other patients who'd called her mommy, it was a lie. Only one other child had expressed the same wish. It was a little boy who had a difficult, unhappy mother. In truth, Zoe was unique. So was the whole situation.

Normally Dottie's students came by bus or private car to the institute throughout the day. Living under the palace roof was an entirely different proposition and invited more intimacy. Zoe was a very intelligent child and should have corrected her own behavior by now, but she chose to keep calling Dottie Mommy. Every time Zoe did that, it blurred the lines for Dottie, who in a short time had allowed the little girl to creep into her heart.

To make matters worse, Dottie was also plagued by guilt because she realized she wanted Alex's approval. That sort of desire bordered on pride. Her aunt had often quoted Gibran. "Generosity is giving more than you can, and pride is taking less than you need." If she wanted his approval, then it was a gift she had to earn.

Did she seek it because he was a prince? She hoped not. Otherwise that put her in the category of those people swayed by a person's station in life. She refused to be a sycophant, the kind of person her aunt had despised. Dottie despised sycophants, too.

"GGGRRRRRR," she said to Zoe, surprising the little girl, who was a quick study and *gggrrrred* back perfectly. Alex gave his daughter a hug before they sat down at the table.

"Wonderful, Zoe." Her gaze flicked to him. "Good morning, Your Highness." Dottie detected the scent of the soap he'd used in the shower. It was the most marvelous smell, reminding her of mornings when her husband—

But the eyes staring at her across the table were a fiery black, not blue. "Aren't you going to *gggrrr* me? I feel left out."

Her pulse raced. "Well, we don't want you to feel like that, do we, Zoe?" The little girl shook her head, causing her shiny brown curls to flounce.

Dottie had a small chalkboard and wrote the word *Bee*. "Go ahead and pronounce this word for us, Your Highness." When he did, she said, "Zoe? Did you hear *bee*?"

"Yes."

"Good. Let's all say *bee* together. One, two three. *Bee*." Zoe couldn't do it, of course. Dottie leaned toward her. "Pretend you're a tiny goldfish looking for food." Pressing her lips together she made the beginning of the *B* sound. "Touch my lips with your index finger." Her daddy helped her. In the process his fingers brushed against Dottie's mouth. She could hardly breathe from the sensation of skin against skin.

"Now feel how it sounds when I say it." Dottie said it a dozen times against Zoe's finger. She giggled. "That tickled, didn't it? Now say the same sound against my finger." She put her finger to Zoe's lips. After five tries she was making the sound.

"Terrific! Now put your lips to your daddy's finger and make the same *B* sound over and over."

As Zoe complied with every ounce of energy in that cute little body, Alex caught Dottie's gaze. The softness, the gratitude she saw in his eyes caused her heart to hammer so hard, she feared he could hear it.

"You're an outstanding pupil, Zoe. Today we're going to work on the *B* sound."

"It's interesting you've brought up the *bee*," Alex interjected.

"They make honey," said Zoe.

"That's right, Zoe. Did you know that just yesterday I met with one of the ministers and we're going to establish beekeeping centers on every island in Hellenica."

"How come?"

"With more bees gathered in hives, we'll have more honey to sell to people here as well as around the world. It's an industry I'd like to see flourish. With all the blossoms and thyme that grow here, it will give jobs to people who don't have one. You know the honey you eat when we're on Aurum?" She nodded. "It comes from two hives Inez and Ari tend on our property."

Zoe's eyes widened. "They do? I've never seen them."

"When we go home, we'll take a look."

Zoe smiled and gave her father a long hug. As he reciprocated, his gaze met Dottie's. He'd taken her suggestion to share more with his daughter and it was paying dividends, thrilling her to pieces.

"I'm going to give your daddy a packet of flash cards, Zoe. Everything on it starts with a *B*. He'll hold up the card and say the word. Then you say it. If you can make three perfect *B* sounds, I have a present for you."

Zoe let out a joyous sound and looked at her daddy with those shiny brown eyes. Dottie sat back in the chair and watched father and daughter at work. Zoe had great incentive to do her best for the man she idolized. The prince took his part seriously and proceeded with care. She marveled to watch them drawing closer together through these teaching moments, forging closer bonds now that he was starting to ease up on his work for the monarchy.

"Bravo!" she said when he'd gone through the pack of thirty. "You said five *B*'s clearly. Do you want your present now or after your lesson?"

Zoe concentrated for a minute. "Now."

Alex laughed that deep male laugh. It resonated through Dottie to parts she'd forgotten were there. Reaching in the bag in the corner, she pulled out one of several gifts she'd brought for rewards. But this one was especially vital because Zoe had been working hard so far and needed a lot of reinforcement.

Dottie handed her the soft, foot-long baby. "This is Baby Betty. She has a *bottle*, a *blanket* and a *bear*."

"Oh—" Zoe cried. Her eyes lit up. She cradled it in her arms, just like a mother. "Thank you, Mommy."

The word slipped out again. Dottie couldn't look at Alex. His daughter had said it again. These days it was coming with more frequency. The moment had become an emotional one for Dottie, who had to fight her own pain over past memories that had been resurrected by being around her new student.

"I'm not your mommy, Zoe. She's in heaven. You know that, don't you."

She finally nodded. "I wish you were my mommy."

"But since I'm not, will you please call me Dot?"

"Yes."

"Good girl. Guess what? Now that you've fed Betty, you have to burp her." Puzzled, Zoe looked up at her. "When a baby drinks milk from a bottle, it drinks in air, too. So you have to pat her back. Then the air will come out and she won't have a tummyache. Your mommy used to pat your back like that when you were a baby, didn't she, Your Highness?"

Dottie had thrown the ball in his court, not knowing what had gone on in their marriage. He'd never discussed his private personal life or asked Dottie about hers.

"Indeed, she did. We took turns walking the floor with you. Sometimes very important people would come in the nursery to see you and you'd just yawn and go to sleep as if you were horribly bored."

At that comment the three of them laughed hard. Dottie realized it provided a release from the tension built up over the last week.

From the corner of her eye she happened to spot Hector, who stood several feet away. He was clearing his throat to get their attention. How long had he been in the room listening?

"Your Highness? The queen has sent for you."

"Is it a medical emergency?"

"No."

"Then I'm afraid she'll have to wait until tonight. After this lesson I'm taking Zoe and Mrs. Richards out on the *boat*," he said emphasizing the B. "We'll work on her *B* sounds while we enjoy a light *buffet* on *board*, won't we, Zoe?" He smiled at his daughter who nodded, still gripping her baby tightly. "But don't worry. I'll be back in time to say good-night to her."

"Very well, Your Highness."

Dottie had to swallow the gasp that almost escaped her throat. Lines bracketed Hector's mouth. She looked at the floor. It really was funny. Alex had a quick, brilliant mind and a surprising imp inside him that made it hard for her to hold back her laughter, but she didn't dare laugh in front of Hector.

After Hector left, Dottie brought out a box containing tubes of blue beads, so Zoe and Alex could make a bracelet together. They counted the beads as they did so, and Dottie was pleased to note that Zoe's *B* sounds were really coming along.

Satisfied with that much progress, Dottie cleaned everything up. "That's the end of our lesson for today." She got up from the chair, suddenly wishing she weren't wearing a T-shirt with a picture of a cartoon bunny on the front. She'd hoped Zoe would ask her about it and they could practice saying the famous rabbit's name. But it was Alex who'd stared at it several times this morning, causing sensual waves to ripple through her.

He swept Zoe in his arms. "I'm very proud of you. Now let's show Dot around the island on the sailboat." His daughter hugged him around the neck. Over her shoulder he stared at Dottie. "Are you ready?"

No. Sailing with him wasn't part of her job. In fact it was out of the question. She didn't want to feel these feelings she had around him. Yearnings…

"That's very kind of you, Your Highness, but I have other things to do this afternoon, including a lot of paperwork to send in to the Institute. In case you don't get back from sailing by dinnertime, I'll see you and Zoe in the morning for her lesson."

He lowered his daughter to the floor. "I insist."

She took a steadying breath. "Did you just give me a command?"

"If I did, would you obey it?"

There was nothing playful about this conversation. The last thing she wanted to do was offend him, but she refused to be anything but Zoe's speech therapist. With his looks and charismatic personality, he could ensnare any woman he wanted. That's what royal playboys did.

Alex might be a widower with a daughter, but as far as she was concerned, he was at the peak of his manhood now and a hundred times more dangerous. She was reminded of that fact when he'd eyed her T-shirt. A little shiver went through her because he was still eyeing her that way and she was too aware of him.

Dottie needed to turn this around and make it right so he wouldn't misunderstand why she was refusing the invitation. Using a different tactic she said, "I gave you that pack of flash cards. You should take your daughter on your sailboat this afternoon and work with her while the lesson is fresh in her mind."

In a lowered voice she added, "I might be her speech therapist, but outside this classroom I can only be a distraction and cause her more confusion over the mommy issue. She wants your undivided attention and will cooperate when you do the cards with her because she'd do anything for you. There's a saying in English. I'm sure you've heard of it. 'Strike while the iron's hot.'"

"There's another saying by the great teacher Plato," he fired back. "'We can easily forgive a child who is afraid of the dark; the real tragedy of life is when men are afraid of the light.'" He turned to his daughter. "Come with me, Zoe."

Dottie trembled as she watched them leave. Alex had her figured out without knowing anything about her. She *was* afraid. Once upon a time her world had been filled with blinding, glorious light. After it had been taken away, she never wanted to feel it or be in it again. One tragedy in life had been too much.

* * *

Alex put his daughter to bed, but he had to face facts. After the outing on the sailboat and all the swimming and fun coaching moments with the flash cards, it still wasn't enough for his little girl. She didn't want Sofia tending to her.

He'd read the good-night book to her six times, but the tears gushed anyway. She was waiting for her favorite person. "Have you forgotten that Dottie had a lot of work to do tonight? You'll see her in the morning. Here's Betty. She's ready to go to sleep with you." He tucked the baby in her arm, but she pushed it away and sat up.

"Tell Dot to come."

Alex groaned because these tears were different. His daughter had found an outlet for her frustration in Dottie who understood her and had become her ally. What child wouldn't want her to be her mommy and stay with her all the time? Alex got it. She made every moment so memorable, no one else could possibly measure up. Dottie was like a force of nature. Her vivacious personality had brought life into the palace.

Earlier, when he'd asked Hector about Dottie's activities, he'd learned she'd refused a car and had left the grounds on foot. Security said that after she'd jogged ten miles in the heat, she'd hiked to the top of Mount Pelos and sat for an hour. After visiting the church, she'd returned to town and jogged back to the palace.

"Zoe? If you'll stay in your bed, I'll go get her."

The tears slowed down. She reached for her baby. "Hurry, Daddy."

Outside the bedroom he called Dottie on his cell phone, something he'd sworn he wouldn't do in order to keep his distance, but this was an emergency. When she picked up, he asked her to come to Zoe's bedroom.

He sensed the hesitation before she said, "I'll be right there."

It pleased him when a minute later he heard footsteps and watched Dottie hurrying towards the suite with another book in her hand.

"Alex—" she cried in surprise as he stepped away from the paneled wall.

He liked it that she'd said his name of her own volition. "I wondered when you would finally break down."

Dottie smoothed the hair away from her flushed cheek. Her eyes searched his. Ignoring his comment she said, "Did Zoe have another nightmare?"

He moved closer. "No. But she's growing more and more upset when you're not with us. Why didn't you come today? I want the truth."

"I told you I had work."

"Then how come it was reported that you went jogging and climbed Mount Pelos, instead of staying in your room? Were you able to see the sail of my boat from the top?"

A hint of pink crept into her cheeks. She *had* been watching for him. "I saw a lot of sailboats."

"The security staff is agog about the way you spent your day. Not one visit to a designer shop. No shopping frenzy. You undoubtedly wore them to a frazzle with your jogging, but it was good for them."

A small laugh escaped her throat. He liked it that she didn't take herself seriously.

"I'll ask the question again. Why didn't you come with us this afternoon?"

"Surely you know why. Because I'm worried over her growing attachment to me."

"So am I, but that's not the only reason you kept your distance from me today. Are you afraid of being on a boat? Don't you know how to swim?"

"Don't be silly," she whispered.

"How else am I to get some honesty out of you? It's apparent you have a problem with me, pure and simple. My earlier reputation in life as Prince Alexius may have prejudiced you against me, but that was a long time ago. I'm a man now and a father the world knows nothing about. Which of those roles alarms you most?"

She folded her arms. "Neither of them," she said in a quiet voice.

His brows met in a frown. "Then what terrible thing do you imagine would have happened to you today if you'd come with us?"

"I'd rather not talk about it, even if you are a prince." She'd said that "even if you are a prince" thing before. After retaining his gaze for a moment, she looked away. "How did your afternoon go with Zoe?"

"Good, but it would have been better if you'd been along. She won't go to sleep until you say good-night. Tonight she fired Sofia."

"What?"

"It's true. She doesn't want a nanny unless it's you. To save poor Hector the trouble of having to summon you every night, why don't you plan to pop in on her at bedtime. In the end it will save my sanity, too."

She slowly nodded. "Since I won't be here much longer, I can do that."

"Let's not talk about your leaving, not when you barely got here."

"I—I'll go in now." Her voice faltered.

"Thank you." For several reasons, he wasn't through with her yet, but it could wait until she'd said good-night to his daughter. Alex followed her into the bedroom. Zoe was sitting up in her bed holding her baby. She glowed after she saw Dottie.

"Hi, Zoe. If I read you a story, will you go to sleep?"

"Yes. Will you sit on the bed?"

"I can read better on this chair." Dottie drew it close to the bed and sat down. Once again Alex was hooked by Dottie's charm as she read the tale about a butterfly that had lost a wing and needed to find it.

She was a master teacher, but it dawned on him she always kept her distance with Zoe. No hugs or kisses. No endearments. Being the total professional, she knew her place. Ironically his daughter didn't want hugs or kisses from her nannies who tried to mother her, but he knew she was waiting for both from Dottie.

Zoe wasn't the only one.

The second she'd gone to sleep, Dottie tiptoed out of the room. Alex caught up to her in the hall. She couldn't seem to get back to her suite fast enough. They walked through the corridors in silence. As she reached out to open the door to her apartment, he grasped her upper arms and turned her around.

They were close enough he could smell her peach fragrance. She was out of breath, but she was in too good a shape for the small exertion of walking to produce that reaction. "Invite me in," he whispered, sensing how withdrawn she'd become with him. "I want an answer from you and prefer that we don't talk out here in the hall where we can be observed."

"I'm sorry, but we have nothing to talk about. I'm very tired."

"Too tired to tell me what has you so frightened, you're trembling?"

A pained expression crossed over her face. "I wish I hadn't come to Hellenica. If I'd known what was awaiting me, I would have refused."

"For the love of heaven, why? If I've done something unforgivable in your eyes, it's only fair you tell me."

"Of course you haven't." She shook her head, but wouldn't look at him. "This has to do with Zoe."

"Because she keeps calling you Mommy?"

"That and much more."

At a total loss, he let go of her with reluctance. "I don't understand."

She eased away from him. "Five years ago my husband and son were killed by a drunk driver in a horrific crash." Tears glistened on her cheeks. "I lost the great loves of my life. Cory was Zoe's age when he died."

Alex was aghast.

"He had an articulation problem like hers, only he couldn't do his vowel sounds. I'd been working with him for a year with the help of a therapist, and he'd just gotten to the point where he could say *Daddy* plainly when—"

Obviously she was too choked up to say the rest. His eyes closed tightly for a moment. He remembered the pain in hers the other day.

"I've worked with all kinds of children, but Zoe is the only one who has ever reminded me of him. The other day when she laughed, it sounded like Cory."

"You didn't let on." His voice grated.

"I'm thankful for that." He thought he heard a little

sob get trapped in her throat. "It's getting harder to be around her without breaking down. That's why I didn't go with you today. I—I thought I'd gotten past my grief," she stammered, "but coming here has proven otherwise."

He sucked in his breath. "You may wish you hadn't come to Hellenica, but keep in mind you're doing something for my daughter only you can do. Watching Zoe respond to your techniques has already caused me to stop grieving over her pain.

"No matter how much you're still mourning your loss, doesn't it make you feel good to be helping her the way you once helped your son? Wouldn't your husband have done anything for your son if your positions were reversed?"

She looked away, moved by his logic. "Yes," came the faint whisper, "but—"

"But what? Tell me everything."

"It's just that I've felt…guilty for not being with them that terrible day."

"You're suffering survivor's guilt."

"Yes."

"In my own way I had the same reaction after Teresa passed away. It took me a long time to convince myself everything possible had been done for her and I had to move on for Zoe's sake."

She nodded.

"Then it's settled. From now on after her morning lessons, we'll have another one during the afternoons in the swimming pool. We'll practice what you've taught her while we play. After finding your strength and solace in furthering your career, don't you see you can make a difference with Zoe and maybe lay those ghosts to rest? It's time to take a risk. With my schedule changed, I can spend as much time as possible with both of you now."

"I've noticed." After a pause, she added, "You're a remarkable man."

"It's because of you, Dottie. You're helping me get close to my daughter in a whole new way. I'll never be able to thank you enough for that."

"You don't need to thank me. I'm just so glad for the two of you." Dottie wiped the moisture from the corners of her eyes. "Tomorrow we'll work on her *W* sounds. Good night, Alex."

CHAPTER FIVE

WHAT luxury! Dottie had never known anything like it until she'd come to the palace ten days ago. After a delicious lunch, it was sheer bliss to lie in the sun on the lounger around the palace pool enjoying an icy fruit drink.

Zoe's morning lesson with her daddy had gone well. Her *B* and G sounds were coming along, but she struggled with the *W*. It might be one of the last sounds she mastered on her long journey to intelligible speech.

Dottie was glad to have the pool to herself. While they were changing into their swimsuits, she was trying to get a grip on her emotions. She'd been doing a lot of thinking, and Alex had been right about one thing. If she'd been the one killed and Cory had been left with his speech problem, then she would have wanted Neil to stop at nothing to find the right person to help their son. At the moment, Dottie was the right person for Zoe.

Deep in her own thoughts, she heard a tremendous splash followed by Zoe's shriek of laughter. Dottie turned her head in time to see Zoe running around the rim of the pool in her red bathing suit, shouting with glee. She was following a giant black whale maybe five feet long skimming the top of the water with a human torpedo propelling it.

Suddenly Alex's dark head emerged, splashing more water everywhere. Zoe got soaked and came flying toward Dottie, who grabbed her own towel and wiped off her shoulders. "You need some sunscreen. Stand still and I'll put it on you." Zoe did her bidding. "I didn't know a whale lived in your pool."

The child giggled. "Come with me." She tugged on Dottie's arm.

"I think I'd rather stay here and watch."

Alex stared at Dottie with a look she couldn't decipher, but didn't say anything. By now Zoe had joined him and was riding on top of the whale while he helped her hold on. The darling little girl was so happy, she seemed to burst with it.

Dottie threw her beach wrap around her to cover her emerald-colored bikini and got up from the lounger. She walked over to the side of the pool and sat down to dangle her legs in the water while she watched their antics.

All of a sudden it occurred to her she was having real fun for the first time in years. This was different than watching from the sidelines of other people's lives. Because of Alex she was an actual participant and was feeling a part of life again. The overpowering sense of oneness with him shook her to the core. So did the desire she felt being near him. That's why she didn't dare get in the water. Her need to touch him was overcoming her good sense.

"I think we need to name Zoe's whale," he called to her.

Dottie nodded. "Preferably a two syllable word starting with *W*."

Both she and Alex suggested a lot of names, laughing into each other's eyes at some of their absurd suggestions. Zoe clapped her hands the minute she heard her daddy say *Wally*. Though it wasn't a name that started with *Wh* like whale, it was the name his daughter wanted. When Zoe pronounced it, the sound came out like *Oye-ee*.

Dottie was secretly impressed when he came up with the idea of Zoe pretending she was a grouper fish. Evidently his daughter knew what one looked like and she formed her mouth in an *O* shape, opening and closing it. After a half hour of playing and practice, the *wa* was starting to make an appearance.

"Well done, Your Highness." Dottie smiled at him. "She wouldn't have made that sound this fast without your help."

He reciprocated with a slow, lazy smile, making jelly of her insides. The afternoon was exhilarating for Dottie, a divine moment out of time. Anyone watching would think they were a happy family. Before she knew it, dinner was served beneath the umbrella of the table on the sun deck. Zoe displayed a healthy appetite, pleasing her father and Dottie.

Toward the end of their meal he said, "Attention, everyone. I have an announcement to make." He looked at Zoe. "Guess who came home today?"

She stopped drinking her juice. "Uncle Stasi?"

"Yes. Your one and only favorite uncle."

"Goody!" she blurted. "He's funny."

"I've missed him, too. Tonight there's going to be a

party to welcome him back. I'm going to take you two ladies with me."

Zoe squealed in delight.

"After we finish dinner, I want you to go upstairs and get ready. Put on your prettiest dresses, because there's going to be dancing. When it's time, I'll come by for you."

Dancing?

Adrenalin surged through Dottie's body at the thought of getting that close to him. Heat poured off her, but she couldn't attribute all of it to the sun. She suspected his announcement had caused a spike in her temperature.

Her mind went through a mental search of her wardrobe. The only thing possibly presentable for such an affair was her simple black dress with her black high heels.

"Will it be a large party, Your Highness?"

He darted her a curious glance. "Thirty or so guests, mostly family friends. If you're both finished with dinner, let's go upstairs."

After gathering their things, Dottie said she'd see them later and she hurried back to her bedroom for a long shower and shampoo. She blowdried her hair and left it loose with a side part, then put on her black dress with the cap sleeves and round neck.

While she was applying her coral-frost lipstick, she thought she heard a noise in the other room. When she went to investigate, she saw Zoe looking like a vision in a long white dress with ruffles and a big yellow sash. But her face was awash in tears. She came running to her.

Without conscious thought, Dottie knelt down and

drew her into her arms. It was the first hug she'd given her, but she could no longer hold back. Zoe clung to her while she wept, exactly the way Cory had done so many hundreds of times when he'd needed comfort.

"What's wrong, darling?"

"Daddy's going to get married."

Dottie was trying to understand. "Don't you mean your uncle?"

"No—I heard *Yiayia* tell Sofia. My daddy's going to marry Princess Genevieve. But I want *you* to be my new mommy. When I kissed *Yiayia* good-night, she told me Princess Genevieve will be at the party and I had to be good."

A stabbing pain attacked Dottie until she could hardly breathe. "I see. Zoe, this is something you need to talk to your daddy about, but not until you go to bed. Does he know you're here with me?"

"No."

Dottie stood up. "I need to phone Hector so he can tell your daddy you ran to my room."

When that was done, she took Zoe in the bathroom. After wetting a washcloth, she wiped the tears off her face. "There. Now we're ready. When we get to the party, I want you to smile and keep smiling. Can you do that for me?"

After a slight hesitation, Zoe nodded.

Dottie clasped her hand and walked her back in the other room. "Have I told you how pretty you look in your new dress?"

"Both of you look absolutely beautiful," came the sound of a deep, familiar voice.

Alex.

Dottie gasped softly when she saw that he'd entered

the room. Since Zoe had left the door open, he must not have felt the need to knock. The prince, tall and dark, had dressed in a formal, midnight-blue suit and tie, taking her breath. His penetrating black eyes swept over her, missing nothing. The look in them sent a river of heat through her body.

"Zoe wanted to show me how she looked, Your Highness. In her haste, she forgot to tell Sofia."

He looked so handsome when he smiled, Dottie felt light-headed. "That's understandable. This is my daughter's first real party. Are you ready?"

When Zoe nodded, he grasped her other hand and the three of them left the room. He led them down the grand staircase where they could hear music and voices. Though Zoe lacked her usual sparkle, she kept smiling like the princess she was. Her training had served her well. Even at her young age, she moved with the grace and dignity of a royal.

Some of the elegantly dressed guests were dancing, others were eating. The three of them passed through a receiving line of titled people and close friends of the Constantinides family.

"Zoe?" her father said. "I'd like you to meet Princess Genevieve."

For a minute, Dottie reeled. She'd seen the lovely young princess in the news. Zoe was a trooper and handled their first meeting beautifully. One royal princess to another. Dottie loved Zoe for her great show of poise in front of the woman she didn't want for her new mother.

Dottie was trying to see the good. It was natural that Alex would marry again, and Zoe desperately needed a mother's love. Plus their match would give Alex more children and Zoe wouldn't have to be the only child. In that respect it was more necessary than ever that her speech improve enough that when Alex married Princess Genevieve, his daughter could make herself understood. Zoe also needed to be strong in her English speech because she would be tested when French was introduced into their household. Princess Genevieve would expect it. The House of Helvetia was located on the south side of Lake Geneva in the French-speaking region.

Now that she knew of Alex's future plans, Dottie had to focus on the additional goal to pursue for his daughter. She needed to help prepare Zoe for the next phase in her life and—

"My, my. What have we here?"

A male voice Dottie didn't recognize broke in on her thoughts. She turned her head to discover another extremely attractive man with black hair standing at the end of the line. Almost the same height as Alex, he bore a superficial resemblance to him, but his features were less rugged. The brothers could be the same age, which she estimated to be early to mid-thirties.

When she realized it was Crown Prince Stasio, she curtsied. "Welcome home, Your Highness."

He flashed her an infectious smile. "You don't need to do that around me. My little brother told me you're working with Zoe. That makes us all family. Did anyone ever tell you you're very easy on the eyes?" His were black, too. "Alex held back on that pertinent fact."

What a tease he was! "Zoe told me you were funny. I think she's right."

The crown prince laughed. She noticed he had a fabulous tan. "Tell me about yourself. Where have you been hiding all my life?" He was incorrigible and so different from Alex, who was more serious minded. Of the two, Dottie privately thought that Zoe's father seemed much more the natural ruler of their country.

"I'm from New York."

His eyes narrowed. "Coming to Hellenica must feel like you dropped off the edge of the planet, right?"

"It's paradise here."

"It is now that I've got my little Zoe to dance with." He reached over and picked up his niece. After they hugged, he set her down again. "Come on. I'm going to spin you around the ballroom."

Zoe's smile lit up for real as he whirled her away. Dancing lessons hadn't been wasted on her either. She moved like a royal princess who was years older, capturing everyone's attention. People started clapping. Dottie couldn't have been prouder of her if she'd been Zoe's real mother.

While she watched, she felt a strong hand slip around her waist. The next thing she knew Alex had drawn her into his arms. His wonderful, clean male scent and the brush of his legs against hers sent sparks of electricity through her system. In her heels, she was a little taller and felt like their bodies had been made for each other.

"Why won't you look at me?" he whispered. "Everyone's going to think you don't like me."

"I'm trying to concentrate on our dancing. It's been a long time." The soft rock had a hypnotizing effect on her. She could stay like this for hours, almost but not quite embracing him.

"For me, too. I've been waiting ages to get you in my arms like this. If it's in plain sight of our guests, so be it. You feel good to me, Dottie. So damn good you're in danger of being carried off. Only my princely duty keeps me from doing what I feel like doing."

Ah… Before Zoe's revelations in the bedroom tonight, Dottie might have allowed herself to be carried away. The clamorings of her body had come to painful life and only he could assuage them.

"I understand. That's why I'm going to say goodnight after this dance. There are other female guests in the ballroom no doubt waiting for their turn around the floor with you. You're a terrific dancer, by the way."

"There's only one woman I want to be with tonight and she's right here within kissing distance. You could have no idea the willpower it's taking not to taste that tempting mouth of yours." He spoke with an intensity that made her legs go weak. "While we were out at the pool, I would have pulled you in if Zoe hadn't been with us."

"It's a good thing you didn't. Otherwise your daughter will be more confused than ever when she sees you ask Princess Genevieve to dance."

His body stiffened. She'd hit a nerve, but he had no clue it had pierced her to the depths. "I know you well enough to realize you had a deliberate reason for bringing up her name. Why did you do it?"

Dottie's heart died a little because the music had stopped, bringing those thrilling moments in his arms to an end. She lifted her head and looked at him for the first time since they'd entered the ballroom. "When you put Zoe to bed tonight, she'll tell you. Thank you for an enchanting evening, Your Highness. I won't forget. See you in the morning."

She eased out of his arms and walked out of the

ballroom. But the second she reached the staircase, she raced up the steps and ran the rest of the way to her room.

"Dot," Zoe called to her the next morning as she and her father came into the classroom. "Look at this?" She held up a CD.

"What's on it?"

"It's a surprise. Put it in your laptop," said Alex.

After giving him a curious glance, Dottie walked around to the end of the table and put it in. After a moment they could all see last night's events at the party on the screen, complete with the music. There she was enclosed in Alex's arms. Princess Genevieve would not have been happy.

Whoever had taken the video had caught everything, including what went on after Dottie had left the ballroom. Her throat swelled with emotion as she watched Alex dance with his daughter. If he'd asked Princess Genevieve to dance, that portion hadn't been put on the CD.

She smiled at Zoe. "You're so lucky to have a video of your first party. Did you love it?"

"Yes!" There weren't any shadows in the little girl's eyes. Whatever conversation had taken place between father and daughter at bedtime, she looked happy. "Uncle Stasi told me I could stand on his feet while he danced with me. He made me laugh."

"The crown prince is a real character." Her gaze swerved to Alex. "He made me laugh, as well. I've decided you and your brother must have given certain people some nervous moments when you were younger."

Alex's grin turned her heart right over. "Our parents

particularly. My brother was upset you left the party before he could dance with you."

"Maybe that was for the best. My high heels might have hurt the tops of his feet."

At that remark both he and Zoe laughed. Dottie was enjoying this too much and suggested they get started on the morning lesson.

They worked in harmony until Alex said it was time for lunch by the pool. After they'd finished eating, Zoe ran into the cabana to get into her swimsuit. Dottie took advantage of the time they were alone to talk to him.

"I'm glad we're by ourselves for a minute. I want to discuss Zoe's preschool situation and wondered how you'd feel if I went with her to class in the morning. You know, just to prop up her confidence. We'll come back here for lunch and enjoy our afternoon session with her out here. What do you think?"

He sipped his coffee. "That's an excellent suggestion. Otherwise she'll keep putting off wanting to go back."

"Exactly."

Alex released a sigh. "Since our talk about her friends, I've worried about her being away from the other children this long."

Dottie was glad they were on her same wavelength. "Is there any particular child she's close to at school?"

Their gazes held. "Not that she has mentioned. As you know, school hasn't been her best experience."

"Then tell me this. Who goes to the school?"

"Besides those who live in Hellenica, there are a few children of some younger diplomats who attend at the various elementary grade levels."

"From where?"

"The U.K., France, Italy, Bosnia, Germany, the States."

The States? "That's interesting." Dottie started to get excited, but she kept her ideas to herself and finished her coffee.

Alex didn't say anything more, yet she felt a strange new tension growing between them. Her awareness of him was so powerful, she couldn't sit there any longer. "If you'll excuse me, I'll go change into my bathing suit."

"Not yet," he countered. "There's something I need to tell you before Zoe comes out."

Her pulse picked up speed. "If it's about her running to my room last eve—"

"It is," he cut in on her. "After what Zoe told me while I was putting her to bed, I realize this matter needs to be cleared up."

"Your marriage to Princess Genevieve is none of my business. As long as—"

"Dottie," he interrupted her again, this time with an underlying trace of impatience. "There will be no marriage. Believe me when I tell you there was never any question of my marrying her. I impressed that on Zoe before she went to sleep."

Dottie had to fight to prevent Alex from seeing her great relief and joy.

"Since Teresa's death, it has been my grandmother's ambition to join the House of Helvetia to our own. Zoe had the great misfortune of overhearing her tell Sofia about her plans. In her innocence, Zoe has expressed her love for you and has told *Yiayia* she wants *you* to be her new mommy."

"I was afraid of that," she whispered.

"Last night I spoke to my grandmother. She admitted that she arranged last night's party for me, not Stasi. She hoped that by inviting Princess Genevieve, it would put an end to Zoe's foolishness."

"Oh, dear."

"The queen has taken great pains to remind me once again what a wonderful mother Teresa was and that it is time I took another wife. Naturally she's grateful you've identified Zoe's problem, but now she wants you to go back to New York. I learned she's already found another speech therapist to replace you."

Dottie's head reared. "Who?"

"I have no idea, but it's not important. My grandmother is running true to form," he said before Dottie could comment further. "She tried to use all her logic with me by reminding me Zoe will have to be taken care of by a nanny until maturity; therefore it won't be good to allow her to get any more attached to you."

"In that regard, she's right."

Anger rose inside him. "Nevertheless, the queen stepped way out of bounds last night. I told her that I had no plans to marry again. She would have to find another way to strengthen the ties with Helvetia because Zoe's welfare was my only concern and you were staying put."

His dark eyes pierced hers. "I'm sure my words have shocked you, but it's necessary you know the truth so there won't be any more misunderstandings."

"Daddy?" They both turned to see Zoe trying to drag out her five-foot inflated whale from the cabana, but it was stuck. "I need help!"

Before he moved in her direction he said, "My grandmother may still be the ruler of Hellenica, but I rule over my own life and Zoe's. My daughter knows she doesn't have to worry about Princess Genevieve ever again, no matter what her *yiayia* might say."

With that declaration, he took a few steps, then paused. "Just so you know, after I've put Zoe to bed tonight, I'm taking you to the old part of the city, so don't plan on an early night."

Alex stayed with Zoe and read stories to her until she fell asleep. Since she realized he wasn't going to marry Princess Genevieve, his daughter actually seemed at peace for a change. With a nod to Sofia in the next room to keep an eye on her, he left for his own suite.

He showered and shaved before dressing in a sport shirt and trousers. On his way out of the room, he called for an unmarked car with smoked glass to be brought around to his private entrance. With Stasio in the palace, Alex didn't need to worry about anything else tonight. He called security and asked them to escort Dottie to the entrance.

After she climbed in the back with him, he explained that they were driving to the city's ancient amphitheater to see the famous sound and light show. "We're going to visit the site of many archaeological ruins. As we walk around, you'll see evidence of the Cycladic civilization and the Byzantium empire."

Alex had seen the show many times before with visiting dignitaries, but tonight he was with Dottie and he'd never felt so alive. The balmy air caused him to forget everything but the exciting woman who sat next to him.

Throughout the program he could tell by her questions and remarks that she loved it. After it was over he lounged against a temple column while she explored.

The tourists had started leaving, yet all he could see was her beautiful silhouette against the night sky. She'd put her hair back so her distinctive profile was revealed. She was dressed in another skirt and blouse, and he was reminded of the first time he'd seen her in his office.

"Dottie?" he called softly in the fragrant night air as he moved behind her. She let out a slight gasp and swung around.

He caught her to him swiftly and kissed her mouth to stop any other sound from escaping. Her lips were warm and tempting, but he didn't deepen the kiss. "Forgive me for doing that," he whispered against them, "but I didn't want you to say *Your Highness* and draw attention. Come and get in the car. It's late."

He helped her into the backseat with him and shut the door. "I'm not going to apologize for what I did," he murmured against her hot cheek. "If you want to slap me, you have my permission. But if I'm going to be punished for it, I'll take my chances now and give you a proper reason."

Alex's compelling mouth closed over Dottie's with a hunger that set her knees knocking. She'd sensed this moment was inevitable. Since her arrival in Hellenica, they'd been together early in the morning, late at night and most of the hours in between. He possessed a lethal sensuality for which she had no immunity.

Knowing he had no plans to marry Princess Genevieve, Dottie settled deeper into his arms and found herself giving him kiss for kiss. It was time she faced an ironic truth about herself. She wasn't any different than the rest of the female population who found the prince so attractive, they'd give anything to be in her position.

Royal scandal might abound, but she'd just discovered there was a reason for it. Forbidden fruit with this gorgeous male made these moments of physical intimacy exquisite. When a man was as incredibly potent and exciting as Alex, you could blot out everything else, even the fact that the driver ferrying them back to the palace was aware of every sound of ecstasy pouring out of her.

She finally put her hands against his chest and tore her mouth from his so she could ease back enough to look at him. Still trying to catch her breath, she asked, "Do you know what we are, Your Highness?" Her voice sounded less than steady to her own ears. She hated her inability to control that part of her.

"Suppose you tell me," he said in a husky voice.

"We're both a cliché. The prince and the hired help, nipping out for a little pleasure. I've just confirmed everything I've ever read in books and have seen on the news about palace intrigue."

"Who are you more angry at?" he murmured, kissing the tips of her fingers. "Me, for having taken unfair advantage? Or you, for having the right of refusal at any time which you didn't exercise? I'm asking myself if I'm fighting your righteous indignation that served you too late, or the ghost of your dead husband."

She squirmed because he'd hit the mark dead center. "Both," she answered honestly.

"Tell me about your husband. Was it love at first sight with him?"

"I don't know. It just seemed right from the beginning."

"Give me a few details. I really want to know what it would be like to have that kind of freedom."

Dottie stirred restlessly, sensing he meant what he said. "We met in Albany, New York, where I was raised. I went to the local pharmacy to pick up a prescription for my aunt. Neil had just been hired as a new pharmacist. It was late and there weren't any other customers.

"He told me it would take a while to get it ready, so we began talking. The next day he phoned and asked me out with the excuse that he'd just moved there from New York City and didn't know anyone. He was fun and kind and very smart.

"On our first date we went to a movie. After it was over, he told me he was going to marry me and there was nothing I could do about it. Four months later we got married and before we knew it, Cory was on the way. I was incredibly happy."

Alex's arm tightened around her. "I envy you for having those kinds of memories."

"Surely you have some wonderful ones, too."

A troubled sigh escaped his lips. "To quote you on several occasions, even if I am a prince, the one thing I've never had power over was my own personal happiness. Duty to my country came first. My marriage to Teresa was planned years before we got together, so any relationships I had before the wedding couldn't be taken seriously.

"She was beautiful in her own way, very accomplished. Sweet. But it was never an affair of the heart or anything close to it. On his deathbed, my father commanded me to marry her. I couldn't tell him I wouldn't."

Dottie shuddered. "Did you love him?"

"Yes."

"I can't comprehend being in your shoes, but I

admire you for being so devoted to your father and your country. Did Teresa love you?"

He took a steadying breath. "Before she died, she told me she'd fallen in love with me. I told her the same thing, not wanting to hurt her. She told me I was a liar, but she said she loved me for it."

"Oh, Alex… How hard for both of you."

"I wanted to fall in love with her, but we both know you can't force something that's not there. Zoe was my one gift from the gods who brood over Mount Pelos."

Her gaze lifted to his. "Not to be in love and have to marry—that's anathema to me. No wonder you seek relief in the shadows with someone handy like me. I get it, Alex. I really do. And you *didn't* take unfair advantage of me. It's been so long since I've been around an attractive man, my hormones are out of kilter right now."

"Is that what this tension is between us? Hormones?" he said with a twinge of bitterness she felt pierce her where it hurt most.

"I don't have a better word for it." She buried her face in her hands. "I loved Neil more than you can imagine. Thank heaven neither of us had a royal bone in our bodies to prevent us from knowing joy."

He stroked the back of her neck in a way that sent fingers of delight down her spine. "How did you manage after they were killed?"

"My aunt. She reminded me not everyone had been as lucky as I'd been. Her boyfriend got killed when he was deployed overseas in the military, so she never married. In her inimitable way she told me to stop pitying myself and get on with something useful.

"Her advice prompted me to go to graduate school

in New York City and become a speech therapist. After graduation I was hired on by the Stillman Institute. Little did I know that all the time I'd been helping Cory with his speech that last year, I was preparing for a lifetime career."

"Is your aunt still alive?"

"No. She died fourteen months ago."

"I'm sorry. I wish she were still living so I could thank her for her inspired advice. My Zoe is thriving because of you." He pulled her closer. "What about your parents?"

"They died in a car crash when I was just a little girl."

"It saddens me you've had to deal with so much grief."

"It comes to us all. In my aunt's case, it was good she passed away. With her chronic pneumonia, she could never recover and every illness made her worse."

"My mother was like that. She had been so ill that Stasi and I were thankful once she took her last breath."

"What about your father?"

"He developed an aggressive cancer of the thyroid. After he was gone, my grandmother took over to make sure we were raised according to her exacting Valleder standards. She was the power behind my grandfather's throne."

"She's done a wonderful job. I'll tell her that when I leave Hellenica." Dottie took a deep breath and sat back in the seat. "And now, despite her disapproval that I haven't left yet, here I am making out in an unmarked car with Prince Alexius Constantinides. How *could* you have given Zoe such an impossible last name? Nine consonants. *Nine!* And two of them are *T*'s," she half sobbed as the dam broke and she felt tears on her cheeks.

Alex reached over and smoothed the moisture from her face. He put his lips where his hand had been. "I'm glad there are nine. I won't let you go until she can pronounce our last name perfectly. That's going to take a long time."

"You'll have gone through at least half a dozen speech therapists by then."

"Possibly, but you'll be there in the background until she no longer needs your services."

"We've been over this ground before."

"We haven't even started," he declared as if announcing an edict. "Shall we get out of the car? We've been back at the palace for the past ten minutes. My driver probably wants to go to bed, which is where we should be."

She didn't think he meant that the way it came out, but with Alex you couldn't be absolutely sure when his teasing side would suddenly show up. All she knew was that her face was suffused with heat. She flung the car door open and ran into the palace, leaving him in the proverbial royal dust.

The death of her husband had put an end to all fairy tales, and that was the only place a prince could stay. She refused to be in the background of his life. It was time to close the storybook for good.

CHAPTER SIX

AT ELEVEN-FORTY-FIVE the next morning, Alex did something unprecedented and drove to the preschool to pick up Zoe and Dottie himself. He'd decided he'd better wear something more formal for this public visit and chose his dove-grey suit with a white shirt and grey vest. He toned it with a darker grey tie that bore the royal crest of the monarchy in silver, wanting to look his best for the woman who'd already turned his world inside out.

The directress of the school accompanied him to the classroom, where he spotted his daughter sitting in front and Dottie seated in the back. As the woman announced the arrival of Prince Alexius Constantinides, Dottie's blue eyes widened in shock. Her gaze clung to his for a moment.

He heard a collective sound of awe from the children, something he was used to in his capacity as prince. Children were always a delight. He was enjoying this immensely, but it was clear Dottie was stunned that he'd decided to come and get them. He knew in his gut her eyes wouldn't have ignited like that if she hadn't been happy to see him.

The teacher, Mrs. Pappas, urged the roomful of

twelve children to stand and bow. Zoe stood up, but she turned and smiled at Dottie before saying good morning to His Royal Highness along with the others. Alex got a kick out of the whole thing as the children kept looking at Zoe, knowing he was her daddy.

He'd never seen his daughter this happy in his life, and he should have done this before now. It lit up her whole being. Dottie was transforming his life in whole new ways. Because of her influence, Alex wanted to give his struggling preschooler a needed boost this morning. But she wasn't so struggling now that she had Dottie in her court.

He shook hands with everyone, then they returned to the palace. After changing into his swimming trunks, he joined them at the pool for lunch. With Zoe running around, he could finally talk to Dottie in private.

"How did my daughter do in class?"

"She participated without hanging back."

"That's because you've given her the confidence."

"You know it's been a team effort. While I've got you alone for a minute, let me tell you something else that happened this morning."

Alex could tell she was excited. "Go ahead."

"I arranged to talk with the directress about Zoe and was given permission to visit the other preschool class. One of the boys enrolled is an American from Pennsylvania named Mark Varney. He's supposed to be in first grade, but his parents put him back in preschool because he has no knowledge of Greek and needs to start with the basics. The situation has made him unhappy and he's turning into a loner."

"And you've decided that two negatives could make a positive?"

"Maybe." She half laughed. "It's scary how well you read my mind. Here's the thing—if you sanctioned it and Mark's parents allowed him to come back to the palace after school next time, he and Zoe could have some one-on-one time here in the pool, or down on the beach. I'd help them with their lessons, but the rest of the time they could have fun together. A play date is what she needs."

"I couldn't agree more."

"Oh, good! The directress says he's feeling inadequate. If his parents understood the circumstances and explained to him about Zoe's speech problem, he might be willing to help her and they could become friends in the process. That would help his confidence level, too."

Alex heard the appeal in Dottie's voice. "I'll ask Hector to handle it and we'll see how the first play date goes."

Light filled her blue eyes, dazzling him. "Thank you for being willing."

"That's rather ironic for you to be thanking me. I'm the one who should be down on my knees to you for thinking of it. She's a different child already because of you."

"You keep saying that, but you don't give yourself enough credit, Alex. When she saw you walk into the schoolroom earlier today, her heart was in her eyes. I wish I'd had a camera on me so I could have taken a picture. Every father should have a daughter who loves him that much. The extra time you've spent with her lately is paying huge dividends. I know it's taking time away from your duties, but if you can keep it up, you'll never regret it."

He rubbed his lower lip with the pad of his thumb,

staring at her through shuttered eyes. "That's why I sent for Stasi to come home. With you showing me the way, I'm well aware Zoe needs me and am doing everything in my power to free myself up."

"I know." She suddenly broke away from his gaze to look at Zoe. "She's waiting for us. Today we'll work on the letter *C*. Her preschool teacher brought her own cat to class. The children learned how to take care of one. Zoe got to pet it and couldn't have been more thrilled."

Dottie had inexplicably changed the subject and was talking faster than usual, a sign that something was going on inside her, making her uncomfortable. When she got up from the chair, he followed her over to the edge of the pool and listened as she engaged his daughter in a conversation that was really a teaching moment. She had a remarkable, unique way of communicating. Zoe ate it up. Why wouldn't she? There was no one else like Dottie.

Dottie was more than a speech therapist for his daughter. She was her advocate. Her selfless efforts to help Zoe lead a normal life couldn't be repaid with gifts or perks or money she'd already refused to accept. The woman wanted his daughter to succeed for the purest of reasons. She wanted it for a stranger's child, too. That made Dottie Richards a person of interest to him in ways that went deep beneath the surface.

Alex took off his sandals and dove into the deep end. After doing some underwater laps, he emerged next to his daughter, causing her to shriek with laughter. The day had been idyllic and it wasn't over.

As he did more laps, his thoughts drifted to his conversation with Dottie last night. When he'd turned eighteen, his family had arranged the betrothal to Princess

Teresa. However, until he'd been ready to commit to marriage, he'd known pleasure and desire with various women over the years. Those women had understood nothing long lasting could come of the relationship. No one woman's memory had lingered long in his mind. Forget his heart.

When Zoe came along, their daughter gave them both something new and wonderful to focus on. With Teresa's passing, Zoe had become the joy of his life. There'd been other women in the past two years, but the part of his psyche that had never been touched was still a void.

Enter Dottie Richards, a woman who'd buried a son and husband. He could still hear her saying she'd lost the great loves of her life. She'd experienced the kind of overwhelming love denied him because of his royal roots. He really envied her the freedom to choose the man who'd satisfied her passion at its deepest level and had given her a child.

Though it was an unworthy sentiment, Alex found himself resenting her husband for that same freedom. If Alex had been a commoner and had met her in his early twenties—before she'd met her husband—would she have been as attracted to him as he was to her? Would they have married?

She wasn't indifferent to Alex. The way she'd kissed him back last night convinced him of her strong attraction to him. He'd also sensed her interest at odd times when he noticed her eyes on him. The way she sometimes breathed faster around him for no apparent reason. But he had no way to gauge the true depth of her emotions until he could get her alone again.

As for his feelings, all he knew was that she'd lit a

fire inside him. In two weeks, even without physical intimacy, Dottie affected him more than Teresa had ever done during the three years of their marriage.

For the first time in his life he was suddenly waking up every morning hardly able to breathe until he saw her. For the only time in his existence he was questioning everything about the royal legacy that made him who he was and dictated his destiny.

His jealousy terrified him. He'd seen his brother's interest in her. Stasi's arranged marriage would be happening on his thirty-fifth birthday, in less than three weeks now. Until then it didn't stop him from enjoying and looking at other women. But it had angered Alex, who felt territorial when it came to Dottie. That's why he hadn't let Stasi dance with her. Alex had no right to feel this way, but the situation had gone way beyond rights.

Alex *wanted* his daughter's speech therapist. But as he'd already learned, a command from him meant nothing to her. A way had to be found so she wouldn't leave, but he had to be careful that he didn't frighten her off.

He swam back to Zoe, who hung on to the edge of the pool, practicing the hard *C* sound with Dottie. Without looking him in the eye, Dottie said, "Here's your daddy. Now that your lesson is over, I have to go inside. Zoe, I need to tell you now that I won't be able come to your bedroom to say good-night later. I have plans I can't break, but I'll see you in the morning." She finally glanced at him. "Your Highness."

Alex had no doubts that if she'd dared and if it wouldn't have alarmed Zoe, Dottie would have run away from him as fast as she could. Fortunately one of the positive benefits of being the prince meant he could keep twenty-four-hour surveillance on her.

After she'd left the sun deck, he spent another half hour in the pool with his daughter before they went inside. But once in her room, Zoe told Sofia to go away. When Alex tried to reason with her and get her to apologize, she broke down in tears, begging him to eat dinner with her in her room. She didn't want to be with *Yiayia*.

Dottie's announcement that she wouldn't be coming in to say good-night had sent the sun behind a black cloud. Naturally Dottie had every right to spend her evenings the way she wished. That's what he told Zoe. He had to help his daughter see that, but the idyllic day had suddenly vanished like a curl of smoke in the air.

"Make her come, Daddy."

A harsh laugh escaped his lips. You didn't make Dottie do anything. He didn't have that kind of power. She had to do it herself because she wanted to.

What if she *didn't* want to? What if the memory of life with her husband trapped her in the past and she couldn't, or didn't want to, reach out? On the heels of those questions came an even more important one.

Why would she reach out? What did a prince have to offer a commoner? An affair? A secret life? The answers to that question not only stared him in the face, they kicked him in the gut with enough violence to knock the wind out of him.

Once Zoe was asleep, Alex left for his suite, taking the palace stairs three steps at a time to the next floor. The last person he expected to find in his living room was Stasio with a glass of scotch in his hand.

He tossed back a drink. "It's about time you made an appearance, little brother." For a while now a cross-grain tone of discontent had lain behind Stasi's speech and it had grown stronger over the last few months. No crystal ball was needed here. The bitter subject of arranged marriages still burned like acid on his tongue as it did on Stasi's.

"Did you and *Yiayia* have another row tonight?" Alex started unbuttoning his shirt and took off his shoes.

"What do you mean, another one?" Stasio slammed his half-empty glass on the coffee table, spilling some of it. "It's been the same argument for seventeen years, but tonight I put an end to it."

"Translate for me," Alex rapped out tersely.

Stasio's mouth thinned to a white line. "I told her I broke it off with Beatriz while I was in Valleder. I can't go through with the wedding."

Alex felt the hairs on the back of his neck stand on end. He stared hard at his brother. All the time Stasi had put off coming home, something in the back of Alex's mind had divined the truth, but he hadn't been able to make his brother open up about it.

Since Stasio had been old enough to comprehend life, he'd been forced to bear the burden of knowing he would be king one day. That was hard enough. But to be married for the rest of his life to a woman he didn't love would have kept him in a living hell. No one knew it better than Alex.

"How is Beatriz dealing with it?"

"Not well," he whispered in agony.

"But she's always known how you truly felt. No matter how much this has hurt her, deep down it couldn't have come as a complete surprise. I thought she would have broken it off a long time ago."

"That miracle never happened. She wanted the marriage, just the way Teresa wanted yours." Alex couldn't deny it. "What always astounded me was that you were able to handle going through with your marriage to her."

Alex wheeled around. "The truth?"

"Always."

"It was the last thing I wanted. I wouldn't have married her, but with Father on his deathbed making me promise to follow through with it, I couldn't take the fight with him any longer and caved. The only thing that kept me sane was the fact that I wouldn't be king one day, so I wouldn't have to be in the public eye every second. And then, Zoe came along. Now I can't imagine my life without her."

Stasio paled. "Neither can I. She's the one ray of sunshine around this tomb." He took a deep breath. "Under the circumstances I should be grateful *Yiayia* isn't taking her last breath because there will be no forced wedding with Beatriz. Philippe has backed me in this and he holds a certain sway with our grandmother."

Alex was afraid that was wishful thinking on Stasio's part. Not only was Philippe his best friend, he'd been one of the lucky royals who'd ended up marrying the American girl he'd loved years earlier. They'd had a son together and the strict rules had been waived in his particular case.

But the queen hadn't approved of Philippe's marriage, so it didn't follow she would give an inch when it came to Stasio's decision. In her eyes he'd created a monumental catastrophe that could never be forgiven.

"So what's going to happen now?"

"Beatriz's parents have given a statement to the press. It's probably all over the news as we speak or will be in a matter of hours. Once the story grows legs, I'll be torn apart. I had to tell *Yiayia* tonight to prepare her for what's coming."

"What was our grandmother's reaction?"

"You know her as well as I do. Putting on her stone face, she said the coronation would go ahead as scheduled to save the integrity of the crown. A suitable marriage with another princess will take place within six months maximum. She gave me her short list of five candidates."

Alex felt a chill go through him. "Putting the cart before the horse has never been done."

"The queen is going to have her way no matter what. Let's face it. She's not well and wants me to take over."

"Stasi—"

Sick for his brother, he walked over and hugged him. "I'm here for you always. You know that."

"I *do*. A fine pair we've turned out to be. She told me you're still resisting marriage to Princess Genevieve."

"Like you, I told her no once and for all," he said through clenched teeth. "I sacrificed myself once. Never again."

"She's not going to give up on Genevieve. I heard it in her voice."

"That's too bad because my only duty now is to raise Zoe to be happy."

With the help of Dottie, he intended that to become a reality. Walking over to the table, he poured himself a drink. He lifted his glass to his brother.

"To you, Stasi," he said in a thick-toned voice. "May God help you find a way to cope." *May God help both of us.*

* * *

After a sleep troubled with thoughts of Alex, Dottie felt out of sorts and anxious and only poked at her breakfast. Since he hadn't brought Zoe for her morning session yet, she checked her emails. Among some posts from her friends at the Institute in New York she'd received a response to the email she'd sent Dr. Rice. With a pounding heart, she opened it first.

Dear Dottie:

Thank you for giving me an update on Princess Zoe. I'm very pleased to hear that she's beginning to make progress. If anyone can work miracles, it's you. In reference to your request, I've interviewed several therapists who I believe would work well with her, but the one I think could be the best fit might not be available as soon as you wanted. She's still working with the parent of another child to teach them coaching skills. I'll let you know when she'll be free to come. Give it a few more days.

By the way, it's all over the news about Crown Prince Stasio calling off his wedding to Princess Beatriz. She's here in Manhattan. I saw her on the news walking into the St. Regis Hotel. What a coincidence that you're working for Prince Alexius. Have you ever met his brother? Well, take care. I'll be in touch before long. Dr. Rice.

She rested her elbow on the table, covering her eyes with her hand. Prince Stasio's teasing facade hid a courageous man who'd just done himself and Princess Beatriz a huge favor, even if talk of it and the judgments that would follow saturated the news.

The world had no idea what went on behind the closed doors of a desperately unhappy couple, royal or otherwise. What woman or man would want to be married to someone who'd been chosen for them years earlier? Alex's first marriage had been forced. It boggled the mind, yet it had happened to the royals of the Constantinides family for hundreds of years in order to keep the monarchy alive.

Poor Zoe. To think that dear little girl would have to grow up knowing an arranged marriage was her fate. Dottie cringed at the prospect. Surely Alex wouldn't do that to his own daughter after what he and his brother had been through, would he?

"Dot?" Zoe came running into the alcove and hugged her so hard, she almost fell off the chair.

Without conscious thought Dottie closed her eyes and hugged her back, aching for this family and its archaic rules that had hung like a pall over their lives. When she opened them again, there was Alex standing there in a navy crew neck and jeans looking bigger than life as he watched the two of them interact.

She saw lines and shadows on his striking face that hadn't been there yesterday. But when their eyes met, the black fire in his took her to the backseat of the car where the other night they'd kissed each other with mindless abandon.

"We're here to invite you out for a day on the water," he explained. "The galley's loaded with food and drink. We'll do lessons and have fun at the same time."

As he spoke, Zoe sat down to do one of the puzzles on the table out of hearing distance. It was a good thing, because Alex's invitation had frightened Dottie. Though her mind was warning her this would be a mistake, that vital organ pumping her life's blood enlarged at the prospect.

The other night she'd almost lost control with him and the experience was still too fresh. To go with him would be like watching a moth enticed to a flame fly straight to its death.

"Perhaps it's time you enjoyed one day without me along. It won't hurt Zoe to miss a lesson." She'd said the first thing to come into her mind, frantically searching for an excuse not to be with him.

Lines marred his arresting features. "I'm afraid this is one time I need your cooperation. There's something critically urgent I must discuss with you."

Dottie looked away from the intensity of his gaze. This had to be about his brother. The distinct possibility that Prince Stasio needed Alex to do double duty for him right now, or to spend more time with him, crossed her mind. Of necessity it would cut short the time he'd been spending with Zoe. If that was the case, she could hardly turn him down while he worked out an alternative plan with her.

"All right. Give me a minute to put some things in the bag for our lesson."

"Take all the time you need." His voice seemed to have a deeper timbre this morning, playing havoc with the butterflies fluttering madly in her chest.

After Zoe helped pack some things they'd need, Dottie changed into a sleeveless top and shorts. When she emerged from the bathroom with her hair freshly brushed, the prince took swift inventory of her face and figure, whipping up a storm of heat that stained her cheeks with color. Once she'd stowed her swimsuit in the bag, she put on her sunglasses and declared she was ready to go.

Dottie had assumed they'd be taking his sailboat. But once they left the palace grounds, Alex informed her he had business on one of the other islands so they were going out on the yacht. The news caused a secret thrill to permeate her body.

That first morning when she and Zoe had gone down to the private beach, she'd seen the gleaming white royal yacht moored in the distance. Like any normal tourist, she'd dreamed of touring the Aegean on a boat while she was in Hellenica. Today the dream had become reality as she boarded the fabulous luxury craft containing every amenity known to man.

With the sparkling blue water so calm, Zoe was in heaven. Wearing another swimsuit, this one in lime-and-blue stripes, she ran up and down the length of it with her father's binoculars, looking for groupers and parrot fish with one of the crew.

Alex settled them in side-by-side loungers while the deck steward placed drinks and treats close enough to reach. With Zoe occupied for a few minutes, Dottie felt this would be the best time to approach him about his brother and turned in his direction. But he'd removed his shirt. One look at his chest with its dusting of black hair, in fact his entire masculine physique, and she had to stifle a moan.

The other night she'd been crushed against him and, heaven help her, she longed to repeat the experience. Fortunately the presence of Zoe and the crew prevented anything like that from happening today.

Admit you want it to happen, Dottie.

After losing Neil, she couldn't believe all these feelings to know a man's possession had come back this strongly. For so long she'd been dead inside. She was frightened by this explosion of need Alex had ignited. She had to hope Dr. Rice would email her the good news that her replacement could be here by next week because she could feel herself being sucked into a situation that could only rebound on her.

Not for a moment did she believe Alex was a womanizer. He was a man, and like any single male was free to find temporary satisfaction with a willing woman when the time and opportunity presented itself. With her full cooperation he'd acted on one of those opportunities and she'd lost her head.

It wasn't his fault. It was *hers*. She'd been an idiot.

Unless she wanted a new form of heartache to plague her for the rest of her life, she couldn't afford another foolish moment because of overwhelming desire for Alex. There was no future in it. She'd be gone from this assignment before long. Nothing but pain could come from indulging in a passionate interlude with a prince. *Nothing*.

"Alex. The head of my department at Stillman's responded to one of my emails this morning."

He removed his sunglasses and shifted his hard-muscled body on the lounger so he faced her. "Was that the one asking him to find another therapist for Zoe?" he inquired in a dangerously silky voice. An underlying tone of ice sent a tremor through her body.

"Yes. He says he'll probably have someone to replace me within another week. By then Zoe ought to have more confidence in herself and will work well with the new speech teacher."

Paralyzing tension stretched between them before

eyes of jet impaled her. "You don't believe that piece
of fiction any more than I do. In any event, there can't
be a question about you leaving, not with the coronation almost upon us."

She sat up in surprise. "You mean there's still going
to be one?"

Like lightning he levered himself from the lounger.
"Why would you ask that question?"

"At the end of Dr. Rice's email, he told me there were
headlines about Prince Stasio calling off his wedding
to Princess Beatriz."

"So it's already today's news in New York." He
sounded far away. She watched him rub the back of
his neck, something he did when he was pondering a
grave problem.

Growing more uneasy, Dottie stood up. "Forgive me
if I've upset you."

He eyed her frankly. "Forgiveness doesn't come into
it. They were never suited, but I didn't know he'd made
the break official until he told me last night."

She rubbed her arms in reaction. "What a traumatic
night it must have been for all of you and your grandmother."

"I won't lie to you about that." His pain was palpable.

Dottie bit her lip. "For both their sakes I'm glad he
couldn't go through with it, but you'll probably think
I'm horrible for saying it."

"On the contrary," Alex ground out. "I'd think something serious was wrong with you if you hadn't. His
life has been a living hell. He should have ended the
betrothal years ago."

Alex... She heard the love for his brother.

"Does it mean the queen will go on ruling?" she

asked quietly. "I'm probably overstepping my bounds to talk to you like this, but after meeting your brother, I can't help but feel terrible for what he must be suffering right now, even if he didn't want the marriage."

"Between us, he's in bad shape," he confided, "but the coronation is still on. Our grandmother is failing in small ways and can't keep up her former pace as sovereign, but she's still in charge. She has given him six months to marry one of the eligible royals on her list."

"But—"

"There are no buts," he cut her off, but she knew his anger wasn't directed at her. "I just have to pray he'll find some common ground with one of the women." His voice throbbed. Again Dottie was horrified by Prince Stasio's untenable situation. "Since there's nothing I can do except stand by him, I'd rather concentrate on Zoe's lesson. What do you have planned for today?"

Heartsick as Dottie felt, she'd been sent to Hellenica to do a job and she wanted desperately to lift his spirits if she could. "Since we're on the yacht, I thought we'd work on the *Y* sound. She can already say *Yiayia* pretty well."

"That's where her Greek ought to help."

"Why don't you say hello to her in Greek and we'll see what happens."

Together they walked toward the railing at the far end. Zoe saw them coming and trained the binoculars on them.

"Yasoo," her father called to her. The cute little girl answered back in a sad facsimile of the greeting.

Dottie smiled. "Do you like being on this boat?"

"Yes."

Today they'd work on *ya*. Another day they'd work

on *yes*. "Do you know what kind of a boat this is?" Zoe shook her head. "It's called a yacht. Say *yasoo* again." Zoe responded. "Now say *ya*." She tried, but the sound was off with both words.

"I can't."

Dottie felt her frustration.

Alex handed Dottie the binoculars and picked up his daughter. "Try it once more." He wanted her to make a good sound for him. Dottie wanted it, too, more than anything. But this was a game of infinite patience. "Be a parrot for daddy, like one of those parrot fish you were watching with its birdlike beak. Parrots can talk. Talk to me. Say *ya*."

"Ya."

"Open your mouth wider like your daddy is doing," Dottie urged her. "Pretend he's the doctor looking down your throat with a stick. He wants to hear you. Can you say *ya* for him?"

She giggled. "Daddy's not a doctor."

The prince sent Dottie a look of defeat. "You're right." He kissed Zoe's cheek. "Come on. Let's have a lemonade." As soon as he put her down, she ran back to the table by the loungers to drink hers.

Clearly Zoe wasn't in the mood for a lesson. Who would be on a beautiful day like this? The translucent blue water was dotted with islands that made Dottie itch to get out and explore everything. She put the binoculars to her eyes to see what was coming next. "What's the name of that island in the distance?"

"Argentum."

"You mine silver there?"

"How did you figure that out?"

"You told me you lived on Aurum. Both islands have Latin names for gold and silver."

His eyes met hers. "You're not only intelligent, but knowledgeable. We'll anchor out in the bay. The head mining engineer is coming aboard for a business lunch. He's also my closest friend."

"Where did you meet?"

"We were getting our mining engineering degrees at the same time, both here and in Colorado at the school of mines."

"That's why your English is amazing. Is your friend married?"

"Yes. He has a new baby."

"That's nice for him."

"Very nice. He's in love with his wife and she with him."

Dottie couldn't bear to talk about that subject. "Tell me about the tall island beyond Argentum with the green patches?"

"That's Aurum, where Zoe and I normally live." He hadn't put on his shirt yet. She could feel his body radiating heat. "As you guessed correctly, rich gold deposits on the other side of the mountain were discovered there centuries ago. Bari and I are both passionate about our work. There are many more mining projects to be explored. I'm anxious to get back to them."

By now she was trembling from their close proximity. Needing a reason to move away from him, she put the binoculars on the table and picked up her lemonade. "Do you miss Aurum?"

"Yes." His dark gaze wandered over her, sending her pulse rate off the charts. "Zoe and I prefer it to Hellenica. The palace there is much smaller with more trees and vegetation that keep it cooler. We'll take you next week so Zoe can show you the garden off her room."

Dottie let the comment pass because if she were still here by then, she had no intention of going there with him. It wouldn't be a good idea. Not a good idea at all. "Do you get her to preschool by helicopter, then?"

He nodded. "Once she's in kindergarten, she'll go to a school on Aurum, but nothing is going to happen until after the coronation." After swallowing the contents of his drink without taking a breath, he reached for his shirt. "Shall we go below and freshen up before Bari comes on board?"

She followed the two of them down the steps of the elegant yacht to the luxurious cabins. "Come with us." Zoe pulled on her hand.

Dottie bent over. "I have my own cabin down the hallway."

"How come?"

"Because I'm a guest."

She looked at her daddy. "Make her come."

"Zoe? We have our room, and she has hers," he said in his princely parental voice as Dottie thought of it.

To the surprise of both of them, Zoe kept hold of Dottie's hand. "I want to be with you."

"It's all right, Your Highness," Dottie said before he could protest. "Zoe and I will freshen up together and meet you on deck in a little while." Their family was going through deep turmoil. The burden of what his brother had done had set off enormous ramifications and Alex was feeling them.

For that matter, so was Zoe, who'd behaved differently today. With the advent of Prince Stasio's stunning news, she couldn't have helped but pick up on the tension radiating from the queen and her father during breakfast. She might not understand all that was going on, but she sensed upheaval. That's why she'd given up on her lesson so easily.

His eyes narrowed in what she assumed was speculation. "You're sure?"

"Do you even have to ask?" Dottie had meant what she'd told him last week about his needing some pampering. He had work to do with Mr. Jouflas, but no one else was there to help him with Zoe the way he needed it. Dottie found she wanted to ease his burden. He'd made sacrifices for the love of his country. Now it was her turn, no matter how small.

"You're operating under an abnormal amount of strain right now. You could use a little help. I don't know how you've been doing this balancing act for such a long time." She smiled at Zoe. "Come on."

Dottie saw the relief on his face and knew she'd said the right thing. "In that case I'll send the steward to your cabin with a fresh change of clothes for her."

"That would be perfect."

CHAPTER SEVEN

DOTTIE felt Alex staring at her before they disappeared inside. Since she'd been trying so hard to keep a professional distance with his daughter, he knew this was an about-face for her. But no one could have foreseen this monarchial disaster.

Alex was being torn apart by his love for his brother, his grandmother and the future of the crown itself. He was Atlas holding up the world with no help in sight. This was a day like no other. If Dottie could ease a little of his burden where Zoe was concerned, then she wanted to.

"I've got an idea, Zoe. After you shower, we'll take a little nap on the beds. The heat has made me sleepy."

"Me, too."

There were two queen beds. Before long she'd tucked Zoe under the covers.

"Dot? Will you please stay with Daddy and me forever? I know you're not my mommy, but Daddy said you were once a mommy."

She struggled for breath. "Yes. I had a little boy named Cory who had to work on his speech, just like you."

"What happened to him?"

"He died in a car accident with my husband."

"So you're all alone."

"Yes," she murmured, but for the first time it wasn't hard to talk about. The conversation with Alex last night had been cathartic.

"My mommy died and now Daddy and I are all alone."

"Except that you have your great-grandmother and your uncle."

"But I want you."

Dottie wanted to be with Zoe all the time, too. Somehow she'd gotten beyond her deep sadness and would love to care permanently for this child. But it was impossible in too many ways to even consider.

"Let's be happy we're together right now, shall we?" she said in a shaky voice.

"Yes." Zoe finally closed her eyes and fell asleep.

Dotti took her own shower and dressed in a clean pair of jeans and a blouse. When she came out of the bathroom, the other bed looked inviting. She thought she'd lie down on top while she waited for Zoe to wake up.

The next thing she knew, she heard a familiar male voice whispering her name. Slightly disoriented, she rolled over and discovered Alex sitting on the side of the bed. She'd been dreaming about him, but to see his gorgeous self in the flesh this close to her gave her heart a serious workout. His eyes were like black fires. They trapped hers, making it impossible for her to look away.

"Thank you for stepping in."

She studied his features. "I wanted to."

"With your help I was able to conclude our business lunch in record time and came in to bring Zoe a change of clothes. Do you have any idea how beautiful you are lying there?"

Dottie couldn't swallow. She tried to move away, but he put an arm across her body so she was tethered to him. "Please let me go," she begged. "Zoe will be awake any minute now."

He leaned over her, running a hand up her arm. The feel of skin against hot skin brought every nerve ending alive. "I'll take any minute I can steal. Being alone with you is all I've been able to think about."

Alex—" she cried as his dark head descended.

"I love it when you say my name in that husky voice." He covered her mouth with his own in an exploratory kiss as if this were their first time and they were in no hurry whatsoever. He took things slow in the beginning, tantalizing her until it wasn't enough. Then their kiss grew deeper and more sensuous. His restless lips traveled over every centimeter of her face and throat before capturing her mouth again and again.

The other night he'd kindled a fire in her that had never died down. Now his mastery conjured the flames licking through her body with the speed of a forest fire in full conflagration.

Out of breath, he buried his face in the side of her neck. "I want you, Dottie. I've never wanted any woman so much, and I know you want me."

"I think that's been established," she admitted against his jaw that hadn't seen a razor since early morning. She delighted in every masculine line and angle of his well-honed body. With legs and arms entwined, their mouths clung as their passion grew more frenzied. They tried to appease their hunger, but no kiss was long enough or deep enough to satisfy the desire building.

He'd taken them to a new level. She felt cherished. Like the wedding vow repeated by the groom, it seemed as if Alex was worshipping her with his body. But in the midst of this rapture only he could have created, she heard the blare of a ship's horn. With it came the realization that this was no wedding night and a groan escaped her throat.

She'd actually been making out with Prince Alexius of Hellenica on his royal yacht! Never mind that it was the middle of the day and his daughter was asleep in the next bed. What if Zoe had awakened and had been watching them?

Horrified to have gotten this carried away, Dottie wrenched her mouth from his and slipped out of his arms. So deep was his entrancement, she'd caught him off guard. Thankfully she was able to get to her feet before he could prevent it, but in her weakened state she almost fell over.

"Dottie?" he called her name in longing, but she didn't dare stay in here and be seduced by the spell he'd cast over her. On the way out of the cabin she grabbed her purse and hurried down the corridor to the stairs.

At the top of the gangway the deck steward smiled at her. "Mrs. Richards? We've docked on Hellenica. You're welcome to go ashore whenever you please."

Could he tell she'd been kissed breathless by the prince? The sun she'd picked up couldn't account for mussed hair and swollen lips, too.

The queen didn't deserve to hear this bit of gossip on top of Prince Stasio's shocking news. Every second Dottie stayed on board, she was contributing to more court intrigue. She couldn't bear it. In fact she couldn't believe they were back at the main island already. She'd been in such a completely different world with Alex, she'd lost track of everything including her wits.

"Th-thank you," her voice faltered. Without hesitation, she left the yacht and got in the waiting limousine. While she was still alone, she brushed her hair and applied some lipstick, trying to make herself presentable.

A few minutes later Alex approached the car with Zoe. "Dot!" she cried and climbed in next to her.

"Did you just wake up?" Dottie concentrated on Zoe, studiously avoiding his eyes. "You were a sleepyhead."

Zoe thought that was funny. She chatted happily with her daddy until they reached the palace where Hector stood outside the entry.

"Welcome back, Your Highness. The queen is waiting for you and the princess to join her and Prince Stasio in her suite."

A royal summons. It didn't surprise Dottie. She'd had visions of the queen herself waiting for them as they drove up to the entrance. For an instant she caught Alex's enigmatic glance before he alighted from the car. All their lives he and Stasio had been forced to obey that summons. A lesser person would have broken long before now.

She might be an outsider, yet she couldn't help but want to rebel against this antiquated system she'd only read about in history books. Unbelievable that it was still going on in the twenty-first century!

Alex helped them out of the backseat. "Come on, Dot." Zoe's hand had slipped into hers. She had to harden herself against Zoe's plea. The child's emotional hold on her was growing stronger with every passing day.

"I'm sorry. The queen has asked for you and your

daddy to come, and I have to speak to my director in New York." Aware Alex's eyes were on her she said, "You have to go with him. I'll see you tomorrow when we leave for your preschool."

Gripping the bag tighter, Dottie hurried inside the palace doors and raced up the stairs. She fled to her suite pursued by demons she'd been fighting from the beginning. Since this afternoon when she'd fallen into Alex's arms like a ripe plum, those demons had gained a foothold, making her situation precarious.

Her instincts told her to pack her bags and fly back to New York tonight. But if she were to just up and leave Hellenica, it would only exacerbate an already volatile situation with Zoe, who'd poured her heart out to her earlier.

Without hesitation she marched over to the bed and reached for the house phone. "This is Mrs. Richards. Could you bring a car around for me? I'm going into the city." She'd eat dinner somewhere and do some more sightseeing. After the nap she'd had, it might take hours before she was ready for bed again.

Alex waited for Hector to alert him on the phone. When the call came, he learned Dottie had just returned to the palace. He checked his watch. Ten to ten.

He left Zoe's bedroom and waited for Dottie at the top of the stairs leading to her suite. This time he didn't step out of the shadows. He stood there in full view. Halfway up she caught sight of him and slowed her steps. Alarm was written all over her beautiful face. She'd picked up some sun earlier in the day, adding appealing color.

"Alex? What's wrong?"

Anyone watching them would never know what had gone on between them on the yacht. He'd nearly made love to her and her passion had equalled his. Her breath-taking response had changed his life today.

"Let's just say there's a lot wrong around here. Since your arrival in Hellenica, you've got me skulking in every conceivable place in order to find time alone with you. At this point you'd have reason to think I'm your personal phantom of the opera." He drew in a harsh breath. "We have to talk, but not here." When he saw her stiffen he said, "I know you can't be commanded, but I'm asking you to come with me as a personal favor." He'd constructed his words carefully.

Tension sizzled between them as he started down the stairs toward her. To his relief she didn't fight him. Slowly she followed him to the main floor. They went down the hallway and out a side door where he'd asked that his sports car be brought around.

Alex saw the question in her eyes. "I bought this ten years ago. It's my getaway car when I need to be alone to think." He intentionally let her get in by herself because he didn't trust himself not to touch her. After leaving the grounds, he headed for the road leading to an isolated portion of the coast with rocky terrain.

"But you're *not* alone," she said in a haunted whisper.

"If you mean the bodyguards, you're right." He felt her nervousness. "Relax. If I had seduction in mind, we wouldn't be in this. I purposely chose it in order to keep my hands off you tonight."

"Alex—"

"Let me finish," he interrupted. "Whatever you may think about me, I'm not in the habit of luring available women to my bed when the mood strikes me. You came to Hellenica at my request in order to test Zoe. Neither of us could have predicted what would happen after you arrived.

"I can't speak for you, but I know for a fact that even if your husband's memory will always be in your heart, the chemistry between us is more powerful than anything I've ever felt in my life. We both know it's not going to go away."

She lowered her head.

"One night with you could never be enough for me." He gripped the steering wheel tighter. "I know you would never consent to be my mistress, and I would never ask you. But until the coronation is over, I'm requesting your help with Zoe."

She shifted in the seat. "In what way?"

"Stasio and my daughter both need me desperately, but I can't be in two places at the same time and still manage the daily affairs of the crown. My brother is going through the blackest period of his life. He's clinging to me and shutting out our grandmother. She's beside herself."

"I can only imagine."

"I'm worried about both of them and asked the doctor to come. He's with them now, seeing what can be done to get them through this nightmare. He says I need to be there for Stasio 24/7. I've asked our cousin Philippe to fly here and stay for a few days so my brother has someone to talk to he trusts."

"I'm so sorry, Alex."

"So am I," he muttered morosely. "This situation is something that's been coming on for years. Unfortunately it's had a negative impact on Zoe. When we got back to the palace today, it took me an hour to settle her down. She wanted to go to your room with you. Tonight she begged me to let you become her official nanny."

Alex heard a half-smothered moan come out of Dottie. The sound tore him up because any kind of connection to keep her with him was fading fast. "It wouldn't work."

"You think I don't know that?" he bit out. "But as a temporary solution, would you be willing to stay at the palace on Aurum with her until the coronation? She loves it there, especially the garden. One of the staff has grandchildren she plays with. I'd fly over each evening in the helicopter to say good-night.

"When the coronation is over, I'll be moving back to Aurum with Zoe, and you can return to New York. Hector will see to your flight arrangements. I assume your replacement will arrive soon after that, if not before. But until then, can I rely on your help?"

She nodded without looking at him. "Of course."

The bands constricting his breathing loosened a little. "Thank you. On Saturday I'll run you and Zoe over in the cruiser. We'll skip her preschool next week."

"Are you still going to go ahead with the arrangements for the Varney boy to come home with Zoe after class tomorrow?"

"Yes," he murmured. "Any distraction would be better than her being around my grandmother, who's not in a good way right now. She's always been a rock, but she never saw this coming with Stasio."

"You sound exhausted, Alex. Tomorrow will be here before we know it. Let's go back to the palace."

She sounded like Hector. *Go back. Do your duty. Forget you're a man with a man's needs.*

Full of rage, he made a sharp U-turn and sped toward the palace tight-lipped, but by the time they reached the entry, he'd turned into one aching entity of pain. He watched the only person who could take it away for good rush away on her gorgeous legs.

Dottie could tell Zoe felt shy around Mark Varney. She stuck close to her daddy at the shallow end of the pool.

They'd just returned home from the preschool. Mark was a cute, dark blond first grader who sported a marine haircut and was a good little swimmer already. He didn't appear to be nervous as he floated on an inner tube at the deep end, kicking his strong legs. Dottie sat on the edge by him.

"My mom told me she talks funny. How come?" he said quietly.

"Sometimes a child can't make sounds come out the way they want. But I'm working on them with her. One day she'll sound like you, but for now I'm hoping to get your help."

He blinked. "How? She's a princess."

She looked at his boyish face with its smattering of freckles. "Forget about that. She's a girl. Just be friends with her. In a way, you can be her best teacher."

His sunny blue eyes widened. "I can?"

"Yes. You're older and you're an American who speaks English very well. If you'll play with her, she'll listen to you when you talk and she'll try to sound like you. You're a guy, and guys like to dare each other, right?"

He grinned. "Yeah."

"Well, start daring her. You know. Tell her you bet she can't say *bat*."

"Bat?" He laughed.

"She's working on her *B*'s and *T*'s. Make a game out of it. Tell her that if she can say *bat* right, you'll show her your MP3 player. I saw you playing with it in the limo on the drive to the palace."

"Don't tell my dad. I'm not supposed to take it to school."

She studied him for a minute. "If he finds out, I'll tell him you're using it to help Zoe. She's never seen one of those. There's an application on it that makes those animal sounds."

"Oh, yeah—"

"It'll fascinate her."

"Cool."

"See if you can get her to say *cool*, too."

"Okay. This is fun."

Dottie was glad he thought so. After trying to learn Greek at school and home, it had to be a big release for him to speak English. "Let's go have a war with her and her daddy." She took off her beach coat and slipped into the water. "You get on the whale. I'll push you over to them and we'll start splashing."

"Won't the prince get mad?"

"Yes." Dottie smiled. "Real mad."

His face lit up and they took off.

Hopefully Alex would get mad enough to forget his own problems for a little while. She'd suffered for him and his family all night. No matter her misgivings about spending full days with Zoe until the coronation, she couldn't have turned Alex down last night. The look in his expression had been a study in anguish, aging him.

Once they reached their destination, the happy shrieks coming out of Zoe were just the thing to get their war started. For a good ten minutes they battled as if their lives depended on it. The best sound of all was Alex's full-bodied laughter. After knowing how deeply he'd been affected by his family's problems, Dottie hadn't expected to hear it again.

When she came up for air after Alex's last powerful dunk, his eyes were leveled on her features. "You've been holding out on me. All this time I thought maybe you couldn't swim well. I was going to offer to teach you, but I was afraid you'd think I was a lecherous old man wanting to get my hands on you. After I showed up in your cabin on the yacht, now you know it's true."

She was thankful for the water that cooled her instantly hot cheeks. In the periphery she noticed Mark pushing Zoe around on the whale. He was talking a blue streak and had captured her full attention. The ice had been broken and they were oblivious to everyone else. Dottie couldn't have been more pleased.

Alex followed her gaze. "Your experiment is working. She's so excited by his attention, she hasn't once called for either of us."

"I've asked him to help her. He's a darling boy." In the next few minutes she told Alex about their conversation. "If all goes well today, how would you feel about Mark coming home with us from school on Friday?"

"I'm open to anything that will help her speech improve and make her happy."

"Mark seems to be doing both. I've learned he's been unhappy, so I was thinking maybe he could even come to Aurum with us on Saturday. Naturally you'd have to talk to his parents. If they're willing, maybe he could make a visit to the island next week. You know, after his morning class at preschool. Zoe would have something exciting to look forward to and I know it would be good for him, too."

His eyes glinted with an emotion she couldn't read. "I can see where you're going with this. If you think his being there will prevent her attachment to you from growing deeper, you couldn't be more wrong. But as a plan to entertain them and help her, I like the idea."

"Honestly?"

He ran suntanned hands through his wet black hair. Adonis couldn't possibly have been as attractive. "I wouldn't have said so otherwise."

She expelled the breath she'd been holding. "Thank you. I was thinking Zoe and I could ride the ferry to Hellenica and meet him at the dock after he's out of class. He could ride back with us and we could eat lunch on board. Mark can help her pronounce the names of foods, and she can teach him some more Greek words."

Alex nodded. "I'll fly him back with me in the helicopter in the evening."

"You'd be willing to do that?"

He frowned. "By now I thought it was clear to you I'd do anything to help my daughter. In order to ensure that you stay with her until her uncle Stasi has been proclaimed king, I've even gone so far as to promise I won't touch you again."

She knew that and already felt the cost of it.

If he had any comprehension of how hard this was for her, too… They had no future together, but that didn't mean she found it easy to keep her distance. She'd come alive in his arms. Because she was unable to assuage these yearnings, the pleasure had turned on her so she was in continual pain. This was the precise reason she didn't want to have feelings for any man, not ever again, but it was far too late for that.

"Your Highness?"

Hector's voice intruded, producing a grimace from Alex. Dottie hadn't realized he'd come out to the pool. It seemed like every time she found herself in a private conversation with Alex, some force was afoot that kept wedging them further apart, At this point she was a mass of contradictions. Her head told her the interruption was for the best, but her heart—oh, her heart. It hammered mercilessly.

"King Alexandre-Philippe has arrived from Valleder and your presence is requested in the queen's drawing room. The ministers have been assembled."

Hearing that news, Alex's face became an inscrutable mask. "Thank you, Hector. Tell her I'll be there shortly."

His gaze shot to Dottie's. "I'm afraid this will be a long night. I'd better slip away now while Zoe's having fun."

"I think that's a good idea. We'll walk Mark out to his parents' car before dinner. She can eat with me. Later I'll take her to her bedroom and put her down."

"You couldn't have any comprehension of what it means to me to know you're taking care of my daughter. Sofia will be there to help. I'll try to get away long enough to kiss her good-night, but I can't promise."

"I understand."

"If I don't make it, I'll see you at nine in the morning. After I've talked to Mark's parents, we'll see if he wants to join us on Saturday. I thought we'd take the cruiser to Aurum. Sofia will know what to pack for Zoe."

"We'll be ready."

She heard his sharp intake of breath. "Zoe trusts you and loves being with you. Under the circumstances, it's an enormous relief to me."

"I'm glad. As for me, she's a joy to be with, Your Highness." She had to keep calling him by his title to remind herself of the great gulf between them no ordinary human could bridge. If she were a princess...

But she wasn't! And if she'd been born a royal, he would have run in the other direction.

For him, any attraction to her stemmed from forbidden fruit. She was a commoner. It was the nature of a man or woman to desire what they couldn't or shouldn't have. In that regard they were both cursed!

Fathoms deep in turmoil, she noticed his eyes lingering on the curve of her mouth for a moment. She glimpsed banked fires in those incredibly dark recesses. He was remembering those moments on the yacht, too. Dottie could feel it and the look he was giving her ignited her senses to a feverish pitch.

With effortless male agility he suddenly levered himself from the pool and disappeared inside the palace. When he was gone, the loss she felt was staggering.

CHAPTER EIGHT

"HI, MARK!"

"Hi!"

He got out of his father's limo and hurried along the dock to get in the cruiser. Zoe's brown eyes lit up when she saw him. The two fathers spoke for a minute longer before Alex joined them and made sure everyone put on a life preserver.

The prince piloted the boat himself and they took off. Excitement suffused Dottie, crowding out any misgivings for the moment. She found the day was too wonderful. It seemed the children did, too. Both wore a perpetual smile on their animated faces. Zoe pointed out more fish and birds as they drew closer to their destination. While they were communicating, Alex darted Dottie an amused glance.

She wondered if he was thinking what she'd been thinking. What if his daughter and Mark were to share a friendship that took them through childhood to the teenage years? What if... But she forced her mind to turn off and think only happy thoughts. The island of Aurum was coming up fast. She'd concentrate on it.

Somehow she'd assumed it shared many of the characterics of Hellenica, but the mountains were higher and woodier. As they pulled up to the royal dock, Dottie had to admit her adrenaline had been surging in anticipation of seeing where they lived. When Alex talked about Aurum, she noticed his voice dropped to a deeper level because he loved it here.

He'd explained that the mountainous part of the island where the palace was located had been walled off from the public. This had been his private residence from the age of eighteen and would continue to be for as long as he retained the title of Duke of Aurum. She'd learned it had its own game preserve, a wildlife sanctuary, a bird refuge and a stable.

Somehow she'd expected this palace to resemble the white Cycladic style of that on Hellenica. Nothing could have been further from the truth. Through the heavy foliage she glimpsed a small gem of Moorish architecture in the form of a square, all on one level.

"Oh!" she cried out in instant delight the second she saw it from the open limo window.

Alex heard her. "This area of the Aegean has known many civilizations. If you'll notice, the other palace leaves the stairs and patios open. Everything tumbles to the sea. You'll see the reverse is true here. The Moors liked their treasures hidden within the walls."

"Whoa!" Mark exclaimed. His eyes widened in amazement. He'd stopped talking to Zoe. *Whoa* was the perfect word, all right.

Dottie marveled over the exterior, a weathered yellow and pale orange combination of seamless blocks delineated by stylized horizontal stripes, exquisite in detail. The limo passed a woman who looked about fifty standing at the arched entry into a courtyard laid out in ancient tiles surrounding a pool and an exquisite garden. At its center stood a latticed gazebo. This was the garden Alex had referred to last week.

As he helped them from the car, a peacock peered from behind some fronds and unexpectedly opened its plumage. The whirring sound startled Dottie and Mark, but Zoe only laughed. It walked slowly, displaying its glorious fan.

"Whoa," their guest said again, incredulous over what he was seeing. It *was* hard to believe.

Dottie eyed Alex. "We're definitely going to have to work on the *P* sound."

One corner of his mouth curved upward. He ran a hand over his chest covered by a cream-colored polo shirt. "Don't look now," he said quietly, "but there's a partridge in the peach tree behind you."

Slowly she turned around, thinking he was teasing her while he made the *P* sounds. But he'd told the truth!

Transfixed, she shook her head, examining everything in sight. A profusion of pink and orange flowers grew against the gazebo. She walked through the scrolling pathway toward it. Inside she discovered a lacy looking set of chairs and a table inlaid with mother-of-pearl. Dottie felt as if she'd just walked inside the pages of a rare first-edition history book of the Ottoman empire. This couldn't possibly be real.

Alex must have understood what she was feeling because he flashed her a white smile. But this one was different because it was carefree. For a brief moment she'd been given a glimpse of what he might have looked like years ago, before he'd had a true understanding that he was Prince Alexius Constantinides with obligations and serious responsibilities he would have to shoulder for the rest of his life.

There was a sweetness in his expression, the same sweetness she saw in Zoe when she was really happy about something, like right now. But the moment was bittersweet for Dottie when she thought of the pain waiting for him back on Hellenica. A myriad of emotions tightened her chest because her pain was mixed up in there, too.

"Do you want to see my room?" Zoe asked Mark.

"I want to follow the peacock first."

"Okay." She tagged along with her new friend, still managing to carry Baby Betty in her hands.

Alex spread his strong arms. "Guys and girls. Human nature doesn't change." Dottie laughed gently, sharing this electric moment with him.

Porticos with bougainvillea and passion flowers joined one section of the palace to the other. The alcoved rooms were hidden behind. Zoe's was a dream of Moorish tiles and unique pieces of furniture with gold leaf carved years ago by a master palace craftsman of that earlier civilization.

A silky, pale pink fabric formed the canopy and covering of her bed. Near a tall hutch filled with her treasures stood an exquisite pink rose tree. When Dottie looked all the way up, she gasped at the sheer beauty of the carved ceiling with hand-painted roses and birds.

Alex had been watching her reaction. "Your room is next door. Would you like to see it?"

Speechless, she nodded and followed him through an alcove to another masterpiece of design similar to Zoe's except for the color scheme. "Whoever painted the cornflowers in this room must have had your eyes in mind, Dottie. They grow wild on the hillsides. You'll see them when you and Zoe go hiking or horseback riding."

She was spellbound. Her eyes fell to the bed canopied with blue silk. "Was this the room you and your wife used? It's breathtaking."

In a flash his facial muscles tensed up. "Teresa never lived here with me. Like my grandmother, she preferred the palace on Hellenica. She thought this place too exotic and isolated, the mountains too savage. This room was used during my mother's time for guests. Since Teresa's death, Zoe's string of nannies have lived in here."

Dottie couldn't help but speculate on how much time he and his wife must have spent apart—that is, when they didn't have to perform certain civic duties together. Separation went on in unhappy marriages all over the planet, but this was different. He'd been born into a family where duty dictated his choice of bride. Even cocooned in this kind of luxury only a few people would ever know, the onlooker could expect such an arrangement to fail.

As Dottie's aunt had often told her, "You're a romantic, Dottie. For that reason you can be hurt the worst. Why set yourself up, honey?" Good question. Dottie's heart ached for Alex and Stasio, for Teresa and Beatriz, for Genevieve, for every royal who had a role and couldn't deviate from it.

"My apartment is through the next alcove. The last section houses two more guest rooms plus the kitchen and dining room. There's a den where I do my work. It has television and a computer. All of it is at your disposal for the time you're here."

"I've never seen anything so unusual and beautiful."

"Those are my sentiments, too. You saw Inez when we drove in. She and her husband, Ari, head the staff here. There's the gamekeeper, of course, and Thomas who runs the stable. All you have to do is pick up the phone and Inez will direct one of the maids to help you."

"Thank you. I didn't expect to find paradise when I came to Hellenica. I don't think your brother believed me when I told him it really does exists here."

"Paradise implies marital bliss. You'll have to forgive him for being cynical over your naïveté."

Alex's comment bordered on mockery, revealing emotions too raw for him to hide. She shuddered and turned away, not wanting to see the bleakness she often saw in his eyes when he didn't know she was looking.

"I'd better go check on Zoe." She hurried through to the other bedroom, but there was still no sign of her.

Alex came up behind Dottie, close enough for her to feel the warmth of his breath on her neck. "I'll give you one guess where she's gone."

"Well, Mark is pretty cute. She doesn't know she's playing with fire yet." The words came out too fast for her to stop them.

"That's true," Alex said in a gravelly voice before she was spun around and crushed against him. "But I do, and right now I don't give a damn. I want you so badly I'm shaking." He put her hand on his chest. "Feel that thundering? It's my heart. That's what you do to me. I know I promised not to touch you, but I'm not strong enough to keep it. You're going to have to give me help."

The moment had caught her unaware. He had a slumberous look in his eyes. His mouth was too close. She couldn't think, couldn't breathe. Dottie tried to remove her hand, but found her limbs had grown weak with longings that had taken over.

"Alex—" She half groaned his name before taking the initiative to kiss him. When she realized she'd been the one to make it happen, it was too late to change her mind. Their mouths met in mutual hunger. She wrapped her arms around his neck, wanting to merge with him.

With one hand cupping the back of her head, his other wandered over her spine and hips, drawing her closer. The kiss she'd started went on and on. She desired him too terribly to do anything that would cut off the divine experience of giving and taking pleasure like this.

In the background she heard the children's muffled laughter. She didn't know if they'd peeked in this room and had seen them or not, but the sound was too close for comfort. Much as she never wanted to leave Alex's arms, she slid her hands back down his chest and tried to ease away from him so he would relinquish her mouth.

"I heard them," he whispered before she could say anything. Alex had the uncanny ability to read her mind.

"I hope Zoe didn't see us."

He sucked in his breath and cupped her face in his hands. "I hate to break this to you, but she woke at the last minute on the yacht."

Guilt swept through her, making her whole body go white-hot.

"Every little four-year-old girl has seen the movie of *Snow White*. My Zoe knows that when Prince Charming kissed the princess awake, it was true love that worked the charm."

What he was telling her now caused Dottie's body to shake with fright. "You don't think she really sees us that way—"

His handsome features hardened. "Who's to say? In her eyes you're her mommy. Zoe has never seen me kiss another woman. I *have* brought you to my castle. The way you and I were devouring each other just now has probably set the seal in her mind."

Aghast, Dottie propelled herself away from him. "Then you have to unset it, Alex."

"I'm afraid it's too late. You might as well know the rest."

She folded her arms to her waist to stay calm. "What more is there?"

"Sofia had a private word with me this morning before I left the palace. Just as Hector spies for my grandmother, Sofia is my eyes and ears where Zoe is concerned. It seems my daughter told her grandmother that you and I were leaving for Aurum today. But she told her not to cry. When we have the baby, we'll bring it to see *Yiayia*."

Dottie didn't know whether to laugh or cry, but the tears won out. The sound that escaped her lips was probably as unintelligible as Zoe's word for Hector. Four consonants. All difficult. "Your grandmother's world truly has come crashing down on her."

She saw his body tauten before he caught her in his arms once more. He shook her gently. "What has happened between you and me wasn't planned. For two years I've been telling the queen I'll never marry again, so it's absurd for you to be feeling guilt of any kind over Genevieve." He kissed her wet eyelids, then her whole face.

"It's not so much guilt as the *fear* I feel for Zoe. She's attached herself to me because of her speech problem. I won't be here much longer, but every day that I stay, it's going to make the ultimate separation that much harder."

A shudder passed through his body she could feel. "You think I'm not aware of that?"

She broke free of him. "I know you are, but we've got to lay down some ground rules. I don't ever want her to see us together like we are now. We can't be alone again. This has to be the end so she won't fantasize about us, Alex. It's no good. I'm going to my room to unpack and settle in. Go be with her and Mark right now. Please."

Blind with pain, she left him standing there ashen-faced.

On Wednesday evening of the following week, Alex's mood was as foul as Stasio's. Five days ago Dottie had virtually told him goodbye on the island, but he couldn't handle it any longer and needed to see her. Something had to be done or he was going to go out of his mind.

Philippe had just left to fly home to Vallader, but he would be coming back with his family to attend the coronation on Saturday just a week off now. Until then Alex and his brother were alone.

Stasio cast him a probing glance. "I do believe you're as restless as I am."

Alex gritted his teeth. "You're right." He shot to his feet. "Alert security and come with me. I'm leaving for Aurum to say good-night to Zoe."

"*And* Dottie?"

"I don't want to talk about her. After Zoe's asleep we'll do some riding and camp out in the mountains."

At least that was what he was telling himself now. Wild with pain, he spun around.

"When it comes to a woman, I can't have what I really want. Even if I could, she wouldn't want me. She adored her husband. Why do you think she's still single? No man measures up. The day after your coronation, she'll be leaving the country whether the new speech therapist replacing her has arrived or not."

"Zoe won't stand for it."

"She'll *have* to," he said in a hoarse whisper. "We're all going to have to go on doing our duty. You've never been able to have what you really wanted. You think I don't know what's been going on inside of you? It's killing me."

Stasio stopped midstride. His tormented expression said it all. "What do you want to do, little brother?"

Alex's brows had formed a black bar above his eyes. "Let's get out of here. Gather anything you need and I'll meet you at the helipad."

Before long they were winging their way to Aurum. Once they'd landed, Zoe came running with a couple of the other children who lived on the estate. Inez chatted with him for a minute.

Alex picked up his daughter and hugged her hard. "I've missed you."

"I've been waiting for you, Daddy. I missed you, too."

He kissed her curls. "Where's Dottie?"

"In town." Tears crept down her cheeks. "She said I couldn't go with her."

Naturally Zoe hadn't been happy about that. Though Alex couldn't argue with Dottie's decision, the news sent his heart plunging to his feet. She'd warned him that she would never be alone with him again and she'd meant it.

"How about a hug for me!" Stasio drew her into his arms to give Alex a chance to pull himself together.

Inez gathered up the other children, leaving the men alone with Zoe. They talked about Mark. "I'm sorry he had a cold and couldn't come today."

"Do you think he can come tomorrow?"

"I'll find out."

"I know he wants to come. Dot told us that after our lesson she'd take us out to look for ducks. He can't wait!"

Of course he couldn't. Any time spent with Dottie was pure enchantment.

"Will you ask his mommy?"

"You know I will."

Stasio put a hand on his shoulder. "I'll be at the stable getting the horses ready."

He nodded. "Come on, my little princess. It's getting late. Time to go to bed."

As she chatted with him, he realized he was starting to hear true sounds coming out of her and she was doing a lot more talking. In a month's time Dottie had already made a profound difference in her. All the thanks in the world would never be able to express his gratitude adequately to her.

For the next half hour he read stories to Zoe, then it was time for her prayers. At the end she said, "Bless my daddy and my Dot."

He blinked. She'd said *Dot* distinctly! He'd heard the *D* and the *T*, plus the *ah* in the middle.

Tears sprang to his eyes. This was Dottie's doing. She'd been trying to get her to say *Dot* instead of *mommy*. Just now the word had passed Zoe's lips naturally. A miracle had happened. He wanted to shout his elation, but he didn't dare because she was ready to go to sleep.

The sudden realization hit Alex hard. He loved Dottie Richards. He loved her to the depth of his being. He wanted her in his life forever and needed to tell her so she wouldn't leave him or Zoe. There had to be a way to keep her here and he was going to find it.

Once his daughter was dead to the world, he stole out of her room and raced to the stable to tell his brother there'd been a major breakthrough with Zoe. It was providential he and Stasio were going riding. Alex did his best thinking on the back of a horse. Tonight he would need all his powers of reasoning to come up with a solution.

But as he approached his brother, Stasio's phone rang. One look at his face after he'd picked up and Alex knew there was trouble.

"That was Hector," he said after ringing off. "*Yiayia* isn't well. The doctor is with her, but he thinks we should come home." They stared at each other. With the queen ill, their best-laid plans would have to wait.

Alex informed Inez. By tacit agreement they left for the helipad. Tonight's shining moment with Zoe had been swallowed up in this new crisis with their grandmother. When they arrived back on Hellenica, Hector was waiting for them in their grandmother's suite.

"The doctor has already left. He says the queen's ulcer is acting up again. He gave her medicine for it and now she's sleeping comfortably. I'm sorry to have bothered you."

Stasio eyed Alex in relief. "Thanks for letting us

know, Hector. It could have been much more serious. We're glad you told us."

"Thank you for your understanding, Your Highness."

"You've been with our grandmother much longer than we have. No one's been more devoted." Stasio's glance rested on Alex. "Shall we go to my suite?"

He nodded at his brother. Both of them needed a good stiff drink about now. As he turned to leave, Hector cleared his throat. "Prince Alexius? If I may have a private word with you first."

Something strange was going on for Hector to address him so formally. Alex eyed his brother who looked equally baffled. "I'll be with you in a minute, Stasi."

After he walked off, Hector said, "Could we talk in your suite, Your Highness?"

"Of course." But the request was unprecedented. As they headed to his apartment, Alex had an unpleasant foreboding. Their grandmother was probably sicker than Hector had let on, but he didn't want to burden Stasio, who walked around with enough guilt for a defeated army. The decision to call off his wedding to Beatriz had dealt a near-lethal blow to their grandmother, and poor Hector had been caught in the fallout.

Once they'd entered the living room, Alex invited the older man to sit down, but he insisted on remaining standing, so they faced each other.

"You have my complete attention, Hector. What is it?"

"When's my daddy coming?"

Dottie had been swimming in the pool on Aurum with Zoe while they waited for Alex. "Last night he told you he would be here after your lesson, didn't he?"

"Yes. I want him to hurry. I hope Mark's still not sick."

"We'll find out soon enough, because I can hear your daddy's helicopter." They both looked up.

When Dottie saw it, the realization that Alex would be walking out here in a few minutes almost put her into cardiac arrest. No mere hormones or physical attraction to a man could cause these feelings that made her world light up just to hear his name or know he was in the vicinity.

She was in love. She knew that now. She was in love again, for the second time in her life, and she cried out at the injustice. Her first love and son had been struck down so cruelly, she'd wondered how she could ever build another life for herself.

Now here she was carrying on with her career and doomed to love again, only this man was a prince who was off-limits to her. By the time of the coronation, Zoe would be snatched from her, too, and she'd be left a totally empty vessel. Blackness weighed her down. *What am I going to do?*

While Zoe shouted with excitement and hurried across the tiles to meet her father, who'd be striding through the entry any second, Dottie got out of the pool and raced to her own room. To be with him would only succeed in pouring acid on a newly opened wound that would never heal.

Knowing Alex needed time alone with his daughter, Dottie would give it to him. Quickly she showered and changed into denims and a top before checking her emails. Dr. Rice had sent her another message.

Dear Mrs. Richards,
Success at last. Your replacement's name is Mrs.
Miriam Hawes. She'll be arriving in Athens to-
morrow. All the arrangements have been made.
When you return to New York, I have a new three-
year-old girl who needs testing. We'll enjoy hav-
ing you back. Good luck and keep me posted.
Dr. Rice.

Dottie read the words again before burying her face in her hands. While she was sobbing, a little princess came running into her room and caught her in the act.

"Why are you crying?" She put her face right up against Dottie's. "Do you have a boo-boo?"

Zoe could say boo-boo well enough to be understood. Nothing could have pleased Dottie more, but right now pain consumed her. Yes. Dottie had a big boo-boo, one that had crumbled her heart into tiny pieces.

She sniffed and wiped the moisture off her face. "I hurt myself getting out of the pool." It wasn't a lie. In her haste she'd scraped her thigh on the side, but she would live. "Did Mark come?"

"Yes. He's running after the peacock." Dottie laughed through the tears. "Can he pull out one of its big feathers?"

"No, darling. That would hurt it."

"Oh." Obviously she hadn't thought about that aspect. "Daddy wants you to come."

Dottie had wondered when the bell would toll. She had no choice but to walk out and say hello to Alex and Mark, who were already in the pool whooping it up. Zoe ran to join them.

"Good afternoon, Your Highness."

His all-encompassing black gaze swept over her. "Good afternoon," he said in his deep, sensuous voice. Her body quickened at the change in him from last Saturday when there'd been nothing but painful tension between them.

"I'm glad you brought Mark with you. How are you feeling today, Mark?"

"Good. I didn't have a temperature, so my mom said I could come."

Dottie took her usual place on the edge and dangled her bare feet in the water. "Well we're very happy you're here, aren't we, Zoe?" She nodded while she hung on to her daddy's neck. "Zoe tells me you'd like to take a peacock feather home for a souvenir."

"Yeah. Could I?"

The sudden glance Alex flashed Dottie was filled with mirth. He wasn't the same man of a few days ago. She hardly recognized him. "What do you say about that, Prince Alexius?"

By now he'd put Zoe up on his powerful shoulders. He looked like a god come to life. "Tell you what, Mark. That peacock is going to moult in another month. When he does, he'll shed his tail feathers. You and Zoe can follow him around. When he drops them, you can take home as many as he leaves."

"Thanks!"

"Cool, Daddy."

Alex burst into laughter. "What did you just say to me?"

"'Cool,'" Mark answered for her.

"That's what I thought she said."

"I've been teaching her."

Zoe patted her daddy's head. "Can Mark come to Uncle Stasi's coronation?"

Alex's black eyes pinned Dottie's body to the tiles at the edge of the pool. The day after she was leaving Hellenica. "His family has already been invited."

"*My* family?" Mark's eyes had rounded like blue marbles.

"*Yiayia* says we have to be quiet," Zoe warned him.

"I won't talk."

"It's going to be a very great occasion in the cathedral," Dottie explained to him. "Hellenica is going to get a new king. You'll be able to see the crown put on his head."

She nodded. "It gave my *pappou* a headache."

Dottie broke down laughing. Despite the fact that part of her was dying inside, she couldn't hold it back.

"Hey—that's not funny!" Stasio's voice broke in. "Do you know the imperial crown of Hellenica weighs over five pounds? I'll have to wear a five-pound sack of flour on my head the whole day before to get used to it."

"Uncle Stasi!" Zoe called to him in delight and clapped her hands. Dottie hadn't realized he'd come with Alex.

"That's my name." He grinned before doing a belly flop in the pool. The splash got everyone wet. When he came up for air, he looked at the children. "You'd better watch out. I heard there was a shark in here."

"Uh-oh." While the children shrieked, Dottie jumped up. "This is where I opt out."

Without looking back she walked across the tiles to her room. She thought she was alone *until* she saw Alex. He'd followed her dressed in nothing more than his wet black swimming trunks. Dottie's heartbeat switched to hyperspeed. "You're not supposed to be in here. That was our agreement."

He stood there with his hands on his hips. "Last night that agreement was rendered null and void."

"Why?" she whispered in nervous bewilderment.

His eyes narrowed on her features. "You may well ask, but now isn't the time to answer that question. The queen has been sick, but she's starting to feel better and is missing Zoe. I promised to take her back to Hellenica. Stasi has volunteered to babysit the children on the flight while you and I take the cruiser. We'll leave here as soon as you're ready. Pack what you want to take for overnight." On that note, he disappeared.

Dottie gathered up some things, not surprised the queen wanted to see Zoe. It would lift her spirits. Before long they were ready and left with Alex for the dock in the limo. Once on board, he maneuvered the cruiser out of the small bay at a wakeless speed, then opened the throttle and the boat shot ahead.

The helicopter dipped low and circled above them so the children could wave to them. Dottie waved back. She could tell they were having the time of their lives. Alex beeped the horn three times before the helicopter flew on.

"That's precious cargo up there," she told him. "The two little sad sacks of a month ago have undergone a big transformation. I had no idea if the experiment would work, but I honestly think they like each other."

He squinted at her. "You only think?"

"Well, I don't know for sure. Mark might be pretending because he wants to haul off some of those peacock feathers."

Alex's shoulders shook in silent laughter. While his spirits seemed so much improved, she decided to tell him about the email from Dr. Rice.

He nodded. "I was already informed by him."

Naturally he was. She cleared her throat. "Under the circumstances I thought the new therapist could come to Aurum and stay in one of the guest rooms. We'll let Zoe get used to her and I'll involve her in our games."

When Alex didn't respond she got nervous and said, "Mrs. Hawes will have her own techniques to try out on your daughter, of course. By the time of the coronation, they'll be used to each other. I know it will be difficult for Zoe to say goodbye to me, so we need to handle that carefully."

"I agree." He sounded remote. "I'll think on it."

With those few words, Alex remained quiet, but she didn't mind because his mellow mood was so different from the way he'd been, she was able to relax. For a little while she could pretend they were a normal couple out enjoying each other on this glorious blue sea with the same color of sky above them. Despite her aunt's warnings, Dottie still had a tendency to dream forbidden thoughts, if only for the few minutes they had until they reached the shore.

In this halcyon state she noticed him turn his dark head toward her. "After we dock, you're free until this evening. At eight-thirty I'll send for you. In light of Mrs. Hawes's imminent arrival, we'll finalize the termination of your contract tonight. For Zoe's sake it will be best if you don't drop by her suite to say good-night."

The trip between islands hadn't taken long. Dottie

had been given her few minutes of dreaming, but that was all. With one royal pronouncement, even that brief time had been dashed to smithereens.

CHAPTER NINE

TONIGHT was different from all the other nights in Alex's life. As he'd told Dottie last week, he couldn't be in two places at once. In order to help his brother, he'd sent her and Zoe to Aurum. But this night he needed to be alone with the woman who'd turned the lights on for him. Only Dottie had known the location of the secret switch. Through her magic, she'd found it and now no power could turn it off.

After eating dinner with Zoe and putting her to bed, Alex asked his brother to read her some stories until she fell asleep. While he did that, Alex slipped away to shower and dress in a black silk shirt and trousers, just formal enough to let Dottie know what this night meant to him.

He flicked his gaze around the private dining room of his own jet. It was one of the few places where they could have privacy and be secure away from the palace. The steward had set up the preparations for their intimate dinner, complete with flickering candlelight.

Alex had never used his plane for anything but transportation and business meetings. Tonight it would serve as his portal to a future he'd never dared dream about. Now that he could, his body throbbed at every pulse point. When he pulled the phone from his pocket to answer it, his hand trembled.

Hector was outside. He'd brought Dottie to the airport in the limousine. "Tell her to come aboard."

He moved to the entrance of the plane. When she saw him, she paused midway up the steps in a pink-and-white-print dress he hadn't seen before. She looked breathtaking. Her honey blond-hair had been swept into a knot.

Though she'd picked up a golden tan over the past month, she had a noticeable pallor. He hoped to heaven it was because the thought of leaving him was killing her. Maybe it had been cruel to set her up this way, but he'd wanted proof that she couldn't live without him either. If he'd misread the radar…

"Come all the way in, Dottie. I've got dinner waiting for us."

She bit her lower lip. "I couldn't possibly eat, Alex. I'm sorry for any trouble you've gone to. We could have taken care of business in your office."

He lounged against the opening, half surprised at that response. "We could have, but the office is too public a place for the proposal I have in mind."

By the look in her blue eyes, she acted as if she'd just had a dagger plunged into her heart. "There can't be anything but indecent proposals between you and me." Her wintry comment might have frozen him if he didn't know certain things she wasn't aware of yet.

His black brows lifted. "If you'll finish that long walk into the plane, I'll enlighten you about a very decent one you wouldn't have thought of."

She remained where she was. "If you've decided to abandon your family and the monarchy and hide away in some distant place for the rest of your life, then you're not the prince I imagined you to be."

Her answer thrilled him because it meant she'd not only thought of every possibility for finding a way the two of them could be together, she'd actually put voice to it.

"Then you like it that I'm Prince Alexius?"

He could tell she was struggling to pretend her breath hadn't almost left her lungs. "That's an absurd question. You couldn't be anyone else. It's who you are."

"In other words I'm *your* highness, and you're *my* lowness."

She averted her eyes. "Don't joke about serious matters like this."

"Joking is how I've gotten through life this far."

Her head flew back. "That's very tragic. Why did you have me driven here?" she cried. "The truth!"

"Can you stand to hear it?" he fired back in a quiet voice.

"Alex—" She'd dispensed with his title. That was progress.

"I have a plan I want to talk over with you."

He could see her throat working. "What plan? There can be no plan."

"If you'll come aboard, I'll tell you. In case you think I'm going to kidnap you, I swear this jet won't leave the ground. But since I'm a target for the press, who have their Telephoto lenses focused on us as we speak, I'd prefer we talked in private."

He felt her hesitation before she took one step, then another, until she'd entered the plane. His steward closed the door behind them.

"This way." Alex refrained from touching her. The

time wasn't right. As soon as they entered the dining room, he heard her soft cry. She looked at everything as if she was in some sort of daze. He'd been in one since last night.

"Why did you go to all this trouble?"

"Because it occurred to me you've done all the work since you came to Hellenica. I thought you deserved a little fuss to be made over *you* for a change." He held out a chair for her, but she didn't budge.

"Alex—it's *me* you're talking to. Mrs. Richards, the speech therapist. If there are lies between us, then this meeting is pointless. Please stop dancing around the subject. What's the purpose in my coming here?"

"More than you know."

"You're being cryptic. I can't do this." She turned away from him but he caught her arm.

"All I ask is that you hear me out."

The beautiful line of her jaw hardened. "What if I don't want to listen?"

They stood there like adversaries. "I thought that after everything we've been through together, you trusted me. I think you know I trust you with my life, but apparently I've made a mistake about you." Alex took a calculated risk and let go of her hand. "If you don't want anything more to do with me, then you're free to leave now."

Dottie stayed planted to the same spot. Her breathing sounded labored. "Is this about Zoe?"

"About Zoe. About you. About me. If you'll sit down, Hector will explain."

Her eyes widened. "Hector—"

"Yes. I'll phone him now."

The older man had a certain gravitas even Dottie recognized. While she continued to stand where she was, he rang the older man. Within a minute, Hector joined them.

"Your Highness?" He bowed.

"Would you please tell Mrs. Richards what you told me last night?"

"Certainly." Hector cleared his throat and proceeded to explain what Stasio had jokingly said earlier was Alex's get-out-of-jail-free card. "Before Prince Alexius married, his father, King Stefano, knew of Princess Teresa's heart condition and worried about it. Eventually he made a legal proviso that cannot be broken.

"Simply stated, it reads that should she precede him in death and he wishes to marry again, he—who is second in line to the crown—would have the constitutional right to choose his own wife whether she be of royal blood or a commoner. However, any children born of that union would have no claim to the throne."

Alex watched Dottie slowly sink to the chair he'd pulled out for her. When the older man had finished, he thanked him.

"I'm happy to be of service, Your Highness. If you need me, I'll be out in the limo." He exited the plane while Dottie rubbed her arms with her hands, as if she were chilly.

"The gods on Mount Pelos have heard me," Alex began. "Until I met you, Dottie, I never wanted to marry again. And now, thanks to my father, I'm now able to ask you to marry me." He stared at her for a long moment. "I'm making you an honorable, legally binding offer of marriage."

She finally looked at him. The pupils of her eyes had grown so large, she was obviously in shock. "I couldn't be happier that because of your father's intervention, you've suddenly been given your free agency to choose your own wife. For him to think that far ahead for your welfare shows he really did love you. What I don't understand is why didn't Hector come forward ages ago so you could have found someone else by now?"

Alex was thunderstruck by her question. Had his proposal of marriage meant nothing to her?

"Hector didn't tell me why, but I suspect it's because he secretly loves Zoe like his own granddaughter. He never married or had children. I'm convinced that seeing her so happy with you and so unhappy at the prospect of becoming the stepdaughter of Princess Genevieve prompted him to come forward. The queen may have his allegiance, but Zoe has his heart. Hector has seen the three of us together and knows I'll always put my daughter first."

"But you've only known me for a month, Alex! You're *young!* You've got years to find the kind of relationship you've dreamed of having."

He leaned forward. "I've already had years of relationships that filled the loneliness from time to time, but now I have a daughter who's as precious to me as your son was to you. If I'd searched the world over, I couldn't have found the more perfect mother for her than you."

"So that's all you want? A mother?"

"After what we've shared, you know better than to ask me that. I'm in love with you and you know it, but even though you've responded to me physically, I'm aware your heart died when you lost your husband and son. I live in the hope that one day you'll come to love me with the same intensity. As for Zoe, she loves you so much, she was calling you mommy almost from the beginning."

"Yes, but—"

"It would be a second chance for both of us to find happiness," he spoke over her. "We could make a home anywhere you want. If you prefer to stay in New York and further your career, we'll buy a house there. Our home will be our castle."

An incredulous expression broke out on her face. "What are you talking about?"

"What all normal couples talk about when they're discussing marriage. I want you to be happy."

"But your place is here in Hellenica!"

"Listen to me, Dottie. I'll always be Prince Alexius, but I don't have to live here. Not now. Thanks to technology, it won't matter where we settle down because I can do my mining engineering work anywhere."

"Be serious—your family and friends are here!"

"Yes, and we'll come for visits."

"I'm talking about your life!"

"My life will be with my own little family. You have no idea how much I want to take care of you. I love you. You'll be my first priority."

"You think the queen is going to stand for that?" She sounded frightened.

"She has no say in this matter."

"You're really serious, aren't you?"

"Of course."

In the quiet that followed, Dottie stared into the candle flames. "I feel like I'm in some kind of strange dream. What if I didn't exist?" she cried out. "What would you be planning to do with this new freedom?"

It appeared he was wrong about her feelings. The

knowledge that they could be together legitimately hadn't changed anything for her.

"It's a moot point. You *do* exist, and you've won Hector around, otherwise he would never have come forward with that document." At this point Alex couldn't comprehend life without her, but maybe he'd been mistaken in thinking there was a future for them. "After the coronation, I plan to live with Zoe on Aurum as always. Shall I consider this your answer?"

When she didn't say anything, Alex's burgeoning hopes disintegrated into blackness. He pushed himself away from the table and got to his feet. "If you're ready to leave, I'll walk you out to the limo and Hector will see you get back to the palace."

Once she'd said good-night to Hector, Dottie hurried to her room so torn up inside she didn't know how she was going to make it through the night. Alex's marriage proposal had turned her world upside down.

He'd told her he'd fallen in love with her, but that had to be his desire talking. She knew he desired her, but feared it would eventually wear off now that she was no longer forbidden fruit. If they married and then he grew tired of her, she couldn't bear it.

She still couldn't comprehend that one minute he was doomed to the life he'd been born into, and the next minute he was free to take a commoner for his wife. It was too convenient. If she hadn't heard it from his own lips—from Hector's—she wouldn't have believed it, not in a million years.

Didn't he realize he could marry any woman he wanted? The idea that he'd move to New York for her was a pipe dream. You didn't take the prince out of the man no matter how hard you tried. She didn't want to do that to him. She loved Alex for who he was, but she wasn't about to ruin his life by condemning him to another prison.

Dottie was painfully in love with him, but she wasn't his grand passion. Once his gratitude to her wore off, he'd want his freedom. She couldn't handle that. It was better to remain single and just do her job. The time had come for her to watch out for herself and what she wanted.

Full of adrenaline, she went to the closet for her luggage and started packing. Mrs. Hawes would be on the job in the morning. Zoe wouldn't be happy about it, but in time she'd adjust. Her speech was improving every day. She was already getting some self-confidence. Alex would keep working with her.

As Dottie cleaned out the schoolroom, she kept telling herself Zoe was going to be fine. She and her daddy had each other. That was the important thing. After another hour she had everything packed and finally crawled into bed, praying for sleep to come. But her pillow was wet before oblivion took over.

The next time she had cognizance of her surroundings, she heard a child crying. The sound tugged at her deepest emotions.

"Cory?" she murmured. Her eyes opened.

"Dot," a voice called out her name clearly in the early morning light. It was Zoe! "Dot?"

"I'm right here."

"Mommy," she cried her other name for her and climbed onto the bed.

Dottie pulled her close and rocked her in her arms. "Did you have a bad dream?"

"No. *Yiayia* says a new teacher has come to help me. Don't go, Mommy. Don't go." Her little body shook from her tears. She clung to Dottie.

"Shh. It's all right." Dottie kissed her wet eyes and cheeks. Her dear little face was flushed. She sang some songs she used to sing to Cory. After a few minutes Zoe started to quiet down. Just when it appeared she'd fallen asleep and Dottie could alert the staff, the palace phone rang, startling both of them.

Zoe lifted her head. "I want to stay here."

Dottie reached for the receiver and said hello.

"Dottie—" The anxiety in Alex's voice was that of any frantic parent who couldn't find his child.

"Zoe's with me. I was just going to let you know."

"Thank heaven. I'll be right there."

Alex must have broken the speed record. By the time she'd thrown on her robe, he'd entered her bedroom out of breath and looking so pale it worried her. He was still dressed in the stunning black silk shirt and trousers he'd worn on the jet. It meant he'd been up all night, which made her feel so guilty she wanted to die.

Zoe stood up in the bed. "Don't be mad, Daddy."

A sound of anguish escaped his throat as he reached for her and hugged her tight. "I went to your room to kiss you good morning, but you weren't there."

"I know. I came to see Dot."

"How did you get past the guards?"

"I ran when they didn't see me."

Dottie heard his groan. "You gave me a fright."

"*Yiayia* said I have a new teacher and Dot is leaving. I don't want a new teacher. Please don't let Dot leave—" The pain in her voice was too much for Dottie, who couldn't stop her own tears.

"I can't make Dottie stay, Zoe." The sound that came out of him seeped from a new level of sadness and despair, finding a responding chord in her.

"Yes, you can," Zoe fought her father.

He shook his dark head and kissed her curls. "You're going to learn you can't force people to do things they don't want to do. Come on. Let's take a walk on the beach and then we'll have breakfast."

"No—" she screamed as he started to carry her out. Still in his arms, Zoe turned her head to look at Dottie. "Don't leave, Mommy. I don't want to go. Stop, Daddy—"

Dottie had a vision of them walking out that door. What if she never saw them again? The day of the car accident Neil had grabbed Cory to take him on an errand. Both of them were smiling as he carried their son out the front door. Dottie never saw them alive again.

The thought of never seeing Alex or Zoe again was unthinkable.

"Wait, Alex—"

He'd already started out the door. The momentum caused him to take a few more steps before he swung around. His haunted expression tore her heart to shreds.

"You really want to marry me?" she whispered shakily.

He slowly lowered Zoe to the marble floor and started toward her. "Would I have asked, otherwise?"

It was the moment of truth. She had to have faith that their marriage could work. He'd told her he loved her. He was willing to move to New York, willing to give her the opportunity of loving his wonderful daughter. What more could a woman ask?

But she'd been thinking about it all night. Her deepest fear was that this royal prince, who'd been denied the possibility of a happy marriage the first time, was jumping impulsively into another marriage he'd regret down the road. He was a free man. If he chose to, he could go where he wanted and live like a commoner with another woman.

After what had happened to Neil and Cory, Dottie wanted a guarantee of happiness. But as her aunt had told her, there were no guarantees. *You're a romantic, Dottie. For that reason you can be hurt the worst. Why set yourself up, honey?*

Her aunt's advice had come too late. For better or worse, Dottie *had* set herself up.

She closed the distance between them. "I love you, Alex. So much, you have no idea." Emotion was almost choking her. "I want to be your wife more than anything in the world."

"Darling—" He crushed her to him, wrapping his arms all the way around her. "I adore you, Dottie. I was up all night plotting how to get you to love me," he whispered against her lips before kissing her long and hard. "We need to get married right away."

"I agree," she cried, kissing him back hungrily. "I think we'd better tell Zoe."

"You think?" His smile lit up her insides before he said, "Why don't we do it right here in the alcove."

His arms reluctantly let her go before he drew Zoe over to the table where they'd spent so many delightful times together. Still trembling from the look he'd just given her, Dottie took her place across from them, her usual teacher position. She checked her watch. It was ten to seven in the morning.

Zoe eyed both of them curiously. She'd seen them

kissing and knew something was going on. "Are we going to have school *now*?"

Alex's lips twitched that way they sometimes did when he was trying to hold back his laughter. When he did that, Dottie thought there could be no more attractive man on earth.

"No," he answered. "This morning is a very special morning and we have plans to make because Dottie has just said she would marry me."

The sweetest smile broke out on Zoe's face. "Then you're going to be my real mommy, like Mark's?"

"Yes." Dottie reached across the table to squeeze her hands.

"They're going to have a baby. Mark told me."

"I didn't know that," he answered, trying to keep a deadpan face. Dottie wasn't as successful.

"Can we have one, too?"

Dottie laughed through the tears. "For now you have Baby Betty."

Alex's dark eyes swerved to hers. The look of desire in them took her breath. "If the gods on Mount Pelos are kind, maybe a new baby will come."

Zoe beamed. "A big boy like you, Daddy!"

He trapped Dottie's gaze midair. Her soon-to-be daughter was precocious to a fault, just like her father. Both of them were remembering the jump-rope game. It was the day she fell so hard for Prince Alexius, she hadn't been the same since. She didn't know which moment was the most surreal. But one thing was absolutely certain. She'd committed herself and there was no going back now.

"I tell you what," Alex said. "Let's all get dressed

and have breakfast in my suite while we make plans. After that we'll tell the family."

Zoe stared at her father before giving him a huge kiss. Then she got down and ran around the table to hug Dottie. "I love you, Mommy."

"I love you, too." Over her brown curls she looked at the man she'd just told she was going to marry. "I love you both beyond belief."

Dottie had been to Alex's apartment once before, but her thoughts had been so focused on her diagnostic session with Zoe, she hadn't really looked around and appreciated the magnificence of her surroundings.

During their fabulous breakfast out on the patio, a delivery came for Dottie. She opened the long florist box and discovered two dozen long-stemmed red roses with the most heavenly fragrance. The little card said, *For the first time in my life, I feel like a king whose every wish has come true.* Coming from Alex, those words had unique significance.

After kissing Dottie hungrily, he excused himself to go visit his grandmother and make sure she was up. He told Dottie and Zoe he'd be coming by for them in a few minutes, at which point they would go to the queen's drawing room and tell her their news.

After Stasio had refused to marry Princess Beatriz, Alex's announcement was going to be another terrible disappointment. Dottie feared it might be too much for Zoe's *yiayia* and she would suffer from something worse than ulcers. In a way Dottie had it in her heart to feel sorry for the dowager whose world was crumbling before her very eyes.

The older woman had grown up knowing nothing

but her duty. Somehow she had made her own marriage work, and so had Alex's parents. Deep down it had to be very hard on her to see her two wonderful grandsons so terribly unhappy up to now.

Dottie played with Zoe out on the patio, but she kept waiting for Alex to appear. A maid brought them some much-appreciated refreshments. Dottie asked for a vase so she could put the gorgeous roses in water. The gesture from Alex was one of the reasons she loved him so much.

After being in the apartment for two hours with no word from him, she started to get nervous. Perhaps his grandmother had suffered a setback from the news. He and Stasio were probably sequestered with her because Alex's news had shattered another dream. Twice Dottie started to pick up the palace phone and ask to speak to him, then thought the better of it.

Zoe seemed perfectly content to play with her toys, but Dottie was turning into a mass of nerves. Another hour went by, still no word about anything. When 7:00 p.m. rolled around, their dinner was brought in, but no news from Alex. When she didn't think she could stand it a second longer, Hector appeared on the patio where they'd started to eat.

"If I might speak to you in private."

Thank goodness. "I'll be right back, Zoe. I'm just going to the living room."

"Okay."

Dottie followed him into the other room. "Obviously something's wrong. It's been ten hours since Alex told me he'd be back."

"He had to fly to Zurich today and might not return until morning."

She blinked. "As in Switzerland?"

"Yes. He asked me to assure you that he would never have left you and the little princess unless it was an emergency. He would like you to stay in his suite."

No doubt Alex had told him they were getting married. "Then we will."

Hector knew what the emergency was, but he would never tell Dottie. Whatever was going on had to be serious for Alex to go away today. She rubbed her arms nervously. "Is he all right?"

The slight hesitation before he said, "Of course," spoke volumes. "If there's anything else you need, you only have to ask."

"We're fine, Hector. Thank you for telling me. Good night."

"Good night."

Hector was always perfectly correct. He'd served the monarchy all his adult life. Like the queen, he didn't deviate from his role. It would be too much to ask of anyone. She thought of Alex who'd told her he would live in New York if she wanted. She had no doubt he could do it and make the most of it, but he'd been raised a prince. That would never change.

Full of musings, she walked out to the patio. "Zoe?"

"Did Daddy come?"

"Not yet. Something came up."

"I know. It's business."

Dottie smiled. Just then Zoe sounded a hundred years old. "Why don't we get you in the tub for a nice bath, then I'll read you some stories."

"Are we going to sleep in Daddy's bed?"

"Yes. At least until he calls or comes."

A little sound of happiness escaped the little girl's lips.

Dottie rang for a maid to bring them some things from their rooms. Within the hour both of them were ready for bed. Zoe picked out the stories she wanted and they climbed under the covers. Dottie looked around the sumptuous room, hardly able to believe she would be marrying the man who slept in this royal bedchamber when he was on Hellenica.

Though she was filled with anxiety over the reason for Alex's absence, the feel of the warm little body nestled against her brought a comfort to her heart she hadn't known in years. When they read the last book, she kissed her. "I'm so thankful you're going to be my daughter soon. I love you, Zoe."

"I love you. Good night, Mommy."

No one slept more peacefully than a child who wasn't worried about anything. Zoe had her new mommy-to-be, her daddy and her Baby Betty. Her world was complete. Dottie wished she could say the same for herself, but without Alex here to tell her what was going on, she was too anxious to sleep.

Instead of lying there tortured by fears she couldn't even identify, she slid out of bed and threw on her robe. Zoe preferred the patio to any other place in the palace. Dottie was drawn to it, too, and wandered out there where she wouldn't disturb Zoe with her restlessness.

CHAPTER TEN

AT ONE in the morning, Alex stepped off his jet into the limo and headed for the palace. He'd been prepared to stay all night in Valleder with Philippe and Stasio, but both men urged him to go back to Hellenica and be with Dottie and Zoe.

There was nothing Alex wanted so much in this life, but since the last time he'd seen Dottie, his entire world had changed. He couldn't reverse time and put it back to the way it was before he'd gone to his grandmother's apartment to let her know he'd returned from Aurum.

He said good-night to Hector, then entered the palace and went straight to his apartment. But he was so torn up in his soul by the events of the past fifteen hours, the burden of what he had to tell Dottie made his limbs heavy. He felt like an old man as he continued up the steps and down the hall to his suite.

No lights had been left on. The place was quiet as a tomb. He tiptoed to the bedroom and was surprised to see Zoe asleep alone. Instinct told him Dottie was out on the patio and he headed for it.

His thoughts flew back to that first day. He'd walked Zoe out there to be tested. When Dottie had thrown him that Ping-Pong ball, she'd set an energy in motion that had turned him into a different man. Now all the dynamics were different because Mrs. Dottie Richards had agreed to become Mrs. Dottie Constantinides. Or so she'd thought.

This happened to be his favorite time of night, when the moon was on the rise over the Aegean. It was the time when the heat of the day released the perfume from the jasmine, filling the warm air with its heavenly scent. Instead of it being day, this was the night of his engagement. It was a singular irony that his daughter occupied his bed.

He stepped out on the patio and glimpsed his bride-to-be at the other end. His pounding heart almost suffocated him as he moved toward her. She stood at the wall and had put her hands on either side of the ledge, taking in the unparalleled view etched in his mind from childhood. With her standing there, a new softly rounded, feminine sculpture had been added to the landscape.

"Dottie?" he murmured. A cry escaped her lips. She turned toward him in surprise. "Enjoying the view?"

"This kind of beauty goes beyond perfection."

He sucked in his breath. "It does now." She looked gorgeous yet maidenlike standing there in the moonlight in her simple pink robe. Alex found it hard to believe she'd given birth to a child in another time and place.

"Hector said you might not be home before morning."

"I thought I might have to stay in Valleder until tomorrow, but my brother and Philippe sent me back."

Her eyes searched his. "Why did you have to go to Philippe's? What's happened?"

"You deserve a full explanation and you're going to

get one, but it's going to take a while. Maybe you should sit down."

"That sounded ominous." Her voice trembled. "I think I'd prefer to stand."

"The bottom line is, Stasio submitted papers to the ministers and has taken the steps to abdicate from the monarchy."

In the silence that followed, he watched her face pale. "*What* did you say?"

"Apparently he's been planning it for a long time. When you suggested that I might have decided to abdicate in order to marry you, the idea wasn't so far-fetched after all. You just happened to apply it to the wrong prince."

A hand went to her throat. "He's really stepping down?"

"Yes. After Stasi called off his betrothal, I should have guessed this would be the next step, but I've been so caught up in my feelings for you, I'm not the same person anymore."

"Darling…"

"It's true, Dottie. The reason he was out of the country so long was because he had to work things out with Philippe."

"What things?"

"Stasi has persuaded our second cousin to rule as king over Hellenica."

She shook her head. "I don't believe it."

"Philippe will be able to reign over both countries without problem. The Houses of Valleder and Constantinides are intrinsically entwined. He's well loved in Valleder. It will be the same here."

She looked shellshocked. "Aren't *you* the second in line to the throne?"

"Yes. But Stasio knows how I feel and would never put me in that position, especially now that I'm going to marry you and move to New York. Zoe is third in line and, if she wishes, will rule one day when Philippe is no longer king."

"So does that mean the coronation has been called off?"

"Yes. The announcement will go out on the news tomorrow evening. My grandmother will continue to be the head of the monarchy until Philippe is installed."

Dottie stared out at the sea. "I'm surprised the queen isn't in the hospital by now."

"She may end up there, but she hasn't given up the fight yet. This change to install Philippe has to be voted on by the ministers of the parliament. She has powerful friends there. So does Stasi. I believe the votes for Philippe will prevail. She's calling for an emergency assembly."

"What if they vote against installing your cousin?"

"Then she'll continue to reign until her death, issuing her edicts through the head of parliament."

"And after that?"

"The parliament will convene to find an heir from the Constantinides line. We have a fourth cousin living on the island of Cuprum in the Thracian Sea. He's in his sixties and could be brought up for consideration. However, we have no idea how long my grandmother will live. She has a strong constitution and could outlive him."

"This is all so unbelievable. Your poor grandmother.

Poor Stasio," she whispered, wringing her hands. "To be so desperate for his freedom, he'd give up everything…"

"Actually, I never saw anyone happier than he was when I left him. He's been in love with a woman from Norway for the past ten years and had to make a choice. In the end he chose Solveig. He's a different man now."

"I can only imagine. The second you said abdicate, I thought there had to be a woman. Only a powerful love could cause him to make a break with your family."

"I told him he was insane if he ever wasted another moment feeling guilty about what he's done."

"You're a wonderful brother to say that to him."

"Stasi would do the same for me. Fortunately our father provided that escape clause for me in his will. Otherwise there would have been two abdications."

"You don't really mean that." Her voice shook.

He gave an elegant shrug of his shoulders. "After Teresa died, I put the idea of marriage completely out of my mind. Much later I realized I wanted to marry you, and knew I would have to have papers drawn up for my abdication because there was no way I was going to let you get away from me. I loved you from the moment I saw you. When Hector heard you were leaving, he acted on my father's wishes and told me about the codicil to his will. As you said, it takes a powerful love."

Her breathing had changed. "You loved me from the beginning?"

"I realize now that I fell for you the moment you walked into my office and treated me like an ordinary man. You had no idea what that did to me. My world changed and I knew I had to have you, even if it meant turning my back on my heritage."

"Alex—

"I love you desperately. When we reach New York, I plan to show you what you mean to me. I'll do whatever I have to in order to make our marriage work."

"So will I," she declared. "Don't you know I'm so crazy about you, I'd do anything for you, too? At first I feared the only reason you wanted to marry me was because I was forbidden fruit and able to be a mother figure for Zoe. But I took the risk and said yes to you anyway because I'm so in love with you, nothing else matters."

"Do you have any concept of what those words mean to me, Dottie? I raced back here from Valleder fearing maybe all this was a fantastic dream. It's so hard to believe that I've found the only woman for me, and she loves me, too."

"Then believe this—I don't want to go back to New York with you. I don't want to live there."

"Of course you do. It's your home."

"It was once, but then I came to your world and I've grown to love it here. *You're* here. I would never expect you to cast aside your whole way of life for me. Being Zoe's therapist has brought me smack-dab into the heart of your world. I've learned so much and I'm still learning."

The blood was pounding in his ears. "You're just saying this because it's what you think I want to hear."

"Well, isn't it? Besides the fact that what I'm telling you is true, what do you think those wedding vows are going to be about? I plan to love, honor and serve you through the good and the bad. This is a bad time for your family. Without Stasio, you need me to help you keep the monarchy together.

"Your grandmother needs you. Even though I haven't

met her, I like her, Alex. I really do. She has tried to do her duty the way she's seen fit and Zoe adores her. Why should King Philippe or any other royal family member have to be brought in when you're the son meant to take up the reins? I believe your father knew that."

Alex couldn't believe what he was hearing.

"Alex, you've already been carrying a lot of the load your whole life. Stasio tried his best to shield you by turning to Philippe. He did everything in his power to help you, but you don't need his help.

"I've watched and listened. Your marriage to Teresa proves to me you cared more for the kingdom than you know, or like Stasio you would have abdicated a long time ago. To my mind, you were born to be king. Your country means everything to you, otherwise you wouldn't have agreed to serve in Stasio's place while he's been away. I love you, Alex. I revere you for wanting to do the noble thing and I love the idea of helping you."

Her brilliant blue eyes flashed like the sapphire of the ring he hadn't given her yet. It was still in his suite on Aurum. Those eyes let him know the truth. It was pouring from her soul. "All you have to do is turn around and accept the crown, my love."

There was a swelling in his chest that felt as though it might be a heart attack.

"You and I will always have each other and you and Stasio will be able to live without any guilt. He can marry the woman he loves. They can come and visit, have children, give Zoe a cousin or two. Hector will be thrilled. The queen can take a well-earned rest and Zoe will always be our darling girl. It's the best of all worlds."

Her logic moved him to tears, but he shook his head. "You don't understand. I can't rule with a commoner for a wife, and I refuse to give you up."

"Who says you can't?" she shot back. "I didn't hear about that when Hector explained the contents of your father's codicil to me. It only said that if we have a child or children together, they won't have claim to the throne. That will be Zoe's privilege."

Alex rubbed the back of his neck. "Everything you've said makes perfect sense, but it's never been done."

"That still doesn't make it impossible. Let's go to the queen right now. Wake her up if you have to and tell her you're willing to rule Hellenica with me at your side. Since your father broke the rules when he made that extension to his will, it stands to reason his mother could be moved to convince the ministers to vote in our favor for the good of the monarchy.

"There's no one who can do greater good for the country than you, Alex. You've already been running everything singlehandedly and doing a brilliant job. Maybe it was a presentiment on my part, but the night of the party I watched you and thought you should be king, not Stasio."

In the next instant he reached blindly for her. "You don't know what you're saying."

"I think I do." She clutched his arms. "All I need to know is one thing. Look me in the eye and tell me you don't want to salvage the House of Constantinides. If you're not truthful with me now, then the marriage we're about to enter into is a sham and won't last."

He crushed her in his arms, rocking her long and hard. With his face buried in her hair he whispered, "What have I ever done to deserve you?"

"It'll take me a lifetime to tell you everything, but first we have to tell the queen. Phone your grandmother now. She needs help. Who better than the father of her beloved Zoe?"

Alex kissed the side of her neck. "Whether or not I become king—whether or not my grandmother decides she wants us to have a public wedding here on Hellenica at the time of the coronation—it doesn't matter as long as for once in my life I do get to do the thing I thought I'd never be able to do."

"What's that?" Dottie asked breathlessly.

He cupped her face in his hands. "Marry the woman of my dreams in the chapel on Aurum tomorrow."

"Alex—"

"It will be a very private ceremony just for us. The tiny church located on the palace grounds isn't open to the public. It was erected for the family's use. Father Gregorius will marry us. I'll ask him to perform the ceremony in English."

"He doesn't have to go to that trouble."

"Yes, he does. I'm marrying the bride of my heart and want to say my vows in English for your sake. My friend Bari will be our witness along with Inez and Ari. And, of course, Zoe."

Dottie clung to Alex's hand as he escorted her and Zoe inside the dark interior of the church that smelled strongly of beeswax candles and incense. She wore her white dress with the yellow sash. Dottie had dressed in the pink print and had left her hair down because Zoe had told her earlier that her daddy loved her hair like that.

Inez stepped forward. She handed Dottie a bouquet

of cornflowers. Against Dottie's ear Alex whispered, "I asked her to gather these this morning. They match the incredible blue of your eyes."

She felt tears start and soon saw that another, smaller bouquet had been picked for Zoe to hold. Alex was wearing a light blue summer suit. After putting two cornflowers inside his lapel, he led her and Zoe to the front where the priest stood at the altar. Inez beckoned Zoe to stand by her.

Despite the fact that Alex would always be a prince, Dottie realized he'd dispensed with all artifice for their wedding. She knew the last thing he wanted was for her to feel overwhelmed. Her heart quivered with her love for him as the ceremony began.

"Do you, Prince Alexius Kristof Rudolph Stefano Valleder Constantinides, Duke of Aurum, take Dorothy Giles Richards to be thy wedded wife? To love, honor and serve her unto death?"

"I do."

Dottie trembled.

"Do you, Dorothy Giles Richards, take Prince Alexius to be thy wedded husband? To love, honor and serve him unto death?"

"I do," she whispered, scarcely able to believe this was really happening.

"Then by the power invested in me, I proclaim you husband and wife from this day forth. What God has blessed, let no man put asunder. In the name of the Trinity, Amen."

"Amen," Alex declared after Dottie spoke.

"You wish to bestow tokens?"

"I do, Father." He reached for Dottie's left hand and slid the one-carat sapphire onto her ring finger.

"You may kiss your bride."

The significance of this moment shook Dottie to her very roots. Alex was her husband now. Her life! Without caring about anything else, she raised her mouth to his, needing his kiss like she needed the sun on her face and air to breathe.

While they stood locked together, Zoe ran over to them and hugged their legs. She felt her little arms, reminding her she and Alex were probably giving Father Gregorius a coronary for letting their kiss go on so long. No doubt she was blushing, but the others wouldn't be able to tell until they went outside.

"Are you married now, Daddy?"

Alex relinquished Dottie's mouth and picked up his daughter to kiss her. "We're very, very married."

She giggled and turned to reach for Dottie, who hugged her.

Bari stepped forward and gave Alex a bear hug before bestowing a kiss on Dottie's cheek.

"Congratulations, Your Highness." Inez and Ari curtsied to him and Dottie, then handed her the bouquet. "Your Highness."

"Thank you," Dottie answered.

Alex shook their hands. "We appreciate all your help."

"It's been our pleasure."

"Let's go outside for some pictures," Bari suggested.

The priest stayed long enough for a group photo in front of the ancient doors, then he had to be on his way to the city. Alex invited Bari to have a drink with them. At Zoe's suggestion they celebrated in the gazebo. Bari drank to their health and happiness. After one more picture, he left to get back to work.

Inez brought out a tray of salad, sandwiches and a pitcher of iced tea. By now they were all hungry, including Zoe. A month ago her appetite had diminished to the point they'd both worried about it, but no longer.

The peacock happened to walk past the gazebo just then. Zoe scrambled out of her chair and went after it, leaving them alone for a minute. Alex caught her in his arms. "Alone at last. Happy wedding day, Mrs. Constantinides."

"I love you, darling," she blurted. "Thank you for the simple, beautiful ceremony. I loved it. I love my ring. I'll treasure this day forever. I'm only sorry I didn't have a ring for you."

He kissed her passionately on the mouth. "I didn't want one. I don't like rings and would prefer not to wear one. Yet I have seven of them, all with precious gems encrusted. The only one that doesn't have stones is this one." He flexed his right hand where he wore the gold ducal crest. "Since I have to wear it, I'll take it off and let you put it on the ring finger of my left hand."

He removed it and handed it to her.

At first she was all thumbs. Finally she took hold of his hand and slid it home. "Did you wear it on this hand when you were married to Zoe's mother?" she asked without looking at him.

"No. She gave me a ring from the House of Valleder. I took it off after she died and put it with the other rings that Zoe will inherit one day."

As she stared into his eyes, she sensed something else was on his mind. "You have news. I can tell."

"Yes. For one thing, Hector explained the situation to Mrs. Hawes and she's been given a free two-week vacation here if she wants. Now you don't have to worry about her needless trip."

"Oh, thank you, darling. That's so generous of you."

"After meeting you, I realized how hard-working and dedicated you therapists are. She deserves every perk we can offer."

Dottie bit her lip. "What else were you going to tell me?"

His expression grew more solemn. She saw the slightest look of vulnerability in his eyes. "Before we left Hellenica this morning, my grandmother told me the vote from the parliament was unanimous. They want me to be king. So does she."

His news was so wonderful, she threw her arms around his neck. "You're going to be the greatest king this country ever had. I'm the luckiest woman in the world because I'm your wife. I promise to help make your life easier. I swear it."

"Dottie—" He pulled her tightly against him. "You realize what this means. The day after tomorrow will be my coronation. The queen wants us to come to the palace immediately to discuss the arrangements for our wedding. We're going to have to go through another ceremony, and then I will be crowned king. She wants to meet the commoner who stole the hearts of her great-granddaughter and grandson."

This time tears rolled down Dottie's cheeks. She grasped his handsome face in her hands. "I can't wait to meet her. I can't wait to say my vows again. I love you," she cried, covering his face with kisses.

The archbishop of Hellenica closed the coronation ceremony with "God Save the King." Dottie adored this great man she'd just married for the second time. He'd now been crowned king in this magnificent cathedral and was so handsome and splendid in his dark blue ceremonial suit and red sash, it hurt to look at him.

Zoe, dressed in a tiara and frilly white floor-length dress, sat on a velvet chair like a perfect little princess between Dottie and her great-grandmother, who'd come in a wheelchair. Stasio sat opposite them in his ceremonial dress. Solveig, the woman he loved, had come and was seated in the crowd. Dottie liked her already and imagined there'd be a wedding soon.

King Philippe and his pregnant American wife sat next to Stasio. Over the past few days Dottie had gotten to know her and couldn't wait to spend more time with her.

When the archbishop bid Princess Dorothy rise to join Alex for the processional out of the church, Dottie realized it was *she* he meant and blushed like mad. Her husband noticed she'd been caught off guard and his black eyes flashed fire as she walked toward him to grasp his hand. Zoe followed to carry the train.

In an intimate appraisal, his gaze swept from the tiara on top of her white lace mantilla, down her white princess-style wedding gown to her satin slippers. He'd given her that same look as she'd started to get out of bed this morning. When she reminded him they should have been up an hour ago, he'd pulled her back on top of him and made love to her again with insatiable hunger.

It was embarrassing how much time they'd spent in the bedroom when there was so much to get done in preparation for the coronation. But obviously not embarrassing enough, because she was the one who always moaned in protest when Hector finally managed to convince Alex he was needed in the office or the queen's drawing room immediately.

Her husband kept squeezing her hand as they slowly made their way toward the great doors. In her heart she knew that if Neil and Cory were looking on, they would be happy for her.

She smiled at the guests standing on either side of the aisle. Everyone looked wonderful in their hats and wedding finery. Halfway down she caught sight of Mark and his parents. He made a little wave to Dottie and Zoe with his hand. It warmed her heart. Next she smiled at Bari and his family. Near the doors she spotted Hector, who beamed back at her.

When she and Alex emerged from the cathedral, a huge roar went up from the crowd in the ancient agora. Alex helped her into the open-air carriage, then assisted Zoe, who sat opposite them. Once he'd climbed inside and closed the door, the bells began to ring throughout the city.

Almost at once a chant went through the crowd for King Alexius to kiss Princess Dot. Somehow word had gotten out that Princess Zoe called her new mother Dot.

"Don't mind if I do," Alex said with a wicked smile before he kissed her so thoroughly her tiara slipped off. The crowd went wild with excitement. The horses began moving.

While Alex fit it back on her, taking his time about it as he stared at her, Zoe said, "Was the crown heavy, Daddy?"

"Very. Your Uncle Stasi wasn't kidding."

"Could Mark ride with us, Mommy?"

"Not today, but you'll see him tomorrow. There are hundreds of children lining the streets with their families. They'd all love to ride in this carriage with you, so wave to them. They're very excited to see you."

"They are?"

"Yes. Just think—today your country got a new king and he's *your* daddy. We need to start working on your K sounds."

Alex's chuckle turned into a deep rumble. He leaned over to give her another kiss that stirred her senses clear down to her toenails. It was a kiss that told her he couldn't wait until they were alone again. As they reached the palace and climbed out of the carriage, the limo carrying the queen and Stasio pulled up behind them.

As they all entered the palace together, Alex's grandmother said, "Really, Alex. Did you have to kiss Dottie like that in front of thousands of people? And you kept doing it! You realize it'll be all over the news."

He grinned at Stasio. "I don't know how to kiss her any other way, *Yiayia*. Worse, I can't seem to stop."

"Are we going to have a baby now?" piped up a little voice.

"Oh, really, Zoe!" her great-grandmother cried out. "You don't ask questions like that in front of people. There's going to be a reception in the grand dining hall and I expect you to behave like the princess you are."

Unabashed, Zoe turned to Hector. "Can Mark sit by me?"

While they were sorting it out, Alex pulled Dottie away from the others and led her to a deserted alcove. Before she could breathe, he kissed her long and deeply. "I needed that," he murmured after lifting his head a few minutes later. "You looked like a vision in the cathedral. Promise me you're not a figment of my imagination. I couldn't take it."

She kissed his hard jaw. "I'll convince you tonight when we're finally alone. I'm so glad I married royalty. I love the idea of going to bed with my husband and *my liege*. It sounds positively decadent and wicked, don't you think?"

"Dottie—"

* * * * *

BETROTHED: TO THE PEOPLE'S PRINCE

MARION LENNOX

CHAPTER ONE

INTO her crowd of beautiful people came…Nikos.

She was taking a last visual sweep of the room, noting descriptions for tomorrow's fashion column.

The men were almost uniformly in black—black T-shirts, black jeans and designer stubble. The women were Audrey Hepburn clones. Cinched waists, wide skirts and pearls. The fifties look was now.

There was little eating. Cinched waists and 'body slimmers' didn't allow for snacking, the waiters were sparse and it wasn't cool to graze.

Nikos was holding a beer, and as the waiter passed with a tray of tiny caviar-loaded blinis he snagged four. He tipped one into his mouth, then turned back to search the room.

For her.

After all these years, he could still stop her world.

She'd forgotten to breathe. It was important to breathe. She took a too-big sip of her too-dry Martini and it went down the wrong way.

Uh-oh. If it wasn't cool to eat, it was even more uncool to choke.

But help was at hand. Smooth and fast as a panther, Nikos moved through the crowd to be by her side in an instant. He took her drink, slapped her back with just the right amount of force, and then calmly waited for her to recover.

Nikos.

She could faint, she thought wildly. An ambulance could take her away and she'd be in a nice, safe emergency room. Safe from the man she'd walked away from almost ten years ago.

But fainting took skills she didn't have. No one seemed about to call for help. No one seemed more than politely interested that she was choking.

Except Nikos.

She didn't remember him as this big. And this...gorgeous? He was wearing faded blue jeans instead of the designer black that was de rigueur in this crowd. His shirt was worn white cotton, missing the top two buttons. He had an ancient leather jacket slung over his arm.

The fashion editor part of her was appreciative. Nice.

More than nice. Nikos.

She coughed on, more than she needed to, trying desperately to give herself space. His dark hair was curly, unruly and a bit too long. His brown-black eyes were crinkled at the edges, weathered from a life at sea. Among this crowd of fake tans, his was undeniably real. His whole body was weathered by his work.

Nikos. Fisherman.

Her childhood love.

He'd grown from a gorgeous boy into a...what? She didn't have words to describe it. She was the fashion editor of one of the world's leading glossies, and she was lost for words.

Words were what she needed. She had to think of something to say. Anything. Almost every eye in the room was on them now. She couldn't retreat to choking again.

'You want your drink back?' His tone was neutrally amused. Deeper than last time she'd heard him. A bit gravelly, with a gorgeous Greek accent.

Sexy as hell.

He was balancing his beer, her Martini and his three remaining blinis. He'd used his spare hand to thump her.

He was large and capable and…

Nikos.

Now she'd stopped choking, the crowd had turned their attention to him. Well, why wouldn't they? The models, designers, media and buyers were openly interested. Maybe more than interested. Their concentrated attention contained more than a hint of lust.

'You going to live?' Nikos asked mildly, and she thought about it. She might. If he went away.

'What are you doing here?'

'Looking for you.'

'It's invitation only.'

'Yep,' he said, as if that hadn't even crossed his mind as something to bother about. How had he done it? People would kill for an invitation to this launch. He'd simply walked in.

'You look cute,' he said, raking her from head to toe.

Right. She'd gone to some trouble with her outfit. Her tiny red skirt was clinging in the right places, she'd managed to make her unruly black curls stay in a knot that was almost sophisticated, but in this crowd of fashion extremists she knew she disappeared.

'Go away,' she said, and he shook his head.

'I can't do that, Princess.'

'Don't call me that.'

'It's what you are.'

'Please, Nikos, not here.'

'Whatever,' he said easily. 'But we need to talk. Phones don't work. You keep hanging up.'

'You don't hang up phones any more.' Very knowledgeable, she thought. What sort of inane talk was this?

'On Argyros we hang up telephones. After we talk to people.'

'I don't live on Argyros.'

'Yeah, that's what I want to talk to you about. It's time you came home.' He handed her back her Martini. He drained his beer and ate his three bite-sized blinis, then looked about for more. Two waiters were beside him in an instant.

He always had been charismatic, Athena thought. People gravitated to him.

She'd gravitated to him.

'So how about it?' he said, smiling his thanks to the waiters. Oh, that smile…

'Why would I want to come home?'

'There's the little matter of the Crown. I'm thinking you must have read the newspapers. Your cousin, Demos, says he's talked to you. I'm thinking Alexandros must have talked to you as well—or did you hang up on him, too?'

'Of course I didn't.'

'So you do know you're Crown Princess of Argyros.'

'I'm not Crown Princess of anything. Demos can have it,' she said savagely. 'He wants it.'

'Demos is second in line. You're first. It has to be you.'

'I have the power to abdicate. Consider me abdicated. Royalty's outdated and absurd, and my life's here. So, if you'll excuse me…'

'Thena, you don't have a choice. You have to come home.'

Thena. He was the only one who'd ever shortened her name. It made her feel…as she had no business feeling.

Just tell it like it is and move on, she told herself. Be blunt and cold and not interested. He was talking history. Argyros was no longer anything to do with her.

'You're right,' she managed. 'I don't have a choice. My life is here.'

But not in this room. All of a sudden the room was claustrophobic. Her past was colliding with her present, and it made her feel as if the ground was shaking underneath her.

She and Nikos in the same room? No, no, no.

She and Nikos in the same city? She and Nikos *and their son?*

No!

Fear had her almost frozen.

'Nikos, this is futile,' she managed. 'There's no use telling me to go home. My home is here. Meanwhile, I have things to attend to, so if you'll excuse me…' She handed her Martini glass back to him and, before he could respond she swivelled and made her way swiftly through the crowd.

She reached the door—and she kept on walking.

She hadn't retrieved her checked coat. It didn't matter. Outside was cold, but she wasn't feeling cold. Her face was burning. She was shaking.

Maybe he'd let her be.

Or maybe not. He hadn't come all the way from Argyros to be ignored.

It was raining. Her stilettos weren't built for walking. She wanted to take them off and run. Because of course he'd follow.

Of course he did.

When he fell in step beside her she felt as if she'd been punched. Nikos… He threatened her world.

'Where are we going?' he asked mildly.

'Nowhere you're welcome.'

'Is this any way to greet family?'

'I'm not your family.'

'Tell that to my mother.'

His mother… She thought of Annia and felt a stab of real regret. She glanced sideways at Nikos—and then looked swiftly away. Annia… Argyros…

Nikos.

She'd walked away from them ten years ago. Leaving had broken her heart.

'It's your heritage,' he said mildly, as if he was simply continuing the conversation from back at the fashion launch.

'I never had a heritage. It was all about Giorgos.'

'The King's dead, Athena. He died without an heir. You know that.'

'And that makes a difference how?'

'It means the Diamond Isles become three Principalities again. The original royal families can resume rule. But you know this. By the way—did you also know that you're beautiful?' And he took her arm and forced her to stop.

She'd been striding. Angry. Fearful. Confused. Rain was turning to sleet. Her heels, her tight skirt and sheer pashmina wrap were designed for cocktail hour, not for street wear.

She should keep going but she wasn't all that sure where to go. She couldn't outwalk Nikos and she surely wasn't leading him back to her apartment. She surely wasn't leading him to her son.

She might as well stop. Get it over with now.

She turned to face him. A blast of icy wind hit full on, and she felt herself shudder.

Nikos's ancient leather jacket was suddenly around her, warm from his body, smelling of old leather and Nikos and…

home. Argyros. Fishing boats in an ancient harbour. White stone villas hugging island cliffs. Sapphire seas and brilliant sun. The Diamond Isles.

Suddenly, stupidly, she wanted to cry.

'We need to get out of this,' Nikos said. His hand was under her elbow and he was steering her into the brightly lit portico of a restaurant, as if this was his town and he wasn't half a world away from where he lived and worked.

Nikos…

'You call those clothes?' he growled, and she remembered how bossy he'd been when they were kids, and how he was always right.

Bossy and arrogant and…fun. Pushing her past her comfort zone. Daring her to join him.

The number of times she'd ended up with skinned knees, battered and bruised because: 'Of course we can get up that cliff; you're not going to sit and watch like some *girl*, are you?'

She never did sit and watch. Even when they'd been older and the boys from the other islands became part of their pack, she'd always been included. Until…

Let's not go there, she told herself. She'd moved on. She was fashion editor for one of the world's best-selling magazines. She lived in New York and she was fine.

So what was Nikos doing, here, ushering her into a restaurant she recognised? This place usually involved queuing, or a month or more's notice. But Nikos was a man who turned heads, who waiters automatically found a place for, because even if they couldn't place him they felt they should. He was obviously someone. He always had been, and his power hadn't waned one bit.

Stunned to speechlessness, she found herself being steered to an isolated table for two, one of the best in the house. The waiter tried to take her jacket—his jacket—but she clung. It was dumb, but she needed its warmth. She needed its comfort.

'What's good?' Nikos asked the waiter, waving away the menu.

'Savoury? Sweet?'

'Definitely something sweet,' he said, and smiled across the table at her. 'The way the lady's feeling right now, we need all the sugar we can get.'

She refused to smile back. She couldn't allow herself to sink into that smile.

'Crêpes?' the waiter proffered. 'Or if you have time…our raspberry soufflé's a house speciality.'

'Crêpes followed by soufflé for both of us then,' he said easily, and the waiter beamed and nodded and backed away, almost as if he sensed he shouldn't turn his back on royalty.

Nikos. Once upon a time…

No. Get a grip.

'I'm not going anywhere,' she muttered into the silence. 'You can't make me go back.'

Nikos smiled again—his smile wide and white, his eyes deep and shaded, an automatic defence against the sun. His smile was a heart stopper in anyone's language. Especially hers.

'You're right. I can't make you. You need to decide yourself. But that's why I'm here—to help you to decide that you need to come home.'

'My home's here.'

'Your career until now has been here,' he agreed. 'You've done very well.'

'There's no need to sound patronising.'

'I'm not patronising.'

'Like you'd know about my career.'

He raised his brows, half mocking. 'There were seven

candidates for the position you're now in,' he said softly.
'Each of them was older, more experienced. You won the job
over all of them and your boss believes he made a brilliant
decision.'

'How do you know…'

'I've made it my business to find out.'

'Well, butt out. There's no need…'

'There is a need. There was always a chance that you'd
inherit, and now you have.'

'I have no intention of inheriting. Demos wants it. Demos
can have it. It should be you, but if that's not possible… Demos.'

'It was never going to be me.'

'You're nephew to the King.'

'You know the score,' he said evenly. 'Yes, my mother was
the King's sister, but the King's lineage has to be direct and
male. That's me out. But the individual island crowns have
male/female equality. First in line for the throne of Argyros
is you. Princess Athena, Crown Princess of Argyros. Sounds
good, hey?' He smiled and tried to take her hand across the
table. She snatched it away as if he burned.

'This is crazy. I've told you, Nikos, I'm not coming home.'

'Can I ask why not?'

'I don't belong there.'

'Of course you do. My family has always welcomed…'

'Your family,' she interrupted flatly. 'Of course. How's
your wife?'

Why had she asked that? What possible difference did it
make? But suddenly—she had to know.

Nikos didn't answer directly. He'd given up trying to take
her hand. Instead he'd clasped his hands loosely on the table
top. He flexed them now, still linked. Big hands and powerful.

He wasn't wearing a wedding ring.

She shouldn't even care. She shouldn't have asked.

But she had asked, and there was something in his face that said the answer was never going to be easy. For a couple of moments she thought he wouldn't answer at all. But finally he beckoned a waiter, ordered a beer and answered.

'Marika and I are divorced. She's remarried and left the island.' His gaze was expressionless, not giving a clue if this still had the power to hurt.

Ten years ago—two months after she'd left the island—her aunt had written.

By the way, Nikos has married Marika. Rumour is there's a baby on the way, but I guess no one worries about such things any more. You know, I always thought you and Nikos would marry, but I know King Giorgos would hate that. So you're best out of it.

Until then she'd hoped, desperately, that Nikos would follow her. But when she'd read that…

Marika was a distant relation of Nikos, giggly, flirtatious and ambitious. She'd always thought Marika was in love with her cousin, Demos—but obviously it had been Nikos all the time.

She'd been so shocked she'd been physically ill.

Then, four months later her aunt had written a much shorter note. 'A baby. A little girl for Nikos and Marika…' Her note had trailed off, unfinished, and the writing on the envelope had been scrawly.

It was no wonder. The letter had been delivered two days after her aunt's death.

She'd wept then, for not going home in time, for not guessing her aunt was ill until she'd received the letter, for knowing her last link to the island was ended. And if she'd wept for the fact that Nikos had a baby with Marika, then so be it, the whole thing was grey.

'I'm sorry,' she said now, feeling useless. 'How…how long?'

'How long ago since she left? Nine years. It wasn't what you might call a long-term marriage.'

His tone was bitter. Oh, Nikos, she thought. You, too? Wounds might heal, but scars remained.

'I'm sorry,' she said again, but then made a belated attempt to pull herself together. 'But…it's nothing to do with me. Nothing from the island's anything to do with me. My aunt was the last family I had, and she's dead.'

'The whole island's your family. You rule.' It was said explosively, with passion, and Athena flinched and couldn't think how to reply.

The crêpes arrived, light and hot, oozing a wonderful lemon liqueur and doused with clotted cream. This was everything she most denied herself in food. Nikos picked up a fork and started in—then paused.

'What's wrong?'

'I didn't really want these.'

'You're ill?'

'No.'

'Then eat,' he said. 'You're stupidly thin.'

'I am not!'

'Are, too,' he said, and grinned and suddenly there it was again—the bossiness, the arguments, the *fun*. Childhood with Nikos had been wonderful. Magic.

'Can't make me,' she responded before she could help herself, a response she'd made over and over as a kid.

His dark eyes gleamed with challenge. 'Want to bet?'

'No!'

'Eat your crêpes, Thene.'

She smiled, despite herself, picked up a fork and ate.

How long since she'd indulged in something this full of calories? They tasted fantastic.

'You're not a model,' Nikos said, halfway through his crêpes and finally pausing for breath. 'Why starve?'

'It's expected,' she said. 'You can never be too rich or too thin.'

'Yeah, I've heard that, too,' he growled. 'So, they'll fire you if you gain a pound or six?'

'That party we were at tonight… If I'd turned up as a size fourteen, you think I'd get a foot in the door?'

'You're invited to write about it. Not be it.'

'I'm part of the scene. They like their scene perfect.'

'And this is a career you like?'

'It beats pulling craypots.'

More silence. But he wasn't angry, she thought. He kept on eating, as if she'd just commented on the weather. She'd never been able to needle him.

Oh, she'd missed him. For ten long years it had felt like an ache, a limb missing, phantom pains shooting when she least expected. Watching him now, it felt as if she was suddenly whole again. He was intent on his pancake, maybe giving her space—who knew with Nikos?

He'd fitted right in with the people at the party, she thought. But then she thought, no. She'd got that wrong.

Nikos was an embodiment of what the people she worked with wanted to be. They went to gyms and solariums and plastic surgeons and every other expensive way to get their bodies to where Nikos had his.

All they had to do was haul fifty or so craypots a day for life, she thought, and found she was smiling.

'What?' he said, and she was suddenly smiling straight at him, almost pleading for him to return the smile.

And he did. In force. His smile had the capacity to knock her sideways.

The waiter, about to descend to take away their plates, paused with the strength of it. This was a classy establishment. Their waiter knew enough not to intrude on such a smile.

'I've missed you, Thene,' Nikos said, and his hand was reaching over the table for hers.

No. She found enough sense to tug her hands off the table and put them sensibly in her lap. But she couldn't stop herself saying the automatic reply. 'I've missed you, too.'

'So come home.'

'Because I've missed you?'

'Because the country needs you.'

Here it was again. Duty. Guilt.

'No.'

She closed her eyes and the waiter decided it was safe to come close. He cleared the plates and set them again, ready for soufflé. Maybe Nikos was watching her. She didn't know.

Duty.

It had torn her in two ten years ago. To go back now…

'You know Demos wants to open the diamond mines again?' he said, almost conversationally, and her eyes flew open.

'What the… Why?'

'He's wanted to for years. It was only Giorgos's greed that stopped him. Giorgos wasn't fussed about mining them—he had more money than he knew what to do with, thankfully. But the royal money chests have gone to Alexandros on Sappheiros. There's little money in the Argyros exchequer.'

'Which mines does he want to open?' She shouldn't care, she thought. She shouldn't!

'All of them.'

'*All?* The island will be ripped apart.'

'You think Demos cares?'

She stared at him, but she was no longer seeing him. Argyros… The Diamond Isles. Three magic island nations in the Mediterranean. All whitewashed stone, steep cliffs, sapphire seas. Three diamonds glittering in the sun.

Home.

Once upon a time the Isles had been three separate nations—Sappheiros, Argyros and Khryseis, but for the last two hundred years they'd been ruled as a Kingdom. Now, however, with the death of King Giorgos without an heir, the islands were Principalities again.

And she was Crown Princess Athena.

Ha. She'd walked away from the royal title when she'd walked away from the island, but it always had been a hollow tag.

Nikos had more right to rule than she, she thought. He'd lived and worked on Argyros all his life. He loved it.

And Demos?

Demos was the son of Athena's uncle. Because his father was younger than Athena's mother, he was second in the ancient lineage where she was first. But neither of them had expected to rule.

From time to time she'd read about Demos in the society pages. Whereas she'd left her title of Princess on the island, Demos still valued the title Prince and he used it.

He'd phoned her a week ago and asked that she abdicate and leave the Crown to him. She'd tentatively agreed, because what was the alternative? Going home…going back herself was impossible.

'Demos arrived back on the island the day after we learned

the King's rule was ended,' Nikos said, and she realised he'd been following her thoughts. 'He wants it so badly he'll do whatever it takes to get it. He's assuming you don't want it. Do you know why?'

'He rang and asked.'

'Alexandros rang you as well.'

'Yes.' Alexandros, the new crown Prince of Sappheiros, was trying to untangle the mess that was the succession.

'And you told him you were confused.'

'I was,' she said. 'Until Demos phoned.'

'So you'd let Demos have it?'

'It's an empty title anyway. Demos will enjoy it. And how can I come home now?' she demanded.

'It's not an empty title. Not if he opens the diamond mines.'

'It doesn't matter. It can't matter. My life is here.'

'It's not much of a life if it doesn't include crêpes. Or soufflé. Hey, look at this!'

The house speciality was arriving. The soufflé. This dish was famous. *How had Nikos manoeuvred his way in here?*

'Who do you think you are?' she demanded, and he grinned.

'A fisherman from Argyros. A kid in a lolly shop. Wow! Shut up and eat, Thene. This food needs serious respect.'

She opened her mouth to deny it. She so did not need another sweet.

Her raspberry soufflé was exploding upward and outward, crusty, dusted with sugar, irresistible. While she thought weakly about denial, the waiter produced a jug and poured a thin, hot trickle of blood-red juice down into the soufflé. The crust burst at the centre, the soufflé swallowed the juice and Athena conceded that maybe Nikos was right. This demanded serious respect.

She shut up and ate.

Heaven. Right here on the plate. Seriously wonderful food…

Missing out on such treats was the price she paid for being where she was. If she got up at five tomorrow and jogged double her normal distance… Maybe…

'Let it go, Thene,' Nick said. He was wiping the inside of his bowl with his forefinger and licking in deep appreciation. 'You had a bigger butt when you were eleven. It's not natural.'

'It's what I do.' She finished and set down her spoon. Who licked their fingers?

She had a sudden blast of memory. Nikos's mother, Annia, standing at her kitchen table, endlessly baking. She remembered a plum pie that was to die for…

Before she could help herself, she let her finger drop into the bowl, ran it round the edges and licked. Not sure whether she was tasting soufflé now, or pie from the past.

'How's your mother?' she asked.

'Great,' Nikos said. 'She sends her love. She says come home—though if I take you home looking like this she'll have forty fits.'

'I loved your mother.'

It was said without thinking. She hadn't meant it. Or…she hadn't meant to say it.

'She hated it when you went away, Thene.'

'Yeah. Well.' Suddenly she'd had enough. More than enough. Emotion was threatening to overwhelm her. She stood up, too fast. It made her feel dizzy. Disoriented. Nikos was beside her in a flash, gripping her elbow, supporting her.

She should wrench away. He made her…melt.

'I need to go home.'

'My car's close.'

'You have a car? Here? In Manhattan?'

'Borrowed from Stefanos.'

Stefanos. Of course. The third member of the guardians.

Stefanos, Alexandros and Nikos had been friends from childhood. Three intelligent boys, bound by one common goal. To free their respective islands.

They'd run together as a pack. Only, of course, while Giorgos was alive they could do nothing. But now…

'Stefanos is still in New York?' she asked. She'd seen him once, when she'd walked into a city hospital to visit a friend. She'd turned and walked out before he'd seen her. She'd even thought of moving to another city because he was here. But that was ridiculous. It was a big city.

'Stefanos is in Australia trying to find the heir to the throne of Khryseis. He's Prince Regent of that island. Like you, he doesn't have a choice.'

'I do have a choice,' she snapped. 'And one of them is to make my own way home. To my home. To where I live now.'

'How do you get home from here?' he asked, as if mildly interested, not taking up her nuances. 'A cab? I'll drive you.'

'I ride the subway.'

'The subway…'

'This is my neighbourhood, Nikos,' she said, and made her voice sound sure and mature and…determined. 'This is where I live. But I need to go. Oscar and Nicholas are expecting me.'

'Who are Oscar and Nicholas?'

'My family,' she said, and the thought of Nicholas brought fear flooding back. 'So…so, if you'll excuse me… Oh, you need to pay? Sorry if I don't wait. Goodnight.'

And she turned and walked from the restaurant.

When she reached the pavement she slipped off her shoes and she started to run.

CHAPTER TWO

CARRIE was watching TV when she let herself into her apartment. Lovely, comforting Carrie, middle-aged and buxom, knitting endless squares to turn into endless blankets for the homeless. She closed the door, leant on it as if to lock the world out and let herself be comforted by the domesticity in front of her.

Oscar was lying draped over Carrie's feet. The big basset hound looked up at her with soulful reproach, as if to say, *You expect me to get up at this time of night? You need to be kidding.*

She smiled. Oscar helped as well.

'Hey, great jacket,' Carrie said equably from the couch. 'You swap jackets with a boy?'

Whoops. She'd forgotten she was wearing it. Or maybe subconsciously she'd known, and she liked it. She fingered the soft, worn leather and found comfort there as well.

'Yep,' she said.

'A good-looking one?'

'Yep to that as well. Really good-looking.'

'Excellent,' Carrie said and dumped her knitting into her carrier bag. 'He ask you out?'

'We did already. We ate soufflé and crêpes.'

'And crêpes? Wow. You going to see him again?'

'Once is enough.' Once in one lifetime.

Carrie's face puckered into disappointment. 'Why the heck?' she demanded, seriously displeased. 'You know I can take Nicky whenever you want. You need a love life.'

'I've had one.'

'But you've kept his jacket,' Carrie said, thoughtful. 'Smart girl. A guy's going to miss a jacket like that. Does he know where you live?'

'No. I'll post it to him.'

'Don't post it for a couple of days,' Carrie said. 'Give the man a challenge.' She pushed her more than ample self to her feet, made her way across the room and gave Athena a hug. 'You deserve some excitement. And Nicky needs a dad.'

'Carrie…'

'Just saying,' Carrie said placidly. 'Just going.'

And she went. Leaving silence.

She sat, on cushions still warm from Carrie. She stared mindlessly at the soap Carrie had been watching. Oscar sighed, heaved himself sideways and redraped himself over her feet.

She needed comfort.

She needed to stop being angry.

Why the anger? After ten years, surely she had no right to still be angry with Nikos.

Or maybe she had. Ten years ago she'd ached for him to follow her. Just one word…something…a message to find out if she was okay. Her aunt had known her address. Nikos had known her aunt.

But it was as if the moment she'd walked off the island she'd walked out of Nikos's life. And now…here he was, demanding she take a part in the island's future. Demanding she think about Argyros.

And all she could think was that she hadn't told him he had a son.

He was here. The time to tell him was now.

The time to tell him was ten years ago. For him to find out now…

It had to happen. She had to find the courage.

Maybe he'd leave without trying to see her again. Maybe she'd have to go to Argyros to tell him.

He was in New York right now. She had to get over her anger and tell him.

And then say goodbye. For to go back to Argyros… Even if Demos were to destroy the island with his greed for diamonds…

No. It couldn't happen. She'd have to do something.

What?

Nothing, she told herself, but there was desperation behind the word.

It had to be nothing. She'd left Argyros behind. That first dreadful year, she'd coped with homesickness, isolation, fear, and the birth of Nicky, and she'd faced it alone. She'd fought to make herself a living, knowing she was all her baby had. *That which doesn't kill us makes us stronger.* The often used platitude had become her mantra.

She'd never again let herself need anyone as she'd needed Nikos. She no longer loved Nikos and she no longer called Argyros home.

Her head hurt. Thinking hurt.

She needed to sleep, but sleep wasn't going to come easily tonight. If she filed her story now… That'd mean tomorrow was free. Saturday—Nicky had the day off school. They could go to the park…something, anything, just to get her away from here, buy her a little time.

She should take off Nikos's jacket.

Not yet. For just a little bit longer she'd allow herself that one small comfort.

* * *

Who the hell were Oscar and Nicholas?

Husband? Son? Sons? He was going nuts not knowing.

He'd hired someone to find her. The firm he'd hired had given him the magazine she worked for and a brief summary of her career. It was hardly personal.

Why had he never thought she could be married?

She wasn't wearing a ring.

That could mean anything. Rings weren't compulsory. Nor was marriage; its lack didn't necessarily mean you were without a long-term partner.

Why had she responded to him with anger?

He'd hardly expected her to fall into his arms as her long lost friend. He'd married someone else.

Marika... He thought of his ex-wife now and fought back anger that stayed with him still. But you needed to move on. *He* needed to move on.

He had.

Or he thought he had until he'd seen Athena tonight. She was every bit the girl he remembered—but now she was a woman. Her eyes had tiny creases—smile lines. Did she smile often? Did the unknown Oscar and Nicholas make her smile?

He'd forgotten how she'd made him feel—or maybe he'd blocked it out. Looking at her across the restaurant table tonight...it had taken all the power he had to keep his voice neutral, to keep his feelings in check.

She was still Athena—the girl he'd loved to the point of madness—and then she'd chosen her career over him. The woman he'd held in a corner of his heart for ten long years.

Oh, there'd been other women—of course there had. As the owner of the biggest fishing fleet in the Diamond Isles he was considered more than eligible. He was never lost for...

companionship, only every woman he dated compared with Athena.

Even the woman he'd married.

Especially the woman he'd married.

The old anger gripped him, tore at him. The old hunger…

Only it wasn't an old hunger. It was as real and as raw tonight as it had ever been.

He opened the door to the adjoining hotel room. The woman from the hotel sitting service rose to leave.

'She's been very good, sir. I read her the book like you said. She even undressed herself. I didn't think…'

'That's great,' he said. He didn't want to hear what she didn't think.

'Goodnight, then,' the woman said and slipped away into the night.

He stood for a moment gazing down at Christa. His daughter was sucking her thumb, even in sleep. She shouldn't—but who cared?

He crossed to the bed and sat down beside his sleeping child. He stroked her pretty dark hair. She opened her eyes and smiled sleepily at him. 'Papa.'

'Go to sleep, kitten,' he said softly.

'N…nice.' She closed her eyes again and was instantly asleep.

How could he still be angry? Athena had moved away but now, in his heart, in her stead, he had his little daughter.

For years he'd tried to think that. It didn't work. It never had.

For years he'd envisaged Athena in a barren, lonely existence in a strange land. He'd almost hoped for it.

She'd left him. He should have cut off all thoughts of her. He shouldn't care.

But it wasn't possible. Not then and not now.

Athena…or his daughter.

Athena and the unknown Oscar and Nicholas.

So she had a family, too. Well, so be it, he thought, trying to be rational. He had his Christa and he was content. What he was feeling now was the echoes of the past. From now on the personal had to be set aside for the good of the island.

Tomorrow he had to find her again. She had to face her duty. She must.

He'd take Christa sightseeing tomorrow morning. Maybe they could take a buggy ride round Central Park. She'd enjoy that. Then, in the afternoon, he'd go to see Athena again.

And get his jacket back.

He thought of his jacket as he'd last seen it, draped round Athena's shoulders as she'd fled the restaurant. Maybe he should have followed her.

But…and it was a big but. There had been fear in her eyes as she'd fled. Real fear.

He didn't know why. He intended to find out, but for now… He was inexplicably glad she'd worn his jacket home.

How could she explain a man's jacket to the unknown Nicholas and Oscar? Unaccountably, he found himself smiling. He hoped they were good to her. Yeah, that was a rational thought. Generous, even.

But…she had to come back to the island, even if it meant she brought this unknown Oscar and Nicholas with her. Though their existence could make things much more complicated.

Whatever. Tomorrow could be faced tomorrow, he told himself, trying to block out the unwanted image of Athena with another man by her side. Trying to block out how it made him feel. After all this time, surely jealousy was crazy.

Of course it was.

He kissed his daughter softly on the forehead, the touch and scent of her soft little body helping him put things into perspective.

'Goodnight, sweetheart,' he whispered. 'We'll have a good time tomorrow; just see if we don't. And then we'll persuade the Princess Athena to come home. Where we belong and where she belongs, too.'

In the morning the sun finally decided to shine. Nikos and his little daughter did the circuit of Central Park twice, and then they did it again. Christa's unalloyed happiness, the sun on her face, the beauty of the horses, the garishness of the decoration on the buggy...she loved it. She clung to him, breathless with excitement, laughing out loud for sheer joy.

Halfway through their third circuit he saw Athena.

And a dog.

And a child.

How could it be? How could fate be this cruel?

Why on earth had she decided to come to a tourist destination this morning?

Stupid, stupid, stupid.

They'd been using their ball-thrower. Dogs were supposed to be on leads here, but she knew a place...most dog owners did. So they'd tossed the ball until Oscar was out of puff. Nicky had run more than the dog. Oscar wasn't the brightest light on the Christmas tree, so about half the time it had been Nicky who'd had to retrieve it. Finally they'd bought ice cream cones and now they were waiting for Oscar to finish his before they walked home.

Oscar, a big, lumbering bear of canine dopiness, took his ice cream eating seriously.

A horse and buggy was wheeling briskly along the path towards them. The horses looked gorgeous, she thought. The day was gorgeous, making up for last night's misery. She was dumb to be anxious on a day like this.

She chuckled at Oscar's pink nose.

The buggy grew closer. The driver raised his crop in salute. It was that sort of day.

She smiled. She waved back.

And then she saw who was in the buggy.

Nikos.

And a child?

The sounds around them faded. Everything faded.

She heard Nikos's snapped order as if it came from a distance. The buggy stopped. Nikos climbed down, paid the driver and lifted the little girl down after him.

The child was little and dark and beautifully dressed, in a pink dress with a wide pink bow, white socks edged with pink lace and shiny pink shoes. A pink Alice band held back her glossy black hair. Shoulder-length with bangs.

Smiling and smiling.

Down's syndrome.

The little girl laughed as Nikos swung her down, and Nikos laughed back.

Athena's heart did a back flip. Landed upside down, somewhere else in her chest than where it should be.

Down's syndrome…

Her aunt's letter came back to her.

'A little girl for Nikos and Marika…'

'Hi,' she managed, and if her voice came out a squeak she couldn't help it.

'Hi,' Nikos said back. He sounded as incredulous as she was—and as wary. The horse and buggy bowled on, leaving Nikos and his daughter on the verge of the path.

Nikos wasn't looking at her. He was looking at Nicky.

Nicky, who was the spitting image of his father—a mirror image of the younger Nikos.

Father…and son.

She should have…she should have…

It was too late for should haves. The time was now.

'This is Christa,' Nikos said at last, and his voice seemed to come from a distance. 'Christa, this is my friend, Athena.'

'Dog,' Christa said in Greek, still smiling. Pointing to Oscar. 'Ice… Ice cream.'

The ice cream vendor was right behind them. 'Would… would you like an ice cream, Christa?' Athena asked, and then thought desperately, what if she had a dairy allergy. What if…

'Yes,' Christa said, very firmly. She looked up at her father, searched for another word and found it. 'Please.'

She smiled again. She was gorgeous, Athena thought, and suddenly found she was blinking back tears. Nikos was holding his little daughter's hand with pride. With tenderness. With love.

'Ice cream, Papa?' Christa asked and Nikos nodded. He hadn't taken his eyes from Nicky.

'Introduce us,' he said.

'This is Nicky,' she said, trying to find the right words. And then, because she didn't want him to get the wrong idea—even if there was no denying the wrong idea was right—she added quickly, 'Nicholas.'

'Of course,' he said. Non-committal. 'And the dog?'

'Oscar.' She turned away—fast. 'I'll buy Christa a cone. Would you like one?'

'No. Thank you.'

It took time to get the cone. There were people queuing ahead of her. Then she thought she should have asked Christa what she wanted. But somehow…she knew. Strawberry.

And she was right. 'Pink,' Christa said with huge pleasure. She looked at the bench where Nicky and Oscar were seated. 'Sit,' she said.

Nicky smiled and shifted, just slightly, so there was room for Christa to sit between him and Oscar.

Athena thought, I'm going to cry.

She was *not* going to cry.

Still Nikos said nothing. Neither did she. Words were too big. Or too small. There was nothing to fill this silence.

Finally Nikos found words that might do. For now. Filler words. 'It's good to meet you, Nicholas. Is Oscar your dog or your mother's?'

'Mine,' Nicky said and she thought, great question. Generally shy, discussions of Oscar made Nicky blossom.

'How old is he?'

'We're not sure. He was in our street one day when we came home. He was dirty and really, really hungry. We took him to the animal shelter 'cos Mama said someone might be looking for him, but no one wanted him so we got him back. I called him Oscar 'cos Mama told me she had a dog called Oscar when she was little. Before my Mama's mama died.'

'I remember Oscar,' Nikos said softly, gravely. 'He was great. If your Oscar's like him he must be really special.'

'He is.'

'Does he eat everything like that?' Oscar was still licking, stretching the experience for as long as he could. Nicky had chosen a rainbow ice cream for him and he'd wedged it between the planks on the bench. Oscar had a paw on either side of the cone so it couldn't tip. His nose colour had changed now to green.

'He enjoys his pleasures, does Oscar,' Athena said, and Nikos finally looked at her. Really looked at her.

The look would stay with her all her life, she thought numbly. Disbelief. Awe. Anger. And raw, undisguised pain.

'He is, isn't he?' he asked, and there was only one way to answer that.

'He is.'

He closed his eyes.

Where to go from here?

'You can't do this, Thena,' he said, and his voice was suddenly harsh. 'No more. You walked away with *this*…'

'I didn't know.' It was a cry of pain but she knew it was no excuse.

'You walked away. And now…' He paused, took a deep breath, then another. 'Leave it,' he said and she wasn't sure if he was talking to himself or to her. 'I can't take it in. Just come back to the island and we'll sort it there. We need to get the succession in place. If you don't come home the island will be ruined. How selfish can you be?'

'Selfish?' She would have gasped if she hadn't felt so winded. 'Me? Selfish.' Then, before she could stop herself she produced the question that had slammed at her heart for almost ten years. 'How old is Christa?'

'Nine.'

'And her birthday is when?'

'June.'

'So there you go,' she snapped, the old, stupid grief welling up in her all over again. 'Nicky's nine and he was born in September. What does that tell you, Nikos?'

'Nothing,' he snapped. 'Except that you should have told me.'

'So maybe you should have asked. When I left…there was nothing.'

'You told me not to follow.'

'I didn't expect you to believe me,' she yelled—really yelled—and everyone looked at her. Even Oscar. Christa's ice cream started to drip on the side she wasn't licking. Nikos automatically stooped and turned it around for her, wiping her chin before it dripped on her dress.

It was a tiny gesture but, for some stupid reason, the sight of it cut through her anger and made her want to weep again.

'It's time we went home,' she whispered, and Nicky looked up at her in surprise.

'We were going to walk right round.'

'I'm tired.'

'I'm not,' he said, clearly astonished.

'Tell you what,' Nikos said. 'Why don't we compromise. Nicky, I'm from the island where your mother was born. I know your mama just shouted at me, but maybe that's because…because we both got a shock. Your mother and I have known each other since we were children, but this is the first time I've been to New York.'

'Yes…' Nicky said, not sure where this conversation was going.

'What if Christa stays here with your mama? Christa gets tired easily—she has a problem with her heart that makes her tired. But she'll be happy here with a dog and an ice cream. So your mama and Christa can rest here. Christa can finish her ice cream and you can show me all the way round.'

Nicky looked doubtfully at his mother. She was too numb to respond.

'Thene,' Nikos said urgently, and she tried to pull herself together. What was he asking? Fine, she decided. Anything. The gods would have to take control from now on. She couldn't.

'Can I take Oscar?' Nicky asked.

'Yes,' Nikos said.

'You really knew my mother when she was little?' her son asked.

'When she was Princess Athena,' Nikos told him. 'Your mother needs to be Princess Athena again. Come with me and I'll tell you why. Will Oscar come with us?'

Nicky was looking at her. Waiting for her approval.

What did it matter? She was no longer in control here. She knew nothing.

'Fine,' she said weakly. 'Take…take your time. Christa and I will look at the zoo.'

She sat on the bench and watched Christa finish her ice cream, and the desire to weep grew almost overwhelming.

What was it with men? How could she have thrown those two birth dates together and have Nikos react without the slightest regret? Or shame. Or guilt.

He'd called her selfish for leaving the island. She'd told him she wanted to leave for an exciting job in New York and he'd looked at her with shock and disbelief—and he'd let her walk away.

But if he knew the true reason… That if she'd stayed his family would be ruined. That the old King had threatened everything Nikos loved if she stayed. How could he never have guessed?

He'd never, ever asked. He'd never so much as written. And, when she'd learned of Christa's birth, she knew the reason why he hadn't.

Her fingers were clenched into her palms so hard they hurt.

'Papa,' Christa said suddenly, as if she'd just realised Nikos was gone. She looked worried.

This wasn't Christa's fault. She had no right to let her own misery and confusion spread to this little girl. 'He'll be back soon,' she said gently.

'Papa.'

'There's a little zoo just near here. Do you like animals?'

The little girl considered. 'Big?' she asked.

'Little. Funny animals. Friends.'

'Friends,' Christa said and put out a hand for Athena to help her to her feet. She smoothed her dress, tucked a sticky hand into Athena's and had another lick of her ice cream. 'Friends.'

There were so many questions… Where to start? An inquisition could be a good way to send Nicky straight back to his mother.

'Where do you go to school?' he asked, and then thought, great, very insightful. Not.

'Over there,' the little boy told him, pointing south east.

Good. That got him places. 'Do you like school?'

'Sometimes. I hafta go to Greek lessons after school, too.'

'You speak Greek?'

'Mama does. She makes me.'

He needed time to take that one in.

They walked along. Kicking stones. Nikos suddenly realised… He was kicking stones in front of him. So was Nicky. With his left foot.

'You're left-handed?'

'Mmm,' Nicky said.

'Your mama's right-handed.'

'Mmm.'

Riveting stuff. Both being left-handed. It meant nothing. It meant everything.

'Has your mother told you about Argyros?'

'Yes,' he said. 'Are you a fisherman?'

'Yes.'

'I like boats.'

'Have you been on boats?'

'Twice. I don't get seasick. Mama does. This is the place where a Beatle was shot.'

'Right,' Nikos said. He gave up. There were too many questions for one small boy to handle.

There were too many questions for him to handle.

They were sitting right where he'd left them, only Christa had replaced her ice cream with a hand puppet. A squirrel.

She wiggled it as they approached, her face lighting up as she saw him.

'Thena bought…me…squirrel.' He grinned and swung her up into his arms. No matter what else was happening here, this mustn't touch her. That had been his mantra for almost ten years and he wasn't budging now.

'Thank you,' he said gravely to Athena.

'We didn't get all the way round,' Nicky said. 'We caught another buggy. Nikos says John was his favourite Beatle. He was yours too, wasn't he, Mama?'

'Yes,' she said, sounding repressive.

'Imagine,' he said softly and watched her wince.

It had been the last night they'd been together. 'I have to go away,' she'd said, but she'd sobbed and clung.

He hadn't understood why she had to leave. She'd completed her university degree by correspondence, far younger than most. Her writing was brilliant. Everyone said so. She could take a job with the local paper and write the novel to end all novels. They'd agreed. She could stand by him in his battle with Giorgos.

That was what they'd planned, but suddenly she was crumpled, broken, sobbing about having to leave.

'I need to go. I just need to go. Please, Nikos, don't make it any harder.'

He'd thought it was her writing that was driving her. 'You'll come back?'

'I don't know. I can't. Nikos…'

She'd run out of words. He'd been angry, shocked, bewildered.

That night in his family's boatshed… Their last night. He'd played music by John Lennon on his tinny little sound system.

Imagine…

He thought now: Nicky must have been conceived that night.

No matter. He had to get rid of the white noise. There was only one absolute. 'You need to come home,' he told her.

'No.'

'Then Demos wins.' He made an almost superhuman effort to rid himself of his emotional tangle and concentrate on what was important. 'I need to go home tomorrow,' he said. 'I thought I had a week to persuade you, but Demos has already contacted mining companies. He's acting as if he owns the place. I daren't stay longer. But it's your birthright, Athena. And,' he added, 'it's your son's.'

'And your…'

'And my daughter's,' he finished for her, harshly. For maybe she was going places he wasn't ready to go just yet. 'Our children's. You must come home.'

'No.'

'Think about it,' he said briefly, harshly. 'There's so much happening here I can't take it in. Whatever's gone on in the past…' He glanced at Nicky and felt as if he was on a shifting deck, unsure of his footing, unsure of anything. 'For now we need to put that aside. If you don't come home, then some time soon I'll be back here to…sort what's mine. But my priority right now has to be the islanders. Thousands of livelihoods, Thena. Princess Athena. They're your people. You answer to them and not to me. Except…'

He hesitated and then said the words that had to be said. The words that had been in his head for the entire tour of the park.

'Except on the question of my son,' he said.

She gasped. 'That's not fair.'

'Life's not fair. Get over it, Athena, and come home. Princess.'

Nicky had been listening on the sidelines, troubled, not understanding but trying. 'You said *my son*,' he pointed out, trying to be helpful. 'Did you mean your daughter?'

Nikos nodded. Grave as Nicky. 'I must have,' he agreed. 'But I'm a bit upset right now. I need your mama to come back to the island where she was born.'

'You called her a princess.'

'She is a princess.'

'She's my Mama.'

'She can be both. I bet your mama says you can be anything you want if you try hard enough.' He turned and faced Athena straight on. She was lovely, he thought. In her casual sweat-shirt, her jeans, her tumbled curls tied back with a piece of red ribbon… She was a mature version of the girl he'd fallen for ten years ago. Longer. The girl he'd loved for ever.

He couldn't think that.

'Your mama can do anything she wants,' he said to Nicky, but he kept right on looking at Athena. 'I think it's time for your mama to do just that. Because I think she wants the island of Argyros to be safe just as much as I do.'

CHAPTER THREE

So two weeks later… Maybe she was out of her mind, but she was going back to a place she'd thought she'd never set foot on again. Argyros. The Silver Island of the Diamond Isles.

If Giorgos had had a son this never would have happened.

Generations of islanders had ached for the islands to revert to the three principalities they had once been. Now with Giorgos's death, they had.

'But why did it have to happen on my watch?' Athena muttered as she stood on the deck of the Athens-Argyros ferry and watched her island home grow bigger.

Beside her was Nicky. He was practically bursting with excitement. He should be in school, she thought. How could he get into the college of his choice if she kept interrupting his education?

That was only one of the arguments she'd thrown at Nikos during the tense phone calls that followed his visit. But always it had returned to the bottom line.

If she backed away from her role as Crown Princess then Demos would open all six diamond mines.

Whereas Nikos had a very different proposal—to open one mine, avoiding mess and with minimal effect on the

island's environment. Profits to go into the island's infrastructure and the island could prosper.

Nikos had told her all of this by phone, talking of nothing
but the island, making no mention of how these children had
happened, how Nicky and Christa affected their future—
nothing, nothing, nothing.

Apart from that one outburst in the park, he'd contained
his rage.

As she'd contained hers. We've been civilised, she thought,
and tried to feel proud of herself.

Instead she felt small. Belittled by the latent anger she
heard behind Nikos's civility. Frightened of what lay ahead.

'How long will we stay?' By her side at the rails, Nicky
suddenly sounded as scared as she was. 'For ever?'

'I've taken a month's leave. I'm hoping by the end of the
month Nikos should be able to take over the running of the
place.'

'Running?'

'Like…the government. If I can organise things then Nikos
will be the government when I leave.'

'Are you the government now?'

'Technically, yes. Though my cousin has been filling in.'

'We don't like your cousin Demos?'

'I'm not sure we do,' she said. 'Nikos says he's greedy. But
let's just see for ourselves, shall we?'

'Okay,' he said and tucked his hand into hers, with the
infinite trust of childhood.

She needed someone to trust too, she thought. What was
she letting herself in for?

'We'll just slip in quietly, do what we have to do and
leave,' she said. 'I'm hoping we'll hardly be noticed. I'll show

you the places where I swam and played when I was a little girl. I'll figure how to stop Demos digging his great big diamond mines. Then we can go home, with as little contact with the locals as possible.'

'So we won't see Nikos and Christa?' He sounded astounded. More. Sad.

'I guess we will,' she said and he lit up again.

'Good. I like them. Christa likes Oscar.'

'Oscar.' She glanced down at the dog on the deck beside her. Crazy. Coming all this way and bringing a dog.

But she needed to. She needed as much family as she could get. Nicky and Oscar were it.

We slip in quietly, do what we need to do and leave, she said to herself again, as she'd told herself countless times before. I'll give Nikos the authority he needs and leave.

But what about…Nicky? The small matter of Nikos's son.

It can't matter, she thought. Yes, Nikos was angry—maybe he even had a right to that anger, but there was still the matter of Christa, conceived three months before Nicky. When he and she…

It didn't bear thinking about.

'We'll get in, do what we have to and get out again,' she said again to Nicky. 'No fuss. Nothing.'

And then the boat passed the headland and turned towards the harbour. And she discovered that no fuss wasn't in the island's equation.

She'd come. Right up until now he'd thought she'd back out. But he knew she'd boarded the ferry in Athens. Short of jumping off, she had to be here.

So he'd let it be known. Demos had been acting Crown Prince. If Athena arrived on the quiet, as if she didn't want the Crown, it would give everyone the wrong idea. The islanders were terrified by Demos's plans. They needed Athena.

And…they knew her.

The only child of a lone and timid mother, home schooled because the King didn't want her to mix with the island children, Athena had every reason to be isolated and aloof. But Athena had been irrepressible. Born a tomboy, she'd declared, aged eight, that Nikos was her very best friend and whatever he did was cool with her.

As children they'd roamed the island, looking for mischief, looking for adventure, looking for fun. Tumbling in and out of trouble. Giving their respective mothers cause for palpitations.

He'd loved her. The islanders had loved her. They had been kids, who together just might make a difference to this island's future.

And now that time had come. He watched the ferry dock and knew that how Athena reacted in the next few moments affected the future of every islander.

Including him.

'Mama, why are all these people here?'

'Uh-oh,' she said.

'What does *uh-oh* mean?'

'It means Nikos is making a statement.'

'What sort of statement?'

'That I'm a princess coming home,' she said.

'So the streamers and balloons and the great big signs…'

'Saying Welcome Home To Our Princess? That would be for us.'

'What do we do?'

'I'm not sure. Stay on board until they get tired of waiting and go home?'

'I don't think that's a good idea,' Nicky said dubiously.

So it wasn't a good idea, she conceded. It was an excellent idea. But she knew Nikos was down there. She knew how much he loved this island and she knew for certain that if she didn't walk back onto her island home he'd come aboard and carry her.

Balloons had drifted into the water. A couple of excited kids had jumped in to retrieve them, and the ferry captain was forced to reverse and wait for his men to verify it was safe to dock.

Nikos watched and waited, feeling as if he shouldn't be here. Feeling as if he had no choice.

The islanders were going crazy. Their pleasure in Athena's arrival was a measure of how terrified they'd been that Demos would destroy them. It was also a measure of confidence that Athena wouldn't betray them.

Did he believe it?

Up until she was nineteen he'd believed it. He and Athena had plotted what they'd do if Giorgos was to die without an heir.

He grinned now as he thought of their plans. They'd build a cinema. They'd set up a surf school—Thena thought she'd make a great surf instructor—and what the heck, they'd invite a few rock groups over. But in their serious moments they'd had a few more solemn ideas. They'd slow-start the diamond mines. They'd ensure every child had the funds to get a decent education. They'd set up a democracy.

All of these things had been discussed over and over, as they'd wandered the island, as she'd come with him in his family's fishing boat and helped him haul pots, as she'd sat at his mother's kitchen table and helped shell peas or stir cakes.

When had he first figured he loved her? It had crept up on him so slowly he hardly knew. But suddenly their laughter had turned to passion, and their intensity for politics had turned to intensity of another kind.

The night her mother had died… She'd been seventeen. He'd cradled her against his heart and thought his own heart would break.

And then…suddenly it had been over. It seemed she had a chance of a journalist apprenticeship in New York.

Leaving had never been in his vocabulary, and he'd never believed it could be in hers.

And now she'd returned—she was standing at the ferry's rail looking lost, and he was standing on the jetty wondering where he could take it from here.

She had Nicky by the hand. Mother and son. And dog. The sight made him feel… Hell, he didn't know how he felt.

'Go on, Nikos.' His mother, Annia, was beside him, holding Christa. 'Go and speak for all the islanders. You know it's your place.'

'It's not my place.'

'It is,' Annia said fiercely. 'No one else will do it.'

And hadn't that always been the case?

As the King's sister, Nikos's mother had always stood up to the old King. She'd fought for the islanders' rights and, as he'd matured, Nikos had taken her fights onto his own shoulders.

He'd built up a fishing fleet that was second to none, but the islanders knew he worked for the whole island. They looked to him now as leader. He was in an uncomfortable position but he had no choice—there was no one else willing or able to take it on.

And now… If the only way Athena would rule was for him to stand beside her and guide her every step of the way, then he'd do it. He'd been raised to love this island, and he would not see it destroyed.

So now… He shoved aside anger, loss, confusion, a host of mixed emotions he wasn't near to understanding, and he strode up the gangplank with the determination of a man who knew where his duty lay. And, as he reached Athena, he took her in his arms and he hugged her. Whether she willed it or not. Whether he willed it or not.

'Welcome home,' he said and lifted her and swung her round in his arms, a precarious thing to do on a gangplank, but jubilation was called for. 'Princess Athena, welcome,' he said in a voice to be heard by all. 'We all welcome you, don't we?' he demanded of the crowd, and the islanders roared their assent.

'It's our royal family,' someone yelled. 'Princess Athena and Prince Nikos.'

'Nikos is only a prince if he marries Athena,' someone else yelled and there was a huge cheer of enthusiasm.

'Hey, Demos is already a prince. Maybe she should marry him,' someone yelled as the applause died, and the crowd laughed. The laughter was derisive.

And Nikos glanced to the back of the crowd and saw Demos. Even from this distance his body language was unmistakable. He was rigid with mortification and with fury.

Athena had a real enemy there, he thought. In the mood he was in, Demos could do harm.

Not if he stayed close.

He had no choice. In order to protect this island then he needed to protect this woman. He intended to stay very close indeed.

Athena's smile looked pinned in place. She was terrified, he thought.

'It's okay,' he murmured.

'No,' she murmured back. 'It's not okay at all. I'm doing

this because I have no choice. If you think I like being hugged by you…'

The crowd's cheers were building. Athena waved and so did Nicky.

And Nikos had no choice either. He waved.

They stood together.

'There's a reception tonight at the palace,' he told her.

'There's a what?'

They were all in the royal limousine, heading for the palace. Nikos hadn't wanted to come with her, but once again there'd been no choice. Someone had to introduce her to the palace staff.

He'd brought Christa along, to lighten the atmosphere a bit. To stop things getting too personal. Oscar lay on the floor looking exhausted. It had been a very long waddle down the gangplank.

Giorgos would have had a fit if he could have seen this dog in his limo, Nikos thought and suppressed a grin.

The limousine, the palace, these trappings of royalty, had been kept so Giorgos could come in state whenever he wished. They could get rid of it all now, Nikos thought, but then he considered the crowd who'd turned up to see Athena arrive. They'd cheered her with joy. She was giving the island its identity back. Did she even realise it?

'A reception,' he repeated, trying to get his head round practicalities. 'Everyone who's anyone on the island and a few more. Three hundred people.'

'*How many?*'

'You need to make a statement.'

'I don't.'

'Of course you do,' he said flatly. 'That's what you've come for.'

'But I'm not staying,' she said, sounding desperate. 'Nikos, I can't do this. A reception. People cheering. It's not who I am.'

'It's what you were born to.'

'I was born to be nothing.'

'That's a dumb statement.'

'Do you need to sound angry?'

'I'm not…'

'What have I done to make you angry, Nikos?' she demanded, suddenly as angry as he was.

'I could tell you.' He glanced across at Nicky. 'But not here.'

'Why not?'

'It's hardly…appropriate.'

'How about if I decide that?' she snapped.

They were being chauffeured along the magnificent coastal road that wound round headland after headland, stretching on until it reached the Royal Palace of Argyros. But Athena wasn't looking at scenery. She was focused on him.

'I don't think…'

'How about we stop thinking?' she snapped. She closed her eyes for a long moment. Then she opened them and she reached for her son's hand.

Nicky had been alternately looking out of the window and looking at his mother. He was a smart kid, Nikos thought. He could hear the undercurrents of her anger. There were things going on that he didn't understand and he obviously didn't like it.

'Nicky, I want you to listen for a bit,' Athena said. 'Full attention.'

He gave it.

Athena glanced at Nikos. Glanced away. Took a deep breath.

'Nicky, when I saw the people at the boat,' she said, faltering for a start and then making her voice firmer. 'I realised there was something that Nikos and I need to tell you. That maybe we should have told you before this. Do you remember asking about who your father is? I told you your father was someone I met when I was very young. I told you that he was my best friend, but then he married someone else. That man is Nikos, Nicky. Nikos is your papa.'

What the…? What had she just said?

She'd taken all the wind out of his sails and then some.

It had clearly astounded Nicholas as well. 'Nikos is… Nikos is…' Nicky said and faltered to a stop, staring at him as if he had two heads.

'Do you see his hair?' All at once Athena sounded weary—strained to breaking point. 'It's the same colour as yours. It curls the same. You see how that little bit sticks up right at the top of Nikos's head? Yours does, too.'

Nicky stuck his hand on top of his head and felt the offending tuft. His eyes grew enormous.

It was all Nikos could do not to do the same.

'I told you that your papa was a fisherman,' Athena said. 'That's what Nikos is. Isn't that right, Nikos?'

She'd given him a son. Just like that. Like it or not.

Where to go from here?

She should have done this nine years ago, he thought, dazed, fighting anger, but knowing instinctively that his anger was no reason to mess with things now. To say no, let's talk about this at a more sensible time. Maybe we need DNA tests. Maybe we need…counselling. Or something?

Nicky was looking at him with eyes that were blank with shock. What happened in the next few moments would affect him for ever. He didn't need a counsellor to tell him that.

He had the power to mess this for life.

So where to go? What to say when you've just been given the gift of a son?

'I should have been there for your mother,' he said softly. 'I should have been around for you. I'm very, very sorry that I wasn't.'

'Why weren't you?' Nicky said.

And there was only one answer. Only the truth would serve.

'I didn't know,' he said heavily. 'Your mother left the island a long time ago, when she was expecting you. And she didn't tell me you were born. Maybe because we were both very young she thought it was the right thing to do. Maybe she thought it would be easier to bring you up on her own when I lived so far away. I wish I'd known, Nicky, but that's in the past. What's important now is that you're my son. I'm so proud that your mother's finally told me about you. I'm so proud to finally have the chance to know you.'

He glanced at Athena and her eyes were brimful of tears. She wrenched her head around so she was looking out of the window, but not before he'd seen those tears.

'I'd like to teach you to fish,' he told Nicky, fighting for something—anything—to say. Hell, there should be a book on what he was doing now. It was too important to mess with, and all he could do was flounder. 'I'd love to take you in my boat.'

'You really own a fishing boat?'

'Really.'

'I don't get seasick,' Nicky said, as if that was important.

'Neither do I,' Nikos said and felt something grow in his chest. *The heart swells to fit all comers.* Maybe the corny saying was right.

His son. The thought was overwhelming.

Nicky and Christa. His son and his daughter.

His family.

'You have a grandma,' he said.

'A grandma.' Nicky was clearly overwhelmed.

'Her name is Annia. She's a princess like your mother.'

'My grandmother's a princess?'

'She's not as pretty a princess as your mother,' Nikos told him. 'And, like your mother, she doesn't wear a tiara. But I hope you'll like… I hope you'll love her. She's a better fisherman than I am.'

'Does she get seasick?'

'No one in my family gets seasick,' he said and he saw Athena flinch.

Nicky fell silent. No one spoke. Athena was looking out of the window as if her life depended on it.

'Why didn't you tell me, Mama?' Nicky asked and the question hung. For a moment he thought she wasn't going to answer. For a moment he thought, how could she?

'I was very young,' she said at last, and her voice sounded as if it came from a long way away. 'I was in America and I was by myself. And I knew…I knew Nikos…your papa…and his wife were having a baby here. That baby is Christa. So I thought your papa needed to stay here to take care of Christa. I knew I could take care of you, and I did.'

And behind those words? Raw, unresolved pain. Bleak. Stark. Dreadful.

How to take that pain away?

Nikos knew that he couldn't. Ten years of pain, and the only way he could alleviate it was a truth that wasn't his to tell.

And he hadn't caused that pain. It was Athena who'd left.

'Why didn't you come back here?' Nicky asked her, obviously fighting to find some sense in all this.

'I have a great job, Nicky,' Athena said. 'I needed to work to support you.'

'But…' Nicky paused and looked from Athena to Nikos

and back again. His mother and his father, and a history he didn't understand.

This was too heavy, Nikos thought. It was way, way too hard. Maybe they should have left this for the future, for some more appropriate time to tell him, but what was done was done. And somewhere in this mess they had to find joy.

He had a son. Yes, there was heartache and regret but he had a son, and his son needed to lose that look of confusion and…and yes, even the echo of his own sense of betrayal.

'See that rock out there in the bay?' he said, fighting for the right note. 'The big one with the flat top about two hundred yards from shore?'

'Mmm,' Nicky said, still dazed.

'I taught your mother to dive off that rock. Or I tried to. She kept doing bellywhackers.'

'I did not,' Athena retorted, struggling not to falter, and he knew that where he went she'd follow. How could she help it now?

'You did, too,' he said, and managed a strained sort of grin. 'You get your mama to take you out and show you her diving skills,' he told Nicky. 'She'll do bellywhackers every single time.'

'Christa, can you swim?' Athena asked, still sounding desperate, and Nikos thought maybe he'd got it right. He'd deflected the father bit, giving Nicky time to come to terms with it as he wanted.

He knew there was a lot more discussion to come. Some of that would have to be personal, between Athena and Nicky.

Some of that needed to be between himself and Athena.

'I like…swimming,' Christa said. She'd pushed her shoes off—she hated shoes—and her feet were resting on Oscar. 'I like…dog.'

'I think Oscar likes you,' Athena said.

'Does this mean Christa is my sister?' Nicky asked and Nikos's thoughts went flying again. The issues were too big. Huge.

'I guess she is,' Athena said softly. 'Your half-sister.' Then she said gently, 'Christa has something called Down's syndrome. That means she was born with something a little different from most children. All the bits that start a baby growing…they're called chromosomes. Christa got an extra one. It makes the tips of her ears a bit small. It makes her tongue a little bit big and her eyes really dark and pretty. And it affects her in other ways too, including her speech.'

'But she likes Oscar.'

'She does,' Athena said gravely, smiling at Christa. 'I think Christa is our friend already. I think having her as your sister might be really cool.'

So much for leading the conversation, Nikos thought. It was now about the three of them. He was right out of the equation.

Somewhere, once, he'd read some scathing comment on fatherhood. Mothers knew all about their children's dramas, their love lives, the spots on the back of their necks. Fathers were vaguely aware there were short people in the house.

Not him, he thought. With Christa, he'd been so much more hands on. But he felt sidelined here.

'I wanted a sister,' Nicky was saying, cautious. 'A little sister. But Christa's nine.'

'I'm nine,' Christa said, nodding grave agreement.

'But she's much shorter than you,' Thena said. 'I think she always will be, so that means she'll always be your little sister.'

'So I get to look after her?'

'If you want.'

'Do I hafta share?'

'I guess you and Christa can work those things out for your-selves,' Athena said, and Christa looked at Nicky and beamed.

'Nicky,' she said.

'Brother,' Nicky said importantly and thumped his chest.

'Brother,' Christa repeated and thumped her chest.

They giggled.

Just like that, Nikos thought, stunned. It was over, just like that. Yeah, there'd be complications. Yeah, there'd be difficul-ties. But, for now…it was sorted.

'Now,' Athena said in a voice that boded ill.

'Now?'

'What about this reception?'

What were they thinking? Talking of social events when she'd casually given him his son? He felt as if all the wind had been sucked from his lungs and he wasn't the least sure how to get it back.

Nicky and Christa were looking at each other, sizing each other up, still grinning. Occasionally giggling. Having a sister was obviously a big deal for Nicky. Bigger than having a father?

He'd missed out on nine years of having a son. He looked back to Athena and she was looking as dazed as he was.

'I wanted to tell you,' she whispered. 'I didn't know how.'

'Like…the phone?' He couldn't keep anger from his voice and he got anger in return.

'You think? So I should have phoned you—and your wife—and thought about the consequences later?'

A host of angry rejoinders crowded his head. None of them could be said in front of the children.

Maybe none could be said at all.

'The reception,' she said again flatly, moving on.

'Seven tonight.' That, at least, was easy. 'The Crown Prince and Princess of Sappheiros will be welcoming home the Crown Princess of Argyros. Officially handing over control.'

'And then what?' He saw panic flare. 'Nikos, I can't do this alone. I can't do this at all. Run this country? I have no experience. I have nothing to qualify me for such a role. I've taken four weeks' leave. That's it.'

'If that's it, then you're handing the Crown to Demos.'

'This isn't fair.'

'Life's not,' he said shortly. He had evidence of this right in front of him. He'd had a son for nine years and he hadn't known.

She stared at him, speechless. He stared out of the window. Tried not to think that yes, it was unfair. As kids they'd planned to do this side by side. They still could if she…if he…

It had to be thought of. The lawyers had demanded he think of it.

How could he think about it?

'You *will* be there tonight,' she said urgently, and a blunt voice inside him said no, let her sink. Not telling him he had a son…

But then he looked at her, he caught the terror, and he caught something else.

The Athena he'd once loved. She was still in there.

And this island… It was his home and he loved it. He had to support her, come what may.

And he had to convince her to stay.

Enough. One step at a time.

'I'll be there,' he told her.

'With me,' she said urgently. 'I won't remember names. People will know me and I won't remember them. I'll say the wrong thing. Nikos, you have to help me.'

'I'll help you.'

He hadn't said it right. He sounded petty, angry, resentful. And she got it. Terror turned to anger again, just like that.

'Don't you dare.'

'Dare what?'

'Dump this on me. You talked me into this. You made me come home. I'm your responsibility, Nikos. I came home because of you.'

'You came home because of the island.'

'I came home because we talked ourselves into loving this island together. If you're even thinking you need me to stay, then you need to support me every step of the way.'

'I'll support you tonight,' he said.

Beyond tonight was a place he was too fearful to think about.

CHAPTER FOUR

THE castle was a time warp.

The limousine pulled up in the castle forecourt. Athena climbed out.

Argyros, circa eighteen hundred. It was almost enough to jerk her out of the emotional mess she'd just landed herself in.

It was almost enough to make her stop thinking about Nikos.

The palace was built of the stone used throughout these islands, whitewashed once but mostly faded to its original soft grey. It was two storeys high in the centre, with long single storey wings at either end. The garden was overgrown to the point of riot. Vast wisteria vines gnarled their way over the buildings like great knots on ancient gift wrapping. There were olive trees, bougainvillea, wild daisies and clumps of blue and yellow irises—a riot of colour. The palace looked half buried by garden—a fantastic wilderness.

And behind the castle was the backdrop of the sea. As a child she'd heard the palace had the best swimming beach on the island, but who knew?

She'd never been in these grounds. The castle had been

protected by vast stone walls for as long as she could re-member. Guard dogs were said to roam at night.

Giorgos had hardly ever come here but he'd deemed it his. What was his he held, fiercely.

'So who does this belong to now?' she whispered to Nikos as she stood in the forecourt, feeling stunned, feeling the warmth of the Mediterranean sun on her face, hearing the wash of the sea under the cliffs.

'The Crown,' Nikos said briefly. 'That would be you. Unless you abdicate. Then it goes to Demos. He's been staying here since Giorgos died—since he phoned you and you told him he could have it. I told him you were coming back and he had to vacate.'

She gulped. 'I hadn't thought...' she whispered. 'Demos must hate me.'

'He hates me, too,' Nikos said, but he touched her arm lightly, in a gesture of reassurance which was supposed to be steadying—and strangely was. 'But we needn't feel guilty. Somehow he wheedled his way into the King's favour. Giorgos left him a personal fortune. Sadly for Demos, a for-tune will never be enough.'

There was so much here to take in... She was fighting to understand it.

Meanwhile staff were waiting, lined up as if in some period play. The women were wearing uniforms that were grim-as-death black. The men wore black too, alleviated only by high starched collars in pristine white. In this Mediterranean paradise they looked...ridiculous.

'You need to meet your staff,' Nikos said, and she thought about backing into the limo and slamming the door. This was scarier than scary.

'You're kidding me, right? I can't employ these people.'

'Maybe you can't,' he said neutrally. 'Giorgos kept the castle fully staffed. Demos intended to sack them and modernise the place, but now it's your call.'

'They can't like working here.' She looked again at the uniforms, at the stoical faces, at their ramrod straight posture. 'Looking like this…'

'Looks don't matter,' he said briefly. 'Apart from a struggling fishing industry, there's very little employment.'

Her head was starting to spin. Nikos knew this place. She didn't. It should be Nikos in charge. But he was giving her information only, and waiting for her to act as she willed.

Waiting for her to fail? Certainly he was judging her.

Anger stirred. She could do this. She would. She was *not* going to fail in front of Nikos.

The staff were in two formal lines. Not a muscle was moving. They looked almost like waxworks. 'Can I afford to pay them?' she demanded.

'The royal coffers are at your disposal,' Nikos said neutrally. 'They're overflowing.'

'How can they be overflowing? I though we were broke.'

'Giorgos taxed everything. Once a year he cleaned out the Argyros accounts and moved the money to Sappheiros. It's been nine months since they've been cleared, and Alexandros is shifting what funds he knows are ours back. You'll need to start road repairs, harbour deepening, the infrastructure. You can provide employment and make this a better place to live in the process.'

'But I'm a fashion editor,' she said and to her horror, she heard herself beginning to wail. 'I can't do this!'

'Your staff are waiting,' Nikos said. He was holding Christa's hand. Standing apart. 'Set Oscar down—hold him by the leash,' he told Nicky. 'Your mother needs to meet the staff, and if you intend to live here then you need to meet them, too.'

'Am I going to live here?' Nicky gazed around in awe. 'Cool!'

'It is cool,' Nikos said gravely. 'I'm not sure if your mother thinks so.'

'I don't think so.' She was fighting for control. She was taking in the crumbling façade of a once magnificent palace. The derelict gardens. Twenty people lined up to see what she would do.

'Do I have a choice?' she muttered.

'No.'

'Fine, then,' she snapped. She was being thrown in at the deep end, like it or not. She had no choice but to swim. 'I can be a princess if I need to.'

He smiled at that. 'Of course you can.'

'Okay,' she muttered.

'Well, then…'

'Well, then.' She took a deep breath. She braced her shoulders and stepped forward. She ignored the sensation of Nikos at her back, watching her. Judging her?

'Hi,' she said, in her best managing-the-staff voice. A voice she hadn't quite perfected. 'You know who I am. I probably should remember all of you but it's been almost ten years since I've been on the island so you need to forgive me. You'll also need to forgive me if I don't get things right—the things I'm supposed to do. But three things I do know, and I might as well say them now. First, not one of you will lose your job for anything except incompetence or dishonesty. Not while I'm here. Second, your salary will stay the same until I have time to review it and even then it won't drop. And finally…I hate your uniforms. Hate 'em. Who's interested in giving me suggestions for change?'

* * *

She was fabulous. She was just as he'd always imagined she'd be.

She'd been here for what—twenty minutes—and the staff were already putty in her hands. Her career had her moving with some of the world's wealthiest, most flamboyant people. She was good at her job. It showed.

He was proud of her.

How corny was that? How patronising?

He didn't have to tell her what to do, he thought. He just had to stand back and watch. And wonder.

She'd already had volunteers to redesign the uniform. She'd already said she'd like to use first names—if that was okay? The staff were already halfway to being in love with her.

Who could blame them?

'So remind me.' She was at the end of the line, looking back at him. 'The reception is at seven?'

'Yes.'

'Will my people have the details?'

My people. Just like that, she'd taken on the mantel of royalty. And once again she'd moved him to the sidelines.

'Yes,' he said shortly. 'Your staff are putting on the reception.'

'So I'll see you then?'

'Yes.'

She nodded. The eyes gazing at him were expressionless. 'We'll be happy to receive you, then,' she said.

And that was that. He'd been dismissed by royalty.

His gaze met hers and held. Then, very slowly, he nodded. And smiled.

'Until then, Your Highness,' he said softly and gave her a gentle, mocking salute. 'Off you go and introduce Oscar to his new home.'

* * *

It took all the courage in the world to watch him go—not to call him back—to stop herself whimpering in terror. But this role was hers. She'd returned to the island as Crown Princess. She had to take the responsibility.

Her dream as a kid—to take on this responsibility with Nikos—was just that—a dream. He'd married someone else. He'd moved on.

Somehow, she must too.

The housekeeper—Mrs Lavros—no first names here!—gave her a cursory tour of the palace, apologising over and over. 'There's not been money for repairs. We're so thankful you're finally here. We're so sorry we couldn't get it how we'd like it.' But neither Athena or Nicky—or Oscar either, for that matter—minded shabby.

'Ooh, it's cool,' Nicky said, and Athena gazed in awe at the vast chandelier in the bedchamber they'd just been ushered into and had to agree. This was the King's bedchamber, with a smaller bedroom leading off to the side. 'The smaller room's for the King's valet,' Mrs Lavros told her. 'It's been years since the King's been here, but we've kept it aired. There's clean linen on the beds…'

Athena was no longer listening. She was staring out of the window at the beach that had been forbidden to mere mortals since Giorgos's ancestors had plundered this place and made it theirs.

Nicky and Oscar were already out on the terrace, scrambling through the balustrades, figuring how they could clamber down to the cliff path.

She was a princess. Did princesses…clamber?

'Has Nikos seen this?' she breathed. The beach was wide and golden, curving from headland to headland. The sea was glistening diamonds—fabulous, romantic.

'I'm not sure,' the housekeeper told her. 'But if you please, ma'am, what will you wear tonight?'

Tonight. A royal reception. *How many people?* She stopped thinking about clambering.

'Something…simple?' she ventured.

The housekeeper's face fell. 'Everyone wants to meet you,' she said. 'We so want our own princess. Prince Alexandros and Princess Lily will be here from Sappheiros, of course, and they're wonderful, but they're not our ruling family. Prince Alexandros will wear his medals,' she said wistfully. 'Don't you have a formal gown?'

It was said without much hope.

And Athena looked at her two suitcases and knew her lack of hope was justified.

She'd packed for four weeks and she'd travelled light. She'd brought one formal little black dress.

Nikos should have warned her. *Nikos should have warned her about the reception*, she thought again, feeling anger build.

But…

But.

Prince Alexandros and Princess Lily would be here.

And…this was really huge…Nikos would be here as well.

Nikos, who'd fathered a child to another woman before she'd left the island. Nikos, who'd married Marika. Nikos, who she'd thought she loved with all her heart. Who'd finally, dreadfully, taught her not to trust…anyone.

He'd thrown her in the deep end here—*but she would not sink.*

He hadn't warned her. He'd expect her to be…ordinary.

She glanced at her watch. It was still only midday. She had seven hours. Could she?

Nikos would be here.

She would be a princess.

Nothing to it, she thought, mentally spitting on her hands and getting down and dusty. She wasn't fashion editor of one of the world's biggest glossies for nothing.

'Mrs Lavros, if my cellphone doesn't work here then I need a landline,' she said. 'And the Internet. I need help to become a princess and I need it fast.'

She didn't come down until seven-thirty. She almost didn't come down then.

She was listening to Nicky read. She and Nicky had changed reader/listener roles about two years back when he'd decreed her choice of stories was boring. Since then this had become her special time of day—to quieten nerves, to remind herself what was important, to focus solely on the two of them.

And this night she needed her quiet time more than she'd ever needed it in her life. This night she was terrified. For the moment she went downstairs she turned into a princess.

Nicky was reading from a manual for a Model T Ford. Gripping stuff. Much more gripping than what was happening downstairs.

But she couldn't stay up here for ever. Finally the housekeeper appeared. 'Ma'am, it's Nikos,' she said apologetically. 'He says if you're not downstairs in two minutes he'll come up and carry you down. And I think he means it.'

'You'd better go, Mama,' Nicky said. 'Nikos is really strong.' He smiled shyly at the housekeeper. 'Nikos is my Papa.'

'He's your…' The housekeeper's chin sagged. 'Well…'

'Mama just told me today,' Nicky said, proud of the effect he'd created. 'Christa is my sister.'

'Well,' the housekeeper said again. 'I can't say I didn't wonder when I saw you, but… Well.' She surveyed Athena with growing concern. 'Oh, my dear, Demos will hate it.

You'll need to be so careful. But you need to get tonight over with first. You look lovely. You do us proud. But…if you don't want the father of your child to carry you forcibly down the staircase, then you'd best come now.'

Nikos was close to being out of his mind. What was Athena playing at, keeping them waiting? And she should have a gown. He hadn't thought of it until everyone had arrived, but every woman here was in an evening gown. His friend, Prince Alexandros, and his wife, Princess Lily, looked positively regal.

But it was Athena who should be a princess tonight, he thought. Dammit, he should have warned her. She'd be a real Cinderella among this splendour. And if she thought he'd orchestrated it so that she looked shabby… Anger wouldn't begin to describe it.

But there was no time left for misgivings. The housekeeper was on the stairs, looking towards him, asking a question with her gaze.

He strode through the crowd and took two steps up, so the crowd could see him. Somewhere above was Athena. He hoped like hell her dress wasn't too dowdy.

There was no time to do anything about it now. She was up on the landing, waiting for his signal to come down.

Waiting for the official introduction.

'Ladies and gentlemen,' he said in a voice that carried to every part of the vast hall. 'I give you Her Royal Highness the Princess Athena, Crown Princess Of Argyros.'

CHAPTER FIVE

THE crowd gasped as one.

Nikos stepped down and turned. And saw. And gasped himself.

She took his breath away.

She took away the breath of every man and woman in the crowded hall. Nikos had never seen her more beautiful.

He'd never seen anyone so beautiful.

She looked to be almost gliding down the stairs. One elegant hand rested on the balustrade to steady herself. Her hand was gloved, long and elegant and beautiful.

And her dress…

Her gown was shimmering silk brocade in rich, deep crimson. Its tiny capped sleeves were slipped to just off her shoulders, and the neckline dropped to show the glorious swell of her beautiful breasts. Her bodice was embroidered, red-black on the deeper crimson, and laced from breast to waist with slivers of silver thread.

From her hips the gown flared into fold on glorious fold of the same richly embroidered fabric, falling to her feet. The skirt was slashed at the front, showing a soft silk underskirt, black, shot with crimson.

Magnificent didn't begin to describe it.

She stepped slowly down the stairs, beneath the great central chandelier, as if she was aware of dramatic effect. Her gown shimmered in the light cast by a thousand crystals above her head.

There were diamonds at her throat and more at her ears. Her shoes were crimson stilettos to match her gown, studded with more diamonds still. Her beautiful black curls were caught in a simple twisting knot, tied with the same silver thread that laced her bodice.

She was an exquisite portrait. She was a royal princess.

She was the Crown Princess Athena, come home to claim her throne.

Around him there were gasps of delight, amazement, disbelief, and the gasps gave way to applause.

Nikos knew why. From the uncertainty of the past months, finally the islanders could glimpse their future. These people would be deeply appreciative of this grand gesture; deeply grateful that their princess was taking up her throne.

Thena.

No. Not Thena. This was Crown Princess Athena, a woman now so far out of his league that suddenly he felt…as if he had no place here.

'What the hell…? Where did she get that dress?' It was Demos, standing beside him, his face a picture of apoplectic fury. 'How long's she been planning this? She told me…'

'She told you she wasn't interested in ruling the island,' Nikos said, his gaze never leaving Athena. Where *had* she got the gown? It surely hadn't been in one of the small cases she'd brought here with her.

Wherever it had come from, it was perfect.

And the islanders were dumbfounded.

Athena had effectively been brought up in isolation. Families

who'd shown her friendship had been harshly warned off by
Giorgos. That she had turned out so full of spirit was a testa-
ment to her strength, and to her courage.

Her mother had home-schooled her, on orders from
Giorgos, so Nikos hadn't met her until they'd been eight years
old. He'd been bird-nesting—not stealing eggs, just observ-
ing, trying to reach the highest nests on the craggy island
cliffs. She'd looked up at him from below, and he'd said,
'Dare you.' To his astonishment she'd come right on up. On
the way down she'd cut her knee. Regardless of her protests,
he'd taken her home so his mother could fix it.

He remembered she'd stopped outside his back door. 'I'm
not allowed into people's houses.'

'Why not?' he'd demanded, astonished.

'The King says I'm not allowed.'

And he remembered his mother's reaction. She'd come out,
breathing fire.

'The King doesn't command who comes into my kitchen,'
she'd retorted. 'Welcome to my home, my love. Nikos, bring
her in. Oh, look at your poor knee.'

Annia had defied the King to marry Nikos's father and,
where Athena was concerned, she defied him again.

'You stay friends with her, Nikos. Giorgos can rant all he
wants—he won't scare us.'

He looked at her now and thought Giorgos had been right
to be worried. She was truly regal.

Princess Lily tucked her hand through Nikos's arm.
'Doesn't she look lovely?' she breathed.

'She does.' There was no denying such a truth.

'Why is Demos looking like thunder?'

'He thought Athena didn't want the Crown. He thought it
was his for the taking.'

'He's scary,' Lily said, watching Demos shove through the crowd and leave. 'He came to see Alex a couple of days ago. I had a feeling…' She shivered. 'Sorry. I just thought…he seems ruthless.'

'There's nothing he can do.'

'Is there not? You look out for her,' Lily said urgently and Nikos frowned.

'What do you mean?'

'I know what people are capable of when there's money at stake,' she said. 'Be careful Nikos. The poor woman's terrified.'

'Are you kidding? She's every inch a princess.'

'You're only seeing the clothes,' she said and sounded disappointed in him.

What was there to see but the clothes?

A lot. He knew—a lot. But hell, it hurt to think that.

'Then there's your son,' Lily said, and he stilled.

'I beg your pardon?'

'Your son.' She was all seriousness now. 'Alex says rumours flew from the time people saw him at the ship. He says the age is right and you and Athena were lovers. No?'

'I…' What the hell…? 'Yes.'

'Then there's another reason to take care of your princess. Your son is now heir to the throne. Any threat to Athena would also be directed at him. Have you thought of that?'

No. No! The thought poleaxed him.

'Lily.' Alexandros was ushering Athena forward. 'Princess Athena, may I present my wife, Princess Lily.'

Lily smiled, then, astonishingly, dropped into a deep curtsey.

'There's no need for curtseys,' Athena said, sounding breathless, bordering on appalled.

'There certainly is,' Lily said. 'If you're about to take on the role of Crown Princess, you need every bit of respect you can get. Nikos, bow or something.'

'We're expected in the great hall,' Nikos growled. 'Princess Athena's kept the kitchen waiting. I hope dinner's not spoiled.'

Which earned him a glance of gentle reproof from Lily. 'Princess Athena's permitted to keep anything she wants waiting,' she said grandly. 'Including you, Nikos. Take the lady's hand and lead the way.'

She was seated in the centre of the head table, at a royal reception just for her. It was almost too much to take in.

To her left was Nikos, then Alexandros and then Lily. They were chatting as old friends. She'd love to be included.

But on her right was the Archbishop, talking and drinking at an alarming rate. He spoke in theological platitudes, and any attempt she made to make the conversation more general—to include Nikos, or to talk to the woman on the other side of him—saw the platitudes grow louder.

Being royal was suddenly boring.

She pecked desultorily at her dinner, not hungry, but then Nikos leaned over and murmured into her ear, ignoring the Archbishop's monotone; 'Thena, the kitchen staff have worked themselves into a lather getting this meal ready tonight. There hasn't been a royal reception on this island for twenty years. I need to tell you that they're likely to fall on their kitchen knives if you don't eat your dinner.'

She stared at him, astonished, and saw he was serious. And she had no comeback. He was already talking again with Alexandros.

Okay, she'd eat her dinner. She'd listen to the Archbishop. She'd be a good princess.

What was she letting herself in for?

She might look like a princess. She didn't feel like one.

Nikos was simply dressed in a black suit, beautifully cut, with a crisp white linen shirt. Alexandros was wearing full royal regimentals.

They looked like two princes, she thought. They *were* two princes. By right, if not by birth.

This Crown should belong to Nikos.

Finally the Archbishop paused for breath. He rose, a little unsteadily, and headed towards the bathroom.

Alexandros rose and slipped into his seat.

Once upon a time Alexandros had been her friend as well as Nikos's friend. Once upon a time, when life had been innocent.

'I'm sorry about this,' he said softly. 'Nikos is throwing you in at the deep end.'

'This should be him—not me.'

He smiled and shook his head. 'He works behind the scenes, our Nikos. His mother's done an extraordinary amount for this island and so has Nikos. But they do it quietly and with no fuss.'

Another woman had made an almost unseemly rush to fill Alexandros's vacant chair beside Nikos. Nikos smiled a welcome at her. The woman simpered.

'Does he have a girlfriend?' Athena asked Alexandros, before she could help herself.

'Not seriously. Lots of short-term encounters but little more. I don't think he's ever got over Marika.'

'That was nine years ago.'

'How long does it take after a bad marriage to trust yourself to a good one?' Alex asked quietly. 'To learn to trust another after such betrayal...?'

They were quiet for a moment. Watching Nikos. Watching the woman inch her chair closer.

'You and he...' he said softly. 'You know, we all thought it'd work.'

'Me included,' she said before she could stop herself.

'Marika was a very attractive woman. And Nikos was very young.'

'The same age as me. Nineteen.'

'So maybe you need to forgive each other? Especially...' He hesitated and then obviously decided to be frank. 'Especially if you have a son.'

'I don't need to forgive Nikos.' She looked at Alex full-on. 'Nikos gave me my son. I regret nothing.'

'So if he forgives you...'

'He'll have it flung back in his face.'

The Archbishop was back, waiting for his chair. She turned to him and smiled sweetly.

'I'm glad you're back. Where were we?'

Nikos could do nothing but watch.

This dinner was interminable. Alexandros had abandoned him to talk to others. The woman hanging on his words was driving him crazy. He wanted out of here.

He could go. But that would mean not watching Thena, and he was mesmerised by her.

He sat and watched. He responded to the laughter and noise around him. The islanders were jubilant that they had their princess home.

He'd brought her home. He'd done his job. He should leave.

Coffee was served. An orchestra, playing gently in the background until now, raised its volume and struck up a waltz.

This had been prearranged. Alexandros was to lead Athena onto the dance floor. Alexandros, in full ceremonial uniform, was every inch a prince.

As Athena was every inch a princess.

In moments she and Alexandros were swirling round the floor with skill and grace. If Lily hadn't been sitting on the sidelines he'd have been jealous.

Jealous? He didn't want any part in this goldfish bowl of royalty. He needed to support Thena from a distance—nothing more.

The waltz ended. There was a moment's pause and he thought they were about to dance another. But Alex whispered something to Athena and strode back to Lily.

Athena stood alone for a moment, as if considering. And then she walked deliberately back to the head table, so she was standing right before him.

'Nikos, it's thanks to you that I'm here tonight,' she said steadily, clearly, so all the room could hear. 'The Prince Alexandros tells me you've taken care of this island—you've worked ceaselessly behind the scenes to protect the islanders from the worst excesses of the old monarchy. I thank you, and I ask you to do me the honour of this dance.'

She was play-acting, he thought. She'd swept down those stairs in her magnificent dress and she'd assumed the mantle of royalty.

Her words to him were those of a Crown Princess, a woman who knew her place in the world and assumed the respect of her birthright.

He'd be proud of her if he wasn't so bewildered.

If he wasn't so angry.

For there was still anger, simmering underneath. There was still Nicky's birth to sort. But now wasn't the time. Not when she was holding out her hand.

There was nothing to do but to take it.

'I'd be honoured, Your Highness,' he told her, and her control ended. It was he who led her back onto the dance floor. It was he who took her into his arms and led her into a waltz.

They could do this.

One wet winter when school was out and Athena was a constant presence, Annia had declared enough with the television and the card games.

'One day, if the gods look favourably on us, you may eventually rule this island,' she'd told Athena. 'And Nikos may well help you. So you need to learn to act as royals.'

So his mother had taught them their royal history, taught them their ancient rights, taught them protocol—and she'd also taught them to dance.

He stepped onto the dance floor, he took Athena into his arms and the years disappeared. They might as well be back in his mother's sitting room, with her complaining on the sidelines… 'Smooth, Nikos, smooth, hold her as if she's precious, not a sack of potatoes…'

Hold her as if she's precious…

How could he help but do that? She was exquisite. Her skirts were swirling around him as she melted into his arms, and he let the dance take them where they willed.

The smell of her… The feel of her…

It felt as if it was yesterday that they'd walked hand in hand over every inch of this island, swearing eternal love, swearing they could never look at another.

She was the most beautiful woman…the most beautiful princess…

The waltz ended but another began, as if the orchestra knew this was no time for interruption.

He had his Thena in his arms again. It felt as natural as life itself.

'It should be you taking the Crown,' she whispered. 'You deserve it.'

The moment—the magic—was broken. He felt it slip away with infinite regret.

'I deserve nothing, Princess.'

'Don't call me that.'

'It's what you are.'

'For four weeks.'

He almost misstepped. He'd have no excuse because dancing with Thena was like breathing.

'You can't leave,' he said. 'You know that.'

'I make up my own mind.'

'As you did last time. Walking away…'

'I believe I ran,' she said. She was smiling, a gentle smile that would have everyone thinking she was enjoying a light conversation with him.

'There was nothing to run from,' he said angrily.

'Oh, but there was,' she said, her smile not slipping. 'And I didn't know the half of it. I should have run much sooner.'

'You're not making sense.'

'Then aren't we a match?' she said.

They danced on. Other couples were joining them on the floor. He had to think of something to say. Anything.

'Where did you get your gown?' he tried.

'You like it?' She sounded strained to breaking point. 'It's worth over ten thousand dollars, which is a fraction of what these diamonds are worth.'

'What the hell…' His brow snapped down in confusion. 'You've managed to get your hands on the royal exchequer?'

Her eyes flashed fire. Somehow her feet kept moving, her smile stayed in place, but daggers could be less lethal than the look she gave him.

'I must have,' she said, and he could see that the effort it cost to keep her smile in place was almost superhuman. 'After all, I only have weeks to strip the place bare.'

'Thena…'

'Nikos,' she snapped. 'You know me better than this.'

'I don't know you.'

She didn't respond. They circled the dance floor, twice, three times more, and the music came to an end.

'Thank you,' she said stiffly and let her hands drop from his. He was aware of a sharp stab of loss. Quickly suppressed. Let's not let emotions get in the way here, he told himself.

But they already had.

'It was my pleasure,' he said, just as formally.

But she wasn't finished with him. 'I'm a fashion editor,' she said coldly, formally. 'I know the value of product placement. So I let it be known that the new Princess Athena of Argyros would be presented to the public for the first time tonight. The fashion houses' marketing teams know me. They know I can carry clothes—see, there are advantages in not eating crepés and soufflés. So they moved fast, flying clothes and jewellery from Athens this afternoon. I get to send them all back, but not before I'm photographed by the world's press—which, if you look to the balcony, also seem to be present. So I've organised my clothes, Nikos, and I've organised them myself. I'd never touch the island coffers. I never will.'

And then she added a more hesitant trailer.

'And Nikos, my feelings for you are messing with my ability to do this job. If this is to work then I need to separate them.'

'You want me to leave you alone?'

'That's it.'

'When you have my son?'

'He's not your son unless you earn the right to call him that.'

'What's that supposed to mean?'

'I don't have a clue,' she said and sighed, and then repinned her smile and turned around to a middle-aged lady who'd clearly been aching to talk to her.

Audience over.

It was so hot in here. She felt as if she was suffocating.

This dress was fabulous but it required a serious waist. She had lacing not only on the dress but also on the less than glamorous undergarment underneath. Move over, Scarlett O'Hara, she thought grimly as the night wore on. What women put up with in the name of vanity!

But the dress, the diamonds, the effort she'd gone to, were working. There were cameras everywhere. She knew the world's press. The glossy magazines liked nothing better than royalty on their front covers. So be it. She'd done the glamorous bit as a clear signal that she was a real princess.

It was a signal to Demos to lay off. It was a signal to Nikos that she was up to the task.

She was dancing with one islander after another. They were treating her with awe. What a difference a frock makes, she thought ruefully. When she was a child these men and women had obeyed the King's ruling and had nothing to do with her.

Only Nikos and his mother had defied the King.

Nikos… He was dancing too, with one beautiful woman after another. Mr Popularity.

That was unfair, she conceded. She'd been here less than a day, but already she was being told how much Nikos had done for this island. He'd fought Giorgos every step of the way.

But…she was his tool, she thought bleakly, as the night wore on. She was a tool for Nikos to use in his fight to save the island. And as for the past… How much of that had been real and how much had it been Nikos's desire to rule this island as he wanted it to be ruled?

The dancing ended. She needed air. She left the ballroom and the crowd parted before her as if she was…royalty.

Could she ever get used to this?

The room next to the ballroom was the great hall where dinner had been served. It was deserted now, cleared and empty. But its vast windows looked onto a balcony, and the balcony looked over the sea.

She walked out and stood at the parapet, gazing out over the ocean. Breathing the night air. Breathe in, breathe out. Try to relax.

She smelled the salt breeze from the sea. There was the scent of flowers she hadn't seen or smelled for ten years.

She loved this island. Loved it.

'What the hell do you think you're playing at?'

She whirled and it was Demos, portly and flaccid and simmering with obvious rage. He walked out and slammed the door behind him. 'Do you seriously think you can get away with this?'

'With what?'

'It's mine,' he said fiercely, stepping towards her with an intent that frightened her. 'Giorgos always meant it to go to me.'

'Giorgos no longer has a say in how this island will be ruled. It's in the hands of the…'

'The gods? Don't give me that. You're not wanted here. You promised me…'

'I meant the people. And I didn't promise you anything.'

'Liar.'

'You lied to me,' she said evenly. 'You said you cared for this island. Now I find it was just greed.'

He was so close to her she could feel his breath. He was pushing his body into her space, so her back was hard against the parapet. 'You left this island to have a kid. Nikos's kid. They're all saying it. You think we want a woman like you to run the island?'

'I care for the island more than you do.'

'You don't know what care is.' He closed his eyes. Regrouped. 'Okay. Here's another solution. You know how much these diamond mines are worth? We can split it. You don't want to live here. Neither do I—it's the pits—but someone has to. You go back to your life in New York and I'll take over. I'll do what has to be done and we'll cut the profits. Fifty-fifty. You can't say fairer than that.'

'Demos,' she said, trying desperately to keep her voice steady, 'I'm not opening the mines.'

'You might have to.'

'I don't know what you mean.'

'There are ways,' he said viciously. 'You care about your kid, don't you. It'd be a shame if anything happened to him. You can't watch him all the time. You go back to Manhattan and he'll be safe again.'

She felt cold and she felt sick.

'You can't hurt us,' she managed.

And he simply smiled. And he raised a hand to hit her.

Only…he didn't. She was backed as far as she could, putting her hands up in a futile attempt to prevent a blow, but the sweeping hand didn't reach her.

A dark shape had sprung from the shadows as if it had always been there. Demos's hand was held before it had a chance to find its mark.

Demos twisted, lashing out with his boots, moving so the shadow was now in the light.

Nikos.

'How dare you touch her?' He let Demos's hand drop as if it was slime. Demos struck out again, but Nikos was before him. He punched, so hard that Demos sprawled backward, crashing over an ornate chair, falling, hitting the ground with a sickening thud. Lying there for one long moment while Thena thought, dear God, he's killed him.

Nikos didn't say a word. His hand came out and took Thena's, holding hard.

An oath came from the tiled floor. Not dead, then.

Nikos tugged her hard against him, putting her slightly behind him, his body between her and her cousin. He watched in grim silence as Demos struggled to his feet.

Demos straightened, swore again and looked at Nikos with murder in his eyes. If he'd had a gun, Athena thought with a shiver of pure dread, then Nikos would be dead. Or if he'd been wearing Alexandros's ceremonial sword…

'What is she to you?' he snarled to Nikos. 'This has nothing to do with you.'

'Princess Athena is the mother of my son,' Nikos said and his voice made Athena shudder. It was as cold as ice, rigid, formal and grim. 'You just threatened my son. And…' he tugged Athena closer '…you were about to strike my woman. I'll defend what's mine, and this woman and her son are mine. Hear me well, Demos, for I mean every word. Get yourself out of this palace and off the royal grounds. If you're seen within sight of Princess Athena or her son again you'll be thrown off the island, never to return.'

Then he turned his back on Demos as if he had no interest in him at all—and he took Athena into his arms.

CHAPTER SIX

ATHENA stayed right where she was, held tight against Nikos.

She was shuddering so hard she couldn't stop, and it was easier to stay than to pull away. For who wanted to pull away?

She no longer knew what Demos was doing. She couldn't see—Nikos didn't let her see. She was aware of heavy breathing, of his sinister presence. Nikos must be watching him, but her face was buried against his chest.

'Leave,' Nikos said again, quietly. There was a loaded silence, then a muttered oath of such invective it took her breath away—and Demos was gone.

'He hates me,' she whispered, feeling ill.

'He doesn't love and he doesn't hate,' Nikos said. 'He wants. He wants wealth and more wealth. Thena...' He put her away from him, holding her at arm's length.

'Thena, you're standing between Demos and a fortune.'

'I don't want it.'

'That's why I brought you home,' he said softly. 'Because you'd never want it. I knew that about you when you were eight years old, and people can't change so much. Demos was greedy from the start. He'll destroy these islands. You can face up to him but...'

'But I don't want to.'

'No. And you also say you're going back to New York. I understand your career is important to you. You put it before the island once before—and I understand you'll do it again. But these people want a figurehead, Thena.'

'I'm not a figurehead. I'm just me.'

He shook his head at that one. 'Look at you,' he said, smiling wryly, and once more he had her at arm's length. 'You're stunning. You're every inch a princess. You're who the people want.'

'I don't want to be royal.'

'Sometimes what we want and don't want doesn't come into it,' he said softly. 'Demos isn't alone, you know. There are heavies behind him.'

'Heavies?'

'Yes.'

'Like…armed thugs. People who could hurt my Nicky?' She whirled away from him and headed for the door but his hand came out and caught her. 'Let me go.' She wrenched back but he didn't release her. He tugged her closer so her breasts were against his chest. He had her by one arm, holding it about her, tugging her in so she was pulled tight against him.

'Where are you going?'

'I'm going to Nicky.' But he was letting her go nowhere.

'He's safe. I've had security guards watch you both from the moment you set foot on the island.' He smiled, apologetic. 'Longer, in fact. Even in Manhattan. You lessened the risk by telling Demos he could have the throne but even then we didn't trust him.'

'We?'

'There are many islanders whose livelihoods hang on you inheriting,' he said. 'Demos's heavies don't have it all their own way. For if Demos succeeds…'

'You really think he'd hurt Nicky?'

'Yes.' It was a flat statement with no equivocation.

'Then I'm leaving. He can have it. I don't want it. Not if it puts Nicky in the slightest danger. Let me go!'

'Thena, do you really want Demos to destroy these islands?'

His voice was grave, low and urgent, and something about his tone stopped the rising hysteria, the rising panic.

This was the real Nikos. The Nikos she'd spent her teenage years with. The Nikos who cared about this place so passionately that he'd taught her to care as well.

Until she'd met Nikos she'd been taught to feel as trapped as her mother was trapped. 'We'd leave if we could afford it,' her mother had told her. 'I'm so sorry you have to stay here. I'm so sorry the royals are destroying your life as well as mine.'

That was how she'd been raised, but then along came Nikos, with his passion, his fire, his certainty that they could make things right.

She'd fallen in love with his fire.

And she heard that fire now, the sheer single-minded determination to create justice for this island, to do whatever needed to be done to achieve that end.

'I can't care,' she whispered. 'Not if Nicky's in danger. You'd feel the same if it was Christa.'

'I feel the same that it's Nicky,' he said. 'He's my son, too.'

Once again he'd taken her breath away. He was still holding her, hand to hand, his hold imparting warmth, strength and urgency.

'He's not… I mean, how can you care?'

'I would have cared for ten years if you'd let me.'

And the old anger stirred. For ten long years… 'Not one call, Nikos.'

'Not one letter, Thena.'

'Dammit, this is past history.'

'It's not. It's here and now. It's two kids we care deeply about, an island we care deeply about, and our future.'

'My future's in Manhattan.'

'You won't be safe in Manhattan. I can't protect you there. Thena, there are six diamond mines at stake. We're talking billions. That money has to be held in trust for the island for ever. It can't stay in royal hands. We need to get the royal thing sorted, the government sorted, so we can finally transfer the mines to the community. So these mines are no longer owned by one man—or one woman—but the island as a whole so they can be worked sensitively as the community needs them. You need to stay for three reasons. One, so I can protect you. Two, so we can keep the mines safe. And three…' He hesitated. 'Three, because Nikos is my son. I've missed ten years of his life, and I believe I have the right to know him now.'

This was doing her head in. The impersonal and the personal were mixing in a combination that was threatening to overwhelm her.

Nikos had been her first love. For the last ten years she'd tried to forget him, but she never could. Every man she'd dated she'd compared with Nikos and they'd fallen short.

She'd finally decided Nikos was a figment of a young girl's romantic longings. Impossible to be true, but also impossible to leave behind.

But here was the dream, come spectacularly to life. Nikos, with a body to die for, a smile to die for… And words so blunt and decisive that she believed him.

There was no reason to believe him, she told herself desperately. Christa. Remember Christa.

'Why can't I sign the diamond mines over now?' she demanded. 'Put them in a community fund or something?'

'There's no community fund. Everything's owned by the Crown.'

'Then set one up.'

'I can't set one up, Princess. Only you can do that.'

'Then I'll do it,' she said wildly. 'Tomorrow. And don't call me Princess.'

'It can't be done tomorrow. You think you can just hand that amount of wealth to the town council and walk away? I need to tell you now that it would be a catastrophe. It'll take years to get this right. So how about it, Thene? Say you'll stay and let me protect you. I've told Demos I'll protect what's mine and I mean just that.'

And amazingly, infuriatingly, he was smiling. That smile was so…so… Seductive. He was seducing her with his voice and with his smile, she thought wildly.

'I'm not yours,' she managed.

'You're the mother of my son.'

Oh, great. What sort of answer was that? One that joined them at the hip for ever?

'You saw the press here tonight,' he said. 'The world has another princess. Do you think you can escape that? The press will follow you all the way to Manhattan. And so will Demos.'

'You're scaring me.'

'You need to be scared.' His smile faded. 'I'm sorry, Thena, but you need to face facts.'

'You didn't tell me these facts when you conned me into coming here,' she snapped. 'That there'd be threats to Nicky…'

'You wouldn't have come.'

'Exactly.'

'You had to come. And I will protect both you and Nicky.'

'You're still angry I didn't tell you about Nicky.'

'How can I not be?'

She wrenched her hands back so strongly that this time he did let her go. 'Well how do you think I feel? You betrayed me in the worst possible way. I thought you were my best friend as well as my lover—and nothing. Nothing!'

'It was your decision to walk away.'

'It wasn't.'

He stilled. 'What do you mean?'

But she wasn't going there. Some things were best left unsaid.

'I need to go to bed, Nikos,' she said wearily, knowing it was true. 'I'm exhausted. It's been some day.'

'You will think about what I've said?'

'I will think about it,' she said. 'Of course I'll think about it. You've scared me. You seriously think Demos could harm me? Yes, he's greedy and shallow, but he's my cousin. I don't know what you stand to gain by my staying…'

'I told you. Nicky.'

'You think I trust you enough to think that's the only reason?'

'You can trust me, Thene.'

'This is nonsense, Nikos,' she said wearily. 'Once upon a time we trusted each other, but that was a long time ago. I'm so confused I can't think straight. So let me be. Tomorrow I'll think about arrangements for when I return to Manhattan. I'll do my best to protect the island from Demos. I'll talk to lawyers—I'll do what I have to do. But trust you? How can I ever do that?'

And she turned and walked back into the ballroom, her gown swishing around her.

Leaving Nikos in the shadows, watching with troubled hooded eyes.

Knowing she was walking further into danger. Knowing

there was only one real way he could protect her but to do that…to trust her that far…

Once upon a time we trusted each other…

It cut both ways.

Finally, thankfully, the interminable evening was at an end. She listened while the Archbishop made his ponderous farewells, she said a formal goodnight to those she must, and then she practically ran upstairs.

Nicky was safe. She opened the adjoining door and saw a mound in the bed by the window, draped by another mound. Nicky with Oscar on top.

He wasn't supposed to let Oscar onto the bed, but who was complaining tonight? Now, all she felt was comfort from the big dog's presence.

A shape rose from a chair beside the door and she practically yelped.

'Ma'am, it's only me.'

Mrs Lavros. Her heart thudded back into place. 'Wh…why are you here?' she stammered.

'Mr Nikos asked me to stay here,' she said. 'His instructions are that we're not to leave the little one alone.'

'What…what right does he have…?'

'No right, more's the pity. But he cares about this island so much.'

'You think…' It was hard to stop her voice from squeaking. On the second try she managed it. 'You think he should be Crown Prince?'

'Everyone knows and trusts him,' the housekeeper said solidly. 'You've been away so long… But Nikos has been here. He's always been the one we've turned to in times of trouble. He's always been ready to stand up to Giorgos. In the last few years we've been left more or less alone, thanks to Nikos. But now…you're here…and Nikos says you'll make a fine Crown Princess and I'm sure you will too, ma'am. It's Demos and his friends who Nikos worries about. He's fearful for you.'

'He shouldn't worry. I'll be fine.'

'I know you'll be fine,' the housekeeper told her. 'For Nikos is keeping you that way. He has guards in place in the corridor and out in the grounds. You're safe.'

She stared, bewildered. 'Are you kidding? He's scaring me witless.'

The housekeeper nodded. 'He said that. He said he couldn't protect you without scaring you a little. But I wouldn't be fearful. He's a good man.'

'He's been talking crazy talk tonight,' she said.

Mrs Lavros raised her brows in polite disbelief. 'Has he now? It's not something I'd credit. All I know is that whatever Nikos does there's reason for. Goodnight, ma'am. Sleep well and safely, for he'll be watching over all of us.'

She sat for a while and watched Nicky and Oscar sleep. She tried to sort the events of the day into some sort of order.

She failed. It was a weird kaleidoscope of emotions, with Nikos front and centre.

Finally, so tired she could scarcely stand, she walked into her bedroom—the King's bedchamber—and started to undress.

Uh-oh.

One of the maids had helped her dress. The gown had something akin to a corset underneath, designed to make her figure a lot more hourglass than it naturally was. There were fine bands of what was surely whalebone inserted inside.

It was laced down the back.

This gown was designed to have people help the wearer in and help the wearer out.

Here there was only her.

She struggled. She struggled some more. She was almost turning herself inside out.

It wouldn't even rip. And where were a pair of scissors when she needed them? She was in a royal palace—where did she go in a royal palace to find scissors?

There was a bell pull by the mantel. She could pull it—but how loud would it be? She might wake the whole palace.

She struggled and swore some more. She was practically breaking her neck trying to see where the lacing was. Even if she could see how it was laced, she couldn't reach.

She could wake Nicky, she thought desperately.

Right, that'd be a help. Once he went to sleep Nicky slept like the dead. She'd wake him and it'd take a cold shower to get him alert enough to unlace her.

Dammit, she could do it. If she could just reach an inch further…

There was a knock on the door.

She froze. It was two in the morning. What the…?

'Who is it?'

'Nikos.' There was no mistaking the voice. Brusque. Urgent. Nikos. She didn't know whether to be relieved or not.

'Are you okay?' he demanded.

'Of course I'm okay,' she managed. 'Why wouldn't I be okay?'

'The security guards in the garden contacted me. They said you appeared to be in trouble.'

'I'm not.'

'They said you were struggling—that you appeared distressed.'

What the…?

She stared at the window.

And winced.

The great bay windows of her bedroom were hung with fine silken netting. That formed the first layer of curtaining. But there was a second layer. Swathes of crimson velvet were pulled back, fastened to the sides with huge golden tassels.

Oh, no.

She glanced through into Nicky's room, checking his windows.

The velvet curtains had been pulled closed.

Until now she hadn't even noticed that there were heavier curtains over the fine ones. But now… She'd been standing before the dresser, trying to see the back of her dress in the mirror.

There was a chandelier in the centre of the room, blazing with light. So she'd been standing in a netted bay window, struggling with her dress, while the chandelier shone its light behind her.

They would have been able to see…

She blushed and blushed, then blushed some more. And ached for her nice anonymous Manhattan apartment.

'I'm fine,' she managed.

'Thena, what's wrong? Is someone in there with you?'

'I'm stuck,' she said, and listened to the silence on the other side of the door.

'Stuck?' he said at last, cautiously.

'Yes, stuck. This damned dress…'

'You're stuck in your dress?'

'In my underskirt. Oh, for heaven's sake, I'll let you in, but if you dare laugh…'

'I won't…laugh,' he said, but laughter was already in his voice. Of course he'd laugh. She knew this man too well.

'Pull the curtains first,' he said, and she could still hear the laughter. 'I need to radio the men to say there's no drama, but if I enter… They can see…'

'I know what they can see.' She hauled the curtains closed with a viciousness she was feeling towards the underskirt—and towards the man in the corridor—and hauled the door open.

Nikos was no longer in his formal black suit. He was in a pair of jeans and a loose battered jacket. His hair was tousled and unkempt.

And she knew…

'They woke you up,' she said, stunned.

'They were worried.'

'I couldn't get my dress off and they contacted you?'

'It looked like…'

'I don't even want to think what it looked like,' she managed. 'Don't you dare grin.'

'I wouldn't dare.' But he was grinning.

'Are you sleeping in the palace?'

'For the time being.'

'Where's Christa?'

'With my mother.'

She stared at him blankly. He gazed back, his laughter fading.

'You really are worried about me,' she whispered.

'We really are, Princess.'

'Don't call me that.' She was close to hysterics, she thought. She was close to…

'Hey, it's not all bad.'

'Isn't it?'

'It's not.' His hands caught her shoulders and held. He was looking down at her, his dark eyes fathomless. 'Thena…'

'Don't.'

'Don't what?'

'I don't know,' she muttered, totally bewildered, backing away from his hold. 'Just unfasten this slip, will you? I'm ready to rip it but the fashion house that lent it to me would have forty fits. Besides,' she added honestly, 'I tried and it wouldn't. Why aren't you wearing a sword?'

'A sword?'

'To slice the thing open.'

'You want me to slice your underclothes off with a sword?' he said cautiously. 'I don't know. It sounds a bit…cavalier…'

'You're laughing.'

'I'm not laughing.'

'Just get it off,' she said, and then looked at his face and thought uh-oh. The royal command wouldn't work here. This was Nikos and he always had been one for trouble.

'Please,' she said before he could make another wisecrack. 'Can you unfasten it?'

'A sword would be more fun. Will you wait until I find one?'

'No! Just unlace me.'

'Okay, Princess,' he said and smiled again. 'I could never resist a damsel in distress. Even without my sword I'll rescue you. Come here.'

'N… No.'

'Sorry?'

But other sensations were surfacing here. Something about the night, the lateness. Something about how damned sexy he looked—laconic, strong and sure, dressed how she'd always known him, battered clothes, a bit unkempt. Gorgeous.

'I…I think I've changed my mind,' she stammered. 'Can you call the housekeeper?'

'You don't think I can unlace you?'

'I don't know if I trust you.'

'That's a harsh thing to say.'

She bit her lip. But she was right. She'd thought she'd known this man as well as she'd known herself. One nine-year-old daughter had put paid to that trust.

But still. This was only lacing. She trusted him enough for lacing, she conceded.

'Okay,' she said begrudgingly and his smile broadened. It was a killer smile. It was a smile to melt a woman's heart.

'Good. But if we're talking undressing here... Let's make doubly sure we lose our audience.'

He flicked the light switch. The chandelier disappeared into darkness. The only light remaining was the fire's soft glow in the grate. It hadn't been tended for hours so it was now a bed of soft-glowing coals.

It was hard to see anything by. It was hard to see Nikos by.

But she knew what he looked like. He'd been her friend for ever. He'd been her lover as well, for just a short, sweet time, but that loving had been a natural and wonderful extension of their friendship.

She hadn't forgotten any of it.

So here he was, her Nikos, in her darkened bedroom. Moving towards her with intent.

She should order him out. But it was as if this was meant, a part of who she was.

She looked up at him in the dim light, not backing away, knowing what was intended, knowing also that his intent matched hers. Knowing he knew it.

She stood, simply waiting. Simply wanting.

He took her in his arms—and he kissed her.

She froze, for a whole three seconds, while her mouth registered his touch, while her body registered his feel, while she realised what was happening and that she wanted it as much as he did.

She should push him away. If she was sensible…

But the sensible part of her was no longer connected to who she was.

For she was suddenly the Athena of ten years ago. Athena in Nikos's arms. Half of the Thena and Nikos partnership, forged when they'd been eight years old, broken but now magically come back together.

It was as if two parts of a whole had finally rejoined, fusing, so the white noise disappeared, the voices muted that said this was crazy, dangerous, stupid…

This wasn't *stupid*. This was Nikos. This was his body against hers, his mouth on hers, his hands holding her tight, tighter… Nikos, making the night disappear.

He was pulling her so close she felt she was sinking into him. Maybe part of her was, and it was sinking back where it belonged.

Crazy, crazy, crazy.

She didn't care.

Her breasts were on fire where they were touching his body, and the fire was spreading. Heat was building, starting low, moving upward, flooding her body with fierce, hot want.

Nikos.

His tongue was in her mouth, exploring, searching and she felt herself stagger. It didn't matter, for his big hands were holding her, cradling her against him, allowing no chance of her falling away from him.

She was his woman. His mouth said it. His hands said it.

Nikos, Nikos, Nikos.

She was surrendering to him. She wanted him so much. Nikos…

But then, cruelly, outside intruded. The radio at his belt crackled into life. 'You okay, boss?' It was a gruff request, full of concern.

He had to respond. She knew he did.

He pulled away with a muttered oath. 'Dammit, I should have… You're distracting me, woman.'

'Is that my fault?' she demanded, even managing to sound indignant, and he grinned. There were electric charges going off everywhere here, zinging around in the darkness like fireflies. She felt light and hot and wonderful.

She hated the voice on the radio.

'It's okay, Zak, just a wardrobe malfunction,' he said into the radio and there was a moment's static-filled silence.

Then… 'You want some help fixing it, boss?'

'I believe we have the situation…in hand,' Nikos said, and the look he gave her was pure need. The zinging started all over again, filling the room with wonder.

He replaced the radio on his belt and took her hands in his.

'Like that's done my reputation some good,' she managed.

He grinned. 'You want a reputation, you just got one.'

But the break had changed things. Just a little, but enough. The first desperate tug of attraction had pulled them together. Now common sense was returning. Just.

'You want that I should unlace this slip?' he asked.

'Yes,' she whispered. 'Then…I think you ought to leave.'

'You want me to leave?'

'Nikos…'

'Okay.' His tone was suddenly flat. 'Yeah, okay. We need to keep some sanity here.'

'I am…I *am* going back to Manhattan.'

'You can't,' he said flatly.

Here it was again, this crazy proposition. But she was too tired. It was doing her head in.

She said nothing. He looked at her for a long considering minute and finally he nodded. 'Okay, Princess. You've had enough for one day. But you do need to see sense. Meanwhile…maybe we should stay away from each other's bodies. It's making me crazy. So let's sleep on what's the sensible course of action for all of us. Your career destroyed what was between us personally. I can't believe you'll let it destroy the island as well.'

'It didn't…'

'Goodnight, Princess,' he said softly, not letting her finish, and it was as if he was closing a door on what had just passed. Locking a door and throwing away the key. 'Think about everything… Please.'

CHAPTER SEVEN

ATHENA woke as two bodies landed on her bed. Nicky and Oscar, zooming in from the other room, launching themselves on top of her, Oscar barking and Nicky whooping.

'Breakfast,' Nicky said. 'Breakfast in bed, Mama. Pancakes.'

There was a soft tap on the door.

'She's awake,' Nicky yelled and a maid appeared, holding a tray.

The maid was dressed in a lovely sapphire-coloured frock, a shirt-waister, buttoned through from throat to waist, the skirt flaring out a little but not too much, tied at the waist.

The difference from the grimly clothed servants she'd seen yesterday was astonishing.

The girl was smiling. 'Please, ma'am, I'm sorry but Nikos said we were to wake you with breakfast at ten.'

'Nikos said…' Her bemusement deepened. There were so many questions she needed answering. 'Nikos gives orders to the palace staff?'

'Yes, ma'am,' the girl said as if her question was a bit foolish. 'For the most part there was no one else to do it.'

'Nikos is a fisherman,' she said cautiously. She had her arms full of dog. Oscar had obviously missed her deeply all night—and was making up for lost time.

'Nikos has six fishing boats and employs many,' the girl said simply. 'When the King started taxing the fishermen so heavily they could no longer operate, Nikos started taking fish to the mainland. He organised funds there that Giorgos couldn't touch. In the end the only way the King could stop him was by arresting him and confiscating his boats, but somehow he found the courage to face his uncle.' She smiled wistfully. 'The islanders love him,' she said simply. 'He would make a wonderful Crown Prince.'

And then…she realised what she'd said and her eyes widened in horror. 'I didn't mean, ma'am… I mean…we believe you'll make a wonderful Crown Princess. It's just that we all know Nikos and trust him.'

Despite the apology, there was still regret in her words. Athena heard it—and she even agreed.

Nikos should be Crown Prince.

He would have been, she thought. If they'd married as they'd once planned.

Marriage to the ruler meant automatic and equal status for the spouse.

So… The thought was suddenly there. What if…?

No. There wasn't enough trust in the world to take her down that path.

Was there?

Marriage… It was such a huge concept that to take it any further seemed terrifying.

Concentrate on now, she told herself, feeling suddenly dizzy. Concentrate on what came next right now. Any more and her head might explode.

Her bed was big enough to hold a small army. Someone must have crept in earlier and rebuilt the fire. It was crackling cheerfully in the grate. The maid was pulling back the curtains. Nicky was already tucking into pancakes—made by the palace staff and brought to her in bed. The morning sun was glimmering across the terrace, and beyond the terrace was the sea.

It made her feel rich. It made her feel ostentatious. It made her feel that she had no right to be here.

'I love your uniform,' she managed, hauling herself back to reality. 'Do you like it?'

The girl smoothed her skirt with pleasure. 'Maria sewed all night. This is the first. She says if you like it she'll make more.'

'I love it,' she said with enthusiasm.

Good. Think of anything but Nikos, she told herself. Anything but Nikos.

Uniforms.

'You know, sapphire looks great on you, but some of the staff might like different colours. How about we leave the choice of colour to each person?'

'Oh,' the girl said, and flushed with pleasure. 'We'd look like a rainbow.'

'It seems there haven't been rainbows round here for a long time. It's a wonder Nikos hasn't suggested change already.'

'Oh, he has no authority to change the King's orders,' the girl said blithely. 'Or yours either, ma'am. And he never would. He knows his place.'

How had they got back to Nikos again? It seemed as if her mind was a whirlpool and, in the centre…Nikos.

Give in, she thought. Just let it come.

'And…and his place is with his fishing fleet?'

'I…yes, ma'am.' The girl didn't understand what she was asking—and who could blame her? 'He has six boats, but the one he uses is the one he built himself when he was a young man. The *Athena*.'

'He has a fishing boat called the *Athena*?' she said, stunned.

'Yes, ma'am,' the girl said and smiled. 'It's nice that he called his boat after his Princess.'

'Yes, Athena said cautiously. 'Um… Is he on his boat now?'

'I believe he left the palace before dawn.'

So…Nikos was fishing.

While she played princess.

What did princesses do all day?

She wouldn't mind going fishing. She wasn't bad at hauling up craypots herself.

'I should talk to my cousin Demos,' she said doubtfully.

'I believe Prince Demos left on the morning ferry for Athens,' the girl said and blushed. 'I…I overheard one of the security guards.'

The day spread before her. No Demos.

No Nikos.

There were probably papers she should be reading, she thought.

She glanced out of the window. The beach looked…fantastic.

'Feel like a swim, Nicky?'

Nicky had been sharing a pancake with Oscar. He paused. She'd said the magic word.

'Swim,' Nicky said cautiously. 'In the sea?'

'That's the one.'

'Yay,' he yelled, and Athena found herself smiling. Life couldn't be all bad.

Threats were a nightmare; something for the dark recesses of the night. Not for now.

Nikos had gone fishing. Long may he stay there. Just as long as he stayed out of her head.

* * *

Was he nuts to go fishing? He had a team of fishermen working for him now, and a solid fleet of boats. He hardly needed to fish himself.

But he hadn't slept. If he couldn't sleep he might as well work.

At least Demos had left the island. It seemed he was on his way to Athens, maybe to confer with lawyers to try to figure a way around Thena's right to rule.

He wouldn't get answers he'd like. Athena's right to the throne was inviolate.

As long as she stayed safe.

But if she left as she said she would… Anything could happen to her back in Manhattan. He couldn't watch over her.

And Nicky… How could he get to know his son if he left? And Demos would still be a threat to him as well.

What the hell to do…

He knew what he wanted to do. He wanted to lift them up, sweep them under his own protection, place them in his house and leave them there.

But he had to concede it wasn't just common sense that was telling him to do that. It was sheer unequivocal lust.

He wanted Thena. He'd wanted her ten years ago and, astonishing or not, his desire was greater than ever. But she'd walked away once because of her career and now she was threatening to walk away again.

Was one career so important? He loved fishing, but would he put it aside if the island's livelihood was in doubt?

Of course he would.

But Thena wasn't him. Once he'd thought he'd known her, but her leaving had shocked his foundations to the core. Not telling him about Nicky had shaken him even further.

He no longer trusted her. And she didn't trust him. He knew why.

But, regardless, it had been Thena's decision to walk away. She hadn't known about Christa or Marika then. So the choice had been hers. One phone call from her and his life would have followed a completely different course.

But it hadn't. And now he had Christa. His little daughter who he'd decided years ago would be protected against everything. *Everything*.

Lay craypots, he told himself sharply. Work with your hands and not with your head.

So he laid craypots. But he just so happened to have taken his trawler around the headland, into the cove below the palace. He could watch the palace from here. He could see the beach.

So he was still laying craypots when they came down for a swim. Athena and Nicky, followed by Oscar.

Unashamedly he found his field glasses and watched. They were skipping down the path leading from the palace. Laughing at their dumb dog. Wearing swimsuits and carrying towels.

Where were his men?

He scoured the cliffs and found two, watching from above. Another was melting into the shadows in the cliff below.

He relaxed. She was safe. She wouldn't be aware of the security men. She could enjoy her swim.

They'd reached the beach. She'd thrown off her towel and was chasing Nicky into the surf.

She was wearing a bikini. Red. He could see every curve of her delectable body.

He wanted her so much… How the hell was he going to control this?

They were swimming now. Nicky was almost as strong a swimmer as his mother. They were stroking out from the shallows, while Oscar barked objections from the shore.

His heart was doing weird things in his chest. He shouldn't be watching.

His son.

His woman?

For the first time since Nikos had found her in Manhattan, she felt at peace.

She'd swum in these waters—not in this cove, but in one like it—as a child. She loved it. In Manhattan, ocean swimming was out of the question, but she used public pools and she'd taught Nicky to swim almost before he could walk. Any time she could she'd take him swimming, and now her salary was good there'd been a couple of magic holidays where she'd been able to introduce him to waves.

He swam as well as she did.

And he loved this. She watched his face as he hit the water—watched his incredulous delight.

She knew he'd been torn since they'd arrived. Telling him Nikos was his papa had pleased him on one level, but he was also confused. He'd responded well initially, but she needed to follow up.

Or…Nikos needed to follow up, she acknowledged, and that scared her. Nikos getting to know her son.

Nikos getting to know *his* son.

They both needed distraction. 'I'll race you to the headland,' she called, and he grinned and put his head down and swam. She could still beat him, she thought, but not for long.

He had Nikos's long, lean body. He had a start on her now—and she'd have a struggle to catch him.

But then… The sound of an incoming boat reverberated through the water. She felt it rather than heard it.

She lifted her head to see…

* * *

Nikos was about to bait a craypot when he heard it. He paused, shielding his eyes from the sun. What the…?

A speedboat was coming in from the north. Fast. This type of boat was almost unknown on Argyros. No islander had money for a boat that didn't pay its keep, and this one looked like a toy of the wealthy. It was built for speed, and right now the thing was almost airborne.

As it grew nearer the noise was almost deafening. It was heading across the entrance to the cove, as if its skipper was intent on circumnavigating the island as some dumb speed challenge.

He didn't like it.

He didn't like it one bit.

Instinctively he reached for the throttle. He was hauling on the rudder. And suddenly he was yelling.

For he knew. Suddenly, sickeningly, he knew.

'Thena,' he yelled. He was hauling his boat around with all the power at his disposal, yelling into the radio. 'Get them out of the water. Get them out…'

Maybe he was mistaken. Maybe they'd pass.

But he was right. At the last minute the boat swerved in towards the beach, its engine still screaming. There were two men crouched low. Dressed in black. Hooded.

There wasn't an identifying mark on the vessel.

All this he saw in the split second before the boat had passed. Heading straight past him, into the cove.

With one aim.

'Thena,' he yelled again, but his boat wouldn't pull round fast enough. The fishing trawler was too big, she wasn't powerful enough, he couldn't get to the woman he loved in time to save her…

* * *

She'd just reached Nicky. She caught his foot and tugged.

He spluttered and came up laughing. 'You little fish,' she said and hugged him—and then glanced sideways at the source of the noise.

And grabbed Nicky, hauling him against her. They hung together in the water, watching. They were close to a beach. They were hardly out of the shallows.

The boat would veer away.

It wouldn't. Instead it turned slightly…

'Dive,' she screamed to her son. 'Dive deep, Nicky, now!'

Nikos was gunning the trawler towards the shore with a speed he'd never pushed it to before. He was yelling uselessly into the radio.

His men were out from their cover, yelling towards the speedboat.

Running down the cliff face, along the beach.

Too late. Too late.

And then the boat was spinning, making a one hundred and eighty degree turn almost on its own axis, and where there'd been woman and child there was nothing.

He was so close… So close…

The wash of the speedboat as it turned had churned the waves, making it impossible to see. It must have hit them square on. There was no sign of them, nothing…

The boat was screaming back past him. One of the hooded figures in the boat had a gun. Nikos saw it, he jerked sideways and felt the zing of a bullet, just touching his cheek.

The other figure grabbed his companion, gesticulating back at the water where they'd come from. Deciding whether to sweep in again.

There was still no sign of them... Dear God, there was no sign.

Nikos was where he'd last seen them now, searching the water. Men were still yelling from the beach. Yelling at him. Yelling at the speedboat. He glanced aside, half expecting it to scream in once more.

Men were wading into the shallows. His men were armed. He saw Zeb raise his rifle and fire.

It was enough. The speedboat's motor screamed to full throttle and it blasted its way out of the cove and around the headland and away.

He didn't see it go. He wasn't looking for the boat.

He was looking for his Thena and he was looking for his son.

Nicky was better than she was at this game. They'd played it over and over—who could go furthest underwater. For the last six months he'd been able to go almost a quarter length of the pool further than she could.

He was one bright kid and he'd caught the urgency. He was pushing himself through the water beside her, at right angles to the boat, towards the rocks.

She'd go as far as he would. She'd go...

Not as far.

She shoved him away from her, gesticulated for him to keep going, and she burst upward.

Into sunlight.

Into air.

The noise of the boat was receding. Instead she heard the heavy thrum of a bigger engine.

She wouldn't go down again. Nicky would surface in seconds—dear God, please let him get far enough away so she could distract whoever it was...the maniac...

A boat was coming nearer. Not a speedboat. Something much bigger. Much more solid.

A fishing boat.

Nikos.

She was there. He saw her surface, glance at his trawler, look frantically around, searching for the threat, searching for her son.

Hell, where was Nicky? The propeller... He cut the motor to silence.

The men on the beach were still shouting.

'Thena,' he called, and she swung round to face him.

'Nicky,' she screamed, and her voice was filled with terror.

But thirty yards away the surface of the water broke. A child's face popped up.

'Miles further,' he yelled to his mother.

And then he burst into tears.

It took him seconds to haul them up, Nicky first, hugging him hard and fast, and Thena after. He hauled her on board, she slithered out of his arms and grabbed Nicky and she held him as if she'd never let go. He looked at them both—Thena and his son—and his world changed.

His trawler was wallowing in the swell close to shore. It'd be grounded if he let it drift any further. It didn't matter—who cared about a boat? He crouched on the deck with them. He put his arms around them and held.

And he knew...

Whatever else happened, whatever Thena decided, whatever course things took from this day, this was his family.

A month ago he'd had his mother and he had Christa.

Now he had Thena and Nicky to love and to cherish as well, and he'd never let them go again.

CHAPTER EIGHT

IT WAS impossible to downplay the seriousness of what had just happened. Or how miserably his measures to keep them safe had failed.

Men were waiting for him on the shore—grim-faced men whose instructions had been to protect this pair and they'd missed an obvious threat.

But it hadn't been an obvious threat. This could never be traced to Demos, he thought. This boat had come from nowhere and had gone to nowhere. It could be traced to no one. Even if Thena and Nicky had died today, it would have been written off as a tragedy. A fool in a fast boat...

A fool who'd gone to lengths not to be recognised. A fool with a lethal boat and a gun...

They'd been lucky. So lucky. That these two could swim like fish and that he'd been there...

There was a jetty by the headland at the side of the cove. He took the boat in and the men were ready to catch his mooring lines, to tell him they'd seen the boat coming and tried to radio him but it had been too late, too late.

They were appalled,

He'd thought Demos was capable of anything to get the Crown. No one had really believed him.

Thena hadn't believed him.

She believed him now. Her face said she knew exactly how close she'd come.

'We'll get you up to the palace,' he said gruffly. He put out a hand to help her to her feet.

She didn't take it.

She was trembling. He wanted to take her in his arms and hold her for ever. But she was backing away.

'We're okay,' she said stiffly. 'Nicky, are you okay? Can you walk?'

'Of course I can.' Nicky was recovering more quickly than his mother. Maybe because he hadn't seen the threat for what it really was. 'They were fools,' he said now, indignant. 'They should know not to go so fast near a beach. Can you have them arrested?'

'If they're found,' Nikos said. 'Though I don't have the power to arrest anyone on this island. Your mother can, though.'

She flashed him a look containing a mixture of fear and anger.

'Don't you dare say that. This is it, Nikos. We're going home.'

'The threat will follow you.'

'It won't. We have police in Manhattan.'

'Demos is rich. He can pay…'

'I don't care. I'm not listening. I won't listen.'

'Thena, we'll leave this,' he said softly and he took her hands whether she liked it or not. 'You can't take this in now. Let my men take you up to the palace. I'll meet you there.'

'What are you going to do?'

'I'll contact the authorities on Sappheiros and Khryseis, and on mainland Greece. I'll get out a description of the boat.'

'There are hundreds of pleasure boats like that all along the Greek coast,' one of his men said. 'There's no chance it will be found.'

'I have to try,' he said heavily. 'Thena, please, let my men take you.'

'I will,' she said and tugged Nicky to his feet. 'And then I'm packing. We're leaving for Manhattan tomorrow.'

He ate a cursory lunch with his mother, and checked on Christa, who was happily drawing pictures of herself and her new brother. He told his mother what he needed her to do, he rang Alexandros, and he set a small army in motion. Then he walked slowly across the headland to the palace.

She had to see sense.

She wasn't in her bedroom. He knocked and when there was no answer he went in. No Thena. He walked across to the adjoining bedroom and twisted the handle.

Dressed simply in jeans and a crisp white blouse, her bare feet tucked up under her, she sat in a big squashy armchair, watching over her sleeping son and her sleeping dog.

She put her finger to her lips, then rose and came out to him, closing the door behind her.

'He was more scared than he'll admit,' she said. 'He heard us talking of Demos. There's a picture of him in the downstairs entrance. Nikos asked if that was the man who was trying to kill us.' She shivered. 'He had a cry, but he's had a bit of lunch and we've talked it out.' She managed a smile. 'He's even talking about what we could do to stop him. And we took down Demos's picture and put it in the trash. So he's okay. But the jet lag's catching up with him as well. I'm glad he's sleeping.'

'You should be sleeping as well,' he said, more roughly than he intended, taking in the shadows under her eyes.

'I can sleep tonight. I won't sleep while Nicky needs me.'

'He's asleep now.' He hesitated. 'Thena, we need to talk.'

'I'm not talking. I'm leaving.'

She was leaning on the closed door. Her hair hadn't been brushed since the swim. She'd obviously showered, tugged on her clothes and that had been enough. There were damp tendrils wisping down her forehead. She obviously didn't care. She was concentrating solely on her son.

Did she have any idea how beautiful she was? Last night in her stunning ball-gown, he'd thought she looked magnificent. But magnificent was too small a word, he thought. He didn't have words to describe how she made him feel.

She was leaning against the door as if she was protecting the child within. If anything happened to Nicky…

It didn't bear thinking about. He'd thought if anything happened to Christa he'd be gutted. Now he had more to care about. Christa. Thena. And now his son.

There was no way he could let her go back to Manhattan. He wanted her to stay. He wanted to get to know Nicky properly, as a father should.

And…he wanted this woman. Despite their differences, he wanted her.

But there wasn't time to voice his emotions. Wanting Thena had to wait. They had to avert this threat first.

'I want you to go to the Eagle's Nest,' he told her. 'I want us all to go there. You, Nicky, me and Christa.'

She stared at him in incomprehension. 'The Eagle's Nest…'

'Someone in this castle told Demos you were down at the cove,' he said. 'There are people here I'd trust with my life, but the staff is too big for me to know everyone. Thena, I need time to sort things out, and I won't have you at risk while I do.'

'I won't be at risk. I'll have left.'

'You can't leave.'

'I can.'

'Then you'll be watching over your shoulder for the rest of your life.' He met her gaze with strength and unwavering conviction. 'Thena, if anything happens to you and your son, Demos inherits. He and his friends. If you leave then I can't protect you. And, Thena, I *will* protect you.'

'You're saying this because you want Nicky,' she stammered.

'I'm saying it because you're in danger.' Somehow he maintained that flat convincing tone. 'But I won't lie to you,' he said softly. 'I do want Nicky. He needs a father.'

'He's managed just fine without one until now.' But her voice faltered.

How much had she wanted her own father? he wondered. Athena's father had been a weak-willed man who Giorgos had bullied and finally bribed to leave the island almost as soon as Thena was born. As far as he knew, Thena had never seen him.

What would it be like, to be raised not knowing your father? He couldn't imagine. His own father had died when he was twelve but he was still a huge part of who he was. And he had grandparents, cousins, uncles and aunts…a huge extended family to constantly remind him he was loved.

Thena had been brought up by a single mother. Maybe she didn't see the advantages of family.

Maybe he had to teach her.

'So…why are you saying the Eagle's Nest?' She'd obviously been doing her own thinking. Asking about the Eagle's Nest was a concession that it could happen.

The Eagle's Nest was an exquisite castle, built for the sole use of the King. It sat perched high on cliffs overlooking the ocean. One road ran in along winding cliffs that soared as granite buttresses, and the cliffs themselves seemed to become its walls.

'It's safe,' he said.

'Have you been in it?' she asked incredulously. As kids the place had fascinated them.

'I have,' he told her. 'It's fabulous. We should have seen it for the first time together, Thene. We tried hard enough as kids.'

They had. The Eagle's Nest explained two matching broken bones. One sheer rock face rising from the sea. Two kids daring each other...

'We can drive in now like normal people,' he said.

'Right. No one drives into the Nest like normal people.'

'I guess they don't.' He smiled. 'Thena, come on. Come to the Eagle's Nest with me.'

She was refusing to meet his gaze. She was staring along the hall, as if looking for an escape route. 'What...what possible purpose can we achieve by locking ourselves in the Eagle's Nest?'

'It'll give us time,' he said, softly now. 'That's what we need. Alexandros is flying to Athens tonight to try and find Demos. Unfortunately, we believe it's not just Demos behind this. The money at stake... He's weak-willed, there'll be real power trying to get him set up as puppet ruler.'

'I hate this,' she whispered.

'So do I.' He tried to touch her hand but she snatched it away. 'I'd like you to come home with me now and talk to my mother,' he said.

'Your mother?'

He smiled wryly. 'Thena, okay, you don't trust me and why should you? But have you ever had reason to distrust Annia?'

'No, I...'

'Then come. Let her talk to you. Please.'

'She'll talk me into staying.'

'You'll be fearful, whether you go or whether you stay. But

if you stay, you'll be safe. We promise you that. Myself. Alexandros. My mother. We'll be your family, Thene.'

'I don't have a family,' she whispered. 'Except Nicky. How can I trust you?'

'You can.'

She stared at him blindly. 'No,' she said at last. 'Not after…' She faltered and then seemed to make a conscious decision to go on. 'Do you know how terrifying it was being pregnant, alone in New York? Do you know how much I depended on you to follow me? How can I trust you, Nikos?'

He grimaced. Christa. Marika. Always the ghost of that long ago nightmare.

But now wasn't the time to talk of the past. He wasn't sure if there ever would be a time, but for now he had to move on.

'What happened in the past is in the past,' he said. 'Maybe we need to remember the time before…before Christa and Nicky were born. We talked of this when we were kids. We wanted this island to prosper. We both wanted it.'

'That was kids. Dreaming.'

'It might have been, but now we can make it a reality.' He took her hands and held them, whether she willed it or not. But she made no move to withdraw.

'Thena, I believe if you leave the island now, then Demos will win. He'll threaten Nicky, you'll cave in to his demands and he'll end up as Crown Prince. I will not stand by and let that happen.'

'You want to be Crown Prince yourself.'

'I want to change this island,' he admitted. 'I won't lie to you. I want this island to be safe and prosperous. I ache for it. But you've known this. You've known it's who I am.'

'I did think I knew you,' she whispered. 'But Marika…she stopped me knowing you.'

'She was my wife for less than a year.'

'It doesn't matter how long she was your wife. I thought you loved me.'

'I did,' he said softly. 'I always have.' He met her gaze directly, refusing to let her look away. 'I believe I still do.'

'No.' She tugged her hands back. 'Stop it, Nikos. Don't you dare say you love me. I have to leave.'

'You can't leave,' he said steadily. 'Not yet. Okay, forget the emotion. Concentrate on necessity. Thene, this island needs you.'

Maybe he shouldn't be throwing this at her, he thought ruefully, but if she was only part of the Athena he remembered then she'd have to share this love. This passion.

'Look at this palace, Thene—look at it,' he told her. 'It's fabulous and if it was restored…the royal family could use part of it, but what a wonderful public place it would be. Alexandros is doing it on Sappheiros. I want to do it, too.'

'You have it all planned.'

'Not me,' he said. 'Us. We dreamed it, Thene. We walked this island as kids and we wanted it.'

'We were kids.'

'And it was dreams,' he said. 'But Giorgos's death without an heir means those dreams can be a reality. Would you willingly stop them happening by handing over to Demos? Does your career mean so much to you that you'd walk away again? That you'd put Nicky's life at risk in doing so?'

'That's not fair.'

'It's not,' he said steadily. 'Life's not. But this is your second chance. Trust me. Move into the Eagle's Nest until we sort Demos out. Put your career on hold. This time it's not just yourself you're choosing for; it's for your son and it's for the whole island.'

'You think I chose last time?' she whispered.

'When you left…' He frowned. 'Of course you did.'

'I had to go.' She bit her lip and closed her eyes. She was trying desperately to make her muddled mind think.

If he was right…if she really was in danger, and after this morning she had to believe him, then maybe she didn't have the luxury of choice

But to trust him…. There were still so many questions she needed answered.

'So…so where does the money come from?' she asked. 'You came to Manhattan to find me. You obviously paid for these security guards. I know your fishing pays—but does it pay that much?'

He smiled at that. 'It does,' he said. 'I've turned into a businessman. When you have a daughter to care for and there's nothing else to distract you, it's amazing how much energy you can put into a passion. I'm a rich man, Thena. But, even if I wasn't… I'm not in this alone. Alexandros cares for these islands, and so does Stefanos. We'll do whatever it takes to protect our own.'

'Your own being Christa.'

'I meant the islands,' he said, softly now and steadily. 'But yes, Christa, too. I know you feel betrayed by her existence and I'm sorry you feel that way. But I make no apologies for her existence. Nothing gets in the way of what I feel for my daughter. But it doesn't make one speck of difference to what we're planning. It's only… You need to be secure and I need to know my son. Where I go, Christa goes. So we'll make it a family holiday if you like. You, me, Nicky and Christa. Oh, and Oscar bringing up the rear.'

She stared up at him. She should pull her hands away, she thought. She should…she should…

'Nothing gets in the way of what I feel for my daughter.'

That was exactly what she felt for Nicky. No apologies. Nothing. Nicky just…*was*.

She gazed at Nikos and he gazed straight back, unflinching. Strong, direct, secure. Demanding she do what was best for the island. Demanding he get to know Nicky.

Declaring his love for his daughter.

'You should be Crown Prince,' she whispered. 'I've never really belonged here anyway. You've always been the people's prince.'

'You don't give yourself credit,' he said. 'You're the true princess.'

'By an accident of birth. Your mother was a princess. If things had been different, you could have inherited the title.'

'I didn't,' he said flatly. 'I don't want it. Why the hell would I?'

Because it'd keep me safe, she thought. Because it would let me get on with my life.

'It doesn't matter,' she said, suddenly weary. 'Okay. I'll stay. I'll stay until Demos is…I don't know… How can you defuse a threat like that? It might take years. It'll ruin my career.'

'You wanted to write a book.'

'Don't even go there,' she whispered. 'You've just told me I have to sacrifice my job because of this island. Don't trivialise it.'

'I wouldn't, Thene.'

'And don't call me Thene.'

'How can I not?' he said. His hold on her hands tightened. 'Athena, then,' he said softly and smiled. 'I know this isn't what you want but we'll make it work, somehow.'

'You did already,' she said steadily. 'More than you can imagine. But in not telling you about Nicky then I hurt you, too. So let's stick to practicalities. Like drying my hair. And agreeing that we sleep in bedrooms separated by at least two kids. Last night you kissed me…we kissed…and it scared me witless. I lost control and I will not go there again. So I control the locks. If I wish to leave I can at any time. I agree to stay at the Nest for a week and then we'll reconsider. That or nothing.'

'Fine,' he said, and rose. 'I'll go home and tell Annia.'

Her eyes flared in sudden panic.

'Nikos…'

'You're safe,' he told her and, before she knew what he was about, he'd placed his fingers under her chin and kissed her lips. It was a feather kiss, over before it was begun. 'Two of my cousins are at the head of the stairs and they'll stay on guard until we move. I promise you're safe.'

'For how long?'

'If I have my way you'll be safe for ever,' he said, and he said it as a vow. 'What's mine I keep.'

Mine? Was he talking about Nicky? But, before she could respond, he'd kissed her again, harder this time, a kiss to seal a vow.

'I'll be back in a couple of hours to collect you,' he said. 'Me and Christa. But now I need to organise a supply of dog food and a surfboard. How safe does that sound?'

He smiled, then he turned and strode down the hallway, with Athena staring blindly after him.

He'd agreed she could be in control.

She wasn't even close to being in control.

She went back into the bedroom, and she started to shake.

She'd just agreed to move into the royal retreat with Nikos.

Nikos, the sexiest man in the known universe. The people's

prince. A fisherman, a businessman. A man who ordered security, who'd saved her life this morning, a man who knew how to protect his own.

She took a couple of deep breaths and tried to steady herself.

Was she overreacting? Maybe she should stop being a drama queen, she told herself. She'd be moving under the umbrella of his protection, for as long as it took to defuse the threat. That was all. Then she'd go back to Manhattan and start her life again.

She looked over to the bed. Her small version of Nikos was still fast asleep.

She wasn't overreacting. The threat this morning had been real and dreadful.

Nikos had saved their son as well.

She closed her eyes—and then suddenly she opened the door again. She flew down the corridor. Down the great marble staircase. Past the two burly fishermen on the stairs. Nikos was already at the grand entrance, striding down to the forecourt.

'Nikos?'

He paused and turned. 'Thene?'

She stopped. He was maybe twelve stairs down from her. She wasn't going any closer.

But she'd run after him for a reason and that reason still held.

'I didn't say thank you,' she said. 'You saved our lives.'

'You saved your own lives by diving.'

'If you and your men hadn't been there…we couldn't have stayed under for ever.'

'Don't think about it,' he said gently. 'Put it behind you.'

'I will,' she said. 'But that doesn't mean…it doesn't mean I don't feel…'

'I don't think we're supposed to feel,' he said dryly. He

raised his hand in a mock salute and turned again, striding down the remaining steps two at a time.

And then he stopped. He swung round to face her.

'Hey,' he said suddenly. 'Come with me and see my mother. We need to tell her what we're planning, and you haven't seen her since we got back.'

'I don't think…'

'Don't think,' he said. 'She's not so scary.'

'I know. I…'

'Nicky's asleep. He's likely to stay that way. My cousins are here watching over him. If you like, you can ask Mrs Lavros to sit with him and phone you the moment he wakes up.' He held out his hand and smiled. 'So Nicky's safe. I promise. And you know my mother would love to see you.'

She looked at his outstretched hand. The urge to take it was almost irresistible.

The urge to trust him was irresistible.

'Why wasn't your mother here last night?' she asked.

'She stayed home and cared for Christa. And she was putting baklava into the oven when I left her this morning.'

Baklava. Nikos's mother's baklava.

'I shouldn't,' she whispered.

'Got you.' He was grinning. 'No one can resist my mother's baklava.'

'For an hour, no more.'

'Excellent,' he said and his hand stayed outstretched.

She walked slowly down the steps towards him. She spent most of the time on the way down staring at that hand.

She shouldn't. She should not.

This was Nikos, taking her to his mother's to eat baklava as he'd done a thousand times before. The temptation to slip back into that time—that life—was irresistible.

'I'll…I'll talk to Mrs Lavros.'

'Already done,' he said, and called to one of his relatives, who was watching from the top step. 'Joe, can you ask Mrs Lavros to watch over Nicky—ring me the moment he wakes?'

'Consider it done,' the man said and disappeared.

'Are you sure you can you trust Joe?'

'He's my cousin,' he said and grinned. 'My father had eight siblings. Half the islanders are my blood relatives.'

'You should so be the prince here.'

'I don't need to be. Not if you stay.'

And his hand was still outstretched. He was still waiting.

Trust wasn't black and white, she thought. Christa's birth meant that on a personal level she couldn't trust this man. But as guardian of this island…as someone she'd hand over the mantle of rule… Yes, she did trust him.

His hand was still outstretched.

Trust… It was a relative thing. She could trust a little. Just a little. Starting now.

Okay. She would.

She stepped down towards him and put her hand in his and he led the way out of the palace grounds.

He hadn't brought a car so they walked as they'd walked so many times before, along the cliff path leading from the palace to the tiny hamlet where Nikos had lived all his life.

Apart from their disastrous attempt to swim, this was the first time she'd been out of the palace grounds since her arrival. She'd forgotten how beautiful the island was. Or maybe she'd blocked it out, too painful to remember.

It was picture-postcard perfect. Houses clung precariously to the cliff face. The cliffs seemed to be almost stepped down to the sea, with tiny jetties jutting out into the water at their base. Boats swung at anchor; there were a couple tied up at the jetties. Fishermen were tossing their catch to brawny helpers, loading it into trucks for the local market.

'We should be exporting,' Nikos said conversationally as they reached the cliff path. She was so aware of his hand holding hers that she could think of nothing else, but he seemed perfectly at ease. 'This place is alive with fish—we could make a great case for a cannery. As it is, most of the fishermen only catch what the local market can absorb.'

'So what about you?' she managed. She should tug her hand away. But it felt too right. It felt too…good.

'My boats are bigger. We can take our catch directly to the mainland.'

'Which made you independent of Giorgos?' His hold was doing strange things to her. She was slipping into the skin of the girl she had once been—the girl she thought she'd left behind for ever.

'Almost,' he said. 'Though he was always a threat.'

That shook her out of her preoccupation. She knew Giorgos's threats only too well. Should she tell him why she'd left the island all those years ago? Should she share the terror that had made her run?

Why?

If she told him…maybe it would make him feel better about her, but it could never alter what she felt in return.

He was silent beside her. They'd always been able to do this, she thought. Talk when there was a need to talk but otherwise relax with each other so words weren't necessary.

Comfortable in each other's company.

'I do need to get to know Nicky,' he said finally into the silence, as if this was simply an extension of his thoughts. 'You realise he's heir to the throne.'

She hadn't thought this through. 'I guess he is,' she whispered, and the thought of a grown-up Nicky taking control of these islands was almost overwhelming.

Maybe she did need to accept the throne. Maybe she had a duty to make these islands safe—for Nicky.

He should inherit from his father, she thought. And then, she thought, maybe he will. He loves boats. Maybe he'll own a fishing fleet like his father.

Maybe he should grow up here. Maybe it was her duty to keep him here.

There were too many maybes to take in.

They rounded the bend on the headland and Nikos's home was in view. And here was another gut wrench.

Nikos's family home was a cottage, tucked into the cliff tops, surrounded by scores of craypots in various stages of building or repair. Two wooden boats, both decrepit, lay upside down. Tomatoes were growing between the boats and runner beans were climbing over them. A big wooden table lay under straggly olive trees and a couple of faded beach umbrellas were giving shade to hens. It should be a mess—but Athena drew breath with delight.

Home.

And when Nikos opened the back door and ushered her in, the feeling of home became almost overwhelming. The door opened straight into the kitchen. Annia was at the table, her hands covered with flour. She glanced up as Athena entered and gave a cry of delight. Athena was promptly enveloped in a floury hug, as wide as it was sincere.

How long since she'd been hugged like this? She hugged Annia back and felt tears sting behind her eyes.

These were her people. This was her island. How could she have walked away ten years ago and not look back?

She hadn't had a choice. She's known it then and she knew it now. But it felt so good to be here.

'She needs feeding, Mama,' Nikos said. 'Look how skinny she is. How goes it, sweetheart?'

For Christa was at the table. She had a pile of dough and was shaping it into balls.

'I'm cooking,' she told her father proudly. 'You will like my cooking.'

'I will.' He swung her out of her chair, hugged her and set her down again, then straddled a kitchen chair and snagged a taste of whatever was in his mother's mixing bowl.

Athena looked blindly down at him, still fighting tears. Everyone trusted this man. He loved his family. He could never betray them.

How could he have betrayed her so badly?

Something of her emotions must be showing, for Annia was suddenly pulling out a chair and pushing her down.

'You've had a terrifying morning,' she said, peering into her face. 'Word's gone right round the island. That Demos…' She shook her head but she was still looking at Athena. Searching for trouble—and obviously finding it. 'You've had a hard time, my Athena. Ten years of hard time?'

And then she moved straight to the big question. The one Athena had known would be asked. 'And…I have a grandson?' she said tentatively. 'That's what they're saying here. Everyone's saying it. That your son is also Nikos's son. I've asked Nikos and he says I need to ask you. So I'm asking you. Is your Nicky my grandson?'

There was no way she could answer this except with the truth. 'He is,' she said and she didn't look at Nikos. She couldn't.

'Well,' Annia said, and put her floury hands on her hips. Her bosom swelled with indignation. 'You bore my grandson

and didn't let us near? You were alone and you didn't tell us?
I would have come. In a heartbeat I would have come.'

No, you wouldn't, she thought. You would have been
helping Marika with Christa. Two grandchildren within three
months. She wanted to yell it at Nikos. Scream it at him.

But Christa was there, happily moulding dough, and
neither she or Annia deserved to be hurt.

Annia held a special role on the island—royal but not
royal. She was Giorgos's sister. There'd been twenty years'
age difference and mutual dislike between brother and sister,
she'd married a fisherman and she'd stepped out of the royal
limelight, but she still knew more than most what royalty
meant to the islanders.

She'd have made a good Crown Princess herself, Athena
thought as she sat at the kitchen table she'd sat at so many
times before. With her earthy good sense—and with her
fabulous son who could have stepped into the role as his right.

'Leave her be, Mama,' Nikos said shortly. 'It's past history.
I'm taking Thene and Nicky and Christa…to the Eagle's Nest.'

Annia's face stilled. She looked from Athena to Nikos and
back again. And then she smiled.

'To the King's love nest?'

'Mama…'

Her smile was broadening. 'Okay, okay, I'll forget it's
other name. So… You're going to the Eagle's Nest—why?'

'To keep Thena safe until we find a way to control Demos.'

Her smile faded for a moment. 'A good idea,' she whispered. 'You'll be safe there.' And then her eyes twinkled into
another smile. 'And maybe while you're there you can enjoy
it. I was there as a child, with my father, the old King. My
Mama showed me their bedroom. It was the closest place to
heaven a woman could get, she told me, and it's one of the

only regrets I had in marrying your father—that I never got to sleep in that bedroom.'

Then, as Nikos looked bemused, she took Athena's face in her floury hands and kissed her. 'You make sure you enjoy it,' she said. 'And enjoy my oh-so-serious son and make him less serious.'

'I… I'm only staying…'

'Until the island is safe,' Annia finished for her. 'How long is a piece of string?' She smiled. 'You and Nikos… You and Nikos. I suppose the answer to your problems hasn't occurred to you?'

'Mama…' Nikos said again, and his mother kissed him.

'Enough. It's occurred to me—ever since I heard Athena was coming home it's occurred to me. And I'm sure it's occurred to you too, for I'm sure neither of you is stupid. But I will say nothing. So Athena…you want some baklava? It's almost cooked.'

'I…no.'

For she was starting to feel overwhelmed. The domesticity. The gentle, loving teasing. The innuendoes of a relationship with Nikos.

The feeling of being on the outside looking in. She'd hated it all her life and she hated it now.

Once upon a time she'd thought she could find her own place within this circle. It wasn't possible, and Annia's tentative suggestion that she might still was threatening to break her heart.

Annia and Christa—and Nikos—were gazing at her now with various levels of interest and of concern. She didn't want their concern.

She didn't know what she wanted.

Or she did but there was no way in the wide world she'd admit it.

'I need to go back to Nicky,' she said, standing so fast she almost tipped her chair.

Nikos stood and caught it as it fell. 'Problem?'

'I…no. I shouldn't have left him.'

'You know he's not awake yet.' He gestured to the phone on his belt. 'They'd have contacted me.'

'I still need to go.'

'Without baklava?'

'Without anything,' she said and she sounded desperate, she knew, but there wasn't anything she could do about it. It was like claustrophobia, only worse. This kitchen table, this man, this family… They were a dream she'd had since she was eight years old, and twenty years on she wasn't one step closer to achieving it. And now she'd be trapped on this island for heaven knew how long, still on the outside looking in.

She felt sick and sad and empty.

'Thena, don't look like that,' Nikos said, and her eyes flew to his and held. He looked… He looked as if he really cared.

He looked as he'd looked when she'd loved him.

She had to get out of here. Now.

'I'll walk you home,' he said as she backed to the door. Annia and Christa were looking at her with concern and confusion. They might well be confused, she thought. She was so confused she might as well share.

'I'm so sorry,' she whispered to Annia. 'We messed it, Nikos and I. But please…don't hope. Don't tease. It's too late to heal it. You know I should have no right to the throne. My rights are an accident of birth. It's you and Nikos… It should be you and Nikos. I've just got to figure a way around it. Thank you, Annia. Thank you for everything. And I'm so sorry.'

And she walked out of the cottage before they could say a word. She closed the door and she started to run.

* * *

'You should go after her.'

Nikos stared at the closed door and his mother's voice came as if from a long way off. 'She doesn't want me.'

'I think she does.'

He shook his head. 'She left, Mama. Ten years ago she left, and she had my son and didn't tell me. She's strong and independent and willful. And she wants to pursue her career.'

'She doesn't look like a woman whose career is everything.' She hesitated. 'Nikos, can I ask…? Maybe I should have asked this ten years ago. I did think of asking…but I knew it was none of my business. But now… When I see Athena so distressed… You and Marika…' She paused. 'Why did you and Marika marry before a Justice of the Peace and not a priest?'

He frowned. 'Marika was pregnant.'

'Father Antonio would still have married you.'

'Neither of us wanted to be married in the church.'

'I know that,' she said thoughtfully. 'We were upset about it—Marika's mother and I. But you were both adamant. Why were you so adamant?'

'Mama, enough. There are so many arrangements to make…'

'Of course there are,' she said softly. And then she smiled. 'Christa, what is it that you're making?'

'A lady,' Christa said. The dough now had a small blob, a bigger blob underneath, two arms, two legs and what might have been a skirt.

'That's lovely,' Annia said and beamed. 'You make yourself a lady. Nikos, you go and make one safe. And if you can make both of you happy in the process… It's time Father Antonio was put to work.'

CHAPTER NINE

THEY took the limousine again, only this time Nikos was driving. Nicky and Christa were delighted to see each other—far too immersed in the novelty of each other to notice scenery. Athena had her nose against the window the whole way.

She and Nikos had been here before—as kids they'd explored most parts of the island, both on foot and on the back of a saddle-tough pony—but they'd never got past the gates of the Eagle's Nest. The gates were twelve feet high and padlocked, with locks big enough to deter the most intrepid of explorers. Mind, a twelve feet high fence wasn't actually what had stopped them. What had stopped them was the pack of dogs left loose to roam the grounds at will.

'So…um…where are the dogs?' Athena asked nervously as the gates swung open at their approach.

'There was only one left when Giorgos died,' Nikos said over his shoulder. 'The old groundsman took him home with him. He says he's turned out to be a pussycat. Do you think you can be royal without killer Dobermans?'

'I'll try,' she said magnanimously, and found herself smiling. Despite the trauma of the morning, despite the confusion of her visit to Annia, suddenly there was a frisson of excitement.

She felt eight years old again, nose pressed against the twelve foot gate—and suddenly the gate swung open.

'Cool, isn't it?' Nikos said, and it was as if he'd guessed her thoughts. 'The place has always been kept in readiness for a royal visit of up to a dozen guests. So there should be room for us.'

'We'll need four bedrooms,' she said as a knee-jerk reaction. He met her gaze in the rear-vision mirror and grinned. And there it was again. That smile. Pure mischief.

The smile of the Nikos she'd once known…

They drew up before the main entrance. Here again were servants. Two servants.

Joe and Mrs Lavros from the palace.

'I figured we'd go with staff we know,' he told her.

'I can make my own bed and we can make our own sand-wiches,' she said, lightness fading. 'Why do we need anyone?'

'I need Joe,' he said flatly.

Once again he met her gaze and the message was unmis-takable. Her lightness faded. Joe. Nikos's cousin. Big, burly and totally dependable. Security.

'And Mrs Lavros makes baklava just like Mama does,' he said. 'No aspersions on your cooking, Princess…'

'You think I can't cook?'

'I didn't say that.'

'Mama makes great hamburgers,' Nicky said, leaping to her defence. Then he hesitated. 'One day last winter we made… bak…bakla…what you were just talking about…'

'Let's not go there,' Athena said hurriedly. Nikos grinned— and Nicky grinned with him—and she suddenly had two guys with identical smiles and it was doing her head in.

'So how did your mama's baklava turn out?' he asked.

'We ate it with spoons,' Nicky said, still grinning. 'It was good but it didn't look like the picture in the recipe book. And Mama had to spend half an hour scrubbing honey off the oven.'

'I rest my case,' Nikos said, opening the door of the car. 'Mrs Lavros is here to stay. Okay, kids, it's yours to explore.'

The kids and Oscar tumbled out of the limousine. Mrs Lavros and Joe smiled a welcome and took themselves off, and they were alone on the steps of a fairy tale. Two kids, two adults and one dog. Her family, Athena thought, and then stomped on the thought and concentrated on this truly excellent building.

It was a true fairy tale castle. Built two hundred years ago by a mad monarch with delusions of grandeur, all white stone, turrets and towers, it was like a sugar confection, a magic, secret fantasy.

'Wow,' Nicky breathed, awed. He was standing dumbstruck, staring upwards, seeing a white flag with blue stars and pale yellow stripes fluttering from the battlements. 'What's the flag for?'

'It means the Crown is in residence,' Nikos said.

'The Crown…'

'That would be your mother. Welcome to the Eagle's Nest, Princess.'

'Don't…don't call me that.'

'We don't have a choice,' he said. 'It's time you acknowledged it. This is your place, Princess. You've come home.'

It was fabulous. The more they saw…it was more and more wonderful. The kids whooped through the castle with joy and wonder, and Nikos thought he'd been right to bring them here. He'd been right to include Christa.

The terrors of this morning had faded to nothing for Nicky. He was a kid in a fairy tale castle, he had an adoring little sister at his heels, he had his dog.

He had his mother.

He had his father.

All was right in his little boy's world, and Nikos watched and listened to his excitement and found a peace settling on his heart that had been missing for ten years.

For ten years Thena had been gone. He had his family here—his daughter, his mother, his aunts and uncles and cousins. He'd built his fishing fleet, he'd succeeded on his own terms, he'd almost thought he had enough.

He hadn't. Now, standing by Thena's side as the kids led them on a tour of exploration, he knew his life had suddenly got better.

How to make it complete?

Ten years ago Thena had thought her career was more important than life on this island. He had one more chance to make her see, he thought. To make her understand how wonderful it could be. To see how right it was.

The castle was three storeys high, with the 'Eagle's Nest', a tower with parapets, as the fourth floor. The kids were whooping from room to room on the second floor, choosing bedrooms.

'This one's ace,' Nicky breathed as he discovered a vast bedchamber with a huge four poster bed amid a décor that was pure medieval, right down to a set of armour on either side of the windows. Nicky leaped onto the big bed, Oscar and Christa gamely followed, Nicky tugged the gold tassels holding back the curtains and they were enclosed in a vast velvet tent. The adults were left firmly on the outside.

Oscar shoved his nose out to look at his mistress, checked she was still there and then dived back to join the kids.

'Can we sleep in here please, Mama?' Nicky breathed from behind the velvet. 'Can we, can we, can we?'

'I guess we can,' she said dubiously. 'It's a pretty big bed. We'll both fit.'

Nicky's head emerged, astonished. 'I didn't mean you, Mama. I meant me and Christa and Oscar.'

'So take that, Mama,' Nikos said at her side, and found himself smiling. For him too, the fears of the morning were dissipating. He should have brought them straight here, he thought. But then…she'd had to go to the palace. She'd had to turn into a princess so she could lay claim to this place.

'I'll sleep next door,' she said, sounding desperate, and both kids launched themselves out from behind their canopy and onto further exploration.

'Don't choose before you've looked at them all,' Nicky ordered, grabbing his mother's hand and tugging her from the room. 'There might be another one as good as this one.'

There wasn't. Not on this floor. Nicky checked them all and declared them ordinary—bedrooms with French windows and terraces that overlooked the sea, with beds big enough to fit a king and half his courtiers, all were rejected as being not as cool as the one Nicky and Christa had claimed.

'I guess we could share,' Nicky said with magnanimity.

'Nicky, I'll take the one next to yours…'

'There's upstairs,' Nikos said, and Nicky beamed.

'See, Mama, there's upstairs. I like this place. Come on, Christa.'

They were flying upstairs, hand in hand.

Christa had a brother, Nikos thought, stunned, and glanced at Thena and saw she was as stunned as he was.

'I thought this might take years,' he said.

'I didn't… I can't…'

'Though maybe they're like us,' he said. 'We met when we were eight years old and we knew right then that we were going to be best friends. Friends for ever.'

'Don't…'

'We were, Thene,' he said softly. 'We still could be. Surely your career can be redirected. I don't mean give it up entirely. But you've given so much for it already…'

'Don't,' she said again and she was close to tears.

He wouldn't push. He mustn't. He had her here. He had time.

And then there was a whoop of absolute joy from above their heads.

'We've found your bedroom. Come on up. Mama, Papa, come on up.'

Mama, Papa… Nicky had shouted the words as naturally as breathing. *Mama, Papa…*

It took their breath away.

'Shall we go take a look?' Nikos said and put his hand out to her.

She took a deep breath. She stared down at his hand.

And then, deliberately, she put her hands behind her back and walked up the stairs.

There was still so much between them. How did you learn to trust again? No matter how desperately you wanted to…how did you take that leap?

But then she reached the top of the stairs and the door to the third floor bedroom, and she stopped thinking of anything else.

The third storey was part of the tower, narrowing to the nest itself on the fourth floor. The top of the tower was a circular fortification on top of the building where one looked over the parapets to see the entire island. Or that was what she'd imagined. She'd just never imagined what lay beneath.

All her childhood she'd seen this part of the castle—a stark white tower seemingly growing from the crags of the northern highlands. The tower could be seen from all over the island, from out at sea, maybe even from the far islands of Sappheiros and Khryseis.

It was almost dusk. The islands, all white stone cliffs and blue-green mountains, glittered like jewels reflecting the tangerine rays of the setting sun. The sea stretched out in every direction, reflecting the sunset. Below them were fishing boats, heading for harbour, heading for home.

She could see everything, because, apart from the tiny vestibule allowing access, there was nothing between them and a three hundred and sixty degree view of sea and sky.

She was on top of the world.

There were no lights, she saw. Instead there were candles. Hundreds of candles, set into wall embrasures. But they weren't lit yet—they didn't need to be. The setting sun gave a tangerine glow to the whole world.

Beneath her feet the carpet was lush and deep, but apart from the view the focus of the room was the bed. How had they ever got it up here? It must have been built on site.

It was a full circle, a great island in the centre of the room. As big as two king-sized beds, it was made up with vast antique quilts of deep crimson and lovely faded silver. The silver and the crimson were caught up in cushions, hundreds of cushions, soft, squishy. Nicky had already picked up an armload and was tossing them indiscriminately at Christa and at Oscar.

Christa was giggling and tentatively tossing a cushion back.

But then Nicky realised Nikos and Athena were at the door, staring in with stunned amazement. 'Look at the sky,' he demanded and grabbed Christa's hand, and they clambered onto the great bed, lay on their backs and gazed upward.

Thena gazed up as well.

And gasped.

The ceiling was a vast glass dome, sweeping upward as

part of the great central tower. It was one enormous window, built of hundreds and hundreds of lead framed glass panels forming one magnificent window to the sky.

The setting sun was glittering in from the windows so Athena's attention had been distracted to the lower level. But now… She gazed up in awe at a vast expanse of sky, the soft scudding clouds of sunset and the first hint of the evening star.

'This is so cool,' Nicky breathed. 'It hasn't got a tent like our bedroom but it's cool anyway. It's like flying.'

She could see the simile. In this room she was on top of the world. She was almost floating.

'Will you and Papa sleep in here?' Nicky demanded and she came down to earth fast.

'I…no. I'll sleep next to your bedroom.'

'It's okay, Mama,' Nicky said magnanimously. 'Christa and Oscar and I don't mind if you sleep up here. I won't be scared if I have Christa. And you won't be scared if you have Papa.'

Papa. The word was part of his vocabulary already.

That was enough to choke her right up, to make her world twist from its axis. Nicky had a papa.

She glanced at Nikos and his eyes were hooded and enigmatic. But she knew this man. She knew this expression. It meant he was struggling hard not to show emotion.

He wanted his son. He was falling in love with her Nicky.

Her son had a father.

Her son was telling her she had to sleep with Nikos.

'Nikos and I don't share a bedroom,' she said, too curtly.

'Why not?' Both the children were gazing at them now. They'd found this room for them. For a moment Athena thought they'd taken it personally if she didn't accept their find as a delight.

'Thena can sleep in here,' Nikos said, and his voice was as

guarded as his expression. 'She probably snores. Grown ups snore a lot. If you guys don't mind, I'll sleep down in one of the downstairs bedrooms so her snores don't drive me crazy.'

'I don't think she snores,' Nicky said doubtfully.

'She has the look of a snorer.'

'Hey.' She was torn between laughter and tears. Laughter was by far the preferred option but tears were certainly close.

'What do snorers look like?' Nicky asked.

'They have fat noses,' Nikos said and looked up to the windows and stroked his own nose. 'As opposed to you and me, Nicky. We have the Andreadis nose. Thin, straight and exceedingly handsome.'

'I do not have a fat nose,' Athena exclaimed.

'Snub, I'd say,' Nikos said indulgently. 'Cute, but definitely not aristocratic.'

The conversation had suddenly veered away from snoring—away from bedrooms—which was definitely a relief.

'I have your nose?' Nicky was supremely unaware of the emotional undercurrents running between the adults. He was concentrating on himself, and on Nikos, and on this new relationship which he'd hardly had a chance to explore. 'And I have your cowlick. And I don't get seasick.'

'So you're a true Andreadis.'

'But I'm Nicholas Christou.'

'Christou's your mother's name,' Nikos said. 'If I'd married your mother you'd be an Andreadis.'

'I like being a Christou.'

'I expect you do,' Nikos said easily but Athena's mind had taken off again.

Christa… Christou…

She was Athena Christou. Something occurred to her which hadn't had time to surface until now. But it hit her then.

How had Marika felt about her daughter being named so closely after Nikos's ex-girlfriend?

Maybe neither of them had ever thought of it. Maybe Marika had never seen her as a threat.

It was so long ago. Why did it still have the capacity to sting now?

'So what do we do now?' Nicky said, moving on.

'Supper and bed?' Nikos suggested and Nicky's face fell. So did Christa's. She'd been gamely following the conversation and she got this.

'Play,' she said very firmly, and Oscar wagged his tail in agreement.

Athena almost groaned. She was so tired she could hardly stand. The emotional strain of the last twenty-four hours was added to sheer physical fatigue. But, of course, Nicky had slept this afternoon and he hadn't spent last night dancing. He was raring to go.

'Tell you what,' Nikos said, and he glanced at Athena with that careful, assessing look she was starting to know. And to fear? The look that said he knew what she was thinking. 'How about we have a light supper and then I take Christa and Nicky down to the beach for a swim before bed?'

'Is it safe?' she demanded before she could stop herself and then could have kicked herself. For Nicky's face registered alarm, and he moved fast to stand beside her.

And Nikos got that, too. 'You needn't worry,' he said, gently but firmly. 'Nicky, what happened this morning will not happen again. We have lookouts now, watching the island's waters. And under this castle, down a secret little path known only to us, there's a tiny cove, rimmed by reefs. The water inside the reef is calm and clear and is only just deep enough for swimming. It's full to the brim with fish—no one's ever been allowed to swim here and the fish show no fear. No boat can get over the reef to reach here. Do you trust me enough to take you there without your mother?'

And it wasn't up to her. It was Nicky himself who decided.

'Yes,' he said, firmly and surely, and he moved confidently away from her side. 'We trust Papa, don't we, Mama?'

'I…yes,' she faltered and was saved from having to say anything more by the whoop of delight as Nicky took her yes to mean not only that she trusted in Nikos, but also that it was okay to swim after dinner. Without her.

It seemed Nicky was now a part of Nikos's family, whether she belonged or not.

The kids went whooping out of the bedroom, up the last remaining flight of stairs to the parapets that capped the tower. Nikos stayed back. There weren't words to express what either of them were feeling. Or maybe neither of them knew what they were feeling.

There were things to be said but neither of them knew where to start.

Finally he stood aside to allow her to precede him from the room.

'He's safe with me, Thene,' he said softly as she passed him, and she thought, yes, I know he is.

Her son was part of Nikos's family.

And she…she was jealous.

CHAPTER TEN

THEY had supper informally in the ancient kitchen at the back of the castle. It was big enough to feed a small army, Athena thought, but it was still…good. The ancient flagstones, the vast old range sending its gentle heat across the room, the scrubbed copper pans hanging from hooks, lavender hanging in bunches from the beams, windows open to let the sounds of the sea drift in, bird feeders hung in the windows…

'This castle doesn't look as if it's been deserted for years,' she said, puzzled, and Mrs Lavros nodded.

'It hasn't. Though Giorgos didn't come here we've loved it. As we've loved the palace. We always knew you'd come home.'

'And now you have,' Nikos said gently and raised his glass to hers. 'Here's to you, our Princess Athena. Long may she reign over us.'

'I'm not… I can't…' She caught her breath in panic. What was he saying? 'We'll be going back to the States…'

'Not yet, Mama,' Nicky said, and he sounded…scared.

As well he might, Thena thought frantically. Her little boy was frightened of leaving this island now. The only safe place for him was…by Nikos's side.

She glanced up and found Nikos's gaze on her, thoughtful, maybe even stern.

'You can't leave, Thena.'

What was she supposed to say to that? She couldn't think of a thing.

'I'm…I'm tired,' she managed. 'If…if you don't mind, thank you, Mrs Lavros, that was lovely, but I'm really tired. Nicky, when you come back from the swim come and tell me about it.'

'You'll be asleep,' Nikos said, teasing.

'I won't be asleep until I've made sure Nicky is safe,' she said and suddenly she inexplicably felt like weeping. It was so hard. It was so, so hard.

Long may she reign over us?

That sounded awfully lonely from where she was sitting.

She didn't sleep. Lying on the huge bed, looking up at the vast expanse of sky, it was as if she'd forgotten who she really was. She was nothing. Insignificant and lost. If she was confused before, she was even more confused now.

That was bad enough—but how could she sleep when Nikos…when the children were playing on the beach right underneath her windows? She got up and walked over to the window. Floodlights set up on the cliff face meant the sheltered little cove was as safe as in daytime. There were lights out on the water as well, tiny buoys floating on the swell. The bigger surf was caught and contained by the circular reef so the waves within were gentle, the light-buoys floating up and down in synchronisation with the gentle waves.

Christa had a rubber surf mat. She was holding on tight, floating in the shallows, giggling, watching her papa teach Nicky to surf. Nikos had produced his surfboard and was already teaching Nicky to catch the waves.

'When it comes you need to be paddling almost as fast as the wave,' Nikos was saying and a trick of sound made his voice carry all the way up to where she stood. 'Okay, here comes a good one. Paddle, paddle, go!'

The wave caught him, and Nicky hung on for dear life as the wave carried him all the way to the sand.

He stood up, exultant, in the shallows. Big with excitement. 'I caught it. I caught it!'

'We'll have you kneeling on the board by tomorrow,' Nikos said. 'And standing by the end of the week.'

But she'd heard enough.

She turned away and walked back to the too big bed, lay down and stared up at herself. Multiplied by plenty.

'Nicky needs his papa,' she told Jupiter—or was it Venus? 'He should stay here.

'You need his papa.' Right. She was talking to a planet.

It was probably a star, she told herself. Surely it was okay to discuss the meaning of life with a star.

'To stay, I'd have to trust him,' she told…what the heck, Venus.

'I think I do trust him.'

But she—or Venus—was lying.

She might not trust him—but she loved him.

That was the only truth. She'd given her heart away when she was eight years old and she'd never taken it back. But that one dreadful betrayal… It didn't mean she loved him less. It was as if there was some part of her that had got it wrong. She'd trusted him so absolutely that his betrayal had destroyed a part of herself.

She hugged herself and Venus tucked herself behind a cloud in sympathy.

There were still a thousand stars. All wanting to talk to her.

She was never going to sleep in this room.

Where, then? On the same floor as Nikos and the children?

'They're together. I'm on my own,' she whispered and then thought, ooh, who's feeling sorry for herself?

There was a shout of laughter from down in the cove. She climbed out of bed—it was almost a marathon to get to the side—and walked back out on the balcony.

They were playing Falafel.

It was a game she and Nikos had played as kids.

When Annia made falafels she formed her little balls of chickpeas and parsley into balls and then rolled them in flour until they were thoroughly coated.

So Athena and Nikos would swim until they were wrinkly as prunes, then race up the beach and roll and roll in the dry sand until every inch of them was coated. Then run round being falafels. They were doing it now—two kids and Nikos. Two kids and their papa.

Completely coated in dry sand, they stood—then Nikos spread his arms and moaned like a great sandy spectre and started chasing them.

The children squealed in delight. The beach at dusk…she'd always thought it was the most magical of times, and here was her son, learning about it for himself. With his papa.

Nicky ran and ran. Christa was far easier to catch but Nikos made it seem as if it was just as hard to catch her. Finally he had them, a child under each arm, and was staggering back to the water to wash them off. Oscar brought up the rear, barking his delight.

And suddenly she was crying.

Damn, she was crying.

Nikos looked up from the beach. And saw her.

He stilled. At his feet the children whooped and splashed in the shallows. But Nikos simply stood—and watched.

And, from nowhere, into her heart came the words he'd used so often.

Dare you.

Dare she take a chance? Dare she forget what had happened ten years ago?

Dare she move forward?

It was too soon. It was too fast.

She had to get rid of these stupid, wussy tears.

She turned and started to go inside.

'Thena!' It was a call from the beach, strong and demanding. She should ignore it. She should...

She turned.

He was still watching her.

'Dare you,' he called, and she gave a gasp of fright. What was it about this man? How did he know what was inside her head?

Did he know that she loved him?

She turned and headed back to her bed and her stars and her confusion.

If she talked to a thousand stars she might just get some answers.

Or not.

She'd left him for a career.

She'd had a career. She'd succeeded on her terms. Surely enough was enough. Surely he could convince her to stay.

He stood in the shallows and watched her back away from the balcony, head indoors and haul the French windows closed after her.

He'd swear she was crying.

'Does your mama cry much?' he asked Nicky conversationally, as if this was a guy to guy discussion of the female sex.

'Only when she thinks I'm asleep,' Nicky told him.

'So she cries at night?'

'I'm not supposed to know,' Nicky said. 'But sometimes when I snuggle into bed with her in the morning her pillow's soggy.'

'Why do you think she gets sad at night?'

'I used to think it was 'cos she was lonely,' Nicky said. 'But she's got me and she's got Oscar. Only now I know about here…' He stood and gazed around him, a small boy taking in a small boy's heaven. 'Now I think it must be 'cos she was lonely for you.'

'For…for this island, you mean?'

'Mama says things and places don't matter,' Nicky said. 'She says only people matter. So I figure it's you.'

He brought the children up from the cove. Mrs Lavros helped bath them and get them to bed. Athena didn't appear. Nikos half expected Nicky to want his mother, but they discussed it and decided if she hadn't wanted to swim she must be very tired indeed. So Nicky himself decided if he was sleeping with Christa and with Oscar there was no need to disturb her.

So Nikos sat beside their tent-cum-bed and started to read them a story—only Nicky objected.

'I have a book in my bag,' he told Nikos. 'It's really good. Mama lets me read to her. Can I read it to you? Is that okay?'

'Sure,' Nikos said, so he sat and watched as his son read his daughter a bedtime story and it was hard not to tear up himself.

It was Thena who wept, he told himself. Real men don't weep.

What was the concept of a real man?

His father had been a real man. He'd died of a heart attack when Nikos was twelve, and Nikos had adored him.

His father had loved Nikos and had been totally, unconditionally proud of him. Even though he'd been dead for many years, that love lingered on. As did the echoes of his care.

'*Anything happens to me, you care for your mother, Nikos. She's the light of my life. You and your mother... You're my whole heart.*'

A real man had a family and loved them unashamedly. A real man would face any terror to keep that family safe.

His parents had had disagreements—loud disagreements—but they'd never frightened him. Because they'd always ended in exasperated laughter, in hugs, in his father saying, 'Your mother is impossible—an impossible woman—how am I to live with such a woman?'—and then cooking his biggest lobster and opening a bottle of wine and playing music his mother didn't like, too loud.

And his parents dancing and him watching in sleepy contentment until they put him to bed and had the night for each other.

So...so what?

What was between him and Thena...it was a disagreement so enormous that no lobster would be big enough.

But to let that betrayal eat away at them for ever...

Maybe his father would say: 'So what if Thena left you ten years ago? So what if she didn't tell you she had your son? You know your actions must have distressed her unutterably, too.'

He couldn't defend his actions. Was it fair therefore to ask her to defend hers?

What if he could simply say that was past history? Move on.

Move onto family.

To two children. A dog.

To a wife?

Ten years ago he'd asked her to marry him and she'd wept with joy. But things had changed. She no longer trusted him.

If he was to ask her to marry him now…she'd assume it was because of the Crown, that he wanted control.

And maybe he did. If he married her he could keep her safe. It would stop Demos in his tracks. He'd be royal himself.

How could he ask her to marry him?

Christa was already fast asleep. Nicky read on, but his voice was starting to stumble. He lifted the book from Nicky's hands, tucked him under the covers and then thought why not? And he kissed his son goodnight.

Such a little thing—but not small at all. Huge.

How could he ask Thena to marry him?

Dare you?

He left the bedroom and closed the door gently behind him. He turned, and Thena was watching him from the shadows.

He stilled. 'Hi,' he said cautiously.

'Hi, yourself.'

'I thought you were asleep.'

She was ready for bed. She was in a pale blue wrap, floor-length. Bare toes, though. Her curls were a tangle—had she been trying to sleep?

'How can I sleep when I keep thinking of you?' she murmured.

'That'd give anyone nightmares.'

She tried to smile but her smile didn't reach her eyes. 'Nikos…'

'Come up to the tower,' he said and put his hand out to take hers. She looked down at his hand—appeared to think about it—and then placed her hand in his.

A tiny step… Why it made his heard thud…

It did. His heart definitely thudded. Whoa, he was in trouble here.

Dare you?

He led her up the stairs. On the landing that led to her bedroom he swiftly led her past. It was a bit too soon to face that room.

The stairs grew narrower the higher they climbed. The tower was just that, an eyrie built for a birds-eye view of the whole island. The tower narrowed the higher they climbed, so he was forced to fall behind.

He'd read somewhere—where was it?—that gentlemen always followed their ladies upstairs and preceded them down so they could catch them either way.

Their hands were still loosely linked—she didn't seem to want to pull away and he'd have rather died—but what he really wanted to do was pick her up and carry her.

She was climbing before him, in her lovely soft robe, her bare feet on the cold stones—if he carried her, then her feet wouldn't get cold.

But he was aware he was holding his breath. There were so many questions that needed answers, and he thought many of those questions were to be resolved in the next few moments.

He mustn't push too fast. Picking her up and carrying her might panic her and that was the last thing he intended.

And then they were at the top—a circular walk, built as battlements around the central dome. He didn't want to think about the dome. The ceiling to Thena's bedroom. *Thena's.*

All around them stretched the warm Mediterranean night. A great moon hung low on the eastern sky, climbing ponderously upward to join the star-filled heavens. The great galaxy of the Milky Way spread above them, stars beyond and beyond and beyond.

'We used to try and count them,' Nikos said softly, and her hand tightened in his.

'It used to scare me—made me feel so small.'

'And do you feel so small now?'

'Smaller,' she whispered. She was leaning back against him as she gazed out in wonder.

To the west was Sappheiros, the largest of the Diamond Isles. North was Khryseis. The lights from the Far Isles glittered through the night, mysterious and beckoning. Closer to home, they could see the lights of boats, riding at anchor; the tiny lights from cottages spread among the mountains; and in the distance the far-off lights of the royal palace. Her royal home?

'This is yours, Thena,' he whispered softly into her hair. 'It's yours to rule as you will. We always dreamed it would come to you, and now it has. You can't walk away from it now. It's your birthright, your heritage…'

'My duty,' she whispered back, and he thought he heard the first faint trace of acceptance. 'Nikos, I can't do this alone.'

'You won't have to, Princess. I'll be beside you every step of the way. If you can put your career on hold… I know it's so important to you…'

'My career is not important.'

For a moment he thought he hadn't heard right. She was leaning into him, her spine curving against his chest, her dark curls just brushing his chin. She was the loveliest creature. His Thena.

But he had to think past her body. He had to think past what her touch was doing to him.

'You mean…your career isn't important any more?' he asked cautiously.

'It never was.' And then, reluctantly it seemed, she pulled away from his grasp. She turned and leaned on the parapet, as if she needed to see him to make him understand what she wanted to say.

'Don't get me wrong; I always wanted to be a writer,' she

said, and he knew she was struggling against the emotion of the moment to make her voice prosaic. 'I always did and maybe I always will. When I was twelve I wanted to be a cutting edge crime reporter. Then I wanted to be a poet. By the time my mother died I wanted to write a history of this island, an exposé of Giorgos's corruption. I wanted to use my writing to save the world. But then…'

'But then you were offered a cadetship on a fashion magazine in New York.'

'No,' she said, tightly now, as if it was desperately important. 'I was given the cadetship. It was paid for. I was told it had been arranged that I start work in Manhattan in two weeks. I was told my accommodation was paid for. I was given a one way airline ticket and enough money to keep me for a year. and I was told to get off the island and never come back.'

He stared at her. Disbelieving. All the breath seemed to have been sucked from his body. 'By?' But he didn't need to ask.

'By Giorgos, of course,' she said.

'But you didn't have to take it.'

'You think?'

'You could have refused.'

She shook her head. She closed her eyes as if remembering a nightmare and opening her eyes on it would start the horror all over again.

'You were just starting to succeed,' she whispered. 'Since your papa died you'd worked so hard to make your boat support you and your mother. And you were starting to make it prosper. That's what Giorgos was afraid of. You were the son of his sister—a royal from his own line. You were starting to make serious money. And you'd just asked me to marry you. If I married the King's sister's child, there'd be royalty on both sides; two people the locals knew and trusted. Giorgos feared the islanders would rebel. He said I had to follow his orders or he'd dynamite every boat in the harbour and he didn't care much if anyone was on them. And he'd run you and your mother off the island. He said the only way I could prevent that happening was by leaving. So…so I left.'

'Thena…' He moved towards her but her hands were out, as if to fend him off.

'No. There's no use being angry. There's no use being anything.'

'If you'd told me…'

'You would have…done something stupid,' she whispered. 'My hero. My Nikos. I knew…or I thought I knew…that your fury on my behalf would know no bounds. I was afraid of him, I was afraid for you and I was afraid for your mother. So I left. I…I hoped you'd follow. That was dumb. Obviously, there were…things that prevented you leaving. So I started work in New York. A couple of months later I realised I was pregnant. I was lucky enough to find a wonderful landlady. I worked right up until Nicky was born, and when he was two months old I went back. I've worked ever since. So…' She took a deep breath. 'So, yes, I'm proud of my career. I'm proud I supported myself and Nicky. I've even enjoyed a lot of it. But don't say I sacrificed everything for my career. Don't say it, Nikos. Because it's just not true and tonight…tonight I want the past to be over. I want to put history behind us. I want to move on.'

'Thena…' It was a groan of pain.

He didn't know where to go from here. He couldn't think. What she'd gone through. And she'd acted out of love, for him, for everyone.

'Don't,' she said and took his head in both her hands and tugged him forward. 'What's done is done. I can't bear to think of ten years ago. I don't want to think of it and why should I? All I know is that you've come back into my life again. Am I misreading the signs, Nikos, as I misread so badly before? Is it you in there? The Nikos I thought I knew? The Nikos who dared to love me?'

'Who dared…'

'Who dared,' she whispered. 'When all the rest of the island avoided me for fear of Giorgos, you dared to be my friend. And then you dared to love me. I don't know what happened after that. I don't want to know. All I know is that I'm home now, exactly where I want to be, and I'm with the man I want more than anything in the world.' She hesitated. 'And I'm trying really hard not to be forward here, but if you don't kiss me I'll very likely explode, or die of humiliation, or…'

Or he'd never know. Because enough was enough. He had her in his arms and he was tugging her close with ruthless strength. She was yielding, her lips were meeting his, her hands were tugging him close, closer, deepening the kiss so the night disappeared, melting into the star-filled sky, transforming with a wonder he thought he'd lost and was now magically his again.

Thena. His Thena. Trusting as she'd trusted once before. Weighing up the sorrow, the hurt he knew he'd caused her with the birth of Christa, with his marriage to Marika, and moving on.

Forgiving…even when she didn't know the truth.

He loved her so much.

He pulled back a little so he could read her face. And what he saw there made his heart twist within him.

She was looking at him as if she loved him.

She loved him. She must love him. That one betrayal had been an aberration—not her Nikos. The Nikos she'd known then could never have done such a thing.

And, even if he had, the Nikos kissing her now could surely never repeat such a betrayal.

But right here, right now, she no longer cared. Nikos was right here, right now, his eyes dark and fathomless, waiting for her to say what she needed to say—if she could ever figure out what that was.

Okay, say it, she told herself. Just say it.

'So…so this is the most romantic place in the Eagle's Nest?' she managed.

'It's not,' he said, fast and sure. 'It's a place of stone and parapet and view—which is all very well if you want stone and parapet and view, but if you want more…'

'If I want more?'

His dark eyes flashed with something she wasn't sure of. Surprise? Laughter? No. Something much, much deeper.

'I'd surely give it,' he said softly. 'But I've hurt you so badly in the past.'

'You have.'

Years ago she'd fallen in love with this man. He'd betrayed that love in the worst possible way, but she'd moved on, she'd grown up and she'd got herself a life. She'd become independent of both Nikos and his island.

But now… She wanted to trust as she'd trusted so long ago. Innocence regained.

Stupid concept, but…

'You think we could maybe learn to trust each other?' Nikos asked, and it was as if he was following her thoughts.

'After so long?'

'You bore my son,' he said steadily. 'You had him alone and I can't begin to imagine how that must have been for you. I can't bear to think that you couldn't contact me—that you couldn't tell me of his existence. But now…I'm finding there are more things I can't bear. Like the thought of you leaving. Once you dreamed of writing freelance. Is there any way you could do that here?'

'So...so you'll have more time with Nicky?'

He placed his hands on her shoulders and he looked at her as if he could read behind her eyes.

'I do want my son,' he said, softly but surely. As if it was a vow. 'Nicky *is* my son and from now on I intend to be a father to him, in any way I can. I want him—but I want you, too. Thena, if I'd known... If I'd guessed...'

'It doesn't matter.' It did, but not tonight. Tonight was hers. Tonight was her dream time, history had never happened and she was surrendering herself to the here and now.

As was Nikos.

'I believe ten years ago is best forgotten,' he whispered, tugging her close, folding her against him and wrapping her in his arms. 'For tonight, at least.'

And then he kissed her, long and hard, as she'd ached to be kissed for ten long years, as she longed to be kissed for ever.

Ten years dissipated just like that. He was her Nikos. Hers! And she was his, with every fibre of her being.

When the kiss ended they both knew it was immutable truth.

'Will you come to my bed, my love?' he asked, in a voice that sounded shaken. And then the loved laughter returned. 'Or...your bed?'

'Aren't there enough stars out here?'

'Not for the serious gazer,' he told her, and the wicked laughter was back. Gloriously back.

'Counting stars beats counting sheep. That is, if we can't think of anything else to do.'

She had to be serious here. Laughter would not do.

'Last time we did what I understand you're suggesting, I

believe we made Nicky,' she said in a voice that was none too steady.

'So we're older and wiser—and a bit more prepared.'

'You're prepared?'

'I believe I am.' He was tugging her close again, kissing her eyelids, each in turn.

'So am I,' she whispered.

The kissing stopped. She was held at arm's length again. Nikos's face showed blank astonishment. 'Did I just hear what I thought I heard?'

'I might be forgetting most of the last ten years,' she said, beginning to laugh. 'But there are a couple of things I need to remember. Like the lecture given to me by my doctor after Nicky's birth. If you think I'd come within a hundred miles of you again without contraception, you're not the man I think you are, Nikos Andreadis.'

'My Thena!' And the laughter was back. The wonderful laughter that had blazed between them since the hour they'd first met.

'Don't you dare laugh,' she said, but she couldn't help herself. She was laughing as well, at his laughter, at his joy, at the assurance of joy to come.

At the knowledge that for this night this man was hers. He always had been, she thought, from the time she'd met him to now. She'd borne his son. She'd carried him in her heart for ever.

'I'm not laughing,' he told her and it was true. The laughter had changed. He was watching her now with eyes as dark as night, with an expression on his face she'd never seen before— of tenderness, of joy, and of something more.

Of hope for the future?

That was what it was, she thought as she melted into him, as he lifted her into his arms and carried her unprotesting down the winding staircase, to a vast bedchamber with windows looking out in every direction to the sea beneath and to the islands beyond. As he laid her tenderly on the bed—a bed big enough for a king or six, piled high with feather pillows so soft she almost disappeared into them. As he pulled the curtains, one after another, cutting out the view, the islands, the sea, the outside world. Everything but the sky.

As he lit the candles, one by one.

And as he came to her where she lay, waiting for the man of her dreams.

He unfastened his shirt and she watched him, awed, fascinated, so deeply in love she thought she could die right now and be happy.

She matched him button for button, unfastening her robe. His dark eyes flared with passion. His shirt was gone long before she had her robe undone—why weren't her fingers working?—but it didn't matter. For he was helping her.

And finally she was free. His hands slipped in beneath her nightgown to cup her breasts and she wanted to cry out with sheer happiness. Sheer joy.

She was pushing her nightgown down, desperate to be closer. He helped her, kissing as he went, touching, tasting, loving, until her body was flames.

Nikos. Her first and last love. Nikos…

She was naked, gloriously, wonderfully naked, and so was he. He was sinking into the pillows beside her, gathering her into his arms.

His body was against her body. Skin against skin—the most erotic sensation in the world.

The heartbreak of years faded to nothing. The children, the island, responsibilities—everything was gone.

There was only this man, this love and this night.

There was only Nikos.

She woke and the world she'd lived in for ten long years had disappeared.

This was a fantasy—a fairy tale. At some time in the future it would end, but for now she was selfish enough, needy enough, to say thank you very much, this is where I belong. Maybe when reality hits I'll have a long time to remember this, so I need to soak up every precious moment.

She was lying in the arms of the man she loved with all her heart. And, whether she believed it or not—and yes, her head was screaming at her to be wary—the feeling seemed to be reciprocated. Nikos was loving her as he'd loved her ten years ago. But this was a grown man now, a businessman, a prince of the people, a lover, a man with strength and gentleness, laughter and tenderness, wonder and hope.

He was hers and she was his. For now they were two lovers exulting in each other's bodies. Drowning in each other's eyes.

And the place where they were loving was over-the-top fantastic.

'I'm hoping this glass is one way,' Nikos murmured in the aftermath of loving. 'Otherwise we could have some very shocked seagulls. You think we should declare this place a fly free zone?'

'And enforce it how?'

'I can't,' he said morosely. 'I believe it's you who's in charge of royal decrees.'

She giggled.

But then… Her giggle was echoed from outside the door. Two giggles.

'Uh-oh,' Nikos said. Athena dived under the covers and Nikos had his pants on and was fastening his shirt before three small faces appeared around the door. Two kids and a dog. Oscar took one look and leaped with joyous abandon onto the bed, and Nicky and Christa landed straight after. Athena was overwhelmed by dog and kids. Nicky hugged her, Christa hugged her too, on the basis of what was good for Nicky was okay by her, and Oscar licked every face in reach.

Her family. She was buried in family. She hugged and sniffed and she glanced up and saw her emotions reflected on Nikos's face.

No. Not her family.

Their family.

'Did you both sleep in here?' Nicky demanded, awed.

'I'm happy to tell you your mother didn't snore—very much,' Nikos said magnanimously. 'I slept on this side of the bed, she slept on the other and if I piled the pillows really high it was just a muted little snortle.'

'Ooh,' Athena said, and emerged from kids and dog long enough to toss a pillow at him. Her aim wasn't bad considering the handicap she was under—clutching bedclothes so the kids wouldn't discover she was naked. But Nikos hadn't defended himself and he was thumped right in the chest.

'Yay,' Nicky said and took his lead from his mother, and in seconds pillows were going everywhere.

Her family.

Their family.

Betrayal was a thing of the past, she thought mistily, giggling and tossing the odd pillow herself. Now was just for…now.

* * *

They had three days and three nights of magic.

Athena asked no questions. She was simply living in the moment. Nikos watched her as the days wore on and thought she was holding the kids to her, holding him to her, as if she feared they could be snatched away at any moment.

Somewhere outside the castle Demos was still plotting. Nikos was sure of it. But Alexandros was working on his behalf. Nikos's job was to keep his little family here; keep them safe until the threat could be defused.

It was no hardship at all. It was pure magic.

He had his kids. He had Thena. As far as he was concerned Alexandros could take as long as he needed to defuse the threat. This time out was theirs.

Only of course reality finally had to intrude.

Nikos had organised the lawyers to come on the third day.

'We need to get things settled before we go back to the palace,' he told her.

'Um…aren't things settled?'

'The affairs of the island aren't,' he said, kissing her on the nose. 'So tomorrow it's lawyers.' Then he hesitated. 'Thene, it's going to be a long, boring day. My mother is asking if she could take Nicky and Christa. They'll be safe—Demos can gain nothing by hurting one of you alone, and I'll send Joe with them to make sure. Do you think Nicky would like to go?'

'We'll ask him,' she said, and did, and Nicky thought the idea of a grandmother was too cool for words.

When Annia came to fetch them in an ancient Land Rover with no roof, he decided she was even cooler. They piled into the back seat, only to discover one of Annia's hens had decided this was a great nesting box. So off they went, with a handful of eggs each, with Oscar squished in the middle and with two grins a mile wide.

For Athena and Nikos the day promised to be far less exciting than the kids'. They needed to announce a coronation date, but first…there were so many papers to read and to sign that her head spun. The contracts and deeds ensuring legal ascension were mind-blowing.

But between the legal stuff, it was great that the kids were happy, she thought. She had visions of her son and Christa at Annia's kitchen table, where she'd spent the happiest part of her childhood. They were safe. And Nikos was right here, reading through the contracts with her, trying to make it less boring.

Her family was where it ought to be. She could cope with a boring day or two. And after she signed… Annia had offered to keep the children until dinner time. That meant Athena had a whole evening with Nikos, and no kids.

She was already thinking of the little cove under the castle. She'd have a secluded beach with only herself and Nikos.

She glanced up from the document she was signing and saw Nikos watching her—and she blushed.

He grinned.

She blushed some more.

She was signing the last contract. The lawyers were starting to pack up documents, beaming, congratulating.

And then Nikos's phone rang.

He listened and his face lost colour. She was at his side in an instant. 'What…what…'

'Mama's just rung,' he said. 'The kids… Demos has the kids.'

He had her hand. He was running, tugging her behind him, down the castle steps to the limousine parked in front. The lawyers were abandoned, shocked to silence.

* * *

She drove while Nikos barked orders into his phone. Then he told her what had happened.

'Mama used the time while she had the kids to cook dinner for a neighbour who's ill. The kids were playing—they were happy and she thought it'd only take five minutes to pop the food next door, the children were in the garden and Joe was in the house. He'd taken his eyes off the children only for a moment. The first he knew of trouble was a scream from the cove below the house. By the time he got down there they were gone.'

Gone…

'Is he sure it's Demos?' Athena asked in a voice she scarcely recognised as hers.

'He saw him,' he said, his voice catching. 'He had both the children in the boat—the same boat that tried to hit you. I've just rung Alexandros on Sappheiros. He has a helicopter. I thought this was safe. I never dreamed…' His voice broke.

She wanted to hold him. She had to keep driving, but it took every ounce of self-restraint not to pull over, take him in her arms and comfort him.

He was her man. She knew it. Whatever had happened in the past, Nikos was her man and she'd fight for him. As she'd fight for her child. Her children, she corrected herself. Her family.

CHAPTER ELEVEN

ANNIA was standing in her kitchen, white-faced and tearful. They walked in, she stepped straight into Nikos's arms and sobbed out her horror on his chest.

Then she tugged back from Nikos and hugged Athena. And then Joe came lumbering in, looking like a dog who'd been kicked. Before Thena knew it, Joe was a part of the hug.

Family.

Despite her terror, here was a glimmer of comfort. She let herself be hugged, she let herself be wept on and if she wept too, it didn't matter.

The hugs were fast; there were too many imperatives to indulge in emotion, but it steadied her. For this moment she'd take comfort where she could find it.

There were more men entering the kitchen now, summoned by Joe—big men, determined, grave-faced. Not knowing what to do.

She held Nikos and Nikos held her. Who was holding who up? It didn't matter. They were facing this as one.

But there was nothing to do. The consensus was that all their hope had to be in Alexandros and his helicopter. It was the only thing fast enough to locate a boat so powerful.

She was trying so hard to think. How to think when you were enmeshed in panic? She must.

'What…what would Demos do with them?' she managed, speaking to the room in general, and the unsayable had been said.

Annia gave one heartrending sob and ended up held again by Nikos.

But Athena wasn't thinking like that. She met Nikos's gaze over his mother's head. She saw his terror, and inexplicably it steadied her.

She knew her cousin. He was a weak-willed man, greedy for riches. Desperate even. But he wasn't completely stupid.

'He wouldn't hurt them,' she said, and the words themselves steadied her, for she knew they were the truth. 'Not deliberately. Yes, he tried to kill Nicky and me, but that was aimed at the two of us, staged to be an accident. Think of all he'd lose by hurting them now. He's been seen. He knows that. If he's known to have hurt them, he could never claim this Crown. Plus, this world doesn't hold a hiding place deep and dark enough if he touches my Nicky.' She shook her head, still puzzled. 'And I don't understand how he got them both onto his boat. Was there only him?'

'Yes,' Joe said. 'He had them in the boat by the time I saw them.'

'If he'd grabbed Christa, Nicky might have decided to stay with her,' Nikos said doubtfully, following her train of thought. 'Was it Nicky who screamed?'

'It surely was,' Joe said. 'I heard him screaming from here, and by the time I reached the beach I could still hear him.'

'If Demos came up here and grabbed them…why didn't he scream here? You'd surely have heard if he had.'

Joe had no answers.

It made less and less sense. She knew her Nicky. 'For Demos

to creep in here and grab them without alerting you… And to get him into the boat… Was he holding him? Why didn't he jump out?'

'I don't know. Maybe Demos tied him up. I couldn't see.'

'He'll be trying to blackmail you into giving up the throne,' Nikos said.

'He must be.' But she'd steadied. She'd heard enough now to be less panicked. 'And if he is then he'll contact us.' She forced herself to say what they all knew they had to do. 'We have to wait.'

But Nikos's face was still strained to breaking.

'Christa has a heart condition,' he said numbly to the room in general, and she felt his wash of absolute fear. Her normally daredevil lover was jelly in the face of a threat to his daughter. 'She's on medication. She has to have it. If we don't find her…'

'He can't have her,' Annia said fiercely. 'He'd never love her. Oh…'

'It's okay, Mama,' Nikos said, hauling himself together again in the face of his mother's terror. 'Demos doesn't want her and, like Thena said, he can't afford to hurt them. We'll find her.'

Oscar was at Thena's feet. She knelt and hugged him while Nikos held his mother. 'Why didn't you bite him, Oscar?' she whispered.

There was no answer.

Her terror had faded a little. This had to be an attempt at blackmail, she thought. But…in her confused mind she found room for more questions. What had Annia said? *'He can't have her. He'd never love her.'*

Why would Demos want Christa? There were undercurrents here she didn't understand.

She straightened and Nikos's arm came round her waist and held. He was more afraid than she was, she thought.

How serious was Christa's heart condition?

Now wasn't the time to ask. Now it seemed all they could do was wait, and to wait seemed the hardest thing in the world.

'I'll make…I'll make coffee,' Annia said, but subsided into her handkerchief instead.

And then Nikos's phone rang.

He flipped it open and listened.

He had the absolute attention of everyone in the room. Even Oscar was looking up, though that probably had more to do with the time and the absence of dinner.

But Oscar's dinner was doomed to wait. Nikos flipped the phone closed again. Frowning.

'Alexandros himself is flying the chopper,' Nikos told them, speaking slowly, thinking it through as he spoke. 'That was Alex now. Demos and the children are indeed in the boat, and they seem fine. But, according to Alexandros, they're going nowhere. Their boat's stopped. He thinks it must have run out of petrol. It's floating half a mile off the northern end of the island. Alexandros is holding position until we can reach them.'

He took a deep breath. Moving on.

'We'll take my runabout. It's faster than the bigger boats,' he snapped. 'Let's go. I'll radio as soon as we know. Can you guys bring one of the bigger boats after us?'

He grabbed Athena's hand, and they were gone.

It took fifteen long minutes to get there. Fifteen minutes with the runabout's motor roaring at full throttle. Smashing through the swells with sickening thumps.

If Demos had restarted the engine… Or if they'd tipped the boat…

She glanced at Nikos and his face was grim as death.

He'd do whatever it took.

She'd never doubted it. Not for a minute. He'd do whatever he must to keep these children safe. To keep the islanders safe.

To keep her…

And suddenly her thoughts were lurching with the boat. Taking her beyond her present fear.

This man had betrayed her. Or she'd thought he had. But…as she watched him at the tiller, as she saw the bleakness behind his eyes, she felt the sense of betrayal finally leave her, and all that remained was the knowledge of his honour.

He'd lost his father when he was twelve. He'd been on the boat with him—his father had a heart attack and by the time twelve-year-old Nikos had managed to get their fishing boat back to harbour his father was dead.

From that day on he'd taken on responsibilities too heavy for a boy. He'd been desperate to care for everyone, to make sure nothing like his father's death happened again.

And Marika… Christa's mother. Nikos's short-term wife. She'd never been able to think of Marika without the pain of betrayal overwhelming her. But, given these moments of enforced thought, the scene they'd just left came back to her. And Annia's words, speaking of Christa.

'He can't have her,' Annia had said fiercely. *'He'd never love her.'*

Marika had been older than she was and a bit…reckless. She'd been infatuated by Demos, desperate to get away from her bully of a father and away from the island. Her mother was one of Nikos's relations—almost family—but her father was a thug. If her father had found out Marika was pregnant… She shuddered to think of his reaction.

The germ of an idea—the germ of truth she'd discovered back in Annia's kitchen—was suddenly turned to full blown certainty.

But now wasn't the time to be talking of this with Nikos. Nikos was sick with worry. She should be sick with worry too—but still things didn't quite fit. She knew her son.

He was very, very like his father.

Dare you...

Nicky knew who Demos was. He'd seen his portrait. He'd understood the threat from the boat.

And now the boat was stranded, according to Alexandros, floundering just outside the reef.

'They'll be okay,' she said, steadily and strongly, to Nikos, and Nikos looked back at her with despair.

'How can you know?'

'Because my son is resourceful and clever and brave,' she told him. 'Because my son will do whatever it takes. Because my son is just like his father.'

And there they were, right where Alexandros directed them. His helicopter was still hovering overhead.

As Alex had told them, there were three people in the boat. Demos. Christa. Nicky.

Demos was leaning over the side.

'He might be armed,' Nikos warned her as they approached but she looked ahead at her cousin and she shook her head.

'He's seasick.'

'He still might be dangerous.'

'You mean he might shoot me? Not Demos.' She shook her head scornfully. 'With Alexandros in the helicopter watching? With the entire Argyros fishing fleet bearing down behind us? When he's totally occupied with his stomach?'

And she was right. Demos was beyond caring. They ran the runabout up beside the speedboat and he barely looked up at them.

Nikos had the two boats fastened together in seconds. He steadied, and then he lifted Christa over.

Thena took her and hugged her close, and Nicky clambered over himself and sat down in the middle and grinned at his mother and grinned at Nikos. He didn't look the least bit worried. He looked supremely pleased with himself.

'Hooray, you came. I knew my plan would work,' he said with smug satisfaction.

'You knew…' Nikos said faintly.

Other boats were approaching now. The bigger fishing boats were slower than Nikos's runabout, but the fishermen of Argyros had gunned their motors as fast as they could to be in the action.

There wasn't a lot of action. Demos was bent over the side. Their villain didn't look the least bit menacing.

The fishing boats were forming a circle. Even if he got the motor going, there was no longer anywhere to run.

'He was all right until the motor stopped,' Nicky said scornfully, as they all looked at Demos. 'But as soon as it stopped, the boat started rolling up and down and up and down and…'

'Do you mind?' Athena said faintly. 'Not so much with the ups and downs. So can you take us back to dry land?' she asked, hugging Christa and looking a plea to Nikos.

Nikos hadn't heard. He was still watching Demos. But Demos was no longer a threat to anyone. He was a bundle of abject misery.

'Tell us what happened,' he said to Nicky, and the little boy's eyes gleamed. He was mischief personified. Just like his father.

'We saw him on the beach from Yia Yia's kitchen window,' he said, and the islander's word for Grandmama resonated with pride. Here, then, was another association Nicky was proud of. 'I knew it was him 'cos of the boat, and 'cos of the picture. He pulled the boat up on the beach, really fast into bushes and I knew he was trying to hide. Then he came up the cliff path. I said to Christa, I know how to stop his boat going again, so we snuck down the cove past the craypots and Joe didn't even see us going. And when we got to the boat it was just like the picture in the book—only it said sometimes the fuel tank's locked—but it wasn't so we opened it up and put a whole lot of sand in. But it was hard getting the top back on 'cos it got sandy and I just got it on when Demos came back. He saw me and tried to grab me but I ran away. But then he grabbed Christa. So I had to go with him.'

'Oh, Nicky…' Athena said, torn between pride and horror. 'You shouldn't have…'

'I couldn't let him just take Christa, could I?' he said, stung by implied criticism of such a great plan. 'She's my sister. He pushed her into the boat and he said he'd hurt her if I didn't come too, and I knew the sand was in the engine so I hopped in anyway. He said you had to agree to ab…to abdicate. He said he'd hurt me if you didn't. So I did get a little bit scared. I thought the boat would stop really fast or not go at all but it went for ages. It sounded sicker and sicker though, but then it stopped and *he* got sick. And he had a gun, but while he was sick I grabbed it from his belt and threw it into the water. And he tried to hit me but he started being sick again. And then the helicopter came and the man up there waved and I knew you'd come. So it was okay, wasn't it, Mama?'

'Yes,' she said and she found she was laughing. Through tears. Her son.

Her men.

And she looked at Nikos and on his face she saw a mixture of pride and love and hope…and awe. Awe, pure and simple.

And in that moment she knew what she had to do.

These were her men.

This was her family.

She was the Crown Princess of Argyros. It was up to her to claim them.

As dusk settled over the island they returned to the Palace. The Eagle's Nest was a hideaway for when there was a threat, but there was no longer a threat. And Athena knew—they all knew—that now was the time to lay claim to the throne so it could never be disputed.

Annia and Mrs Lavros took the children to be bathed and fed and put to bed. When Athena came downstairs it seemed half the men of Argyros had come to tie the threads together. Nikos and Alexandros were seated at the head of the long table in the ancient meeting room, where decisions on the rule of this island had been made for generation upon generation.

Nikos signalled that she sit between them. But she couldn't. Not yet. There were things she had to sort in her own mind first.

There were words she had to find. For now she'd leave the speaking to Nikos.

'We found the thugs who nearly killed the Princess Athena and Prince Nicholas.' Nikos was talking to everyone in the room, but he was watching her. 'They were guns-for-hire from Athens. Alexandros traced the boat, he found them, and we had the link we needed to Demos. But Demos obviously took fright. He's had an informer on the island. We know now who he is—a man my mother thought of as a friend, a man who forfeited that friendship for pay. He's already fled to Greece, but before he left he told Demos that today the children would be with my mother.'

The men in the room were silent. Shocked. As was Nikos,

Thena thought. He still looked gaunt—the terror of this afternoon would probably stay with him for ever—but he had himself in hand, her Prince of the People.

'We know it all now,' Nikos said, and managed a wry smile. 'It seems that seasickness is better than torture for getting information. The men who towed Demos to shore told him he'd stay in his boat until he told us everything, and now he has.'

'He wrote it down,' Alexandros added gravely. 'We handed him pen and paper and he wrote and signed a confession. Jail's looking pretty good to Demos. Anywhere where the ground's solid.'

He smiled, but Nikos didn't return the smile. The events of the day had shaken him too deeply for humour.

'He wasn't as unprepared as he seemed,' Nikos said heavily. 'He had a gun. Nicky described it to me, and…'

He broke off, his voice cracking. Alexandros put his hand on his friend's shoulder and Athena thought blindly, these two men cared deeply for each other.

Her mind steadied. Focused. Knew what had to be done.

'Enough,' Nikos said and forced himself to go on. 'So… Demos beached the boat, he went up to the cottage and found no one. He returned to the boat—furious—to find the children, seemingly waiting for him.'

He hesitated, and Thena could see him repress a shudder. 'Maybe…maybe that was the best thing that could have happened. For if Joe had been in the garden and Annia had been at home…there could well have been a bloodbath as he seized Nicky and decided to eliminate witnesses.' He closed his eyes.

Alexandros took over. 'We know now that Demos has a king-sized gambling problem,' he added. 'He's been gambling on the assumption he'd have access to all the Argyros diamond mines. He was desperate enough to do anything to get his hands on that stream of wealth.'

Athena shivered. She was standing by the door, leaning against the wall. She'd said she wanted to be able to leave easily if the kids needed her. But in reality she just needed to watch, listen and figure what had to be said. And how she was going to say it.

'So he's in jail,' Alexandros said, and glanced across at Athena. 'If it's okay by you, Princess Athena, I'll take care of him on Sappheiros.'

The men were all watching her now. Waiting for her to speak. She took a deep breath. She looked at Nikos's haggard face. She knew what had to be said.

'Thank you for your offer, Alexandros,' she said, forcing her voice to be steady. Forcing her words to be clear enough to be heard the length of the great room. 'But Demos will be tried here. We'd be thankful if you'd hold him for us until we have the facilities for a full and fair trial. But Prince Nikos and I will build this island's court system as one of our earliest priorities.'

'Prince Nikos,' Alexandros said blankly.

'Prince Nikos,' she repeated.

'If you abdicate, Nikos can't…' he began.

'I have no intention of abdicating.'

Maybe she should have dressed in her royal gear again, she thought. She'd dressed neatly this morning, for the lawyers, in smart casual trousers and a crisp white blouse. But since then she'd been hammered by the sea. Oscar had jumped up on her when they'd docked and she was covered in sand. Her hair was a wild tangle from the wind. She'd abandoned her soaked shoes and she was still barefoot—and she didn't care.

She was Crown Princess Athena and it was time for her to claim what was hers.

'Ten years ago Nikos Andreadis asked me to marry him,' she said, and she left the relative obscurity of her alcove near the door and walked deliberately around the table to its head. She stood between the two men—the two princes—and she looked out over the men of power from this island. Her people.

'Ten years ago there were misunderstandings and threats,' she said. 'I left this island because I believed harm would come to it's people if I stayed. Nikos let me go because he thought I was intent on a career. For ten years there's been misunderstanding and grief. But no more. This day is a watershed for this island. This day I say to you all—to the entire island—that I'm here to stay. That ten years ago Nikos asked me to marry me. I accepted his offer, and now, if he'll have me, I'd like to hold him to that contract. I would like Nikos and I to rule this island as man and wife. Prince Nikos and Princess Athena of Argyros.'

She turned and looked at Nikos. Who was looking…stunned.

'Nikos, you're a man of honour,' she said. 'I know—we all know—that you would never ask me to marry you if there was a hint that your offer would be taken as a desire to rule this island yourself. Everyone in this room knows you're an honourable man. Everyone in this room knows the island is your home, your heart. Is there any man in this room who would say Prince Nikos shouldn't take what I see as his rightful role? As ruler beside me?'

There wasn't a sound. Not a sound.

Nikos was staring at her blindly, as if he couldn't believe what she'd just said. The silence stretched on and on.

And then one lone person, far up the back of the long hall, started to clap. And then another started beside him. And then another.

And then the whole room was clapping. They were on their feet, cheering, shouting, clapping each other on the back.

And Nikos was simply staring at Athena. Saying nothing.

The applause died. Athena watched the men regain their seats.

Still Nikos said nothing.

'I believe,' she said softly into the silence, 'that you'll have to excuse us. Nikos and I have a few things to discuss.'

There was a delighted roar of laughter. Nikos was looking as thrown as a man could be, and their audience was loving it.

'So can we call this meeting closed?' she said. 'I think we've achieved everything we wished for. Oh, and when the council next meets… I want this room to hold at least as many women as it does men.'

'You'll be under petticoat rule now,' someone called to Nikos.

'And he'll love it,' someone else called.

'Our Princess isn't one for petticoats as far as I can see,' someone else added. 'I'm thinking climbing trees and saving kids and making us proud of her is where she is. That's where they both are. Our royal couple.'

But Athena wasn't listening. She was watching Nikos.

'Well?' she said softly. 'How about the beach? Is it private enough? Or should we go back to our sky dome?'

'Thena…'

'Your call, but we have to talk,' she said, and he stared at her for a long moment—and then he smiled, that wonderful heart-twisting smile she loved so much. He rose and he took her hand.

And the men of the island council rose again and cheered as one, as the people's Prince led his Princess from the room.

CHAPTER TWELVE

THEY didn't need to go far. Just as far as the cliff path, where they could look out on the rising moon, the moonbeams glittering over the ocean, where there was only silence and each other.

'What have you done?' Nikos asked gently, and Athena smiled because she knew that even now he'd be honourable.

'I've claimed my own.'

'You don't need to marry me to be a princess.'

'I never did,' she said. 'But I do need to marry you because I love you and I need you by my side.'

He took a deep breath. He turned to face her and he took both her hands in his.

'Thena, I hurt you…'

'So you did,' she said. 'And I hurt you. It's in the past.'

'But you explained…'

'And you can't.' She hesitated, but it had to be said. Once and then never again.

'Nikos, when I left the island… You know I went hoping you'd follow. I knew you'd be hurt but I hoped…I hoped so much that I could explain my reasons for leaving. But then I found I was pregnant. And, while I was working up the courage to phone you, I was told that Marika was pregnant.

And that you'd promised to marry her. And that she was further gone in her pregnancy than I was.'

He groaned.

All she wanted to do was hold him—kiss him—but this had to be said. She had to sort this in her head. Get it right.

'So I thought you'd betrayed me,' she said softly. 'Until today…'

'So what's happened today?' he demanded in a voice she hardly recognised. 'To make you change your mind.'

And somehow she found the strength and certainty to answer.

'When Annia said: *"He can't have her. He'd never love her,"* I knew then what had happened. I knew.'

'How can you know? No one…'

'No one will ever know from me,' she whispered. 'You know, and Annia knows—or maybe she's just guessing as well. But when I left the island I was heartbroken, and I can only imagine how you must have felt. Maybe, given time, you'd have contacted me, seen how things really were. But along came Marika. Sure, I'm guessing, but I know I'm right. I'm guessing Marika came begging for your help. Pregnant by Demos. Abandoned by Demos. Terrified that her bully of a father might well kill her if he found out.'

She couldn't bear to watch him. She couldn't bear to see the pain. Nikos said nothing but the bleakness in his eyes told her all she'd ever want to know. She was speaking the truth.

'So I'm guessing you thought why not? You thought I'd betrayed you and abandoned the island, so why not help Marika? So you went with Marika to her parents and said yes, Marika's pregnant, but the two of you wanted to marry. Instead of being appalled, her father would have welcomed you with open arms. So you married.

'But then a baby was born,' she whispered. 'A little girl

with Down's syndrome. A child who Demos would never have cared for. Marika herself obviously couldn't cope and she chose to run.'

Still he said nothing. His silence was frightening her. But she'd come this far—there was no choice but to take it to its conclusion.

'But you…' she said, and she knew in her heart that she spoke the absolute truth. 'You stood with Christa in your arms and you declared to all the island that she was yours. With the respect you and your mother are held on this island, affection for Christa is guaranteed. She has Annia as a grandmama. She has you as her papa. She's safe.'

And at last he broke his silence. 'You're just guessing,' he said explosively.

'So tell me I'm wrong. Look at me straight, Nikos and tell me I'm wrong.'

He didn't. He couldn't. The pain that had wrapped itself around her heart ten long years ago dissolved and faded to nothing.

He'd do…*whatever it took*.

Her Prince. Her Nikos.

'I'll never ask you to confirm it,' she said softly, seeing raw pain. 'But I know I'm right.' She forced a rueful smile. 'Christa is your daughter. She stays your daughter, no matter what else happens. My only regret is that I've been so stupid. A bit of terror and fifteen minutes in an open boat and I've guessed it all. Oh, Nikos, I love what you did. I love what you are.' She hesitated then, but she'd come so far… Why not go on.

'So…I know it's not the woman who's supposed to say these things,' she whispered. 'But your honour won't let you. So here it is. Nikos, I'm saying, right here, right now, that I love you with all my heart. That if you demand it of me, then I'll rule this island alone, but only if you refuse what I'm asking. Because it seems to me that we've had ten years alone and why wait one minute longer? You asked me to marry you ten years ago and I accepted. Only then Giorgos destroyed it. So today I've accepted again, in front of the full island council. And I accept again now.'

His hands were tight on hers. His face was expressionless again, but she knew what that meant. It meant he was hiding what he felt. She knew this man as she knew herself.

'I love you, Nikos,' she whispered. 'I've loved you since I was eight years old and I love you still. If you want me to be your wife, it would be an honour and it would be my joy to accept.'

'If I want you,' he whispered.

'So?' she said, and tilted her chin and even managed a smile. 'So, Nikos Andreadis? Prince of my heart. Dare you.'

'Dare to marry you?'

'I'll make a very demanding wife,' she whispered, venturing a smile. 'Plus I have it on the best authority that I snortle.'

'I love your snortle.'

'I don't snortle.'

'I believe you just said…'

'Nikos!'

'I like to get my facts right,' he said, mischief emerging, the wicked grin that had her heart doing handsprings causing its normal damage again—and more. 'I need to let myself know what I'm getting into,' he said. 'One wife?'

'Only one,' she said. 'No Henry the Eighth absurdity for this royal couple.'

'Agreed,' he said promptly.

'One son?'

'And one daughter,' she said serenely. 'And…and maybe even more?' And his answering smile was enough to make her heart turn over.

'I guess you'll expect me to adopt Oscar as well,' he said, struggling for a martyred tone.

'Of course I will.'

'So…'

'So?' she whispered and held her breath.

'So,' he said and dropped to his knee before her.

She gasped. 'Nikos…'

'So let's get this right,' he said softly. 'As my Princess, to whom I owe fidelity and all honour, you've asked me to marry you.'

'Yes,' she said, suddenly doubtful. 'But it doesn't mean you must.'

'No, but there are connotations of duty to my Crown Princess,' he said. 'And I'd hate you to think I'd just said yes to stop myself being thrown in a dungeon.'

'Do we have dungeons?'

'We'll find out together,' he whispered. 'Meanwhile, Princess Athena Christou of Argyros, would you let me get a word in edgeways?'

'Yes,' she said—and did.

'Will you do me the great honour of becoming my wife?'

'Of course I will,' she said, and tugged him up to stand before her. 'If you really want me.'

'How can you ask?'

'I'll never ask again,' she whispered. 'I'll never need to ask again. Oh, Nikos. My one and only love.'

'My Thena,' he whispered into her hair. 'My Princess and my life.'

And then he put her away from him. He held her at arm's

length and his face broke into a smile she'd never seen before. It was a look of exultation, triumph and pride. 'My Thena.' It was a shout of pure joy and it echoed down into the cove below, back into the palace behind them, out onto the sea breezes blowing over the whole island.

He swung her round and round and round, and then he set her down before him and he kissed her, long and hard and true.

And then, finally, he set her back from him again.

He held her hands and he held her heart.

'Thena, I've loved you for ever,' he said softly. 'So…you'll really be my wife?'

'Yes.'

'Princess to my Prince?'

'Absolutely.'

'Mama to my Papa?'

'That, too.'

'My lover?'

'You're very demanding.'

'You have no idea how demanding,' he said. His hands were tugging her into him, his eyes were dark and fathomless and she was against his heart, held tight, his hand cupping her chin so her mouth was just under his.

'We're family,' he said fiercely, and it was as if he was making a vow. 'You'll be my wife and I'll not let you go again. I love you Athena. I've loved you since I was eight years old and I don't intend stopping until I'm a hundred and eight. Or longer if I'm granted more years by your side.'

'Stupid,' she said softly, lovingly, and as an echo to a vow it was pretty dumb—but it didn't matter.

She was kissing him.

He was kissing her back.

And, on the steps of the Royal Palace of Argyros, half the

island council and practically all the palace staff were craning their heads to see.

The island had its royal family.

And the Prince and his Princess didn't notice their audience at all.

The combined wedding and coronation of the Crown Prince and Crown Princess of Argyros was a day to remember for ever. The sun shone gently on the rugged cliffs and distant mountains. The ocean glittered in its sapphire and diamond brilliance. The warm breeze from the sea was almost a caress.

Coronations and royal weddings should take place in a formal setting—most properly in the Great Hall of the Royal Palace. That was a problem, for the Great Hall only held five hundred, and all the island wanted to see.

So they held the ceremony on the wide sweep of lawn between the palace and what had once been the most private of beaches. No invitation was necessary. Whosoever loved this island and wished it well was welcome, to see the beginning of its future.

And its future was assured. In the best of monarchies, the royal family was an embodiment of the hopes and dreams of the people and, in Nikos and Athena, the islanders of Argyros had found that dream.

Nikos, in royal uniform—jet-black jacket and trousers, shining boots, tassels, braid, dress sword—was eye-candy enough to have at least half their audience sighing with pure enchantment. And Athena, in her clouds of swirling silk and lace, was a bride to turn the most hardened islander misty-eyed. She made her vows clearly and solemnly and she looked so happy there was hardly a dry eye on the island.

Even Father Antonio… The old priest married them with

love and with pride, and there was definitely a tear or two rolling down his wrinkled cheek. As he blessed the bride and groom, his old voice became redolent with joy.

His blessing was supposed to be just for the bride and groom—the Prince and Princess—but he didn't stop there. He blessed the ancient ring on Athena's finger, the ring of Argyros, ancient silver, gnarled and twisted and lovely, with three magnificent diamonds embedded in its depths. He blessed the islanders looking on. He blessed Alexandros and Lily from the Isle of Sappheiros. And he blessed Stefanos, even now trying to sort the future of the third and last island.

And of course he blessed the children. Nicky was pageboy, torn a little between embarrassment and pride. Pride was definitely winning. Christa was flower girl, with so many pink and white flounces she'd announced that any minute now she might float. Indulging her fancy, the dressmaker had attached a tiny pair of gossamer wings to her back. Christa's happiness was complete. She had a mama and a papa, a brother and a dog. And wings. She was tossing her rose petals with delight, and she was making Nicky toss them with her.

Two royal children…and even now the island grandmothers were dusting off their knitting needles in hope.

But knitting was for the future. Everything was for the future. For now the royal couple knelt to receive the ancient crowns that had lain in storage for over two hundred years. They rose to thunderous applause.

To a happy beginning.

Crown Princess Athena and Crown Prince Nikos stood hand in hand on the raised dais and looked out on the island of their birth, and if there were tears shed in the crowd then the islanders' tears found reflection in the face of the new Crown Princess of Argyros.

The Crown was secure. The Argyros diamonds were confirmed as belonging to the people, and legal proceedings were already underway to ensure no royal held such terrifying powers again.

Demos was stripped of his title and waiting for the courts to administer justice. Exile, Athena thought, for there was room in her heart to almost feel sorry for the man.

So what was next?

It had been leaked by the media that Prince Nikos had decreed a month's honeymoon was the minimum required to cement their union. The islanders, deliriously happy at their good fortune, could only smile their agreement.

Nikos had offered his wife any place in the world for their time out. A deserted island in the Maldives, a tropical *bure*, nights alone by candlelight…

She'd chosen…the Eagle's Nest. They'd leave for there tonight. With Nicky and with Christa and with Oscar.

'For I have a daughter now,' she'd whispered proudly to Nikos.

He'd held her close, he'd kissed her eyelids and he'd felt so much in love that surely his heart must burst.

They'd face the future together, he thought, and if the worst happened… They were a family. They'd face their future with love and with courage.

And with a dog called Oscar. And with a grandmother called Annia. And uncles and aunts and cousins. And thousands of islanders who loved this place as they did.

Their island home.

'It's perfect,' he whispered to Athena as they stood side by side and waved to the assembled population of Argyros. 'I can't imagine anything more perfect than this.'

'I can't imagine anyone more perfect than you,' she whispered back.

'Then you need to look in the mirror,' he retorted, and then this very serious ceremonial occasion was marred.

This ceremony had been timed to the last nanosecond. There was no room for improvisation. Right now the Crown Prince was supposed to take the Crown Princess's hand and solemnly lead her to the pair of gold and crimson thrones at the middle of the crimson-carpeted dais.

He didn't.

Instead, for three whole minutes—for one whole trumpet chorale that was supposed to see them taking the throne together—the Crown Prince of Argyros took the Crown Princess of Argyros into his arms and he kissed her.

As he intended to kiss her for the rest of her life.

CROWN PRINCE, PREGNANT BRIDE!

RAYE MORGAN

This book is dedicated to Baby Kate

CHAPTER ONE

THOUGH MONTE COULDN'T see her, Pellea Marallis passed so close to the Crown Prince's hiding place, he easily caught a hint of her intoxicating perfume. That gave him an unexpected jolt. It brought back a panoply of memories, like flipping through the pages of a book—a vision of sunlight shining through a gauzy white dress, silhouetting a slim, beautifully rounded female form, a flashing picture of drops of water cascading like a thousand diamonds onto creamy silken skin, a sense of cool satin sheets and caresses that set his flesh on fire.

He bit down hard on his lower lip to stop the wave of sensuality that threatened to wash over him. He wasn't here to renew the romance. He was here to kidnap her. And he wasn't about to let that beguiling man-woman thing get in the way this time.

She passed close again and he could hear the rustle of her long skirt as it brushed against the wall he was leaning on. She was pacing back and forth in her courtyard, a garden retreat built right into this side of the castle, giving her a small lush forest where she spent most of her time. The surrounding rooms—a huge closet filled with clothes and a small sitting room, a neighboring compact office stacked to the ceiling with books, a sumptuously decorated bedroom—each opened onto the courtyard with French doors, making her living space a mixture of indoors and outdoors in an enchanting maze of exciting colors and provocative scents.

She was living like a princess.

Did he resent it all? Of course. How could he not?

But this was not the side of the castle where his family had lived before the overthrow of their royal rule. That area had been burned the night his parents were murdered by the Granvillis, the thugs who still ruled Ambria, this small island country that had once been home to his family. He understood that part of the castle was only now being renovated, twenty-five years later.

And that he resented.

But Pellea had nothing to do with the way his family had been robbed of their birthright. He had no intention of holding her accountable. Her father was another matter. His long-time status as the Grand Counselor to the Granvillis was what gave Pellea the right to live in this luxury—and his treachery twenty-five years ago was considered a subject of dusty history.

Not to Monte. But that was a matter for another time.

He hadn't seen her yet. He'd slipped into the dressing room as soon as he'd emerged from the secret passageway. And now he was just biding his time before he revealed his presence.

He was taking this slowly, because no matter what

he'd told himself, she affected him in ways no other woman ever had. In fact, she'd been known to send his restraint reeling, and he knew he had to take this at a cautious pace if he didn't want things to spin out of control again.

He heard her voice and his head rose. Listening hard, he tried to figure out if she had someone with her. No. She was talking on her mobile, and when she turned in his direction, he could just make out what she was saying.

"Seed pearls of course. And little pink rosebuds. I think that ought to do it."

He wasn't really listening to the words. Just the sound of her had him mesmerized. He'd never noticed before how appealing her voice was, just as an instrument. He hadn't heard it for some time, and it caught the ear the way a lilting acoustic guitar solo might, each note crisp, crystal clear and sweet in a way that touched the soul.

As she talked, he listened to the sound and smiled. He wanted to see her and the need was growing in him.

But to do that, he would have to move to a riskier position so that he could see out through the open French doors. Though he'd slipped easily into her huge dressing room, he needed to move to a niche beside a tall wardrobe where he could see everything without being seen himself. Carefully, he made his move.

And there she was. His heart was thudding so hard, he could barely breathe.

The thing about Pellea, and part of the reason she so completely captivated him, was that she seemed to embody a sense of royal command even though there wasn't a royal bone in her body. She was classically beautiful, like a Greek statue, only slimmer, like an angel in a Renaissance painting, only earthier, like a dancer drawn by Toulouse-Lautrec, only more graceful, like a thirties-era film star, only more mysteriously luminescent. She was all a woman could be and still be of this earth.

Barely.

To a casual glance, she looked like a normal woman. Her face was exceptionally pretty, but there were others with dark eyes as almond-shaped, with long, lustrous lashes that seemed to sweep the air. Her hair floated about her face like a misty cloud of spun gold and her form was trim and nicely rounded. Her lips were red and full and inviting. Perfection.

But there were others who had much the same advantages. Others had caught his eye through the years, but not many had filled his mind and touched off the sense of longing that she had.

There was something more to Pellea, something in the dignity with which she held herself, an inner fire that burned behind a certain sadness in her eyes, an inner drive, a sense of purpose, that set her apart. She could be playful as a kitten one minute, then smoldering with a provocative allure, and just as suddenly, aflame with righteous anger.

From the moment he'd first seen her, he'd known she was special. And for a few days two months ago, she'd been his.

"Didn't I give you my sketches?" she was saying into the phone. "I tend to lean a little more toward tradtional. Not too modern. No off-the-shoulder stuff. Not for this."

He frowned, wondering what on earth she was talking about. Designing a ball gown maybe? He could see her on the dance floor, drawing all eyes. Would he ever get the chance to dance with her? Not in a ballroom, but maybe here, in her courtyard. Why not?

It was a beautiful setting. When he'd been here before, it had been winter and everything had been lifeless and stark. But spring was here now, and the space was a riot of color.

A fountain spilled water in the center of the area, making music that was a pleasant, tinkling background. Tiled pathways meandered through the area, weaving in among rosebushes and tropical plants, palms and a small bamboo forest.

Yes, they would have to turn on some music and dance. He could almost feel her in his arms. He stole another glance at her, at the way she held her long, graceful neck, at the way her free hand fluttered like a bird as she made her point, at the way her dressing gown gaped open, revealing the lacy shift she wore underneath.

"Diamonds?" she was saying into the phone. "Oh, no. No diamonds. Just the one, of course. That's customary. I'm not really a shower-me-with-diamonds sort of girl, you know what I mean?"

He reached out and just barely touched the fluttering hem of her flowing sleeve as she passed. She turned quickly, as though she'd sensed something, but he'd pulled back just in time and she didn't see him. He smiled, pleased with himself. He would let her know he was here when he was good and ready.

"As I remember it, the veil is more of an ivory shade. There are seed pearls scattered all over the crown area, and then down along the edges on both sides. I think that will be enough."

Veil? Monte frowned. Finally, a picture swam into stark relief and he realized what she must be talking about. It sounded like a wedding. She was planning her wedding ensemble.

She was getting married.

He stared at her, appalled. What business did she have getting married? Had she forgotten all about him so quickly? Anger curled through him like smoke and he only barely held back the impulse to stride out and confront her.

She couldn't get married. He wouldn't allow it.

And yet, he realized with a twinge of conscience, it wasn't as though he was planning to marry her himself. Of course not. He had bigger fish to fry. He had an invasion to orchestrate and manage. Besides, there was no way he would ever marry the daughter of the biggest betrayer still alive of his family—the DeAngelis Royalty.

And yet, to think she was planning to marry someone else so soon after their time together burned like a scorpion's sting.

What the hell!

A muted gong sounded, making him jerk in surprise. That was new. There had been a brass knocker a few weeks ago. What else had she changed since he'd been here before?

Getting married—hah! It was a good thing he'd shown up to kidnap her just in time.

Pellea had just rung off with her clothing designer, and she raised her head at the sound of her new entry gong. She sighed, shoulders drooping. The last thing she wanted was company, and she was afraid she knew who this was anyway. Her husband-to-be. Oh, joy.

"Enter," she called out.

There was a heavy metal clang as the gate was pulled open and then the sound of boots on the tile. A tall man entered, his neatly trimmed hair too short to identify the color, but cut close to his perfectly formed head. His shoulders were wide, his body neatly proportioned and very fit-looking. His long face would have been handsome if he could have trained himself to get rid of the perpetual sneer he wore like a mark of superiority at all times.

Leonardo Granvilli was the oldest son of Georges Granvilli, leader of the rebellion that had taken over this island nation twenty-five years before, the man who now ruled as *The General*, a term that somewhat softened the edges of his relatively despotic regime.

"My darling," Leonardo said coolly in a deep, sonorous voice. "You're radiant as the dawn on this beautiful day."

"Oh, spare me, Leonardo," she said dismissively. Her tone held casual disregard but wasn't in any way meant to offend. "No need for empty words of praise. We've known each other since we were children. I think by now we've taken the measure, each of the other. I don't need a daily snow job."

Leonardo made a guttural sound in his throat and threw a hand up to cover his forehead in annoyance. "Pellea, why can't you be like other women and just accept the phony flattery for what it is? It's nothing but form, darling. A way to get through the awkward moments. A little sugar to help the medicine go down."

Pellea laughed shortly, but cut it off almost before it had begun. Pretending to be obedient, she went into mock royal mode for him.

"Pray tell me, kind sir, what brings my noble knight to my private chambers on such a day as this?"

He actually smiled. "That's more like it."

She curtsied low and long and his smile widened.

"Bravo. This marriage may just work out after all."

Her glare shot daggers his way, as though to say, *In your dreams*, but he ignored that.

"I came with news. We may have to postpone our wedding."

"What?" Involuntarily, her hands went to her belly—and the moment she realized what she'd done, she snatched them away again. "Why?"

"That old fool, the last duke of the DeAngelis clan, has finally died. This means a certain level of upheaval is probable in the expatriate Ambrian community. They will have to buzz about and try to find a new patriarch, it seems. We need to be alert and ready to move on any sort of threat that might occur to our regime."

"Do you expect anything specific?"

He shook his head. "Not really. Just the usual gnashing of teeth and bellowing of threats. We can easily handle it."

She frowned, shaking her head. "Then why postpone? Why not move the date up instead?"

He reached out and tousled her hair. "Ah, my little buttercup. So eager to be wed."

She pushed his hand away, then turned toward the fountain in the middle of the courtyard and shrugged elaborately. "'If it were done when 'tis done, then 'twere well it were done quickly,'" she muttered darkly.

"What's that my sweet?" he said, following into the sunshine.

"Nothing." She turned back to face him. "I will, of course, comply with your wishes. But for my own purposes, a quick wedding would be best."

He nodded, though his eyes were hooded. "I understand. Your father's condition and all that." He shrugged. "I'll talk to my father and we'll hit upon a date, I'm sure." His gaze flickered over her and he smiled. "To think that after all this time, and all the effort you've always gone to in putting me off, I'm finally going to end up with the woman of my dreams." He almost seemed to tear up a bit. "It restores one's faith, doesn't it?"

"Absolutely." She couldn't help but smile back at him, though she was shaking her head at the same time. "Oh,

Leonardo, I sometimes think it would be better if you found someone to love."

He looked shocked. "What are you talking about? You know very well you've always been my choice."

"I said *love*," she retorted. "Not *desire to possess*."

He shrugged. "To each his own."

Pellea sighed but she was still smiling.

Monte watched this exchange while cold anger spread through him like a spell, turning him from a normal man into something akin to a raging monster. And yet, he didn't move a muscle. He stood frozen, as though cast in stone. Only his mind and his emotions were alive.

And his hatred. He hated Leonardo, hated Leonardo's father, hated his entire family.

Bit by bit, the anger was banked and set aside to smolder. He was experienced enough to know white-hot emotional ire led to mistakes every time. He wouldn't make any mistakes. He needed to keep his head clear and his emotions in check.

All of them, good and bad.

One step at a time, he made himself relax. His body control was exceptional and he used it now. He wanted to keep cool so that he would catch the exact right time to strike. It wouldn't be now. That would be foolish. But it would be soon.

He hadn't been prepared for something like this. The time he and Pellea had spent together just a few weeks before had been magical. He'd been hungry to see her again, aching to touch her, eager to catch her lips with his and feel that soaring sense of wonder again. He had promised himself there would be no lovemaking to distract him this time—but he'd been kidding himself. The moment he saw her he knew he had to have her in his arms again.

That was all. Nothing serious, nothing permanent. A part of him had known she would have to marry someone—eventually. But still, to think that she would marry this…this…

Words failed him.

"I'd like you to come down to the library. We need to look at the plans for the route to the retreat in the gilded carriage after we are joined as one," Leonardo was saying.

"No honeymoon," she said emphatically, raising both hands as though to emphasize her words. "I told you that from the beginning."

He looked startled, but before he could protest, she went on.

"As long as my father is ill, I won't leave Ambria."

He sighed, making a face but seemingly reconciled to her decision. "People will think it strange," he noted.

"Let them."

She knew that disappointed him but it couldn't be helped. Right now her father was everything to her. He had been her rock all her life, the only human being in this world she could fully trust and believe in and she wasn't about to abandon him now.

Still, she needed this marriage. Leonardo understood

why and was willing to accept the terms she'd agreed to this on. Everything was ready, the wheels had begun to turn, the path was set. As long as nothing got in the way, she should be married within the next week. Until then, she could only hope that nothing would happen to upset the apple cart.

"I'll come with you," she said. "Just give me a minute to do a quick change into something more suitable."

She turned and stepped into her dressing room, pulling the door closed behind her. Moving quickly, she opened her gown and began unbuttoning her lacy dress from the neck down. And then she caught sight of his boots. Her fingers froze on the buttons as she stared at the boots. Her head snapped up and her dark eyes met Monte's brilliant blue gaze. Every sinew constructing her body went numb.

She was much more than shocked. She was horrified. As the implications of this visit came into focus, she had to clasp her free hand over her mouth to keep from letting out a shriek. For just a moment, she went into a tailspin and could barely keep her balance.

Eyes wide, she stared at him. A thousand thoughts ricocheted through her, bouncing like ping-pong balls against her emotions. Anger, remorse, resentment, joy—even love—they were all there and all aimed straight into those gorgeous blue eyes, rapid-fire. If looks could kill, he would be lying on the floor, shot through the heart.

A part of her was tempted to turn on her heel, summon Leonardo and be done with it. Because she knew as sure as she knew her own name that this would all end badly.

Monte couldn't be a part of her life. There was no way she could even admit to anyone here in the castle that she knew him. All she had to do was have Leonardo call the guard, and it would be over. They would dispose of him. She would never see him again—never have to think about him again, never again have to cry into her pillow until it was a soggy sponge.

But she knew that was all just bravado. She would never, ever do anything to hurt him if she could help it.

He gave her a crooked grin as though to say, "Didn't you know I'd be back?"

No, she didn't know. She hadn't known. And she still didn't want to believe it. She didn't say a word.

Quickly, she turned and looked out into the courtyard. Leonardo was waiting patiently, humming a little tune as he looked at the fountain. Biting her lower lip, she turned and managed to stagger out of the dressing room towards him, stumbling a bit and panting for breath.

"What is it?" he said in alarm, stepping forward to catch her by the shoulders. He'd obviously noted that she was uncharacteristically disheveled. "Are you all right?"

"No." She flickered a glance his way, thinking fast, then took a deep breath and shook her head. "No. Migraine."

"Oh, no." He looked puzzled, but concerned.

She pulled away from his grip on her shoulders, regaining her equilibrium with effort.

"I…I'm sorry, but I don't think I can come with you right now. I can hardly even think straight."

"But you were fine thirty seconds ago," he noted, completely at sea.

"Migraines come on fast," she told him, putting a hand to the side of her head and wincing. "But a good lie-down will fix me up. How about…after tea?" She looked at him earnestly. "I'll meet you then. Say, five o'clock?"

Leonardo frowned, but he nodded. "All right. I've got a tennis match at three, so that will work out fine." He looked at her with real concern, but just a touch of wariness.

"I hope this won't affect your ability to go to the ball tonight."

"Oh, no, of course not."

"Everyone is expecting our announcement to be made there. And you will be wearing the tiara, won't you?"

She waved him away. "Leonardo, don't worry. I'll be wearing the tiara and all will be as planned. I should be fine by tonight."

"Good." He still seemed wary. "But you should see Dr. Dracken. I'll send him up."

"No!" She shook her head. "I just need to rest. Give me a few hours. I'll be good as new."

He studied her for a moment, then shrugged. "As you wish." He bent over her hand like a true suitor. "Until we meet again, my beloved betrothed."

She nodded, almost pushing him toward the gate. "Likewise, I'm sure," she said out of the corner of her mouth.

"Pip pip." And he was off.

She waited until she heard the outer gate clang, then turned like a fury and marched back into the dressing room. She ripped open the door and glared at Monte with a look in her eyes that should have frozen the blood in his veins.

"How dare you? How dare you do this?"

Her vehemence was actually throwing him off his game a bit. He had expected a little more joy at seeing him again. He was enjoying the sight of her. Why couldn't she feel the same?

She really was a feast for the senses. Her eyes were bright—even if that seemed to be anger for the moment—and her cheeks were smudged pink.

"How dare you do this to me again?" she demanded.

"This isn't like before," he protested. "This is totally different."

"Really? Here you are, sneaking into my country, just like before. Here you are, hiding in my chambers again. Just like before."

His smile was meant to be beguiling. "But this time, when I leave, you're going with me."

She stared at him, hating him and loving him at the same time. Going with him! What a dream that was. She could no more go with him than she could swim the channel. If only...

For just a split second, she allowed herself to give in to her emotions. If only things were different. How she would love to throw herself into his arms and hold him tight, to feel his hard face against hers, to sense his heart pound as his interest quickened…

But she couldn't do that. She couldn't even think about it. She'd spent too many nights dreaming of him, dreaming of his tender touch. She had to forget all that. Too many lives depended on her. She couldn't let him see the slightest crack in her armor.

And most of all, she couldn't let him know about the baby.

"How did you get in here?" she demanded coldly. "Oh, wait. Don't even try to tell me. You'll just lie."

The provocative expression in his eyes changed to ice in an instant.

"Pellea, I'm not a liar," he said in a low, urgent tone. "I'll tell you or I won't, but what I say will be the truth as I know it every time. Count on it."

Their gazes locked in mutual indignation. Pellea was truly angry with him for showing up like this, for complicating her life and endangering them both, and yet she knew she was using that anger as a shield. If he touched her, she would surely melt. Just looking at him did enough damage to her determined stance.

Why did he have to be so beautiful? With his dark hair and shocking blue eyes, he had film-star looks, but that wasn't all. He was tall, muscular, strong in a way that would make any woman swoon. He looked tough, capable of holding his own in a fight, and yet there was nothing cocky about him. He had a quiet confidence that made any form of showing off unnecessary. You just knew by looking at him that he was ready for any challenge—physical or intellectual.

But how about emotional? Despite all his strength, there was a certain sensitivity deep in his blue eyes. The sort of hint of vulnerability only a woman might notice. Or was that just hopeful dreaming on her part?

"Never mind all that," she said firmly. "We've got to get you out of here."

His anger drifted away like morning fog and his eyes were smiling again. "After I've gone to so much trouble to get in?"

Oh, please don't smile at me! she begged silently. This was difficult enough without this charm offensive clouding her mind. She glared back.

"You are going. This very moment would be a good time to do it."

His gaze caressed her cheek. "How can I leave now that I've found you again?"

She gritted her teeth. "You're not going to mesmerize me like you did last time. You're not staying here at all." She pointed toward the gate. "I want you to go."

He raised one dark eyebrow and made no move toward the door. "You going to call the guard?"

Her eyes blazed at him. "If I have to."

He looked pained. "Actually, I'd rather you didn't."

"Then you'd better go, hadn't you?"

He sighed and managed to look as though he regretted all this. "I can't leave yet. Not without what I came for."

She threw up her hands. "That has nothing to do with me."

His smile was back. "That's where you're wrong. You see, it's you that I came for. How do you feel about a good old-fashioned kidnapping?"

CHAPTER TWO

PELLEA BLINKED QUICKLY, but that was the only sign she allowed to show his words had shocked her—rocked her, actually, to the point where she almost needed to reach out and hold on to something to keep from falling over.

Monte had come to kidnap her? Was he joking? Or was he crazy?

"Really?" With effort, she managed to fill her look with mock disdain. "How do you propose to get me past all the guards and barriers? How do you think you'll manage that without someone noticing? Especially when I'll be fighting you every step of the way and creating a scene and doing everything else I can think of to ruin your silly kidnapping scheme?"

"I've got a plan." He favored her with a knowing grin.

"Oh, I see." Eyes wide, she turned with a shrug, as though asking the world to judge him. "He's got a plan. Say no more."

He followed her. "You scoff, Pellea. But you'll soon see things my way."

She whirled to face him and her gaze sharpened as she remembered his last visit. "How do you get in here, anyway? You've never explained that." She shook her head, considering him from another angle. "There are guards everywhere. How do you get past them?"

His grin widened. "Secrets of the trade, my dear."

"And just what is your trade these days?" she asked archly. "Second-story man?"

"No, Pellea." His grin faded. Now they were talking about serious things. "Actually, I still consider myself the royal heir to the Ambrian throne."

She rolled her eyes. "Good luck with that one."

He turned and met her gaze with an intensity that burned. "I'm the Crown Prince of Ambria. Hadn't you heard? I thought you understood that."

She stared back at him. "That's over," she said softly, searching his eyes. "Long over."

He shook his head slowly, his blue eyes burning with a surreal light. "No. It's real and it's now. And very soon, the world will know it."

Fear gripped her heart. What he was suggesting was war. People she loved would be hurt. And yet…

Reaching out, she touched him, forgetting her vow not to. She flattened her palm against his chest and felt his heartbeat, felt the heat and the flesh of him.

"Oh, please, Monte," she whispered, her eyes filled with the sadness of a long future of suffering. "Please, don't…"

He took her hand and brought it to his lips, kissing the center of her palm without losing his hold on her gaze for a moment. "I won't let anything hurt you," he promised, though he knew he might as well whistle into the wind. Once his operation went into action, all bets would be off. "You know that."

She shook her head, rejecting what he'd said. "No, Monte, I don't know that. You plan to come in here and rip our lives apart. Once you start a revolution, you start a fire in the people and you can't control where that fire will burn. There will be pain and agony on all sides. There always is."

His shrug was elaborate on purpose. "There was pain and agony that night twenty-five years ago when my mother and my father were killed by the Granvillis. When I and my brothers and sisters were spirited off into the night and told to forget we were royal. In one fire-ravaged night, we lost our home, our kingdom, our destiny and our parents." His head went back and he winced as though the pain was still fresh. "What do you want me to do? Forgive those who did that to me and mine?"

A look of pure determination froze his face into the mask of a warrior. "I'll never do that. They need to pay."

She winced. Fear gripped her heart. She knew what this meant. Her own beloved father was counted among Monte's enemies. But she also knew that he was strong and determined, and he meant what he threatened. Wasn't there any way she could stop this from happening?

The entry gong sounded, making them both jump.

"Yes?" she called out, hiding her alarm.

"Excuse me, Miss Marallis," a voice called in. "It's Sergeant Fromer. I just wanted to check what time you wanted us to bring the tiara by."

"The guard," she whispered, looking at Monte sharply. "I should ask him in right now."

He held her gaze. "But you won't," he said softly.

She stared at him for a long moment. She wanted with all her heart to prove him wrong. She should do it. It would be so easy, wouldn't it?

"Miss?" the guard called in again.

"Uh, sorry, Sergeant Fromer." She looked at Monte again and knew she wouldn't do it. She shook her head, ashamed of herself. "About seven would be best," she called to him. "The hairdresser should be here by then."

"Will do. Thank you, miss."

And he was gone, carrying with him all hope for sanity. She stared at the area of the gate.

There it was—another chance to do the right thing and rid herself of this menace to her peace of mind forever. Why couldn't she follow through? She turned and looked at Monte, her heart sinking. Was she doomed? Not if she stayed strong. This couldn't be like it was before. She'd been vulnerable the last time. She'd just had the horrible fight with her father that she had been dreading for years, and when Monte had jumped into her life, she was in the mood to do dangerous things.

The first time she'd seen him, he'd appeared seemingly out of nowhere and found her sobbing beside her fountain. She'd just come back to her chambers from that fight and she'd been sick at heart, hating that she'd hurt the man she loved most in the world—her father. And so afraid that she would have to do what he wanted her to do anyway.

Her father's health had begun to fade at that point, but he wasn't bedridden yet, as he was now. He'd summoned her to his room and told her in no uncertain terms that he expected her to marry Leonardo. And she'd told him in similar fashion that she would have to be dragged kicking and screaming to the altar. No other way would work. He'd called her an ungrateful child and had brought up the fact that she was looking to be an old maid soon if she didn't get herself a husband. She'd called him an overbearing parent and threatened to marry the gardener.

That certainly got a response, but it was mainly negative and she regretted having said such a thing now. But he'd been passionate, almost obsessive about the need for her to marry Leonardo.

"Marry the man. You've known him all your life. You get along fine. He wants you, and as his wife, you'll have so much power…"

"Power!" she'd responded with disdain. "All you care about is power."

His face had gone white. "Power is important," he told her in a clipped, hard voice. "As much as you may try to pretend otherwise, it rules our lives." And then, haltingly, he'd told her the story of what had happened to her mother—the real story this time, not the one she'd grown up believing.

"Victor Halma wanted her," he said, naming the man who had been the Granvillis' top enforcer when Pellea was a very small child.

"Wha-what do you mean?" she'd stammered. There was a sick feeling in the pit of her stomach and she was afraid she understood only too well.

"He was always searching her out in the halls, showing up unexpectedly whenever she thought she was safe. He wouldn't leave her alone. She was in a panic."

She closed her eyes and murmured, "My poor mother."

"There was still a lot of hostility toward me because I had worked with the DeAngelis royal family before the revolution," he went on. "I wasn't trusted then as I am now. I tried to fight him, but it was soon apparent I had no one on my side." He drew in a deep breath. "I was sent on a business trip to Paris. He made his move while I was gone."

"Father…"

"You see, I had no power." His face, already pale, took on a haggard look. "I couldn't refuse to go. And once I was gone, he forced her to go to his quarters."

Pellea gasped, shivering as though an icy blast had swept into the room.

"She tried to run away, but he had the guard drag her into his chamber and lock her in. And there, while she was waiting, she found a knife and killed herself before he could…" His voice trailed off.

Pellea's hands clutched her throat. "You always told me she died during an influenza epidemic," she choked out. She was overwhelmed with this news, and yet, deep down, she'd always known there was something she wasn't being told.

He nodded. "That was what I told you. That was what I told everyone. And there was an epidemic at the time. But she didn't die of influenza. She died of shame."

Pellea swayed. The room seemed to dip and swerve around her. "And the man?" she asked hoarsely.

"He had an unfortunate accident soon after," her father said dryly, making it clear he wasn't about to go into details. "But you understand me, don't you? You see the position we were in? That's what happens when you don't have power."

"Or when you work for horrible people," she shot back passionately.

Shaking his head, he almost smiled. "The strange thing was, the Granvillis started to trust me after that. I moved up in the ranks. I gained power." He looked at his daughter sternly. "Today, nothing like that could happen to me. And what I want for you is that same sort of immunity from harm."

She understood what he wanted for her. She ached with love for him, ached for what he'd gone through, ached for what her own mother had endured. Her heart broke for them all.

But she still hadn't been able to contemplate marrying Leonardo. Not then.

To some degree, she could relate to his obsession to get and hold power. Still, it was his obsession, not hers and she had no interest in making the sort of down payment on a sense of control that marrying Leonardo would entail.

But this had been the condition she'd been in when she'd first looked up and found Monte standing in her courtyard. She knew she'd never seen him before, and that was unusual. This was a small country and most in the castle had been there for years. You tended to know everyone you ran into, at least by sight. She'd jumped up and looked toward the gate, as though to run.

But he'd smiled. Something in that smile captivated her every time, and it had all begun that afternoon.

"Hi," he'd said. "I'm running from some castle guards. Mind if I hide in here?"

Even as he spoke, she heard the guards at the gate. And just that quickly, she became a renegade.

"Hurry, hide in there," she'd said, pointing to her bedroom. "Behind the bookcase." She'd turned toward the gate. "I'll deal with the guards."

And so began her life as an accomplice to a criminal—and so also her infatuation with the most wrong man she could have fallen in love with.

Monte didn't really appreciate the effort all this had cost her. He'd taken it for granted that she would send the guard away. She'd done the same thing the last time he was here—and that had been more dangerous for them both—because they'd already seen him in the halls at that point. The whole castle was turned upside down for the next two days as they hunted for him. And the entire time, she'd had him hidden in her bedroom.

No one knew he was here now except Pellea—so far.

"Was that the DeAngelis tiara you were talking about just now?" he asked her. "I thought I heard Leonardo bring it up."

She glared at him. "How long have you been here spying on me? What else did you hear?"

He raised an eyebrow. "What else didn't you want me to hear?"

She threw her hands up.

"Don't worry," he said. "The wedding-dress-design discussion and your talk with Leonardo were about it."

They both turned to look at the beautiful gown hanging against a tall, mahogany wardrobe. "Is this the gown you're wearing to the ball tonight?"

"Yes."

It was stunning. Black velvet swirled against deep green satin. It hung before him looking as though it was already filled with a warm, womanly body. Reaching out, he spanned the waist of it with his hands and imagined dancing with her.

"The DeAngelis tiara will look spectacular with this," he told her.

"Do you remember what it looks like?" she asked in surprise.

"Not in great detail. But I've seen pictures." He gave her a sideways look of irony. "My mother's tiara."

She shivered, pulling her arms in close about her. "It hasn't been your mother's tiara for a long, long time," she said, wishing she didn't sound so defensive.

He nodded slowly. "My mother's and that of every

other queen of Ambria going back at least three centuries," he added softly, almost to himself.

She shivered again. "I'm sure you're right."

His smile was humorless. "To the victor go the spoils."

"I didn't make the rules." Inside, she groaned. Still defensive. But she did feel the guilt of the past. How could she not?

"And yet, it will take more than twenty-five years to erase the memories that are centuries old. Memories of what my family accomplished here."

She bit her lip, then looked at him, looked at the sense of tragedy in his beautiful blue eyes, and felt the tug on her heart.

"I'm sorry," she said quickly, reaching for him and putting a hand on his upper arm. "I'm sorry that I have to wear your mother's tiara. They've asked me to do it and I said yes."

He covered her hand with his own and turned toward her. She recognized the light in his eyes and knew he wanted to kiss her. Her pulse raced, but she couldn't let it happen. Quickly, she pulled away.

He sighed, shaking his head in regret, but his mind was still on something else.

"Where is it?" he asked, looking around the wardrobe. "Where do you keep it?"

"The tiara?" She searched his eyes. What was he thinking? "It's in its case in the museum room, where it always is. Didn't you hear Sergeant Fromer? The guards will bring it to me just before I leave for the ball. And they will accompany me to the ballroom. The tiara is under guard at all times."

He nodded, eyeing her speculatively. "And so shall you be, once you put it on."

"I imagine so."

He nodded again, looking thoughtful. "I was just reading an article about it the other day," he said, half musing. "Diamonds, rubies, emeralds, all huge and of superior quality. Not to mention the wonderful craftsmanship of the tiara itself. It's estimated to be worth more than some small countries are."

Suddenly she drew her breath in. She hadn't known him long, but she was pretty sure she knew a certain side of him all too well.

"Oh, no you don't!" she cried, all outrage.

He looked at her in surprise. "What?"

She glared at him. "You're thinking about grabbing it, aren't you?"

"The tiara?" He stared at her for a moment and then he threw his head back and laughed. That was actually a fabulous idea. He liked the way she thought.

"Pellea," he said, taking her by the shoulders and dropping a kiss on her forehead. "You are perfection itself. You can't marry Leonardo."

She shivered. She couldn't help it. His touch was like agony and ecstasy, all rolled into one. But she kept her head about her.

"Who shall I marry then?" she responded quickly. "Are you ready to give me an offer?"

He stared at her, not responding. How could he say

anything? He couldn't make her an offer. He couldn't marry her. And anyway, he might be dead by the end of the summer.

Besides, there was another factor. If he was going to be ruler of Ambria, could he marry the daughter of his family's biggest betrayer? Not likely.

"I think kidnapping will work out better," he told her, and he wasn't joking.

She'd known he would say that, or something similar. She knew he was attracted to her. That, he couldn't hide. But she was a realist and she also knew he hated her father and the current regime with which she was allied. How could it be any other way? He could talk about taking her with him all he wanted, she knew there was no future for her there.

"I'll fight you all the way," she said flatly.

He smiled down into her fierce eyes. "There's always the best option, of course."

"And what is that?"

"That you come with me willingly."

She snorted. "Right. Before or after I marry Leonardo?"

He looked pained. "I can't believe you're serious."

She raised her chin and glared at him. "I am marrying Leonardo in four days. I hope."

He brushed the stray hairs back off her cheek and his fingers lingered, caressing her silken skin. "But why?" he asked softly.

"Because I want to," she responded stoutly. "I've promised I will do it and I mean to keep that promise."

Resolutely, she turned away from him and began searching through a clothes rack, looking for the clothes she meant to change into.

He came up behind her. "Is it because of your father?"

She whirled and stared at him. "Leave my father out of this."

"Ah-hah. So it is your father."

She turned back to searching through the hangers. He watched her for a moment, thinking that he'd never known a woman whose movements were so fluid. Every move she made was almost a part of a dance. And watching her turned him on in ways that were bound to cripple his ability to think clearly. He shook his head. He couldn't let that happen, not if he wanted to succeed here.

"Leonardo," he scoffed. "Please. Why Leonardo?"

Unconsciously, she cupped her hand over her belly. There was a tiny baby growing inside. He must never know that. He was the last person she could tell—ever. "It's my father's fondest wish."

"Because he might become ruler of Ambria?"

"Yes." How could she deny it? "And because he asked."

That set him back a moment. "What if I asked?" he ventured.

She turned to him, but his eyes showed nothing that could give her any hope. "Ah, but you won't, will you?"

He looked away. "Probably not."

"There's your answer."

"Where is Georges?" he asked, naming the Granvilli who had killed his parents. "What does he say about all this?"

She hesitated, choosing her words carefully. "The General seems to be unwell right now. I'm not sure what the specific problem is, but he's resting in the seaside villa at Grapevine Bay. Leonardo has been taking over more and more of the responsibilities of power himself." She raised her head and looked him squarely in the eye. "And the work seems to suit him."

"Does it? I hope he's enjoying himself. He won't have much longer to do that, as I intend to take that job away from him shortly."

She threw up her hands, not sure if he meant it or if this was just typical male bombast. "What exactly do you mean to do?" she asked, trying to pin him down.

He looked at her and smiled, coming closer, touching her hair with one hand.

"Nothing that you need to worry about."

But his thoughts were not nearly as sanguine as he pretended. She really had no conception of how deep his anger lay and how his hatred had eaten away at him for most of his life. Ever since that night when the castle had burned and his parents were murdered by the Granvilli clan. Payment was due. Retribution was pending.

"Is your father really very ill?" he asked quietly.

"Yes." She found the shirt she wanted and pulled it down.

"And you want to make him happy before he…"

He swallowed his next words even before she snapped her head around and ordered curtly, "Don't say it!"

He bit his tongue. That was a stupid thing to have thought, even if he never actually got the words out. He didn't mind annoying her about things he didn't think she should care so much about, but to annoy her about her father was just plain counterproductive.

"Well, he would like to see you become the future first lady of the land, wouldn't he?" he amended lamely.

He tried to think of what he knew about her father. Marallis had been considered an up-and-coming advisor in his own father's regime. From what he'd been able to glean, the king had recognized his superior abilities and planned to place him in a top job. And then the rebellion had swept over them, and it turned out Vaneck Marallis had signed on with the other side. Was it any wonder he should feel betrayed by the man? He was the enemy. He very likely gave the rebels the inside information they needed to win the day. There was no little corner of his heart that had any intention of working on forgiveness for the man.

"Okay, it's getting late," she said impatiently. "I have to go check on my father."

"Because he's ill?"

"Because he's very ill." She knew she needed to elaborate, but when she tried to speak, her throat choked and she had to pause, waiting for her voice to clear again. "I always go in to see him for a few minutes at this time in the afternoon." She looked at him. "When I get back, we'll have to decide what I'm going to do with you."

"Will we?" His grin was ample evidence of his opinion on the matter, but she turned away and didn't bother to challenge him.

Going to her clothes rack, she pulled out a trim, cream-colored linen suit with slacks and a crisp jacket and slipped behind a privacy screen to change into them. He watched as she emerged, looking quietly efficient and good at whatever job she might be attempting. And ravishingly beautiful at the same time. He'd never known another woman who impressed him as much as this one did. Once again he had a pressing urge to find a way to take her with him.

It wouldn't be impossible. She thought he would have to get her past the guards, but she was wrong. He had his own way into the castle and he could easily get her out. But only if she was at least halfway cooperative. It was up to him to convince her to be.

"I don't have time to decide what to do with you right now," she told him, her gaze hooded as she met his eyes. "I have to go check on my father, and it's getting late. You stay here and hold down the fort. I'll be back in about half an hour."

"I may be here," he offered casually. "Or not."

She hesitated. She didn't like that answer. "Tell me now, are you going to stay here and wait, or are you going to go looking for Leonardo and get killed?" she demanded of him.

He laughed shortly. "I think I can handle myself around your so-called fiancé," he said dismissively.

Her gaze sharpened and she looked seriously into his

eyes. "Watch out for Leonardo. He'll kill you without batting an eye."

"Are you serious? That prancing prig?"

She shook her head. "Don't be fooled by his veneer of urbanity. He's hard as nails. When I suggested you might be killed, I meant it."

He searched her eyes for evidence that she really cared. It was there, much as she tried to hide it. He smiled.

"I'm not too keen on the 'killed' part. But as for the rest…"

She glanced at her watch. Time was fleeting. "I'm running out of time," she told him. "Go out and wait in the courtyard. I just have one last thing to check."

"What's that?" he asked.

She looked pained. "None of your business. I do have my privacy to maintain. Now go out and wait."

He walked out into the lush courtyard and heard the door click shut behind him. Turning, he could see her through the glass door, walking back into her closet again. Probably changed her mind on what to wear, he thought to himself. And he had a twinge of regret. He didn't have all that much time here and he hated to think of missing a moment with her.

Did that mean he'd given up on the kidnapping? No. Not at all. Still, there was more to this trip than just seeing Pellea.

He scanned the courtyard and breathed in the atmosphere. The castle of his ancestors was all around him.

For a few minutes, he thought about his place in history. Would he be able to restore the monarchy? Would he bring his family back to their rightful place, where they should have been all along?

Of course he would. He didn't allow doubts. His family belonged here and he would see that it happened. He'd already found two of his brothers, part of the group of "Lost Royals" who had escaped when the castle was burned and had hidden from the wrath of the Granvillis ever since. There were two more brothers and two sisters he hadn't found yet. But he hoped to. He hoped to bring them all back here to Ambria by the end of the summer.

He turned and looked through the French doors into her bedroom and saw the huge, soft bed where he'd spent most of the two and a half days when he'd been here before. Memories flooded back. He remembered her and her luscious body and he groaned softly, feeling the surge of desire again.

Pellea was special. He couldn't remember another woman who had ever stuck in his mind the way she did. She'd embedded herself into his heart, his soul, his imagination, and he didn't even want to be free of her. And that was a revelation.

If he survived this summer…

No, he couldn't promise anything, not even to himself. After all, her father was the man who had betrayed his family. He couldn't let himself forget that.

But where was she? She'd been gone a long time. He turned back and looked at the closed doors to her dressing room, then moved to them and called softly, "Pellea."

There was no response.

"Pellea?"

Still nothing. He didn't want to make his call any louder. You never knew who might be at the gate or near enough to it to hear his voice. He tried the knob instead, pushing the door open a bit and calling again, "Pellea?"

There was no answer. It was quite apparent she wasn't there.

CHAPTER THREE

ALARM BELLS RANG IN Monte's head and adrenaline flooded his system. Where had she gone? How had she escaped without him seeing her? What was she doing? Had he overestimated his ability to charm, compared to Leonardo's ability to hand out a power position? Was she a traitor, just like her father?

All that flashed through his mind, sending him reeling. But that only lasted seconds before he'd dismissed it out of hand. She wouldn't do that. There had to be a reason.

The last he'd seen of her she was heading into her large, walk-in closet at the far side of the dressing room. He was there in two strides, and that is when he saw, behind a clothing bar loaded with fluffy gowns, the glimmer of something electronic just beyond a door that had been left slightly ajar.

A secret room behind the clothing storage. Who knew? He certainly hadn't known anything about it when he'd been here before.

Reaching in through the gowns, he pushed the door fully open. And there was Pellea, sitting before a large computer screen that was displaying a number of windows, all showing places in the castle itself. She had a whole command center in here.

"Why you little vixen," he said, astounded. "What do you have here? You've tapped into a gold mine."

She looked up at him, startled, and then resigned.

"I knew I should have closed that door all the way," she muttered to herself.

But he was still captured by the computer screen. "This is the castle security system, isn't it?"

She sighed. "Yes. You caught me."

He shook his head, staring at the screen. "How did you do that?" he asked in wonder.

She shrugged. "My father had this secret room installed years ago. Whenever he wanted to take a look at what was going on, he came to me for a visit. I didn't use it myself at first. I didn't see any need for it. But lately, I've found it quite handy."

"And you can keep things running properly on your own?"

"I've got a certain amount of IT talent. I've read a few books."

He looked at her and smiled. "My admiration grows."

She colored a bit and looked away.

"So you can see what's going on at all the major interior intersections, and a few of the outside venues as well. How convenient." His mind was racing with possibilities.

She pushed away from the desk and sighed again. "Monte, I shouldn't have let you see this."

"You didn't let me. I did it all on my own." He shook his head, still impressed. "Are you going to tell me why?"

She sighed again. "There are times when one might want to do things without being observed. Here in the castle, someone is always watching." She shrugged. "I like a little anonymity in my life. This way I can get a pretty good idea of who is doing what and I can bide my time."

"I see."

She rose and turned toward the door. "And now I really am late." She looked back. He followed her out reluctantly and she closed the door carefully. It seemed to disappear into the background of paneling and molding strips that surrounded it.

"See you later," she said, leading him away from the area. "And stay out of that room."

He frowned as she started off. He didn't want her to leave, and he also didn't want to miss out on anything he didn't have to. On impulse, he called after her, "I want to go with you."

She whirled and stared at him. "What?"

"I'd like to see your father."

She came back towards him, shocked and looking for a way to refuse. "But you can't. He's bedridden. He's in no condition…"

"I won't show myself to him. I won't hurt him." He shook his head and frowned. "But, Pellea, he's one of the few remaining ties to my parents left alive. He's from their generation. He knew them, worked with them. He was close to them at one time." He shrugged, looking oddly vulnerable in his emotional reactions. "I just want to see him, hear his voice. I promise I won't do anything to jeopardize his health—or even his emotional well-being in any way."

She studied him and wondered what she really knew about him. The way he felt about her father had been clear almost from the first. He was wrong about her father. She'd spent a lot of time agonizing over that, wondering how she could make him understand that her father was just a part of his time and place, that he had only done what he had to do, that he was really a man of great compassion and honesty. Maybe this would be a chance to do just that.

"You won't confront him about anything?"

"No. I swear." He half smiled. "I swear on my parents' memories. Do you trust me?"

She groaned. "God help me, I do." She searched his eyes. "All right. But you'll have to be careful. If you're caught, I'll claim you forced me to take you with me."

He smiled at her sideways, knowing she was lying. If he were caught, she would do her best to free him. She talked a good game, but deep down, she had a lot of integrity. And she was at least half in love with him. That gave him a twinge. More the fool was she.

"I only go when no one else is there," she was telling him. "I know when the nurse goes on her break and how long she takes."

He nodded. He'd always known she was quick and

sure at everything she did. He would have expected as much from her.

"Keep your eyes downcast," she lectured as they prepared to head into the hallway. "I try to go at a quiet time of day, but there might be someone in the halls. Don't make eye contact with anyone or you'll surely blow your cover. You can't help but look regal, can you? Take smaller steps. Try to slump your shoulders a little. A little more." She made a face. "Here." She whacked one shoulder to make it droop, and then the other, a tiny smile on her lips. "That's better," she said with satisfaction.

He was suspicious. She hadn't held back much. "You enjoyed that, didn't you?"

"Giving you a whack?" She allowed herself a tight smile. "Certainly not. I don't believe in corporal punishment."

"Liar." He was laughing at her. "Are you going to try to convince me that it hurt you more than it hurt me?"

She didn't bother to respond. Giving him a look, she stepped out into the hallway, wondering if she was crazy to do this. But she was being honest when she said she trusted him to come along and see her father with her. Was she letting her heart rule her head? Probably. But she'd made her decision and she would stick to it.

Still, that didn't mean she was sanguine about it all. Why had he come back? Why now, just when she had everything set the way it had to be?

And why was her heart beating like a caged bird inside her chest? It didn't matter that she loved him. She couldn't ever be with him again. She had a baby to think about. And no time to indulge in emotions. Taking Monte with her was a risk, but she didn't really have a lot of choice—unless she wanted to turn him in to the guard.

She thought about doing exactly that for a few seconds, a smile playing on her lips. That would take them back full circle, wouldn't it? But it wasn't going to happen.

Don't worry, sweet baby, she said silently to her child. *I won't let anything hurt your father.* She said a tiny prayer and added, *I hope.*

Monte wasn't often haunted by self-doubt. In fact, his opinions and decisions were usually rock-solid. Once made, no wavering. But watching Pellea with her father gave him a sense that the earth might not be quite as firm under his feet as he'd assumed.

In the first place, he wasn't really sure why she'd let him come with her. She knew how the need for retribution burned in him and yet she'd let him come here where he would have a full view of the man, his enemy, lying there, helpless. Didn't she know how dangerous that was?

It would be easy to harm the old man. He was still handsome in an aged, fragile way, like a relic of past power. His face was drawn and lined, his color pale, his thin hair silver. Blue veins stood out in his slender hands. He was so vulnerable, so completely defenseless. Someone who moved on pure gut reaction would have done him in by now. Luckily, that wasn't Monte's style.

He would never do such a thing, but she didn't really know that. She'd taken a risk. But for what?

He watched as the object of his long, deep hatred struggled to talk to the daughter he obviously loved more than life itself, and he found his emotions tangling a bit. Could he really feel pity for a man who had helped ruin his family?

No. That couldn't happen.

Still, an element confused the issue. And to be this close to someone who had lived with and worked with his parents gave him a special sense of his own history. He couldn't deny that.

And there was something else, a certain primal longing that he couldn't control. He'd had it ever since that day twenty-five years ago when he'd been rushed out of the burning castle, and he had forever lost his parents. He'd grown up with all the privileges of his class: the schools, the high life, the international relationships. But he would have thrown it all out if that could have bought him a real, loving family—the kind you saw in movies, the kind you dreamed about in the middle of the night. Instead, he had this empty ache in his heart.

And that made watching Pellea and her father all the more effective. From his position in the entryway, he could see her bending lovingly over her father and dropping a kiss on his forehead. She talked softly to him, wiping his forehead with a cool, damp cloth, straightening his covers, plumping his pillow. The love she had for the man radiated from her every move. And he felt very similarly. She was obviously a brilliant bit of sun in his rather dark life.

"How are you feeling?" she asked.

"Much better now that you're here, my dear."

"I'm only here for a moment. I must get back. The masked ball is tonight."

"Ah, yes." He took hold of her hand. "So tonight you and Leonardo will announce your engagement?"

"Yes. Leonardo is prepared."

"What a relief to have this coming so quickly. To be able to see you protected before I go…"

"Don't talk about going."

"We all have to do it, my dear. My time has come."

Pellea made a dove-like noise and bent down to kiss his cheek. "No. You just need to get out more. See some people." Rising a bit, she had a thought. "I know. I'll have the nurse bring you to the ball so that you can see for yourself…."

"Hush, Pellea," he said, shaking his head. "I'm not going anywhere. I'm comfortable here and I'm too weak to leave this bed."

Reluctantly, she nodded. She'd known he would say that, but she'd hoped he might change his mind and try to take a step back into the world. A deep, abiding sadness settled into her soul as she faced the fact that he wasn't even tempted to try. He was preparing for the end, and nothing she said or did would change that. Tears threatened and she forced them back. She would have to save her grieving for another time.

Right now, she had another goal in mind. She was

hoping to prove something to Monte, and she was gambling that her father would respond in the tone and tenor that she'd heard from him so often before. If he went in a different direction, there was no telling what might happen. Glancing back at where Monte stood in the shadows, she made her decision. She was going to risk it—her leap of faith.

"Father, do you ever think of the past? About how we got here and why we are the way we are?"

He coughed and nodded. "I think of very little else these days."

"Do you think about the night the castle burned?"

"That was before you were born."

"Yes. But I feel as though that night molded my life in many ways."

He grasped her hand as though to make her stop it. "But why? It had nothing to do with you."

"But it was such a terrible way to start a new regime, the regime I've lived under all my life."

"Ugly things always happen in war." He turned his face away as though he didn't want to talk about it. "These things can't be helped."

She could feel Monte's anger beginning to simmer even though she didn't look at him. She hesitated. If her father wasn't going to express his remorse, she might only be doing damage by making him talk. Could Monte control his emotions? Was it worth it to push this further?

She had to try. She leaned forward.

"But, Father, you always say so many mistakes were made."

"Mistakes are human. That is just the way it is."

Monte made a sound that was very close to a growl. She shook her head, still unwilling to look his way, but ready to give up. What she'd hoped for just wasn't going to happen.

"All right, Father," she began, straightening and preparing to get Monte out of here before he did something ugly.

But suddenly her father was speaking again. "The burning of the castle was a terrible thing," he was saying, though he was speaking so softly she wondered if Monte could hear him. "And the assassination of the king and queen was even worse."

Relief bloomed in her chest. "What happened?" she prompted him. "How did it get so out of control?"

"You can go into a war with all sorts of lofty ambitions, but once the fuse is lit, the fire can be uncontrollable. It wasn't supposed to happen that way. Many of us were sick at heart for years afterwards. I still think of it with pain and deep, deep regret."

This was more like it. She only hoped Monte could hear it and that he was taking it as a sincere recollection, not a rationalization. She laced her fingers with her father's long, trembling ones.

"Tell me again, why did you sign on with the rebels?"

"I was very callow and I felt the DeAngelis family had grown arrogant with too much power. They were rejecting all forms of modernization. Something was needed to shake the country up. We were impatient. We thought something had to be done."

"And now?"

"Now I think that we should have moved more slowly, attempted dialogue instead of attack."

"So you regret how things developed?"

"I regret it deeply."

She glanced back at Monte. His face looked like a storm cloud. Wasn't he getting it? Didn't he see how her father had suffered as well? Maybe not. Maybe she was tilting at windmills. She turned back to her father and asked a question for herself.

"Then why do you want me to marry Leonardo and just perpetuate this regime?"

Her father coughed again and held a handkerchief to his lips. "He'll be better than his father. He has some good ideas. And your influence on him will work wonders." He managed a weak smile for his beloved daughter. "Once you are married to Leonardo, it will be much more difficult for anyone to hurt you."

She smiled down at him and blotted his forehead with the damp cloth. He wouldn't be so sure of that if he knew that at this very moment, danger lurked around her on all sides. Better he should never know that she was carrying Monte's child.

"I must go, Father. I've got to prepare for the ball."

"Yes. Go, my darling. Have a wonderful time."

"I'll be back in the morning to tell you all about it," she promised as she rose from his side.

She hurried toward the door, jerking her head at Monte to follow. She didn't like the look on his face. It seemed his hatred for her father was too strong for him to see what a dear and wonderful man he really was. Well, so be it. She'd done her best to show him the truth. You could lead a horse to water and all that.

But they were late. She had a path laid out and a routine, and now she knew she was venturing out into the unknown. At her usual time, she never met anyone in the halls. Now—who knew?

"We have to hurry," she said once they were outside the room. She quickly looked up and down the empty hallway. "I've got to meet Leonardo in just a short time." She started off. "Quickly. We don't want to meet anyone if we can help it."

The words were barely out of her mouth when she heard loud footsteps coming from around the bend in the walkway. Only boots could make such a racket. It had to be the guards. It sounded like two of them.

"Quick," she said, reaching for the closest door. "In here."

Though she knew the castle well, she wasn't sure what door she'd reached for. There was a library along this corridor, and a few bedrooms of lower-ranking relatives of the Granvillis. Any one of them could have yielded disaster. But for once, she was in luck. The door she'd chosen opened to reveal a very small broom closet.

Monte looked in and didn't see room for them both. He turned back to tell her, but she wasn't listening.

"In," she whispered urgently, and gave him a shove,

then came pushing in behind him, closing the door as quietly as she could. But was it quietly enough? Pressed close together, they each held their breath, listening as the boots came closer. And closer. And then stopped, right outside the door.

Pellea looked up at Monte, her eyes huge and anxious. He looked down at her and smiled. It was dark in the closet, but enough light came in around the door to let him make out her features. She was so beautiful and so close against him. He wanted to kiss her. But more important things had cropped up. So he reached around her and took hold of the knob from the inside.

There was a muttering conversation they couldn't make out, and then one of the guards tried the knob. Monte clamped down on his lower lip, holding the knob with all his might.

"It's locked," one of the guards said. "We'll have to find the concierge and get a key."

The other guard swore, but they began to drift off, walking slowly this time and chattering among themselves.

Monte relaxed and let go of the knob, letting out a long sigh of relief. When he looked down, she was smiling up at him, and this time he kissed her.

He'd been thinking about this kiss for so long, and now, finally, here it was. Her lips were smooth as silk, warm and inviting, and for just a moment, she opened enough to let his tongue flicker into the heat she held deeper. Then she tried to pull away, but he took her head in his hands and kissed her longer, deeper, and he felt her begin to melt in his arms.

Her body was molded to his and he could feel her heart begin to pound again, just as it had when they'd almost been caught. The excitement lit a flame in him and he pulled her closer, kissed her harder, wanted her all to himself, body and soul.

It was as though he'd forgotten where they were, what was happening around them. But Pellea hadn't.

"Monte," she finally managed to gasp, pushing him as hard as she could. "We have to go while we have the chance!"

He knew she was right and he let her pull away, but reluctantly. Still, he'd found out what he needed to know. The magic still lived between them and they could turn it on effortlessly. And, he hoped, a bit later, they would.

But now she opened the door tentatively and looked out. There was no one in the hall. She slipped out and he followed and they hurried to her gate, alert for any hint of anyone else coming their way. But they were lucky. She used a remote to open the gate as they approached. In seconds, they were safely inside.

The moment the gate closed, Monte turned and tried to take her into his arms again, but she backed away, trying hard to glare at him.

"Just stop it," she told him.

But he was shaking his head. "You can't marry Leonardo. Not when you can kiss me like that."

She stared at him for a moment. How could she have let this happen? He knew, he could tell that she was so in love with him, she could hardly contain it. She could protest all she wanted, he wasn't going to believe her. If she wasn't very careful, he would realize the precious secret that she was keeping from him, and if that happened, they would both be in terrible trouble.

Feeling overwhelmed, she groaned, her head in her hands. "Why are you torturing me like this?

He put a finger under her chin and forced her head up to meet his gaze. "Maybe a little torture will make you see the light."

"There's no light," she said sadly, her eyes huge with tragedy. "There's only darkness."

He'd been about to try to kiss her again, but something in her tone stopped him and he hesitated. Just a few weeks before, their relationship had been light and exciting, a romp despite the dangers they faced. They had made love, but they had also laughed a lot, and teased and played and generally enjoyed each other. Something had changed since then. Was it doubt? Wariness? Or fear?

He wasn't sure, but it bothered him and it held him off long enough for her to pivot out of his control.

"Gotta go," she said as she started for the gate, prepared to dash off again.

He took a step after her. "You're not planning to tell Leonardo I'm here, are you?" he said. His tone was teasing, as though he was confident she had no such plans.

She turned and looked at him, tempted to do or say something that would shake that annoying surety he had.

But she resisted that temptation. Instead, she told the truth.

"I'm hoping you won't be here any longer by the time I get back."

He appeared surprised. "Where would I go?"

She shook her head. It was obviously no use to try, but she had to make her case quickly and clearly. "Please, Monte," she said earnestly. "Go back the way you came in. Just do this for me. It will make my life a whole lot easier."

"Pellea, this is not your problem. I'll handle it."

She half laughed at his confidence. "What do you mean, not my problem? That's exactly what you are. My problem."

"Relax," he advised. "I'm just going to work on my objective."

"Which is?"

"I told you. I'm here to kidnap you and take you back to the continent with me."

"Oh, get off it. You can't kidnap me. I'm guarded day and night."

"Really? Well, where were your wonderful guards when I found my way into your chambers?"

She didn't have an answer for that one so she changed the subject. "What's the point? Why would you kidnap me?"

He shrugged. "To show them I can."

She threw up her hands. "Oh, brother."

"I want to show the Granvillis that I've been here and taken something precious to them."

Her eyes widened. "You think I'm precious?"

His smile was almost too personal. "I know you are. You're their most beautiful, desirable woman."

That gave her pause. Was she supposed to feel flattered by that? Well, she sort of did, but she wouldn't admit it.

"Gee, thanks. You make me feel like a prize horse." She shook her head. "So to you, this is just part of some war game?"

The laughter left his gaze. "Oh, no. This is no game. This is deadly serious."

There was something chilling in the way he said that. She shivered and tried to pretend she hadn't.

"So you grab me. You throw me over your shoulder and carry me back to your cave. You go 'nah nah nah' to the powers that be in Ambria." She shrugged. "What does that gain you?"

He watched her steadily, making her wonder what he saw. "The purpose is not just to thumb my nose at the Granvillis. The purpose is to cast them into disarray, to make them feel vulnerable and stupid. To throw them off their game. Let them spend their time obsessing on how I could have possibly gotten into the castle, how I could have possibly taken you out without someone seeing. Let them worry. It will make them weaker."

"You're crazy," she said for lack of anything else to say. And he was crazy if he thought the Granvillis would tumble into ruin because of a kidnapping or two.

"I'd like to see them tightening their defenses all around," he went on, "and begin scurrying about, looking for the chinks in their armor. There are people here who watch what they do and report to us. This will give us a better idea of where the weak spots are."

She nodded. She understood the theory behind all this. But it didn't make her any happier with it.

"So when you get right down to it, it doesn't have to be me," she noted. "You could take back something else of importance. The tiara, for instance."

Something moved behind his eyes, but he only smiled. "I'd rather take you."

"Well, you're not going to. So why not just get out of my hair and go back where you came from?"

He shook his head slowly, his blue eyes dark with shadows. "Sorry, Pellea. I've got things I must do here."

She sighed. She knew exactly what he would be doing while she was gone. He would be in her secret room, checking out what was going on all over the castle. Making his plans. Ruining her life. A wave of despair flooded through her. What had she done? Why hadn't she been more careful?

"Arrgghh!" she said, making a small wail of agony.

But right now she couldn't think about that. She had to go meet Leonardo or he would show up here.

"You stay out of my closet room," she told him with a warning look, knowing he wouldn't listen to a word she said. "Okay?" She glared at him, not bothering to wait for an answer. "I'll be back quicker than you think."

He laughed, watching her go, enjoying the way her

hips swayed in time with her gorgeous hair. And then she was gone and he headed straight for the closet.

To the casual eye, there was nothing of note to suggest a door to another room. The wall seemed solid enough. He tried to remember what she'd done to close it, but he hadn't been paying attention at the time. There had to be something—a special knock or a latch or a pressure point. He banged and pushed and tried to slide things, but nothing gave way.

"If this needs a magic password, I'm out of luck," he muttered to himself as he made his various attempts.

He kicked a little side panel, more in frustration than hope, and the door began to creak open. "It's always the ones you don't suspect," he said, laughing.

The small room inside was unprepossessing, having space only for a computer and a small table. And there on the screen was access to views of practically every public area, all over the castle. A secret room with centralized power no one else knew about. Ingenious.

Still, someone had built it. Someone had wired it. Someone had to know electronics were constantly running in here. The use of electricity alone would tip off the suspicious. So someone in the workings of the place was on her side.

But what was "her side" exactly? That was something he still had to find out.

The sound of Pellea's entry gong made him jerk. He lifted his head and listened. A woman's voice seemed to be calling out, and then, a moment later, singing. She'd obviously come into the courtyard.

Moving silently, he made his way out of the secret room, closing the door firmly. He moved carefully into the dressing area, planning to use the high wardrobe as a shield as he had done earlier, in order to see who it was without being seen. As he came out of the closet and made his way to slip behind the tall piece of furniture, a pretty, pleasantly rounded young woman stepped into the room, catching sight of him just before he found his hiding place.

She gasped. Their gazes met. Her mouth opened. He reached out to stop her, but he was too late.

She screamed at the top of her lungs.

CHAPTER FOUR

MONTE MOVED LIKE LIGHTNING but it felt like slow motion to him. In no time his hand was over the intruder's mouth and he was pulling her roughly into the room and kicking the French door closed with such a snap, he was afraid for a moment that the glass would crack.

Pulling her tightly against his chest, he snarled in her ear, "Shut the hell up and do it now."

She pulled her breath into her lungs in hysterical gasps, and he yanked her more tightly.

"Now!" he demanded.

She closed her eyes and tried very hard. He could feel the effort she put into it, and he began to relax. They waited, counting off the seconds, to see if anyone had heard the scream and was coming to the rescue. Nothing seemed to stir. At last, he decided the time for alarm was over and he began to release her slowly, ready to reassert control if she tried to scream again.

"Okay," he whispered close to her ear. "I'm going to let go now. If you make a sound, I'll have to knock you flat."

She nodded, accepting his terms. But she didn't seem

to have any intention of a repeat. As he freed her, she turned, her gaze sweeping over him in wonder.

"Wait," she said, eyes like saucers. "I've seen you before. You were here a couple of months ago."

By now, he'd recognized her as well. She was Pellea's favorite maid. He hadn't interacted with her when he'd been here before, but he'd seen her when she'd dropped by to deal with some things Pellea needed done. Pellea had trusted her to keep his presence a secret then. He only hoped that trust was warranted—and could hold for now.

But signs were good. He liked the sparkle in her eyes. He gave her a lopsided smile. "I'm back."

"So I see." She cocked her head to the side, looking him over, then narrowing her gaze. "And is my mistress happy that you're here?"

He shrugged. "Hard to tell. But she didn't throw anything at me."

Her smile was open-hearted. "That's a good sign."

He drew in a deep breath, feeling better about the situation. "What's your name?" he asked.

"Pellea calls me Kimmee."

"Then I shall do the same." He didn't offer his own name and wondered if she knew who he was. He doubted it. Pellea wouldn't be that reckless, would she?

"I've been here for a couple of hours now," he told her. "Pellea has seen me. We've been chatting, going over old times."

Kimmee grinned. "Delightful."

He smiled back, but added a warning look. "I'm

sure you don't talk about your mistress's assignations to others."

"Of course not," she said brightly. "I only wish she had a few."

He blinked. "What do you mean?"

She shrugged, giving him a sly look. "You're the only one I know of."

He laughed. She had said the one thing that would warm his heart and she probably knew it, but it made him happy anyway.

"You're not trying to tell me your mistress has no suitors, are you?" he teased skeptically.

"Oh, no, of course not. But she generally scorns them all."

He looked at her levelly. "Even Leonardo?" he asked.

She hesitated, obviously reluctant to give her candid opinion on that score. He let her off the hook with a shrug.

"Never mind. I know she's promised to him at this point." He cocked an eyebrow. "I just don't accept it."

She nodded. "Good," she whispered softly, then shook her head as though wishing she hadn't spoken. Turning away, she reached for the ball gown hanging in front of the wardrobe. "I just came by to check that the gown was properly hung and wrinkle-free," she said, smoothing the skirt a bit. "Isn't it gorgeous?"

"Yes, it is."

"I can't wait to see her dancing in this," Kimmee added.

"Neither can I," he murmured, and at the same time, an idea came to him. He frowned, wondering if he should trust thoughts spurred on by his overwhelming desire for all things Pellea. It was a crazy idea, but the more he mulled it over, the more he realized it could serve more than one purpose and fit into much of what he hoped to accomplish. So why not give it a try?

He studied the pretty maid for a moment, trying to evaluate just how much he dared depend on her. Her eyes sparkled in a way that made him wonder how a fun-loving girl like this would keep such a secret. He knew he had better be prepared to deal with the fallout, should there be any. After all, he didn't have much choice. Either he would tie her up and gag her and throw her into a closet, or he would appeal to her better nature.

"Tell me, Kimmee, do you love your mistress?"

"Oh, yes." Kimmee smiled. "She's my best friend. We've been mates since we were five years old."

He nodded, frowning thoughtfully. "Then you'll keep a secret," he said. "A secret that could get me killed if you reveal it."

Her eyes widened and she went very still. "Of course."

His own gaze was hard and assessing as he pinned her with it. "You swear on your honor?"

She shook her head, looking completely earnest. "I swear on my honor. I swear on my life. I swear on my…"

He held a hand up. "I get the idea, Kimmee. You really mean it. So I'm going to trust you."

She waited, wide-eyed.

He looked into her face, his own deadly serious.

"I want to go to the ball."

"Oh, sir!" She threw her hands up to her mouth. "Oh, my goodness! Where? How?"

"That's where you come in. Find me a costume and a nice, secure mask." He cocked an eyebrow and smiled at her. "Can you do that?"

"Impossible," she cried. "Simply impossible." But a smile was beginning to tease the corners of her mouth. "Well, maybe." She thought a moment longer, then smiled impishly. "It would be fun, wouldn't it?"

He grinned at her.

"Will you want a sword?" she asked, her enthusiasm growing by leaps and bounds.

He grimaced. "I think not. It might be too tempting to use it on Leonardo."

"I know what you mean," she said, nodding wisely.

He got a real kick out of her. She was so ready to join in on his plans and at the same time, she seemed to be thoroughly loyal to the mistress she considered her best friend. It was a helpful combination to work with.

He lifted his head, looking at the ball gown and thinking of how it would look with his favorite woman filling it out in all the right places. "All I want to do is go to the ball and dance with Pellea."

"How romantic," Kimmee said, sighing. Then her gaze sharpened as she realized what he might be describing. "You mean…?"

"Yes." He nodded. "Secretly. I want to surprise Pellea."

Kimmee gave a bubbling laugh, obviously delighted with the concept. "I think Leonardo will be even more surprised."

He shook his head and gave her a warning look. "That is something I'll have to guard against."

She sighed. "I understand. But it would be fun to see his face."

He frowned, wondering if he was letting her get a little too much into this.

"See what you can do," he said. "But don't forget. If Leonardo finds out…" He drew his finger across his throat like a knife and made a cutting sound. "I'll be dead and Pellea will be in big trouble."

She shook her head, eyes wide and sincere. "You can count on me, sir. And as for the costume…" She put her hand over her heart. "I'll do my best."

Pellea returned a half hour later, bristling with determination.

"I've brought you something to eat," she said, handing him a neatly wrapped, grilled chicken leg and a small loaf of artisan bread. He was sitting at a small table near her fountain, looking for all the world like a Parisian playboy at a sidewalk café. "And I've brought you news."

"News, huh? Let me guess." He put his hand to his forehead as though taking transmissions from space.

"Leonardo has decided to join the national ballet and forget all about this crazy marriage stuff. Am I right?"

She glared at him. "I'm warning you, don't take the man lightly."

"Oh, I don't. Believe me." He began to unwrap the chicken leg. He hadn't eaten for hours and he was more than ready to partake of what she'd brought him. "So what is the news?"

"Leonardo talked to his father and we've decided to move the wedding up." Her chin rose defiantly. "We're getting married in two days."

He put down the chicken leg, hunger forgotten, and stared at her with eyes that had turned icy silver. "What's the rush?" he asked with deceptive calm.

The look in his gaze made her nervous. He seemed utterly peaceful, and yet there was a sense in the air that a keg of dynamite was about to blow.

She turned away, pacing, thinking about how nice and simple life had been before she'd found him lurking in her garden that day. Her path had been relatively clear at the time. True, she had been fighting her father over his wish that she marry Leonardo. But that was relatively easy to deal with compared to what she had now.

The irony was that her father would get his wish, and she'd done it to herself. She would marry Leonardo. She would be the first lady of the land and just about impervious to attack. Just as her father so obsessively craved, she would be as safe as she could possibly be.

But even that wasn't perfect safety. There were a thousand chinks in her armor and the path ahead was perilous. Everything she did, every decision she made, could have unforeseen repercussions. She had set a course and now the winds would take her to her destination. Was it the best destination for her or was it a mirage? Was she right or was she wrong? If only she knew.

Looking out into the courtyard, Pellea shivered with a premonition of what might be to come.

Monte watched her from under lowered brows, munching on a bite of chicken. Much as she was trying to hide it, he could see that she was in a special sort of agony and he couldn't for the life of him understand why. What was her hurry to marry Leonardo? What made her so anxious to cement those ties?

Motivations were often difficult to untangle and understand. What were hers? Did it really mean everything to her to have her father satisfied that she was safe, and to do it before it was too late? Evidence did suggest that he was fading fast. Was that what moved her? He couldn't think what else it could be. But was that really enough to make her rush to Leonardo's arms? Or was there something going on that he didn't know about?

"I suppose the powers that be are in favor of this wedding?" he mentioned casually.

She nodded. "Believe me, everything around here is planned to the nth degree. Public-relations values hold sway over everything."

"I've noticed. That's what makes me wonder. What's the deal with this wedding coming on so suddenly? I would think the regime would try to milk all the publicity they could possibly get out of a long engagement."

"Interesting theory," she said softly, pretending to be busy folding clothes away.

"Why?" he asked bluntly. "Why so soon?"

"You'd have to ask Leonardo about that," she said evasively.

"Maybe I will. If I get the chance." He looked at her sharply, trying to read her mind. "I can't help but think he has a plan in mind. There has to be a reason."

"Sometimes people just want to do things quickly," she said, getting annoyed with his persistence.

"Um-hmm." He didn't buy that for a minute. The more he let the idea of such a marriage—the ultimate marriage of convenience—linger in his mind, the more he hated it. Pellea couldn't be with Leonardo. Everything in him rebelled at the thought.

Pellea belonged to him.

That was nonsense, of course. How could she be his when he wouldn't do what needed to be done to take that responsibility in hand himself? After all, he'd refused to step up and do the things a man did when making a woman his own. As his old tutor might say, he craved the honey but refused to tend to the bees.

Still in some deep, gut-level part of him, she was his and had been since the moment he'd first laid eyes on her. He'd put his stamp on her, his brand, his seal. He'd held her and loved her, body and soul, and he wanted her available for more of the same. She was his, damn it!

But what was he prepared to do about it?

That was the question.

He watched her, taking in the grace and loveliness of her form and movement, the full, luscious temptation of her exciting body, the beauty of her perfect face, and the question burned inside him. What was he prepared to do? It was working into a drumbeat in his head and in his heart. What? Just exactly what?

"You don't love him."

The words came out loud and clear and yet he was surprised when he said them. He hadn't planned to say anything of the sort. Still, once it was out, he was glad he'd said it. The truth was out now, like a flag, a banner, a warning that couldn't be ignored any longer. And why not? Truth was supposed to set you free.

And she didn't love Leonardo. It was obvious in the way she talked to him and talked about him. She was using him and he was using her. They had practically said as much in front of him—though neither had known it at the time. Why not leave it out there in the open where it could be dealt with?

"You don't love him," he said again, even more firmly this time.

She whirled to face him, her arms folded, her eyes flashing. "How do you know?" she challenged, her chin high.

A slow smile began to curl his lips. As long as they were speaking truth, why not add a bit more?

"I know, Pellea. I know very well. Because..." He paused, not really for dramatic effect, although that was what he ended up with. He paused because for just a second, he wondered if he really dared say this.

"Because you love me," he said at last.

The shock of his words seemed to crackle in the air.

She gasped. "Oh! Of all the…" Her cheeks turned bright red and she choked and had to cough for a moment. "I never told you that!"

He sat back and surveyed her levelly. "You didn't have to tell me with words. Your body told me all I would ever need to know." His gaze skimmed over her creamy skin. "Every time I touch you your body resonates like a fine instrument. You were born to play to my tune."

She stood staring at him, shaking her head as though she couldn't believe anyone would have the gall to say such things. "Of all the egos in the world…"

"Mine's the best?" he prompted, then shrugged with a lopsided grin. "Of course."

She held her breath and counted to ten, not really sure if she was trying to hold back anger or a smile. He did appear ridiculously adorable sitting there looking pleased with himself. She let her breath back out and tried for logic and reason. It would obviously be best to leave flights of fancy and leaps of faith behind.

"I don't love you," she lied with all her heart. Tears suddenly threatened, but she wouldn't allow them. Not now. "I can't love you. Don't you see that? Don't ever say that to me again."

Something in her voice reached in and made a grab for his heartstrings. Had he actually hurt her with his careless words? That was the last thing he would ever want to do.

"Pellea." He rose and reached for her.

She tried to turn away but he wouldn't let her. His arms came around her, holding her close against his chest, and he stroked her hair.

"Pellea, darling…"

She lifted her face, her lips trembling. He looked down and melted. No woman had ever been softer in his arms. Instantly, his mouth was on hers, touching, testing, probing, lighting her pulse on fire. She kissed him in return for as long as she dared, then pulled back, though she was still in the circle of his embrace. She tried to frown.

"You taste like chicken," she said, blinking up at him.

He smiled, and a warm sense of his affection for her was plain to see. "You taste like heaven," he countered.

She closed her eyes and shook her head. "Oh, please, Monte. Let me go."

He did so reluctantly, and she drew back slowly, looking toward him with large, sad eyes and thinking, *If only…*

He watched her, feeling strangely helpless, though he wasn't really sure why. With a sigh, she turned and went back to pacing.

"We have to get you out of here," she fretted while he sat down again and leaned back in his chair. "If I can get you out of the castle, do you have a way to get back to the continent?"

He waved away the very concept. "I'm not going anywhere," he said confidently. "And when I do go, I'll take care of myself. I've got resources. No need to worry about me."

She stopped, shaking her head as she looked at him. How could she not worry about him? That was pretty much all she was thinking about right now. She needed him to leave before he found out about the baby. And even more important, she wanted him to go because she wanted him to stay alive. But there was no point in bringing that up. He would only laugh at the danger. Still, she had to try to get him to see reason.

"There is more news," she told him, leaning against the opposite chair. "Rumors are flying."

He paused, the chicken leg halfway to his mouth. He put it down again and gazed at her. "What kind of rumors?"

She turned and sank into the chair she'd been leaning on. "There's talk of a force preparing for an Ambrian invasion."

He raised one sleek eyebrow and looked amused. "By whom?"

"Ex-Ambrians, naturally. Trying to take the country back."

His sharp, all-knowing gaze seemed to see right into her soul as he leaned closer across the table. "And you believe that?"

"Are you kidding?" She threw her hands up. "I can see it with my own eyes. What else are you doing here?"

He gave her another view of his slow, sexy smile. "I came to kidnap you, not to start a revolution. I thought I'd made that perfectly clear."

She leaned forward, searching his eyes. "So it's true. You are planning to take over this country."

He shrugged, all careless confidence. "Someday, sure." His smile was especially knowing and provocative. "Not this weekend though. I've got other plans."

He had other plans. Well, wasn't that just dandy? He had plans and she had issues of life and death to contend with. She wanted to strangle him. Or at least make him wince a little. She rose, towering over him and pointing toward her gateway.

"You've got to go. Now!"

He looked surprised at her vehemence, and then as though his feelings were hurt, he said, "I'm eating."

"You can take the food with you."

He frowned. "But I'm almost done." He took another bite. "This is actually pretty good chicken."

She stared at him, at her wit's end, then sank slowly back into the chair, her head in her hands. What could she do? She couldn't scream for help. That could get him killed. She couldn't pick him up and carry him to the doorway. That would get *her* killed. Or at least badly injured. She was stuck here in her chambers, stuck with the man she loved, the father of her child, the man whose kisses sent her into orbit every time, and everything depended on getting rid of him somehow. What on earth was she going to do?

"I hate you," she said, though it was more of a moan than a sentence.

"Good," he responded. "I like a woman with passion."

She rolled her eyes. Why couldn't he ever be serious? It was maddening. "My hatred would be more effective if I had a dagger instead," she commented dryly.

He waved a finger at her. "No threats. There's nothing quite so deadly to a good relationship. Don't go down that road."

She pouted, feeling grumpy and as though she wasn't being taken seriously. "Who said we had a good relationship?"

He looked surprised. "Don't we?" Reaching out, he took her hand. "It's certainly the best I've ever had," he said softly, his eyes glowing with the sort of affection that made her breath catch in her throat.

She curled her fingers around his. She couldn't help it. She did love him so.

She wasn't sure why. He had done little so far other than make her life more difficult. He hadn't promised her anything but kisses and lovemaking. Was that enough to give your heart for?

Hardly. Pellea was a student of history and she knew very well that people living on love tended to starve pretty quickly. What began with excitement and promises usually ended in bleak prospects and recriminations.

The gong sounded, making her jump. She pulled away

her hand and looked at him. He shrugged as though he regretted the interruption.

"I'll take my food into the library," he offered. "Just don't forget and bring your guest in there."

"I won't," she said back softly, watching him go and then hurrying to the entryway.

It was Magda, her hairdresser, making plans for their session. The older woman was dressed like a gypsy with scarves and belts everywhere. She was a bit of a character, but she had a definite talent with hair.

"I'll be back in half an hour," she warned. "You be ready. I'm going to need extra time to weave your hair around the tiara. It's not what I usually do, you know."

"Yes, I know, Magda," Pellea said, smiling. "And I appreciate that you are willing to give it a try. I'm sure we'll work something out together."

Magda grumbled a bit, but she seemed to be looking forward to the challenge. "Half an hour," she warned again as she started off toward the supply room to prepare for the session.

Pellea had just begun to close the gate when Kimmee came breezing around the corner.

"Hi," she called, rushing forward. "Don't close me out."

Pellea gave her a welcoming smile but didn't encourage her to come into the courtyard. "I'm in a bit of a hurry tonight," she warned her. "I've got the hairdresser coming and…"

"I just need to give your gown a last-minute check

for wrinkles," Kimmee said cheerfully, ignoring Pellea's obvious hint and coming right on in.

"Where is he?" she whispered, eyes sparkling, as she squeezed past.

"Who?" Pellea responded, startled.

Kimmee grinned. "I saw him when I was here earlier. You were out, but he was here." She winked. "I said hello." She looked around, merrily furtive. "We spoke."

"Oh."

Pellea swallowed hard with regret. This was not good. This was exactly what she'd hoped to avoid. Kimmee had kept the secret before, but would she again?

"He is so gorgeous," Kimmee whispered happily. "I'm so glad for you. You needed someone gorgeous in your life."

Pellea shook her head, worried and not sure how to deal with this. "But, Kimmee, it's not like that. You know I'm going to marry Leonardo and…"

"All the more reason you need a gorgeous man. No one said it had to be a forever man." Her smile was impish. "Just take some happiness where you can. You deserve it."

She looked at her maid in despair. It was all very well for her to be giving shallow comfort for activities that were clearly not in good taste. But here she was, hoisted on her own petard, as it were—taking advice that could ruin her life. But what was she going to do—beg a servant not to gossip? Might as well ask a bird not to fly.

Of course, Kimmee was more than a mere servant.

In many ways, she had always been her best friend. That might make a difference. It had in the past. But not being sure was nerve-wracking. After all, this was pretty much a life-or-death situation.

She closed her eyes and said a little prayer. "Kimmee," she began nervously.

"Don't worry, Pel," Kimmee said softly. She reached out and touched her mistress's arm, her eyes warm with an abiding affection. She'd used the name she'd called Pellea when they were young playmates. "I'm just happy that…" She shrugged, but they both knew what she was talking about. "I'd never, ever tell anyone else. It's just you and me."

Tears filled Pellea's eyes. "Thank you," she whispered.

Kimmee kissed Pellea's cheek, as though on impulse and nodded. Then suddenly, as she noticed Monte coming into the doorway to the library, she was the dutiful servant once again. "Oh, miss, let me take a look at that gown."

Monte leaned against the doorjamb, his shirt open, his hair mussed, looking for all the world like an incredibly handsome buccaneer.

"Hey, Kimmee," he said.

"Hello, sir." She waved, then had second thoughts and curtsied. As she rose from her deep bow, Pellea was behind her and Kimmee risked an A-OK wink to show him plans were afoot and all was going swimmingly. "I hope things are going well with you," she added politely.

"Absolutely," he told her. "I've just had a nice little meal and I'm feeling pretty chipper."

She laughed and turned back to her work, completed it quickly, and turned to go.

"Well, miss, I just wanted to check on the gown and remind you I'll be here to help you get into it in about an hour. Will that suit?"

"That will suit. Magda should be through by then." She smiled at the young woman. "Thank you, Kimmee," she said, giving her a hug as she passed. "I hope you know how much I appreciate you."

"Of course, miss. My only wish is for your happiness. You should know that by now."

"I do. You're a treasure."

The maid waved at them both. "I'll be back in a bit. See you."

"Goodbye, Kimmee," Monte said, retreating into the library again.

But Pellea watched her go, deep in thought. In a few hours, she would be at the ball, dancing with Leonardo and preparing to have their engagement announced. People would applaud. Some might even cheer. A couple of serving girls would toss confetti in the air. A new phase of her life would open. She ought to be excited. Instead, she had a sick feeling in the pit of her stomach.

"Get over it," she told herself roughly. She had to do what she had to do. There was no choice in the matter. But instead of a bride going to join her fiancé, she felt like a traitor going to her doom.

Was she doing the right thing? How could she know for sure?

She pressed both hands to her belly and thought of the child inside. The "right thing" was whatever was best for her baby. That, at least, was clear. Now if she could just be sure what that was, maybe she could stop feeling like a tightrope walker halfway across the rope.

And in the meantime, there was someone who seemed to take great delight in jiggling that rope she was so anxiously trying to get across.

CHAPTER FIVE

TURNING, PELLEA MARCHED into the library and confronted Monte.

He looked up and nodded as she approached. "She's a good one," he commented on Kimmee. "I'm glad you've got such a strong supporter nearby."

"Why didn't you tell me you'd seen her, actually chatted with her?" Pellea said, in no mood to be mollified. "Don't you see how dangerous that is? What if she talks?"

He eyed her quizzically. "You know her better than I do. What do you think? Will she?"

Pellea shook her head. "I don't know," she said softly. "I don't think so, but…"

She threw up her hands. It occurred to her how awful it was to live like this, always suspicious, always on edge. She wanted to trust her best friend. Actually, she did trust her. But knowing the penalty one paid for being wrong in this society kept her on her toes.

"Who knows?" she said, staring at him, wondering how this all would end.

It was tempting, in her darkest moments, to blame it

all on him. He came, he saw, he sent her into a frenzy of excitement and—she had to face it—love, blinding her to what was really going on, making her crazy, allowing things to happen that should never have happened.

But he was just the temptor. She was the temptee. From the very first, she should have stopped him in his tracks, and she'd done nothing of the sort. In fact, she'd immediately gone into a deep swoon and hadn't come out of it until he was gone. She had no one to blame but herself.

Still, she wished it was clearer just what he'd been doing here two months ago, and why he'd picked her to cast a spell over.

"Why did you come here to my chambers that first time?" she asked him, getting serious. "That day you found me by the fountain. What were you doing here? What was your purpose? And why did you let me distract you from it?"

He looked at her coolly. He'd finished the chicken and eaten a good portion of the little loaf of bread. He was feeling full and happy. But her questions were a bit irksome.

"I came to get the lay of the land," he said, leaning back in his chair. "And to see my ancestral castle. To see my natural home." He looked a bit pained.

"The place I was created to rule," he added, giving it emphasis that only confirmed her fears.

"See, I knew it," she said, feeling dismal. "You were prepared to do something, weren't you?"

"Not then. Not yet." He met her gaze candidly. "But soon."

She shook her head, hands on her hips. "You want to send Leonardo and his entire family packing, don't you?" That was putting a pleasant face on something that might be very ugly, but she couldn't really face just how bad it could be.

He shrugged. "There's no denying it. It's been my obsession since I was a child." He gave her a riveting look. "Of course I'm going to take my country back. What else do I exist for?"

She felt faint. His obsession was her nightmare. She had to find a way to stop it.

"That is exactly where you go wrong," she told him, beginning to pace again. "Don't you see? You don't have to be royal. You don't have to restore your monarchy. Millions of people live perfectly happy lives without that."

He blinked at her as though he didn't quite get what she was talking about. "Yes, but do they make a difference? Do their lives have meaning in the larger scheme of things?"

She threw out her arms. "Of course they do. They fall in love and marry and have children and have careers and make friends and do things together and they're happy. They don't need to be king of anything." She appealed to him in all earnestness, wishing there was some way to convince him, knowing there was very little hope. "Why can't you be like that?"

He rose from the desk and she backed away quickly,

as though afraid he would try to take her in his arms
again.

But he showed no intention of doing that. Instead, he
began a slow survey of the books in her bookcases that
lined the walls.

"You don't really understand me, Pellea," he said at
last as he moved slowly through her collection. "I could
live very happily without ever being king."

She sighed. "I wish I could believe that," she said
softly.

He glanced back over his shoulder at her as she stood
by the doorway, then turned to face her.

"I don't need to be king, Pellea. But there is something
I do need." He went perfectly still and held her gaze with
his own, his eyes burning.

"Revenge. I can never be fulfilled until I have my
revenge."

She drew her breath in. Her heart beat hard, as though
she was about to make a run for her life.

"That's just wicked," she said softly.

He held her gaze for a moment longer, then shrugged
and turned away, shoving his hands down deep into
his pockets and staring out into her miniature tropical
forest.

"Then I'm wicked. I can't help it. Vengeance must
be mine. I must make amends for what happened to my
family."

She trembled. It was hopeless. His words felt like a
dark and painful destiny to her. Like a forecast of doom.

There was no doubt in her mind that this would all end badly.

It was very true, what Monte had said. His character needed some kind of answer for what had happened to his family, some kind of retribution. Pellea knew that and on a certain level, she could hardly blame him. But didn't he see, and wasn't there any way she could make him see, that his satisfaction would only bring new misery for others? In order for him to feel relief, someone would have to pay very dearly.

"It's just selfish," she noted angrily.

He shrugged and looked at her coolly. "So I'm selfish. What else is new?"

She put her hand to her forehead and heaved a deep sigh. "There are those who live for themselves and their own gratification, and there are those who devote their lives to helping the downtrodden and the weak and oppressed. To make life better for the most miserable among us."

"You're absolutely right. You pay your money and you take your chances. I'd love to help the downtrodden and the poor and the oppressed in Ambria. Those are my people and I want to take care of them." He searched her eyes again. "But in order for me to do that, a few heads will have to roll."

The chimes on her elegant wall clock sounded and Pellea gasped.

"Oh, no! Look at the time. They're going to be here any minute. I wanted to get you out of here by now."

She looked around as though she didn't know where to hide him.

He stretched and yawned, comfortable as a cat, and then he rose and half sat on the corner of the desk. "It's all right. I'll just take a little nap while you're having your hair done."

"No, you will not!"

"As I remember it, your sleeping arrangements are quite comfortable. I think I'll spend a little quality time with your bedroom." He grinned, enjoying the outrage his words conjured up in her.

"I want you gone," she was saying fretfully, grabbing his arm for emphasis. "How do you get in here, anyway? Tell me how you do it. However you get in, that's the way you're going out. Tell me!"

He covered her hand with his own and caressed it. "I'll do better than that," he said, looking down at her with blunt affection. "I'll show you. But it will have to wait until we leave together."

She looked at his hand on hers. It felt hot and lovely. "I'm not going with you," she said in a voice that was almost a whimper.

"Yes, you are." He said it in a comforting tone.

Her eyes widened as she glanced up at him. He was doing it again—mesmerizing her. It was some sort of tantalizing magic and she had to resist it. "No, I'm not!" she insisted, but she couldn't gather the strength to pull her hand away.

He lifted her chin and kissed her softly on the lips.

"You are," he told her kindly. "You belong with me and you know it."

She felt helpless. Every time he touched her, she wanted to purr. She sighed in a sort of temporary surrender. "What are you going to do while I'm at the ball?" she asked.

"Don't worry. I'll find something to while away the time with." He raised an eyebrow. "Perfect opportunity, don't you think? To come and go at will."

She frowned. "There are guards everywhere. Surely you've seen that by now."

"Yes. But I do have your security setup to monitor things. That will help a lot."

"Oh." She groaned. She should never have let him see that.

She shook her head. "I should call the guards right now and take care of this once and for all."

"But you won't."

Suddenly, a surge of adrenaline gave her the spunk she needed to pull away from his touch, and once she was on her own, she felt emboldened again.

"Dare me!" she said, glaring at him with her hands on her hips.

He stared back at her for a long moment, then a slow grin spread over his handsome face. "I may be careless at times, my darling, but I'm not foolhardy. Even I know better than to challenge you like that."

The entry gong sounded. She sighed, all the fight ebbing out of her. "Just stay out of sight," she warned him. "I'll check in on you one last time before I go to the ball." She gave him a look of chagrin. "Unless, of course, you've left by then." She shrugged. "But I guess I won't hold my breath over that one."

He nodded. "Wise woman," he murmured as he watched her go. Then he slipped into her bedroom and closed the door before she'd let the hairdresser into the compound.

It was a beautiful room. The bedding was thick and luxurious, the headboard beautifully carved. Large oils of ancient landscapes, painted by masters of centuries past, covered the walls. He wondered what they had done with all the old portraits of his ancestors. Burned them, probably. Just another reason he needed his revenge.

But that was a matter to come. Right now he needed sleep.

He sat on the edge of her bed and looked at her bedside table, wondering what she was reading these days. What he saw gave him a bit of a jolt.

Beginning Pregnancy 101.

Interesting. It would seem Pellea was already thinking about having children. With Leonardo? That gave him a shudder. Surely she wasn't hoping to have a baby in order to reassure her father. That would be a step too far. And if she just had a yen for children, why choose Leonardo to have them with?

Making a face, he pushed the subject away. It was too depressing to give it any more attention.

He lay down on her sumptuous bed and groaned softly as he thought of the times he'd spent here. Two months ago everything had seemed so clean and simple.

A hungry man. A soft and willing woman. Great love-making. Good food. Luxurious surroundings. What could be better? He'd come back thinking it would all be easy to recreate. But he'd been dead wrong.

The wall clock struck the quarter hour again and tweaked a memory. There had been a huge, ancient grandfather clock in his mother's room when he was a child. There was a carved wooden tiger draped around the face of the timepiece and it had fascinated him. But even as he thought of that, he remembered that his mother had kept copies of her jewelry in a secret compartment in that clock.

What a strange and interesting castle this was. There were secret compartments and passageways and hiding places of all kinds just about everywhere. A few hundred years of the need to hide things had spurred his ancestors into developing ingenious and creative places to hide their most precious objects from the prying eyes and itching fingers of the servants and even of the courtiers. Life in the castle was a constant battle, it seemed, and it probably wasn't much different now.

Looking around Pellea's room, he wondered how many secret places had been found, and how many were still waiting, unused and unopened, after all these years. He knew of one, for sure, and that was the passageway that had brought him here twice now. He was pretty sure no one else had used it in twenty-five years. What else would he find if he tapped on a few walls and pressed on a few pieces of wood trim? It might be interesting to find out.

Later. Right now he needed a bit of sleep. Closing his eyes, he dreamed of Pellea and their nights together. He slept.

Pellea stood looking down at Monte, her heart so full of love, she had to choke back the tears that threatened. Tears would ruin her makeup and that was the last thing she would have been able to handle right now. She was on the edge of an emotional storm as it was.

Everyone had gone. She'd even sent the two men who were supposed to guard the tiara out into the hall to wait for her. And now she was ready to go and make the announcement that would set in stone her future life and that of her baby. But she needed just one more moment to look at the man she loved, the man she wished she were planning to marry.

If only they had met in another time, another place. If only circumstances were different. They could have been so happy together, the two of them. If there was no royalty for him to fight for, if her father was still as hale and hearty as he'd been most of her life, if her place weren't so precarious that she needed it bolstered by marrying Leonardo...

There were just too many things that would have to be different in order for things to work out the way they should, and for them to have a happy life. Unfortunately that didn't seem to be in the cards for her.

As for him—oh, he would get over it. He would never know that the baby she would have in a few months was really his. He was the only man she'd ever loved, but she had been very careful not to tell him that. She was pretty sure he'd had romances of one kind or another for years. It wouldn't be that hard for him. There would always be beautiful and talented women ready to throw themselves at him in a heartbeat.

Of course, if he did do as he threatened and try to take his country back by force, the entire question would be moot and they might all have to pay the ultimate price. Who knew?

In the meantime, she wanted just a moment more to watch him and dream….

When he woke an hour or so later, she was standing at the side of the bed. His first impression was benignness, but by the time he'd cleared his eyes, her expression had changed and she was glaring down at him.

"I don't know why you're still here," she said a bit mournfully. "Please don't get yourself killed while I'm at the ball."

He stretched and looked up at her sleepily. She was dressed to the hilt and the most beautiful thing he'd ever seen. His mother's tiara had been worked into a gorgeous coiffure that made her look as regal as any queen. Her creamy breasts swelled just above the neckline of her gown in old-fashioned allure. The bodice was tight, making her waist look tiny, as though he could reach out and pick her up with his two hands and pull her down…

His mouth went dry with desire and he reached for her. Deftly, she sidestepped his move and held him at bay.

"Don't touch," she warned. "I'm a staged work of art right now and I'm off to the photographer for pictures."

A piece of art was exactly what she was, looking just as she appeared before him. She could have walked right out of a huge portrait by John Singer Sargent, burnished lighting and rich velvet trimmings and all.

He sighed, truly pained. She looked good enough to ravish. But then she always did, didn't she?

"Forget the ball," he coaxed, though he knew it was all for naught. "Stay here with me. We'll lock the gate and recreate old times together."

"Right," she said, dismissing that out of hand, not even bothering to roll her eyes. She had other things on her mind right now. "The pictures will take at least an hour, I'm sure. Leonardo will meet me there and we'll go directly to the ball."

He frowned, feeling grumpy and overlooked for the moment. "Unless he has an unfortunate accident before he gets there," he suggested.

She looked at him sharply. "None of that, Monte. Promise me."

He stretched again and pouted. "When do you plan to make the big announcement?" he asked instead of making promises he might not be able to keep.

She frowned. "What does that matter?" she asked.

He grinned. "You are so suspicious of my every mood and plan."

Her eyes flashed. "With good reason, it seems."

He shrugged. "So I won't see you again until later?"

"No. Unless you decide to go away. As you should." She hesitated. She needed to make a few thing clear to him. He had to follow rules or she was going to have to get the guard to come help her keep him in line.

Right. That was a great idea. She made a face at herself. She was truly caught in a trap. She needed to keep him in line, but in order to do that, she would be signing his death warrant. There was no way that was going to happen.

At the same time, he showed no appreciation for the bind she was in. If he didn't feel it necessary to respect the rules she made, she couldn't have him here. He would have to understand that.

Taking a deep breath, she gave him the facts as she needed them to be.

"Once the announcement is made, our engagement will be official and there will be no more of anything like this," she warned him, a sweep of her hand indicating their entire relationship. "You understand that, don't you?"

His eyes were hooded as he looked up at her. "I understand what you're saying,"

"Monte, please don't do anything. You can't. I can't let you. Please have some respect."

His slow, insolent smile was his answer. "I would never do anything to hurt you."

She stared at him, then finally did roll her eyes. "Of

course not. Everything you do would be for my own good, wouldn't it?"

There was no escaping the tone of sarcasm in her voice. She sighed with exasperation and then the expression in her eyes changed. She hesitated. "Will you be gone?" she asked.

He met her gaze and held it. "Is that really what you hope?"

She started to say, "Of course," but then she stopped, bit her lip and sighed. "How can I analyze what I'm hoping right now?" she said instead, her voice trembling. "How can I even think clearly when you're looking at me like that?"

One last glare and she whirled, leaving the room as elegantly as any queen might do.

He rose and followed, going to the doorway so that he could watch her leave her chambers, a uniformed guard on either side. She could have been royalty from another century. She could have been Anne Boleyn on her way to the tower. He thought she was pretty special. He wanted her to be his, but just how that would work was not really clear.

Right now he had a purpose in mind—exploring the other side of the castle where his family's living quarters had been. That was the section that had burned and he knew it had been recently renovated. He only hoped enough would be left of what had been so that he could find something he remembered.

It would seem the perfect time to do it. With the ball beginning, no one would be manning their usual places.

Everyone would be gravitating toward the ballroom for a look at the festivities. A quick trip to Pellea's surveillance room was in order, and then he would take his chances in the halls.

The long, tedious picture-taking session was wrapping up and Pellea waited with Kimmee for Leonardo to come out. The photographers were taking a few last individual portraits of him.

"Shall I go check on the preparations for your entrance to the ballroom?" Kimmee asked, and Pellea nodded her assent.

It had been her experience that double-checking never hurt and taking things for granted usually led to disaster. Besides, she needed a moment to be alone and settle her feelings.

Turning slowly, she appraised herself in the long, full-length mirror. Was that the face of a happy woman? Was that the demeanor of a bride?

Not quite. But it was the face of a rather regal-looking woman, if she did say so herself. But why was she even thinking such a thing? She would never be queen, no matter what. Monte might be king someday, but he would never pick her to be his wife. He couldn't pick someone from a traitor's family to help him rule Ambria, now could he?

The closest she would get to that was to marry Leonardo. Did that really matter to her? She searched her soul, looking for even the tiniest hint of ambition and couldn't find it. That sort of thing was important to her father, but not to her. If her father weren't involved, she would leave with Monte and never look back. But that was impossible under the circumstances.

Still, it was nice to dream about. What if she and Monte were free? They might get on a yacht and sail to the South Seas and live on an island. Not an island like Ambria with its factions always in contention and undermining each other. A pretty island with coconut trees and waterfalls, a place that was quiet and warm and peaceful with turquoise waters and silver-blue fish and white-sand beaches.

But there was no time to live in dreams. She had to live in the here and now. And that meant she had to deal with Leonardo.

She smiled at him as he came out of the sitting room.

"All done?" she asked.

"So it seems," he replied, then leaned close. "Ah, so beautiful," he murmured as he tried to nuzzle her neck.

"Don't touch," she warned him, pulling back.

"Yes, yes, I know. You're all painted up and ready to go." He took her hand and kissed her fingers. "But I want to warn you, my beauty, I plan to touch you a lot on our wedding night."

That sent a chill down her spine. She looked at him in surprise. He'd never shown any sexual interest in her before. This put an ominous pall on her future, didn't it? She'd heard lurid tales about his many mistresses and she'd assumed that he knew their marriage would be for advantage and convenience only, and not for love or for anything physical. Now he seemed to be having second thoughts. What was going on here?

She glanced at Kimmee who'd just returned and had heard him as well, and they exchanged a startled glance.

Leonardo took a call on his mobile, then snapped it shut and frowned. "I'm sorry, my love," he told her. "I'm afraid I'm going to have to let the guards escort you to the ballroom. I'll be along later. I have a matter that must be taken care of immediately."

Something in his words sent warning signals through her.

"What is it, Leonardo?" she asked, carefully putting on a careless attitude. "Do we need to man the barricades?"

"Nothing that should trouble you, my sweet," he said, giving her a shallow smile that didn't reach his eyes. "It seems we may have an interloper in the castle."

"Oh?" Her blood ran cold and she clenched her fists behind the folds of her skirt. "What sort of interloper?"

He waved a hand in the air. "It may be nothing, but a few of the guards seem to think they saw a stranger on one of the monitors this afternoon." He shook his head. "We don't allow intruders in the castle, especially on a night like this."

He sighed. "I just have to go and check out what they caught on the recorder. I'll be back in no time."

"Hurry back, my dear," she said absentmindedly,

thinking hard about how she was going to warn Monte.

"I will, my love." He bowed in her direction and smiled at her. "Don't do any dancing without me," he warned. Turning, he disappeared out the door.

Pellea reached out to steady herself to keep from keeling over. She met Kimmee's gaze and they both stared at each other with worried eyes.

"I told him to go," she fretted to her lifelong friend and servant. "Now he's probably out running around the castle and about to get caught. Oh, Kimmee!"

Kimmee leaned close. "Don't worry, Pel," she whispered, scanning the area to make sure no one could overhear them. "I'll find him and I'll warn him. You can count on me."

Pellea grabbed her arm. "Tell him there is no more room for error. He has to get out of the castle right now!"

"I will. Don't you worry. He'll get the message."

And she dashed off into the hallway.

Pellea took a deep breath and tried to quiet her nerves. She had to forget all about Monte and the trouble he might be in. She had to act as though everything were normal. In other words, she would have to pretend. And it occurred to her that this might be a lesson for the way things would be for the rest of her life.

CHAPTER SIX

MONTE WAS BACK FROM EXPLORING and he was waiting impatiently for Kimmee to make good on her promises and show up with a costume he could wear to the ball.

He'd been to the other side of the castle and he'd seen things that would take him time to assimilate and deal with emotionally. It could have been overwhelming if he'd let it be. He'd barely skimmed through the area and not much remained of the home he'd lived in with his loving family. Most of what was rebuilt had a new, more modern cast.

But he had found something important. He'd found a storeroom where some of the rescued items and furniture from his family's reign had been shoved aside and forgotten for years. A treasure trove that he would have to explore when he got the chance. But in the short run, he'd found his mother's prized grandfather clock. More important, he'd found her secret compartment, untouched after all these years. That alone had given him a sense of satisfaction.

And one of the items he had found in that secret

hiding place was likely to come in very handy this very night.

But right now, he just wanted to see Kimmee appear in the gateway. He knew she'd been helping with the photo shoot, but surely that was over by now. If she didn't come soon, he would have to find a way to go without a special costume—and that would be dangerous enough to make him think at least twice.

"Don't give up on me!"

Kimmee's voice rang out before the gong sounded and she came rushing in bearing bulky gifts and a wide smile.

"I've got everything you need right here," she claimed, spreading out her bounty before him. "Though I'm afraid it's all for naught."

"Once more, you save the day," he told her as he looked through the items, thoroughly impressed. "I'm going to have to recommend you for a medal."

"A reward for costume procurement?" she asked with a laugh. "But there's more. I'm afraid you won't be able to use this after all."

"No?" He stopped and looked at her. "Why not?"

"The castle is on stranger alert." She sighed. "You must have gone exploring because some of the guards claim they saw you—or somebody—on one of the hall monitors."

"Oh. Bad luck."

She shrugged. "Leonardo is looking into it and he seems pretty serious about it. So Pellea sent me to tell you to get out while the getting's good, because there's no time left." She shook her head, looking at him earnestly. "I went ahead and brought you the costume, because I promised I would, and I knew you'd want to see this. But I don't think it would be wise to use it. You're going to have to go, and go quickly."

"Am I?" He held up the coat to the uniform and gazed at it.

"Oh, I think you'd better," she said.

"And I will." He smiled at her. "All in good time. But first, I want to dance with Pellea."

Her face was filled with doubt but her eyes were shining. "But if you get caught…?"

"Then I'll just have to get away again," he told her. "But I don't plan to get caught. I've got a mask, don't I? No one will be sure who I really am, and I'll keep a sharp eye out." He grinned. "Don't worry about me. I'm going to go try this on."

"Well, what do you know?" She sighed, wary but rather happy he wasn't going to give up so easily. "Go ahead and try it on. I'll wait and help with any last-minute adjustments."

He took the costume up as though it were precious—and in a way it was. He recognized what she'd found for him—the official dress uniform of Ambrian royalty from the nineteenth century—a uniform one of his great-great-grandfathers had probably worn. He slipped into it quickly. It all fitted like a glove. Looking in the mirror, he had to smile. He looked damn good in gold braid and a stiff collar. As though he was born to wear it.

When he walked out, Kimmee applauded, delighted with how it had worked out.

"Here's your mask," she said, handing it to him. "As you say, it will be very important in keeping your identity hidden. And it's a special one. Very tight. Very secure." She gave it a sharp test, pulling on the band at the back. "No one will be able to pull it off."

"Exactly what I need. Kimmee, you're a genius."

"I am, aren't I?" She grinned, pleased as punch. "Believe me, sir, I take pride in my work—underhanded as it may be."

He shook his head. "I don't consider this underhanded at all."

And actually, she agreed. "I'll just think of it this way—anything I can do to help you is for the good of the country."

He looked at her closely, wondering if she realized who he was. But her smile was open and bland. If she knew, she wasn't going to let it out. Still, it was interesting that she'd put it that way.

"I've got to hurry back," she said as she started toward the gate. "I'm helping in the ladies' powder room. You pick up all the best rumors in there."

"Ah, the ladies like to talk, do they?" he responded, adjusting his stand-up collar.

"They like to impress each other and they forget that we servants can hear, too." She gave him a happy wave. "I'll let you know if anything good turns up."

He nodded. "The juicier the better."

She laughed as she left, and he sobered. He'd been

lighthearted with Kimmee, but in truth, this was quite an emotional experience for him.

He took one last look in the mirror. For the first time in many years, he felt as if he'd found something he really belonged to, something that appealed to his heart as well as his head. It was almost a feeling of coming home.

And home was what he'd missed all these years. Without real parents, without a real family, he'd ached for something of his own.

He'd had an odd and rather disjointed life. For his first eight years, he'd been the much beloved, much cosseted Crown Prince of Ambria, living in the rarified air of royal pomp and celebrity. His mother and father had doted on him. He'd shown every evidence of being as talented and intelligent as his position in life warranted, and also as pleasant and handsome as a prince should be. Everyone in his milieu was in awe of him. The newspapers and magazines were full of pictures of him—his first steps, his first puppy, his new Easter clothes, his first bicycle. It was a charmed life.

And then came the coup. He still remembered the night the castle burned, could still smell the fire, feel the fear. He'd known right away that his parents were probably dead. For an eight-year-old boy, that was a heavy burden to bear.

That night, as he and his brother Darius were rushed away from the castle and hustled to the continent in a rickety boat, he'd looked back and seen the fire, and even at his young age, he'd known his way of life was crumbling into dust just as surely as the castle of his royal ancestors was.

He and Darius were quickly separated and wouldn't see each other again until they were well into adulthood. For the first few weeks after his escape, he was passed from place to place by agents of the Ambrian royalty, always seeing new contacts, never sure who these people were or why he was with them. People were afraid to be associated with him, yet determined to keep him safe.

As the regime's crown prince, he was in special danger. The Granvillis had taken over Ambria and it was known that they had sent agents out to find all the royal children and kill them. They didn't want any remnants of the royal family around to challenge their rule.

Monte finally found himself living in Paris with an older couple, the Stephols, who had ties to the monarchy but also a certain distance that protected them from scrutiny. At first, he had to hide day and night, but after a year or so, the Stephols got employment with the foreign service and from then on, they were constantly moving from one assignment to another, and Monte lived all over the world, openly claiming to be their child.

He grew up with the best of everything—elite private schools, vacations in Switzerland, university training in business. But he was always aware that he was in danger and had to keep his real identity a secret. The couple treated him with polite reserve and not a lot of affection—as though he were a museum piece they were protecting from vandals but would return to its proper shelf when the time came. They had no other children and were sometimes too cool for comfort. The couple was very closely knit and Monte often felt like an interloper—which he probably was. They were kind to him, but somewhat reserved, and it was a lonely life. They obviously knew he was special, though he wasn't sure if they knew exactly who he was.

He knew, though. He remembered a lot and never forgot his family, his country or that he was royal. That in itself made him careful. He remembered the danger, still had nightmares about it. As he got older, it was hard not being able to talk to anyone about his background, not having someone he could question, but he read everything he could about his homeland and began to understand why he had to maintain his anonymity. He knew that some saw him as cold and removed from normal emotions. That wasn't true. His emotions were simmering inside, ready to explode when the time was right.

Coming back to Ambria had done a lot to help put things in order in his mind. Finding Pellea had confused the issue a bit, but he thought he could handle that. Now, putting on the uniform that should have been his by rights cemented a feeling of belonging in him. He was the Crown Prince of Ambria, and he wanted his country back.

Monte DeAngelis, Crown Prince of Ambria, walked into the ballroom annex in a uniform that reflected his position, and he did it proudly. He knew the authorities were looking for him and it would only take one careless action, one moment of inattention, to make them realize he was the intruder they were searching for.

But he was willing to risk it. He had to. He needed to do this and he was counting on his natural abilities and intelligence to keep him from harm. After all, he'd had to count on exactly those for most of his life, and his talents had so far stood him in good stead. Now for the ultimate test. He definitely expected to pass it.

The announcer looked up at him in surprise and frowned, knowing that he'd never seen this man before in his life. He got up from his chair and came over busily, carrying papers and trying to look as though he were comfortably in charge.

"Welcome," he said shortly, with a bow. "May I have the name to be announced?"

Monte stood tall and smiled at him.

"Yes, you may. Please announce me as the Count of Revanche," he said with an appropriately incomprehensible Mediterranean accent, though he was blatantly using the French word for revenge.

The man blinked, appearing puzzled. "And Revanche is…?"

"My good man, you've never visited our wonderful region?" Monte looked shocked. "We're called the wine country of the southern coast. You must make a visit on your next holiday."

"Oh," the man responded dutifully, still baffled. "Of course." He bowed deeply and held out his arm with a flourish. "If you please, Your Highness."

He reached for the loudspeaker and made the announcement.

"Ladies and gentleman, may I present His Highness, the Count of Revanche?"

And Monte held his head high as he navigated the steep stairway into the ballroom.

Heads turned. And why not? Obviously, no one had ever heard of him before, and yet he was a commanding presence. He could see the wave of whispering his entrance had set off, but he ignored it, looking for Pellea.

He picked her out of the crowd quickly enough. For a moment the sight of all those masks blinded him, but he found her and once he'd done that, she was all he could see. She stood in the midst of a small group of women and it seemed to him as though a spotlight shone down on her. In contrast to the others around her, the mask she wore was simple, a smooth black accent that set off the exotic shape of her dark eyes and allowed the sparkling jewels of the tiara to take center stage. At the same time, the porcelain translucence of her skin, the delicate set of her jaw, the lushness if her lips, all added to the stunning picture she made in her gorgeous gown. She was so utterly beautiful, his heart stopped in his chest.

He began to head in her direction, but he didn't want to seem over-anxious, so he made a few bows and gave out a few smiles along the way.

Only a few stately couples were dancing as he entered the cavernous room, but he knew how this sort of ball operated, having been to enough of them on the continent. The older people did most of the dancing at first, and the music was calm and traditional. Then the younger ones would filter in. By a certain hour, rocking rhythms and Latin beats would be the order of the day, and the older people would have retreated to drink in the bar or queue for the midnight buffet table.

That was the structure, but it wasn't really relevant to his plans. He just wanted Pellea in his arms. Now all he had to do was to get there and claim her.

Many of the women had noticed him right away. In fact, a few were blatantly looking him over. One pretty little redhead had actually lowered her mask in order to wink at him in outright invitation.

Meanwhile, Pellea hadn't even noticed his arrival. She was deep in conversation with another woman, both of them very earnest. It was quite evident that the subject of their talk was more likely to be the state of world affairs than the latest tart recipe. But what did that matter? She was looking so beautiful, if one had to pick out a queen from the assemblage, she would take the night.

Why did that thought keep echoing in his mind? He turned away, reminding himself that the question was out of order. He wasn't going to think about anything beyond the dancing tonight. And in order to get things started, he decided to take the little redhead up on her offer.

She accepted his invitation like a shot and very soon they were on the dance floor. It was a Viennese waltz, but they managed to liven it up considerably. She chatted away but he hardly heard a word she said. His attention was all on Pellea.

As he watched, Leonardo asked her to dance, and she refused him, shaking her head. He looked a bit disgruntled as he walked away, but his friends crowded around him and in a moment, they all went straight for the hard liquor bar, where he quickly downed a stiff one.

Monte smiled. Fate seemed to be playing right into his hands. The music ended and Monte returned the redhead to her companions. He gave her a smile, but not many words to cherish after he was gone. Turning, he headed straight toward Pellea.

As he approached, she looked up and he saw her eyes widen with recognition behind her mask. She knew who he was right away, and that disappointed him. He'd hoped to get a bit of play out of the costume and mask before he had to defend himself for showing up here.

But then he realized the truth, and it warmed his heart. They would know each other in the dark, wouldn't they?

Not to say that she was pleased to see him.

"You!" she hissed at him, eyes blazing. "Are you crazy? What are you doing here?"

"Asking the most stunning woman in the room to dance with me." He gave her a deep bow. "May I have the honor?"

"No!" She glared at him and lifted her fan to her face. She was obviously finding it hard to show her anger to him and hide it from the rest of the people in the room at the same time. "Didn't Kimmee tell you that you'd been seen?" she whispered.

"Kimmee delivered your message and I acknowledge it. But I won't be cowed by it." He gave her a flourish and a flamboyant smile that his mask couldn't hide. "I have a life to live you know."

"And this stupid ball is that important to your life?" she demanded, trying to keep her voice down and astounded that he could be so careless.

Didn't he care? Or did he see himself as some kind of superhero, so over-confident in his own abilities that he scoffed at danger? In any case, it was brainless and dangerous and it made her crazy.

"Oh, yes, this ball is very important," he answered her question. His smile was slow and sensual. "It may be my last chance to dance with you. Believe me, Pellea, there is nothing more important than that."

She was speechless, then angry. How did he do it, again and again? Somehow he always touched her emotions, even when she knew very well that was exactly what he was aiming at. She felt like a fool, but she had to admit, a part of her that she wasn't very proud of loved it.

Monte knew he'd weakened her defenses with that one and he smiled. It might sound glib and superficial, but he meant every word of it.

She was beautiful, from head to toe, and as he gazed at the way the tiara worked perfectly with her elaborate ensemble, he thought about his memories of his own mother wearing it, and a mist seemed to cloud his eyes for a moment. In many ways, Pellea fitted into the continuity of culture here in Ambria the way no other woman he'd ever met could do. It was something to keep in mind, wasn't it?

Out of the corner of his eye, he saw Leonardo coming back into the room and looking their way, frowning fiercely. Monte smiled and glanced at Pellea. She'd seen him, too.

"We'd better get out on the dance floor or we'll be answering questions from Leonardo in no time," he noted. "He has that mad inquisitioner look to him tonight."

Quickly, she nodded and raised her arms. He took her into his embrace and they began to sway to the music.

"This is all so wrong," she murmured, leaning against his shoulder. "You know this is only going to anger him."

He glanced over at Leonardo, who was scowling, his friends gathered around him. Angering Leonardo was the least of his worries right now. He was gambling that the man wouldn't see him as the intruder he'd been studying on the castle monitoring system.

If he'd arrived in more normal attire, that might have been a problem. But because he'd appeared in such an elaborate costume, claimed to be royal and seemed to fit so well with the others who were here, he hoped Leonardo wouldn't connect him with the intruder until it was too late.

At first glance, he would have to say that he'd been right. Everything was influenced by context.

"I see that your handsome and valorous swain is celebrating his fool head off tonight," he noted as Leonardo threw back another shot of Scotch.

"Yes," she whispered. "He's already had too much. It's becoming a habit of his lately. I'm going to have to work on that."

He gazed down at her and barely contained the sneer he felt like using at her words. "Are you?"

"Yes." She lifted her chin and met his gaze defiantly. "After we're married."

She said the word loud and clear, emphasizing it to make sure he got her drift. And now he did sneer. He got it all right. He just didn't want to accept it.

He whirled her in a fancy turn, then dipped her in a way that took her breath away. But she was half laughing at the same time.

"Oh, that was lovely," she told him, clinging to him in a way that sent his pulse soaring.

"Your lover boy didn't like it," he told her blithely.

"Maybe not," she admitted, looking back at where Leonardo was standing a bit apart from his friends and watching her. "But you have to admit, until you arrived, all in all, he seems to be happy tonight."

"Why wouldn't he be?" He pulled her up against his chest and held her there for a beat too long, enjoying the soft, rounded feel of her body against his. "And you, my darling," he added softly. "Are you happy?"

Her dark eyed gaze flickered up at him, then away again. "You know the answer to that. But I'm prepared to do my duty."

That was an answer that infuriated him and he was silent for a moment, trying to control himself. But he couldn't stay angry with her in his arms. He looked down at her and his heart swelled. When was he going to admit it? This trip had been completely unnecessary. He'd already gathered all the reconnaissance data he needed on his last visit to Ambria. He'd only come for one thing. Trying to turn it into a Helen-of-Troy kidnapping of the enemy's most beautiful woman was just fanciful rationalizing. He'd come to find Pellea because he needed to see her. That was all there was to it. But now that he knew about this insane wedding to a Granvilli monster, he wanted to get her out of here with more urgency. She had to go. She couldn't marry Leonardo. What a crime against nature that would be!

And yet, there was the problem of her father. No matter what he might think of the man, if he ripped her away from him by force, without first convincing her to go, she would never forgive him. Knowing how important family was, and how traumatic it could be when it was torn apart, he might never forgive himself.

He had to find a way to make her come with him. Somehow.

He dipped her again, pulling her in close and bending over her in a rather provocative way. "I promise you, Pellea," he said, his voice rough and husky. "I swear it on my parents' graves. You will be happy."

Her heart was beating hard. She stared at him, not sure what he was up to. He was making promises he couldn't possibly keep. She didn't believe a word of it.

"You can't decide on my happiness," she told him bluntly. "It's not up to you."

"Of course not," he said, his bitterness showing. "I suppose it's up to your father, isn't it?"

She drew her breath in and let resentment flow through her for a moment. Then she pushed it back. It did no good to let emotions take over at a time like this.

"I know you hate my father," she said softly, "and you may have good reason to, from your point of view."

"You mean from a reasonable perspective?"

She ignored his taunt and went on.

"But I don't hate him. I love him very much. My mother died when I was very young and he and I have been our only family ever since. He's been everything to me. I love him dearly."

He pulled back, still holding her loosely in his arms. "You'd choose him over me?" he asked, his voice rough as sandpaper.

Her eyes widened. His words startled her. In fact, he took her breath away with the very concept. What was he asking of her? Whatever he was thinking, he had no right to put it to her that way.

And so she nodded. "Of course I would choose him. He and I have a real relationship. With you, I have…"

Her voice trailed off. Even now she was reluctant to analyze what exactly it was that they had together. "With you I had something that was never meant to last," she said finally.

He stared at her, wondering why her words stung so deeply. Wondering why there was an urge down in him that was clawing its way to the surface, an urge to do what he'd only bantered about, an urge to throw her over his shoulder as his own personal trophy, and fight his way out of the castle.

Kidnap her. That was the answer. He would carry her off and hide her away somewhere only he could find her. The need swelled inside him, almost choking him with its intensity. He was flying high on fantasy.

But he came back down to earth with a thump. What the hell was wrong with him? That whole scenario was just sick. He had no more right to force her into anything than he had to force anyone. If he really wanted her that badly, he would have to find a way to convince her to want him just as much. And so far, that wasn't working.

She preferred to stay with her father.

But that wasn't fair, to put it that way. Her father was her only living relative and he was very ill. Of course she was protective of him and wanted to stay with him. Her tenderness and compassion were part of what he loved about her.

"So I guess I come in third," he mentioned with deceptive calm. "Behind your father and Leonardo." He glanced back at her fiancé waiting for this long dance to end. "Maybe I ought to have a talk with your lover boy."

She drew her breath in sharply. "Stay away from him, Monte. The more he drinks the more dangerous he'll be."

She was passionate and worried, but also confused and torn and not at all sure how to handle this. Here she was in the same room with the man she loved and even in his arms, and just a stone's throw away from the man she was pledged to marry.

Let's face it, he was the man she *had* to marry, no way around it. She was pregnant. She needed a husband. Without one, she would be persona non grata in this community. And if those in charge ever figured out who the baby's father was, her child would be an outcast as well.

She really didn't have much choice in the matter. In a country like this, living in this rarefied sliver of the society as she did, and caring for her father as she did, there was no option to play the free spirit and defy the culture's norms. She needed protection. It was all very well to love Monte, but he would never marry her. She had to provide for her child—and herself. No one else was prepared to do it for her.

No one but Leonardo, and for that—though Monte might never understand it—she would be forever grateful to the man.

Leonardo knew she was pregnant, though he didn't know who the father was. He didn't really care. It wasn't love he was looking for in their relationship. It was the factions she represented, the power she could help him assemble, and the prestige of her name. Though her father had been mistrusted for a time because he had worked with the old DeAngelis regime, years had passed now, and his reputation was clear. Now, the magic of the old days and the old regime was what mattered. People were said to hold him in such high esteem, his reputation rivaled that of the Granvillis. And that was one reason Leonardo wanted her on his side.

It was well understood between the two of them. She was getting something she needed from him and he was getting something he needed from her. If Monte had just stayed away, everything would be going along as planned.

But Monte had appeared out of nowhere once again and upset the apple cart. She loved him. She couldn't deny it. And he was the father of her child, although he didn't know it. And here he was, inserting himself into the equation in a way that was sure to bring misery to them all. Did she have the strength to stop him? So far, it didn't seem possible.

The music finally came to an end. She knew Leonardo was waiting for her to return to her spot and she was resigned to it. Reluctantly, she began to slip out of Monte's arms.

But he didn't want to let her go.

"Do you find it oppressively hot in here?" he murmured close to her ear, his warm breath tickling her skin.

"Oh, I don't know, I guess…"

He didn't wait for a full answer. In the confusion of couples coming and going every which way to get on and off the dance floor, he maneuvered her right out the open French doors onto the dimly lit and almost empty terrace. As the small orchestra struck up a new tune, they continued their dance.

"Monte," she remonstrated with him. "You can't do

this. You're not the only one who wants to dance with me, you know."

"I know that very well," he said. "Why do you think I felt I had to resort to these guerilla tactics to have my way with you?"

She laughed low in her throat and he pulled her into the shadows and kissed her. His kiss was music by Mozart, sculpture by Michelangelo, the dancing of Fred Astaire. He was the best.

Of course, she wasn't exactly an expert on such things. Her experience wasn't extensive. But she'd had make-out sessions with incredibly attractive men in her time, and she knew this was top-tier kissing.

He started slowly, just barely nipping at her lips, and, as she felt herself enjoying the sensation and reaching for more of it, he found his way into the honey-sweet heat of her mouth, using his tongue to explore the terrain and sample the most tender and sensitive places.

She knew she was being hypnotized again and for the moment, she didn't care. His slow, provocative touch was narcotic, and she fell for the magic gladly. If he had picked her up and carried her off at that moment, she wouldn't have protested at all.

But he'd kept the clearer head and he pulled back.

"Oh, Monte, no," she sighed, the sweetness of his lips still branding hers. She felt so wonderful in his arms, like a rose petal floating downstream. The music, the cool night air, his strong arms around her—what could be better?

"Please," she whispered, reaching for him again.

"Not now, my darling," he whispered back, nuzzling behind her ear. "There are people nearby. And there are things that must be done."

"Like what?" she murmured rather sulkily, but she was beginning to come back to her senses as well and she sighed, realizing that he was perfectly right to deflect her. "Oh, bother," she muttered, annoyed with herself as her head cleared. "There you go, flying me to the moon again."

He laughed softly, dropping one last kiss on her lips. "There will be plenty of time for that later," he promised.

"No there won't," she said sensibly. "I'll be married. And if you think you're going to be hanging around once that has happened, you'd better think again."

She couldn't help but wince as she let herself imagine just how bereft her world was going to be.

But she managed to keep a fiercely independent demeanor. "There are certain lines I swear I will never cross."

He gazed at her, his blue eyes clouded and unreadable. "What time is the announcement planned for?" he asked her.

She looked up at him in surprise. "Just before the midnight buffet," she answered, then frowned, alarmed. "Wait. Monte! What are you planning to do?"

"Who, me? Why would you think I was planning anything at all?"

"Because I know you." She planted her hands on his

shoulders and shook him. "Don't do it! Whatever you're planning, don't!"

He pretended to be wounded by her suspicion, though his eyes were sparkling with laughter. "I can't believe you have so little faith in me," he said.

She started to respond, but then her gaze caught sight of something that sent her pulse racing. "Leonardo," she whispered to Monte. "He's found us."

"Oh, good," he said. "I've been wanting to talk to him."

CHAPTER SEVEN

PELLEA DREW IN A SHARP BREATH, filled with dread as she watched Leonardo approach.

"I'll hold him off if you want to make a run for it," she told Monte urgently, one hand gripping his shoulder. "But go quickly!"

"Why would I run?" he said, turning to meet the man, still holding her other hand. "I've been looking forward to this."

"Oh, Monte," she whimpered softly, wishing she could cast a spell and take them anywhere else.

Leonardo's face was filled with a cold fury that his silver mask couldn't hide.

"Unhand my fiancée, sir," he ordered, his lip curling and one hand on the hilt of the sword at his side. "And identify yourself, if you please."

Monte's smile was all pure, easy confidence. "You don't allow hand holding with old friends?" he asked, holding Pellea's hand up where Leonardo could see his fingers wrapped around hers. "Pellea and I have a special connection, but it's nothing that should concern you."

"A special connection?" Leonardo repeated, seeming momentarily uncertain. "In what way?"

"Family connections," Monte explained vaguely. "We go way back." But he dropped her hand and clicked his heels before giving Leonardo a stiff little bow. "Allow me to introduce myself. I'm the Count of Revanche. Perhaps you've heard of me?"

Leonardo looked a bit puzzled, but much of his fury had evaporated and a new look of interest appeared on his long face. "Revanche, is it?"

"Yes." Monte stuck out his hand and gave the man a broad smile. It was fascinating how the hint of royalty always worked magic, especially with dictator types. They always seemed a little starstruck by a title, at least at first. He only hoped the sense of awe would last long enough to save him from ending up in a jail cell.

"It is a pleasure to meet you at last, Leonardo," he said heartily. "I've heard so much about you. I'm hoping the reality can compete with the legend."

Leonardo hesitated only a moment, then stuck out his own hand and Monte shook it warmly.

"Have I heard of you before?" he asked.

Monte gave a grand shrug. "That's as may be. But I've heard of you." He laughed as though that was quite a joke. "Your father and I go way back."

"My father?" Leonardo brightened. "How so?"

Monte nodded wisely. "He's meant a great deal to me in my life. In fact, I wouldn't be the man I am today without his strong hand in my early training."

"Ah, I see." Leonardo began to look downright welcoming. "So he has mentored you in some way."

Monte smiled. "One might say that. We were once thick as thieves."

Leonardo actually smiled. "Then you will be happy to know he is going to make an appearance here tonight."

Monte's confidence slipped just a bit, but he didn't let it show. "Is he? What a treat it will be to see him again. I'll be happy to have a drink with him."

"Well, why not have a drink with me while we await his arrival?" Leonardo suggested. He was obviously warming to this visiting count and had forgotten all about the manhandling of his future bride. "Come along, Pellea," he said, sweeping them back into the ballroom with him. "We must make sure our guest is well supplied with refreshment."

Her gaze met Monte's and she bit her lip. She could see what he was doing, but she didn't like it at all. The moment an opportunity arose, she would help him make a run for it. That was the only thing she could see that would save him. This manly bonding thing couldn't last once the truth began to seep out.

But Monte gave her a wink and his eyes crackled with amusement. He was obviously having the time of his life fooling someone who didn't even realize he was dealing with his worst enemy.

They made their way to the bar, and by the time they got there, a crowd of Leonardo's friends and hangers-on had joined them.

"Come," Leonardo said expansively. "We must drink together."

"Of course," Monte agreed cordially. "What are we drinking?"

The bartender slapped a bottle of something dark and powerful-looking on the bar and everyone cheered.

"We must share a toast," Monte said, holding his glass high. "Let us drink to destiny."

"To destiny!"

Each man downed his drink and looked up happily for more. The bartender obliged.

"And to fathers everywhere," Monte said, holding his glass up again. "And to General Georges Granvilli in particular."

"Well. Why not?" Leonardo had just about decided Monte was the best friend he'd ever had by now. He pounded him on the back at every opportunity and merrily downed every drink Monte put before him.

Pellea watched this spectacle in amazement. But when Monte offered her a glass, she shook her head.

"Pellea, come share a toast with us," he coaxed, trying to tempt her. "I'll get you something fruity if you like."

She shook her head firmly. "No. I don't drink."

He blinked at her, remembering otherwise and sidling a bit closer. "You drank happily enough two months ago," he said to her quietly. "We practically bathed in champagne, as I remember. What's changed?"

She flashed him a warning look. "That was then. This is now."

He frowned, ready to take that up and pursue an answer, but Leonardo wrapped an arm around his neck and proclaimed, "I love you, man."

"Of course," Monte said with a sly smile. "You and I are like blood brothers."

Pellea blanched. Was she the only one who got a chill at hearing his words?

"Blood brothers." Leonardo had imbibed too much to be able to make head nor tails of that, but it sounded good to him.

Monte watched him with pity. "You don't understand that," he allowed. "I'm going to have to explain it to you. But for now, trust me." He raised his glass into the light, glad no one seemed to notice that he had never actually drunk what was in it. "Blood brothers under the skin."

"Are we, by God?" Leonardo was almost in tears at the thought.

"Yes," Monte said with an appropriate sense of irony. "We are."

Pellea shook her head. She could see where this was inevitably going and knew there would probably be no announcement of their engagement tonight. Unless Monte volunteered to prop the man up for it, and that wasn't likely.

All in all, this appeared to be a part of his plan. Didn't he understand that it would do no good? The announcement would be made, one way or another, before the wedding, and that was only two days away. He couldn't stop it. She couldn't let him.

He caught her eye, gesturing for her to come closer.

"Do you think Georges will really make an appearance?" he whispered to her.

She shook her head. "I have no idea. I haven't seen him in months. They always say he is in France, taking the waters for his health. For all I know, he's been right here this whole time, watching television in his room."

Monte glanced at Leonardo, who was laughing uproariously with a couple of his mates. One more toast and it was pretty obvious he wouldn't be capable of making an engagement announcement.

"Wait here, my love," he said softly. "I have to finish what I've started."

"Monte, no!" She grabbed his arm to keep him with her, but he pulled away and joined the men at the bar.

"A final toast," he offered to Leonardo. "To our new and everlasting friendship."

"Our friendship!" cried Leonardo, turning up his glass and taking in the contents in one gulp. Then, slowly, he put the glass down. Staring straight ahead, his eyes glassy, he began to crumble. His knees went first, and then his legs. Monte and a couple of the others grabbed him before he hit the ground. A sigh went through the crowd. And, at the same time, bugles sounded in the hallway.

"The General is coming!" someone cried out. "It's General Georges."

"Prepare for the arrival of the General."

Shock went through the crowd in waves, as though no one knew exactly what to do, but all realized something had to be done. Their leader was coming. He had to be welcomed in style.

One of Leonardo's friends sidled up to Monte. "We've got to get him out of here before his father comes," he whispered urgently. "There'll be hell to pay. Believe me, the old man will kill him."

Monte looked at the limp young gentleman who thought he was going to marry Pellea and had a moment of indecision. What did he care if Georges saw his son like this? It wasn't his problem.

And yet, in a way, it *was* his fault. Leonardo was not his enemy. His rival, yes. But it was Leonardo's father who was his mortal enemy. And perhaps it would be just as well if Georges wasn't distracted by focusing his rage on his hapless son.

Because he did plan to face him. How could he avoid the confrontation he'd spent his life preparing for?

"Let's go," he said to the man who'd approached him. "Let's get him to his chambers before his father gets here."

He looked back at Pellea, signaling her to his intentions. But she wasn't paying attention any longer. A servant had come to find her.

"My lady, your father is ill and asking for you," he said nervously.

Pellea reacted immediately. "My father! Oh, I must go."

Monte stopped her for only a moment. "I'll meet you at your father's room as soon as I can make it," he told her.

She nodded, her eyes wide and anxious. "I must go," she muttered distractedly, and she hurried away.

Monte looked back at the task at hand and gritted his teeth. It wasn't going to be a pretty chore, but it had to be done.

"Let's get him out of here," he said, hoisting Leonardo up with the assistance of two other men. And, just as they heard Georges arrive at the main ballroom entrance, they slipped out the side door.

"I'll be back, Georges," Monte whispered under his breath. "Get ready. We've got business between us to settle. Old business."

Monte slipped into Pellea's father's room and folded his form between the drapes to keep from being seen. Pellea was talking to the doctor and her father seemed to be sleeping.

The doctor began to pack his black bag and Pellea went to her father's bedside. Monte watched and saw the anguished love in her face as she leaned over the man. There was no denying this simple truth—she adored her father and she wouldn't leave him.

Monte closed his eyes for a moment, letting that sink in. There was no way he would be able to take her with him. All his kidnapping plans—in the dust. In order to get her to leave he would have to render her unconscious and drag her off, and that wasn't going to happen.

When the idea had first formed, he'd assumed she would come at least semi-willingly. Now he knew that was a fantasy. Her love for her father was palpable. She would never leave while he was still alive. And yet, how could he leave her behind? How could he leave her to the tender mercies of the Granvillis? The more he saw of her, the more he got to know her, the more he felt a special connection, something he'd never felt with a woman before. He wanted her with him.

But more than that, he wanted her safe. Leaving her here with Leonardo would be torture. But what could he do?

Invade, a voice deep in his soul said urgently. *The sooner the better.*

Yes. There really was no other option left.

So he would return to the continent empty-handed. Not quite what he'd promised his supporters waiting for him in Italy.

But all was not lost on that score. He had another plan—something new. Instead of kidnapping their most desirable woman, he would take their most valuable possession.

He was going to steal the tiara.

"Please tell me how he really is," she said anxiously to the doctor. "Don't sugarcoat anything. I need to know the truth." She took a deep breath and asked, "Is he in danger?"

"In other words, is he going to die tonight?" Dr. Dracken translated. "Not likely. Don't worry. But he is very weak. His heart is not keeping up as it should." He hesitated, then added, "If you really want me to be blunt, I'd have to say I wouldn't give him much more than six months. But this sort of thing is hugely unpredictable. Next year at this time, you might be chiding me for being so pessimistic."

"Oh, I hope so," she said fervently as she accompanied him to the door. "Please, do anything for him that you can think of."

"Of course. That's my job, Pellea, and I do the best I can."

The doctor left and Monte reached out and touched her as she came back into the room.

"Oh!" She jumped back, then put her hand over her heart when she realized it was him. "Monte! You scared me."

"Sorry, but once I was in, I was going to startle you no matter how I approached it."

She looked at him with tragic eyes. "My father…" Her face crumpled and she went straight into his arms and clung to him.

"Yes," he said, holding her tenderly, stroking her hair. "I heard what the doctor said. I'm so sorry, Pellea. I truly am."

She nodded. She believed him.

"He's sleeping now. The doctor gave him something. But a little while ago he was just ranting, not himself at all." She looked up into his face. "They are bringing in a nurse to stay with him tonight and tomorrow I'm going to sit with him all day."

He nodded, and then he frowned, realizing his fingers were tangling in her loosened hair. She was wearing it down. All the fancy work Magda had put into her coiffure was gone with the wind.

"Pellea, what happened to the tiara?" he asked.

She drew back and reached up as though she'd forgotten it was gone. "The guards took it back to its museum case," she said. She shook her head sadly. "I wonder if I'll ever get to wear it again."

He scowled, regretting that he'd let her get away before doing what he'd planned to do. Unfortunately, this threw a spanner into the works. Oh, he was still going to steal the thing. But now he was afraid he would have to do some actual breaking and entering in order to achieve his objective.

But when he looked at her again, he found her studying him critically, looking him up and down, admiring the uniform, and the man wearing it. He'd lost the mask somewhere, but for the rest, he looked as fresh as he had at the beginning of the evening.

"You know what?" she said at last, her head to the side, her eyes sparkling. "You would make one incredibly attractive Ambrian king."

He laughed and pulled her back into his arms, kissing her soundly. Her arms came up and circled his neck, and she kissed him back. Their bodies seemed to meet and fit together perfectly. He had a quick, fleeting thought that this might be what heaven was made of, but it was over all too soon.

She checked that her father was sleeping peacefully, then turned to Monte again. "Come sit down and wait with me," she said, pulling him by the hand. "And tell me what happened in the ballroom after I left. Did the General actually appear?"

He shook his head. "I didn't stay any longer than you did. With all the chaos that ensued upon Leonardo's… shall we call it a fall from grace…?"

He flashed her a quick grin, but she frowned in response and he sobered quickly, looking abashed.

"There you were, rushing off to see to your father. People were shouting. No one knew exactly what was going on for quite some time. And I and all my new mates picked up your fiancé and carried him to his rooms."

"I'm glad you did that," she said. "I would hate to think of what would have happened if his father had seen him like that."

"Yes," he said a bit doubtfully. "Well, we tucked him into his bed and I nosed around a little."

"Oh?"

"And I find I need to warn you of something."

She smiled. "You warning me? That's a twist on an old theme, isn't it?"

"I'm quite serious, Pellea." He hesitated until he had her complete attention. "Did it ever occur to you that you might not be the only one with a video monitoring system in this castle?"

She shrugged. "Of course. There's the main security center. Everyone knows that."

"Indeed." He gave her a significant look. "And then there's the smaller panel of screens I found in a small room off Leonardo's bedroom suite. The one that includes a crystal-clear view of your entryway."

Her eyes widened in shock. "What?"

He nodded. "I thought that might surprise you. He can see everyone who is coming in to see you, as well as when you leave."

She blanched, thinking back over what she'd done and who she'd been with in the recent past. "But not…" She looked at him sideways and swallowed hard.

"Your bedroom?" He couldn't help but smile at her reaction. "No. I didn't see any evidence of that."

"Thank God." But her relief was short-lived as she began to realize fully the implications of this news.

She frowned. "But how is it monitored? I mean…did he see you when you arrived? Or any of the other times you've come and gone?"

"I'm sure he doesn't spend most of his time sitting in front of the monitor, any more than you do."

"It would only take once."

"True."

"And how about when you arrived this time?"

Monte hesitated, then shrugged and shook his head. "I didn't come in through your entryway."

She stared at him, reminded that his mode of entering the castle was still a mystery. But for him to say flat-out that he didn't use the door—that was something of a revelation. "Then how…?"

He waved it away. "Never mind."

"But, Monte, I do mind. I want to know. How do

you get into my courtyard if you don't come in the way everyone else does?"

"I'm sorry, Pellea. I'm not going to tell you."

She frowned, not liking that at all. "You do realize that this leaves me in jeopardy of having you arrive at any inopportune moment and me not able to do anything about it."

He'd said it before and now he said it again. "I would never do anything to hurt you."

"No." She shook her head, her eyes deeply troubled. "No, Monte. That's not good enough."

He shrugged. He understood how she felt and sympathized. But what could he do? It was something he couldn't tell anyone about.

"It will have to do. I'm sorry, Pellea. I can't give away my advantage on this score. It has nothing to do with you. It has everything to do with my ability to take this country back when the time comes."

She searched his eyes, and finally gave up on the point. But she didn't like it at all. Still, the fact that Leonardo was secretly watching who came to her door was a more immediate outrage.

"Oh, I just can't believe he's watching my entry-way!"

Monte grinned. "Why are you so upset? After all, you're watching pretty much everyone in the castle yourself."

"Yes, but I'm just watching general walkways, not private entrances."

"Ah, yes," he teased. "That makes all the difference."

"It does. I wouldn't dream of setting up a monitor on Leonardo's gate."

He raised one eyebrow wisely. "Yes, but you're not interested in him. And he is very interested in you."

She thought about that for a few seconds and made a face. "I'm going to find his camera and tape it up," she vowed.

He looked pained. "Don't do that. Then he'll know you're on to him and he'll just find another way to watch you, and you might like that even less. The fact that you know about the camera gives you the advantage now. You can avoid it when you need to."

She sighed. "You're probably right," she said regretfully. It would have felt good taping over his window into her world.

There was a strange gurgling sound and they both turned to see Pellea's father rising up against his pillows.

"Father!" she cried, running to his side. "Don't try to sit up. Let me help you."

But he wasn't looking at his daughter. It was Monte he had in his sights.

"Your Majesty," he groaned painfully. "Your Royal Highness, King of Ambria."

Monte rose and faced him, hoping he would realize the man standing in his bedroom was not the king he'd served all those years ago, but that king's son. This was the first time anyone had mistaken him for his father. He felt a strange mix of honor and repulsion over it.

"My liege," Pellea's father cried, slurring his words. His thin, aged face was still handsome and his silver hair still as carefully groomed and distinguished as ever. "Wait, don't go. I need to tell you. I need to explain. It wasn't supposed to happen that way. I…I didn't mean for it to be like that."

"Father," Pellea said, trying to calm him. "Please, lie back down. Don't try to talk. Just rest."

"Don't you see?" he went on passionately, ignoring her and talking directly to the man he thought was King Grandor. "They had promised, they'd sworn you would be treated with respect. And your queen, the beautiful Elineas. No one should have touched her. It was a travesty and I swear it cursed our enterprise from the beginning."

Monte stood frozen to the spot. He heard the old man's words and they pierced his heart. It was obvious he had a message he'd been waiting a long time to deliver to Monte's father. Well, he was about twenty-five years too late.

He slid down into his covers again, now babbling almost incoherently. Pellea looked up with tears in her eyes.

"He doesn't know what he's saying," she said. "Please go, Monte. You're only upsetting him. I'll stay until the nurse comes."

Monte turned and did as she asked. His emotions were churning. He knew Pellea's father was trying to make amends of sorts, but it was a little too late. Still, it was good that he recognized that wrong had been done.

Wrong that still had to be avenged.

CHAPTER EIGHT

KNOWING PELLEA WOULD BE BUSY with her father for some time, Monte made a decision. He planned to make a visit to General Georges. Why not do it now?

A deadly calm came over him as he prepared to go. This meeting with the most evil man in his country's history was something he'd gone over a thousand times in his mind and each time there had been a different scenario, a different outcome. Which one would he choose? It didn't matter, really. They all ended up with the General mortally wounded or already dead.

The fact that his own survival might be in doubt in such an encounter he barely acknowledged and didn't worry about at all. His destiny was already set and included a confrontation with the General. That was just the way it had to be.

He strode down the hallways with confidence. He knew where the cameras were and he avoided them with ease. One of Leonardo's compadres had pointed out the General's suite to him as they'd carried Leonardo past it, and he went there now.

Breaking into the room was a simple matter. There

were no guards and the lock was a basic one. He'd learned this sort of thing as a teenager and it had stood him in good stead many times over the years.

Quietly, he slipped into the darkened room. He could hear the General snoring, and he went directly into his bedroom and yanked back the covers on his bed, ready to counter any move the older man made, whether he pulled out a gun or a cell phone.

But the man didn't move. He slept on. He seemed to have none of the effete elegance his son wore so proudly. Instead, he was large and heavy-set, but strangely amorphous, like a sculpture that had begun to melt back into a lump of clay.

"Wake up," Monte ordered. "I want to talk to you."

No response. Monte moved closer and touched the dictator. Nothing changed.

He glanced at the things on the bedside table. Bottles of fluid and a box of hypodermic needles sat waiting. His heart sank and he turned on the light and looked at the General again.

His eyes were open. He was awake.

The man was drugged. He lay, staring into space, a mere burnt-out shell of the human being he had once been. There wasn't much left. Monte realized that he could easily pick up a pillow and put it over the General's face…and that would be that. It would be a cinch. No problem at all. There wasn't an ounce of fight left in his enemy.

He stood staring down at the General for a long, long time and finally had to admit that he couldn't do it. He'd always thought he would kill Georges Granvilli if he found him. But now that he'd come face to face with him, he knew there was nothing left to kill. The man who had murdered his parents and destroyed his family was gone. This thing that was left was hardly even human.

Killing Georges Granvilli wouldn't make anything any better. He would just be a killer himself if he did it. He wasn't worth killing. The entire situation wasn't worth pursuing.

Slowly, Monte walked away in disgust.

He got back to the courtyard just moments before Pellea arrived. He thought about telling her where he'd been and what he'd seen, but he decided against it. There was no point in putting more ugliness in her thoughts right now. He could at least spare her that.

He was sitting by the fountain in the twilight atmosphere created by all the tiny fairy lights in her shrubbery when she came hurrying in through the gate.

"Monte?" she asked softly, then came straight for him like a swooping bird. As she reached him, she seized his face in her hands and kissed him on the lips, hard.

"You've got to go," she said urgently, tears in her eyes. "Go now, quickly, before they come for you."

"What have you heard?" he asked her, reaching to pull her down into his lap so that he could kiss her sweet lips once more.

"It's not what I've heard," she told him, snuggling in closely. "It's what I know. It's only logic. When all this chaos dies down and they begin to put two and two together, they'll come straight here looking for you. And you know what they'll find."

He searched her dark eyes, loving the way her long lashes made soft shadows on her cheeks. "Then we'd better get the heck out of here," he said calmly.

"No." She shook her head and looked away. "You're going. I'm staying."

He grimaced, afraid she still didn't understand the consequences of staying. "How can I leave you behind to pick up the pieces?"

"You have to go," she told him earnestly. She turned back to look at him, then reached up to run her fingers across the roughness of his barely visible beard, as though she just couldn't help herself. "When Leonardo wakes up, he's going to start asking around and trying to find out just who that man at the ball was. He'll want to know all about you and where you've been staying. And this time, they won't leave my chambers alone. They'll search with a fine-tooth comb and any evidence that you've been here will be…"

Her voice trailed off as she began to face the unavoidable fact that she was in as much danger as he was. She looked at him, eyes wide.

He was just thinking the same thing. It was torture to imagine leaving her behind. He'd turned and twisted every angle in his mind, trying to think of some way out, but the more he agonized, the more he knew there was no good answer. Unless she just gave up this obsession with staying with her father, what could he do to make sure she was protected while he was gone?

Nothing. Nothing at all.

He did have one idea, but he rejected it right away. And yet, it kept nagging at him. What if he showed her the tunnel to the outside? Then, if she was threatened, she could use it to escape.

They were bound to come after her, and even if they couldn't find any solid evidence of her ties to him, they would have their suspicions. Luckily her position and the fact that her father was so highly placed in the hierarchy would mean the most they would do at first was place her under house surveillance—meaning she would be confined to her chambers. But if her father died, or Leonardo became insanely jealous, or something else happened, all that might fall apart. In that case, it would be important for her to have a way to escape that others didn't know about. That was what made it so tempting to give her the information she needed.

Still, it was crazy even to contemplate doing that. Deep down, he didn't believe she would betray him on purpose. But what if she was discovered? What if someone saw her? His ace in the hole, his secret opening back into the castle which he and his invading force would need when he returned to claim his country back would be useless. He just couldn't risk that. Could he?

"And Monte," she was saying, getting back to the subject of her thoughts. "Leonardo's father is not a nice man."

"No?" Monte thought of the burned-out hulk he'd just been visiting. "What a surprise."

"I'm serious. Leonardo has at least some redeeming qualities. His father? None."

He looked at her seriously. "And do those redeeming qualities make him into a man you can stomach marrying?"

She avoided his eyes. "Monte…"

His arms tightened around her. "You can't kiss me the way you just did and then talk about marrying Leonardo. It doesn't work, Pellea. I've told you that before and nothing's changed." He kissed her again on her mouth, once, twice, three times, with quick hunger that grew more urgent with each kiss. He pulled her up hard against his strong body, her softness molding against him in a way that could quickly drive him crazy. Burying his face in her hair, he wanted to breathe her in, wanted to merge every part of her with every part of him.

She turned in his arms, reaching up to circle his neck, arching her body into his as though she felt the same compulsion. He dropped kisses down the length of her neck and heard her make a soft moaning sound deep in her throat. That alone almost sent him over the top, and the way her small hands felt gliding under his shirt and sliding over the muscles of his back pretty much completed the effort.

He wanted her as he'd never wanted a woman before, relentlessly, fiercely, with an insatiable need that raged through him like a hurricane. He'd felt this way about her before, but he hadn't let her know. Now, for just a few moments, he let her feel it, let her have a hint of what rode just on the other side of his patience.

She could have been shocked. She could have considered his ardor a step too far and drawn back in complete rejection. But as she felt his passion overtaking him and his desire for her so manifest, she accepted it with a willingness of her own. She wanted him, too. His marriage of the emotional need for her with the physical hunger was totally in tune with her own reactions.

But this wasn't the time. Resolutely, she pushed him back before things went too far.

He accepted her lead on it, but he had to add one thing as she slipped out of his arms.

"You belong to me," he said fiercely, his hand holding the back of her head like a globe. "Leonardo can't have you."

She tried to shake her head. "I'm going to marry him," she insisted, and though her voice was mournful, she sounded determined. "I've told you that from the moment you came today. I don't know why you won't listen."

This would be so much easier if she could tell him the truth, but that was impossible. How could he understand that she needed Leonardo even more than he needed her? She was caught in a web. If she didn't marry Leonardo, she would be considered an outcast in Ambrian traditional society.

Out-of-wedlock births were not uncommon, but they were considered beyond the pale. Once you had a baby out of wedlock, you could never be prominent in society. You would always have the taint of bad behavior about you. No one would trust your judgment and everyone would slightly despise you.

It wasn't fair, but it was the way things were.

He held her in a curiously stiff manner that left her feeling distinctly uncomfortable.

"You don't love Leonardo," he said. He'd said it before, but she didn't seem to want to accept it and act upon the fact. Maybe he should say it again and keep saying it until she realized that some things were hard, basic truths that couldn't be denied or swept under the rug.

She pulled away from him and folded her arms across her chest as though she were feeling a frost.

"I hate to repeat a cliché," she said tartly, "but here goes. What's love got to do with it?"

He nodded, his face twisted cynically. "So you admit this is a royal contract sort of wedding. A business deal."

"A power deal is more like it. Our union will cement the power arrangements necessary to run this country successfully."

"And you still think he'll want you, even if he begins to suspect…"

"I told you, love isn't involved. It's a power trade, and he wants it as much as I need it."

"Need it?" He stared at her. "Why do you 'need' it?"

She closed her eyes and shook her head. "Maybe I put it a little too strongly," she said. "I just meant… Well, you know. For my father and all."

He wasn't sure he bought that. There was something else here, something she wasn't telling him. He frowned, looking at her narrowly. He found it hard to believe that she would prefer that sort of thing to a love match. But then, he hadn't offered her a love match, had he? He hadn't even offered her a permanent friendship. So who was he to complain? And yet, he had to. He had to stop this somehow.

"Okay, I see the power from Leonardo's side," he said, mulling it over. "But where do you get yours?"

She rose and swayed in front of him, anger sparking from her eyes. She didn't like being grilled this way, mostly because she didn't have any good answers.

"For someone who wants to be ruler of Ambria, you don't know much about local politics, do you?"

He turned his hands palms-up. "If you weren't such a closed society, maybe I could be a bit more in the know," he pointed out.

She considered that and nodded reluctantly. "That's a fair point. Okay, here's the deal. Over the years, there have been many factions who have—shall we say—strained under the Granvilli rule for various reasons. A large group of dissenters, called the Practicals, have been arguing that our system is archaic and needs updating. For some reason they seem to have gravitated toward my father as their symbolic leader."

Monte grunted. "That must make life a bit dodgy for your father," he noted.

"A bit. But he has been invaluable to the rulers and

they don't dare do anything to him. And anyway, the Practicals would come unglued if they did."

"Interesting."

"The Practicals look to me as well. In fact, it may just be a couple of speeches I gave last year that set them in our direction, made them think we were kindred souls. So in allying himself with me, Leonardo hopes to blunt some of that unrest."

He gazed at her in admiration and surprise. "Who knew you were a mover and a shaker?" he said.

She actually looked a bit embarrassed. "I'm not. Not really. But I do sympathize with many of their criticisms of the way things are run. Once I marry Leonardo, I hope to make some changes."

Was that it? Did she crave the power as much as her father did? Was it really all a bid for control with her? He found that hard to believe, but when she said these things, what was he to think?

He studied her for another moment, then shrugged. "That's what they all say," he muttered, mostly to himself.

She was tempted to say something biting back, but she held her tongue. There was no point in going on with this. They didn't have much more time together and there were so many other things they could be talking about.

"Have you noticed that so far, no one seems to know who you really are?" she pointed out. As long as they didn't know who he was, his freedom might be imperiled, but his life wouldn't be. And if they should somehow realize who it was they had in their clutches… She hated to think what they might do.

"No, they don't, do they?" He frowned, not totally pleased with that. "How did *you* know, anyway? From the other time, I mean."

"You told me." She smiled at him, remembering.

"Oh. Did I?" That didn't seem logical or even realistic. He never told anyone.

"Yes, right from the first." She gave him a flirtatious look. "Right after I saved you from the guards, you kissed me and then you said, 'You can tell everyone you've been kissed by the future king of Ambria. Consider yourself blessed.'"

"I said that?" He winced a bit and laughed softly. "I guess you might be right about me having something of an ego problem."

"No kidding." She made a face. "Maybe it goes with being royal or something."

"Oh, I don't know about that." After all, he hadn't blown his cover all these years—except, it seemed, with her. "I think I do pretty well. Don't you think I blend in nicely with the average Joes?"

She shook her head, though there was a hint of laughter in her eyes. "Are you crazy? No, you do not blend in, as you so colorfully put it. Look at the way you carry yourself. The arrogance. There's no humility about you."

"No humility?" He was offended. "What are you talking about? I'm probably the most humble guy you would ever meet."

She made a sound of deprecation. "A little self-awareness would go a long way here," she noted as she looked him over critically. "But I could see that from the start. It was written all over you. And yet, I didn't kick you out as I should have."

"No, you didn't." Their gazes met and held. "But we did have an awfully good weekend, didn't we?"

"Yes." She said it softly, loving him, thinking of the child they had made together. If only she could tell him about that. Would he be happy? Probably not. That was just the way things were going to be. She loved him and he felt something pretty deep for her. But that was all they were destined to have of each other. How she would love to spend the next fifty years in his arms.

If only he weren't royal and she weren't tied to this place. If only he didn't care so much about Ambria. They could have done so well together, the two of them. She could imagine them walking on a sandy beach, chasing waves, or having a picnic by a babbling brook, skipping stones in the water, or driving around France, looking at vineyards and trying to identify the grapes.

Instead, he was planning to invade her country. And that would, of necessity, kill people she cared about. How could she stand it? Why hadn't she turned him in?

"Why does it matter so much to you, Monte?" she asked at last. "Why can't you just leave things alone?"

He looked up, his eyes dark and haunted. "Because a very large wrong was done to my family. And to this

country. I need to make things right again. That's all I
live for."

His words stabbed into her soul like sharp knives.
If this was all he lived for, what could she ever be to
him?

"Isn't there someone else who could do it?" she asked
softly. "Does it have to be you?"

Reaching out, he put his hand under the water raining
down from the fountain. Drops bounced out and scattered across his face, but he seemed to welcome them.
"I'm the crown prince. I can't let others fight my battles
for me."

"But you have brothers, don't you?"

He nodded. "There were five of us that night. Or
rather, seven. Five boys and twin girls." He was quiet
for a moment, remembering. "I hunted for them all for
years. I started once I enrolled in university in England. I
studied hard, but I spent a lot of time poring over record
books in obscure villages, hoping to find some clue.
There was nothing."

He sighed, in his own milieu now. "Once I entered the
business world and then did some work for the Foreign
Office, I developed contacts all over the world. And
those have just begun to pan out. As I think I told you,
I've made contact with two of my brothers, the two closest to me in age. But the others are still a mystery."

"Are you still looking?"

"Of course. I'll be looking until I find them all. For
the rest of my life if need be." He shrugged. "I don't
know if they are alive or not. But I'll keep looking." He

turned and looked at her, his eyes burning. "Once we're all together, there will be no stopping us."

She shook her head, unable to imagine how growing up without any contact with his family would have affected this young Ambrian prince.

"What was it like?" she asked him. "What happened to you as a child? It must have been terrible to grow up alone."

He nodded. "It wasn't great. I had a wonderful family until I was eight years old. After that, it was hit or miss. I stayed with people who didn't necessarily know who I was, but who knew I had to be hidden. I ended up with a couple who were kind to me but hardly loving." He shrugged. "Not that it mattered. I wasn't looking for a replacement for my mother, nor for my father. No one could replace either one of them and I didn't expect it."

"Why were they hiding you?"

"They were trying to keep the Granvillis from having me killed."

"Oh." She colored as though that were somehow her fault. "I see."

"We were all hidden. From each other, even. You understand that any surviving royals were a threat to the Granvilli rule, and I, being the crown prince, am the biggest threat of all."

"Of course. I get it."

"We traveled a lot. I went to great schools. I had the sort of upbringing you would expect of a royal child, minus the love. But I survived and in fact, I think I did pretty well."

"It wasn't until I found my brother Darius that I could reignite that family feeling and I began to come alive again. Family is everything and I had lost mine."

"And your other brother?"

"A young woman who worked for an Ambrian news agency in the U.S. found Cassius. He was only four during the coup and he didn't remember that he was royal. He'd grown up as a California surfer and spent time in the military. Finding out his place in life has been quite a culture shock to him. He's trying to learn how to be royal, but it isn't easy for a surfer boy. I only hope he can hold it all together until we retake our country."

The old wall clock struck the time and it was very late, well after midnight. She looked at him and sighed. "You must go," she told him.

He looked back at her and wondered how he could leave her here. "Come with me, Pellea," he said, his voice crackling with intensity. "Come with me tonight. By late morning, we'll be in France."

She closed her eyes. She was so tired. "You know I can't," she whispered.

He rose and came over to kiss her softly on her full, red lips. "Then come and get some sleep," he told her. "I'll go just before dawn."

"Will you wake me up when you go?" she asked groggily.

"Yes. I'll wake you."

And would he show her his escape secrets? That was

probably a step too far. He couldn't risk it. He had to think of more lives than just their two. So he promised he would wake her, but he didn't promise he would let her see him go.

She lay down in her big, fluffy bed and he lay down on her long couch, which was almost as comfortable. He didn't understand why she wouldn't let him sleep beside her. She seemed to have some strange sense of a moral duty to Leonardo. Well, if it was important to her, he wasn't going to mess with it. She had to do what she had to do, just like he did. Lying still and listening to her breathe on the bed so near and yet so far, he almost slept.

CHAPTER NINE

THE MOMENT PELLEA WOKE, she knew Monte was gone. It was still dark and nowhere near dawn, but he was gone. Just as she'd thought.

She curled into a ball of misery and wept. Someday she would have his child to console her, but right now there was nothing good and beautiful and strong and true in her life but Monte. And he was gone.

But wait. She lifted her head and thought for a moment. He'd promised to say goodbye. He wouldn't break his promise. If he didn't tell her in person, he would at least have left a note, and there was nothing. That meant…he was still somewhere in the castle.

Her heart stopped in her throat. What now? Where could he be? Dread filled her since, surely, he would get caught. He would be killed. He would have to leave without saying goodbye! She couldn't stand it. None of the above was tolerable. She had to act fast.

Rising quickly, she went to the surveillance room with the security monitors and began to study them. All looked quiet. It was about three in the morning, and she detected no movement.

Maybe she was wrong. Maybe he had gone without saying goodbye. Darn it all!

That's when she saw something moving in the museum. A form. A tall, graceful masculine form. Monte! What was he doing in the museum room?

The tiara!

She groaned. "No, Monte!" she cried, but of course he couldn't hear her.

And then, on another panel, she saw the guards. There were three of them and they were moving slowly down the hallway toward the museum, looking like men gearing up for action. There was no doubt in her mind. They'd been alerted to his presence and would nab him.

Her heart was pounding out of her chest. She had to act fast. She couldn't let them catch him like this. They would throw him in jail and Leonardo would hear of it and Monte's identity would be revealed and he would be a dead man. She groaned.

She couldn't let that happen. There was only one thing she could do. She had to go there and stop it.

In another moment she was racing through the hallways, her white nightgown billowing behind her, her hair a cloud of golden blond, and her bare feet making a soft padding sound on the carpeted floors.

She ran, heedless of camera positions, heedless of anyone who might step out and see her. Who would be watching at this time of night anyway? Only the very men she'd seen going after Monte. She had one goal and that was to save his singularly annoying life. If only she could get there in time.

The museum door was ajar. She burst in and came face to face with Monte, but he was standing before her in handcuffs, with a guard on either side. Behind them, she could see the tiara, glistening on its mount inside the glass case. At least he didn't have it in his hands.

She stared into Monte's eyes for only a second or two, long enough to note the look of chagrin he wore at being caught, and then she swung her attention onto the guards.

"What is going on here?" she demanded, her stern gaze brooking no attitude from any of them. She knew how to pour on the superior pose when she had to and she was playing it to the hilt right now. Even standing there barefoot and in her nightgown she radiated control.

The guards were wide-eyed. They knew who she was but they'd never seen her like this. After a moment of surprised reaction, the captain stepped forward.

"Miss, we have captured the intruder." He nodded toward Monte and looked quite pleased with himself.

She blinked, then gestured toward Monte with a sweep of her hand. "You call this an intruder?" she said sternly, her lip curling a bit in disdain.

"Uh." The captain looked at her and then looked away again. "We caught him red-handed, Miss. He was trying to steal the tiara. Look, you can see that the lock was forced open."

"Uh." The second in command tugged on the captain's shirt and whispered in his ear.

The captain frowned and turned back to Pellea, looking most disapproving.

"I'm told you might have been dancing with this gentleman at the ball, Miss," he said. "Perhaps you can identify him for us."

"Certainly," she said in a sprightly manner. "He's a good friend of Leonardo's."

"Oh." All three appeared shocked and Monte actually gave her a triumphant wink which she ignored as best she could. "Well, there may be something there. Mr. Leonardo, is it?"

Just his name threw them for a loop. Everyone was terrified of Leonardo. They shuffled their feet but the captain wasn't cowed.

"Still, we found him breaking into the museum case," he noted. "You can't do that."

"Is anything missing?" she asked, looking bored with it all.

"No. We caught him in time."

"Well then." She gave a grand shrug. "All's well that ends well, isn't it?"

The captain frowned. "Not exactly. I'm afraid I have to make a report of this to the General. He'll want to know the particulars and might even want to interview the intruder himself."

Not a good outcome. Monte gave her a look that reminded her that this would be a bad ending to this case. But she already knew as much.

"Oh, I doubt that," she said airily. "If you have some time to question him yourself, I think you will find the problem that is at the root of all this."

The captain frowned. He obviously wasn't sure he

liked the interference being run by this know-it-all from the regime hierarchy. "And that is?"

She sighed as though it was just so tedious to have to go over the particulars.

"My good man, it was a ball. You know how men get. This one and Leonardo were challenging each other to a drinking contest." She shrugged elaborately. "Leonardo is now out cold in his room. I'm sure you'll find this fellow…" She gestured his way. "…who you may know as the Count of Revanche, isn't in much better shape. He may not show it but he has no clue what he's doing."

The guards looked at Monte. He gave them a particularly mindless grin. They frowned as Monte added a mock fierce look for good measure. The guards glanced away and shuffled their feet again.

"Well, miss," said the captain, "What you say may be true and all. But he was still found in the museum room, and the lock was tampered with and that just isn't right."

Pellea bit her lip, biding for time. They were going to be sticklers, weren't they? She felt the need of some reinforcement. For that, she turned to Monte.

"Please, Your Highness, tell us what you were doing in the museum room."

He gave her a fish-eyed look before he turned to the guards and gave it a try.

"I was…" He managed to look a little woozy. "I was attempting to steal the tiara." He said it as though it were a grand announcement.

"What on earth!" she cried, feeling all was lost and wondering what he was up to.

"Don't you understand?" he said wistfully. "It's so beautiful. I wanted to give it back to you so that you could wear it again."

She stared at him, dumbfounded at how he could think this was a good excuse.

"To me?" she repeated softly.

"Yes. You looked enchanting in it, like a fairy-tale princess, and I thought you should have it, always." His huge, puppy-dog eyes were doing him a service, but some might call it over the top for this job.

"But, it's not mine," she reminded him sadly.

"No?" He looked a bit puzzled by that. "Well, it should be."

She turned to the guards. "You see?" she said, throwing out her hands. "He's not in his right mind. I think you should let me take him off your hands. You don't really want to bother the General with this trifle, especially at this time of night. Do you?"

The captain tried to look stern. "Well, now that you mention it, miss…"

She breathed a sigh of relief. "Good, I'll just take him along then."

They were shuffling their feet again. That seemed to be a sign that they weren't really sure what they should be doing.

"Would you like one of us to come along and help you handle him?" the captain asked, groping for his place in all this.

"No, I think he'll be all right." She took hold of his hands, bound by the handcuffs, and the captain handed her the key. "He usually does just what I tell him," she lied happily. She'd saved him. She could hardly contain her excitement.

"I see, miss. Good night, then."

"Good night, Captain. Men." She waved at them merrily and began to lead Monte away. "Come along now, Count," she murmured to him teasingly. "I've got you under house arrest. You'd better do what I tell you to from now on."

"That'll be the day," he said under his breath, but his eyes were smiling.

Once back in her courtyard, they sat side by side on the garden bench and leaned back, sighing with relief.

"You're crazy," she told him matter-of-factly. "To risk everything for a tiara."

"It's a very special tiara," he reminded her. "And by all rights, it belongs to my family."

"Maybe so, but there are others who would fight you for it," she said, half closing her eyes and thinking about getting more sleep. "You almost pulled it off," she added.

"Yes."

She turned to look at him. "And you actually seemed to know what you were doing. Why was that? Have you been moonlighting as a jewel thief or something?"

He settled back and smiled at her. "In fact, I do know what I'm doing around jewelry heists," he stated calmly.

"I apprenticed myself to a master jewel thief one summer. He taught me everything he knew."

She frowned at him for a long moment. It was late. Perhaps she hadn't heard him correctly. But did he say…?

"What in the name of common sense are you talking about?" she said, shaking her head in bewilderment. "Why would you do such a thing?"

He shrugged. "I wanted to learn all I could about breaking into reinforced and security-protected buildings. I thought it would be a handy talent to have when it came time to reassert my monarchy on this island nation."

She stared at him in wonder, not sure if she was impressed or appalled. But it did show another piece of evidence of the strength of his determination to get his country back. This was pretty obviously an ambition she wasn't going to be able to fight.

Sighing, she shook her head and turned away. "Well, maybe you should go back for a refresher course," she noted.

He raised an eyebrow. "What are you talking about?"

She looked back at him. "Well, you didn't get the tiara, did you?"

"What makes you say that?" He smiled and reached back and pulled something out of the back of his shirt and held it up to the light, where it glittered spectacularly.

"You mean this tiara?" he asked her.

She stared at it as it flashed color and fire all around the room. "But I saw it in the case in the museum."

"You saw a copy in the case." He held it even higher and looked at it, admiring its beauty. "This is the real thing."

She was once again bewildered by him. "I don't understand."

"What you saw was a replica. My grandmother had it made years ago. I remembered that my mother had it in a secret hiding place. I went over to that side of the castle and, lo and behold, I found it."

"That's amazing. After all this time? I can hardly believe it."

"Yes. It seems that most of my family's private belongings were shoved into a big empty room and have been forgotten. Luckily for me."

She shook her head. "But now that you have the tiara, what are you going to do with it?"

"Take it back with me." He tucked it away and leaned over to take her hand in his. "If I can't take their most beautiful woman from them, at least I can take their prized royal artifact." He smiled. "And when you think about it, the tiara actually belongs to me. Surely you see that."

She laced her fingers with his and yearned toward him. "You're just trying to humiliate them, aren't you? You would have preferred to do it by stealing me away, but since that's not possible, you take the tiara instead."

"Yes," he said simply. "The answer is yes."

"But…"

"Don't you understand, Pellea? I want them thrown off-center. I want them to wonder what my next move might be. I want them to doubt themselves." The spirit of the royal warrior was back in his eyes. "Because when I come back, I'm going to take this country away from them."

He sounded sure of himself, but in truth, here in the middle of the night, he was filled with misgivings and doubts. Would he really be able to restore the monarchy? Would he get his family back into the position they'd lost twenty-five years before? Night whispers attacked his confidence and he had to fight them back.

Because he had to succeed. And he would, damn it, or die trying. No doubts could be allowed. His family belonged here and they would be back. This was what his whole life had been aimed at.

It was time to go. Actually, it was way past time to go, but he had run up against the wall by now. He had to follow the rules of logic and get out of here before someone showed up at Pellea's gate. It was just a matter of time.

But there was something else. He had made a decision. He was going to show Pellea the tunnel. There was no other option. If he couldn't take her with him, he had to give her some way to escape if things got too bad.

He was well aware of what he was doing—acting like a fool under the spell of a woman. If he were watching a friend in the same circumstances, he would be yelling, "Stop!" right now. Every bit of common sense argued against it. You just didn't risk your most important advantages like that.

After all, there were so many imponderables. Could he trust her? He was sure he could, and yet, how many men had said that and come out the loser in the end? Could he really take a woman who claimed she was going to marry into the family of the enemy and expect her to keep his confidences? Was he crazy to do this? He knew he was risking everything by placing a bet on her integrity and her fidelity—a bet that could be lost so easily. How many men had been destroyed putting too much trust in love?

For some reason the lyrics to "Blues in the Night" came drifting into his head. But who took their advice from old songs, anyway?

He had to trust her, because he had to protect her. There was nothing else he could do.

"Pellea," he said, taking her into his arms. "I'm going."

"Oh, thank God!" She held his face in her hands and looked at him with all the love she possessed. "I won't rest easy until you get to Italy."

He kissed her softly. "But I need you to do me a favor."

"Anything."

He was looking very serious. "I want you to keep a secret."

She smiled. "Another one?"

He touched her face and winced, as though she was

almost too beautiful to bear. "I'm going to show you how I get into the castle."

Her face lost its humor and went totally still. She understood right away how drastic this was for him. He'd refused even to hint at this to her all along. Now he was going to show her the one ace in the hole he had—the chink in the castle's armor. Her heart began to beat a bit faster. She knew very well that this was a heavy responsibility.

"All right," she said quietly. "And Monte, please don't worry. I will never, ever show this to anyone."

He looked at her and loved her, loved her noble face, loved her noble intentions. He knew she meant that with all her heart and soul, but he also knew that circumstances could change. Stranger things had happened. Still, he had to do it. He couldn't live with himself if he didn't leave behind some sort of escape route for her.

He frowned, thinking of what he was doing. It wouldn't be enough to show her where it was. The tunnel was old and dark and scary. He remembered when he'd first tried to negotiate it a few weeks before. He'd always known about it—it was the way he and his brothers had escaped on that terrible night all those years ago. And it had been immediately obvious no one had used it since. That was the benefit of having strangers take over your castle. If they made themselves hateful enough, no one would tell them the castle secrets.

When he'd come through, in order to pass he'd had to cut aside huge roots which had grown in through cracks. For someone like Pellea, it might be almost impassable.

It would be better if she came partway with him so that she would see what it was like and wouldn't be intimidated by the unknown.

"Bring a flashlight," he told her. "You're going to need it."

She followed him. He took her behind the fountain, behind the clump of ancient shrubs that seemed to grow right out of the rocks. He moved some smaller stones, then pushed aside a boulder that was actually made of pumice and was much lighter than it looked. And there, just underfoot, was a set of crumbling steps and a dank, dark tunnel that spiraled down.

"Here it is," he told her. "Think you can manage it?"

She looked down. It would be full of spiders and insects and slimy moss and things that would make her scream if she saw them. But she swallowed hard and nodded.

"Of course," she said, trying hard to sound nonchalant. "Let's go."

He showed her how to fill in the opening behind her, and then they started off. And it was just as unpleasant a journey as she'd suspected it would be. In twenty-five years, lots of steps had crumbled and roots had torn apart some walls. The natural breakdown of age was continuing apace and wouldn't be reversed until someone began maintaining the passageway. Even with a flashlight, the trip was dark and foreboding and she was glad she had Monte with her.

"Just ahead there is a small window," he told her. "We'll stop there and you can go back."

"All right," she said, shuddering to think what it was going to be like when she was alone.

"How are you feeling?" he said.

"Nauseated," she said before she thought. "But I'm always sick in the morning lately."

As soon as the words were past her lips she regretted them. How was it that she could feel so free and open to saying anything that came into her head when she was with him? And then she ended up saying too much. She glanced at him, wondering if he'd noticed.

He gave no sign of it. He helped her down the last set of stairs and there was the thin slit of a window, just beginning to show the dawn coming out over the ocean. They stopped and sat to rest. He pulled her close, tightening his arm around her and kissing her cheek.

She turned her face to accept his lips and he gave her more. Startled, she found in the heat of his mouth a quick arousal, calling up a passionate response from her that would have shocked her if she hadn't already admitted to herself that this man was all she ever wanted, body and soul. She drew back, breathless, heart racing and he groaned as she turned away.

"Pellea, you can't marry Leonardo. I don't care how much your father wants you to. It won't end up the way he hopes anyway. Nothing like that ever does. You can't sell your soul for security. It doesn't work."

"Monte, you don't really know everything. And you can't orchestrate things from afar. I've got to deal with the hand I've been dealt. You won't be here and you won't figure in. That's just the way it has to be."

"You don't understand. This is different. I'm making you a promise." He hesitated, steeling himself for what he had to do. "I'm going to move up operations. We'll invade by midsummer. I'll come and get you." He brushed the loose curls back from her face and looked at her with loving intensity. Here in the gloom, she was like a shining beacon in the dark.

"Leonardo's brand of protection won't do you any good by then. I'll be the one your father will have to look to."

His words struck fear into her heart. She turned, imploring him.

"No, Monte. You can't do that. You'll put yourself and all your men in danger if you try to come before your forces are ready. You can't risk everything just for me." She reached up and grabbed the front of his shirt in both hands. "I can't let you do that."

He gazed back steadily. "We'll have right and emotion on our side. We'll win anyway."

"Monte, don't be crazy. You know life doesn't work like that. Just being right, or good, or the nicest, doesn't win you a war. You need training and equipment and the manpower and…"

He was laughing at her and she stopped, nonplussed. "What is it?"

"You sound as though you've taken an army into the field yourself," he told her. "If I didn't know better, I would think you were a natural-born queen."

She flushed, not sure whether he was making fun of her. "I only know I want you safe," she said, her voice trembling a bit.

He took her into his arms. "I'll be safe. You're the one who needs protecting. You're the one ready to put your trust in the Granvillis."

She shook her head. "It's not like that," she said, but he wasn't listening.

He gazed at her, his blue eyes troubled. "I'll do anything I have to do to keep you from harm."

"You can't do it. You can't invade until you're ready."

"We'll get ready." He lifted her chin with his finger. "Just don't ruin everything by marrying Leonardo."

She turned away. Another wave of nausea was turning her breathless.

"What is it?" he said.

She shook her head. "I'm…I'm just a little sick."

He sat back a moment, watching her. "Have you been having that a lot lately?"

She couldn't deny it. She looked up and tried to make a joke out of it. "Yes. I imagine the situation in the world brings on nausea in most sane people at least once a day."

He frowned. "Possibly." A few bits of scattered elements came together and formed a thought. He remembered the way she seemed to want to protect her belly. The book at her bedside. The sudden aversion to alcohol. "Or maybe you're pregnant."

She went very still.

"Are you, Pellea? Are you pregnant?"

She paled, then tried to answer, but no words came out of her mouth.

"You are."

Suddenly the entire picture cleared for him. Of course. That explained everything—the reluctance to recreate the love they'd shared, the hurry to get him out of her hair, the rush to marry Leonardo. But something else was also clear. If she was pregnant, he had no doubt at all that the baby was his.

What the hell!

"You're pregnant with my baby and you weren't going to tell me about it?"

Outrage filled his voice and generated from his body. He shook his head, unable to understand how she could have done this. "And you plan to marry Leonardo?" he added in disbelief.

That rocked him back on his heels. He couldn't accept these things. They made no sense.

"Pellea…" He shook his head, unable to find the words to express how devastated he was…and angry.

She turned on him defensively. "I have to marry *some-one*," she said crisply. "And you aren't going to marry me, are you?"

She held her breath, waiting for his response to that one, hoping beyond all logic.

He stared at her, rage mixing with confusion. He couldn't marry her. Could he? But if she was carry-ing his child… This was something new, something he hadn't even considered. Did it change everything? Or was everything already set in stone and unchangeable?

He turned away, staring out at the ocean through the tiny window in the wall. She waited and watched the emotions crossing in his face and knew he wrestled with his feelings for her, his brand-new feelings for his child, and his role as the crown prince and a warrior king. He was torn, unprepared for such big questions all at once. She had to give him a bit of space. But she'd hoped for more. It wasn't like him to be so indecisive.

And, as he didn't seem to be able to find words that would heal things between them, her heart began to sink. What was the use of him telling her that they had to be together if he wasn't prepared to take the steps that might lead to something real? If he would never even consider making her his wife?

He had a lot of pride as the royal heir to Ambria. Well, she had a bit of pride herself. And she wasn't going anywhere without a promise of official status. If she wasn't good enough to marry, she would find another way to raise her child.

He turned back, eyes hard and cold as ice. "You have to come with me," he said flatly.

She was already shaking her head. "You know I can't go with you while my father lives."

Frustration filled his face and he turned away again, swearing softly. "I know," he said at last, his hands balled into fists. "And I can't ask you to abandon him."

"Never."

"But, Pellea, you have to listen…"

Whatever he was about to say was lost to history. An alarm went off like a bomb, echoing against the walls of the castle, shaking it to its foundations. They turned, reaching for each other, and then clinging together as the walls seemed to shake.

He looked questioningly at her. "What is it?" he asked her roughly.

"The castle alarm," she said. "Something must have happened. I haven't heard an alarm like this since…since Leonardo's mother died."

He stepped back, listening. "I thought for a moment it was an earthquake," he muttered, frowning. "Do you think…?"

"I don't know," she said, answering his unspoken question.

The alarm continued to sound. Pellea put her hands over her ears.

And just as suddenly as it had begun, it stopped. They stared at each other for a long moment.

"I'm going back," she said.

He nodded. He'd known she would. He had never wanted anything more strongly than he wanted her to come with him and yet he knew she couldn't do it. He was sunk in misery such as he'd never known before— misery in his own inability to control things. Misery in leaving behind all that he loved. And even the concept of a new baby that he would take some time to deal with.

"One more thing," he noted quickly. "Come here to the window." He waited while she positioned herself to look out. "Listen to me carefully. When you escape, wait until you get out into the sunlight, then look out across that wide, mowed field and you will see a small cottage that looks like something left over from a fairy tale. Go directly to it, ask for Jacob. I'll warn him that you may be coming. He will take you to the boat that will transfer you to the continent."

"If I escape," she amended softly, feeling hopeless.

He grasped her by the shoulders. "You will. One way or another, you will. And when you do, you'll come to me. Do you swear it?"

She nodded, eyes filling with tears.

"Say the words," he ordered.

"I swear I'll come to you," she said, looking up through her tears.

He stared into her eyes for a long moment, then kissed her.

"Goodbye," she said, pulling away and starting up the steps. "Good luck." She looked back and gave him a watery smile. "Until Ambria is free," she said, throwing him a kiss.

"Until Ambria is free," he saluted back. "I love you, Pellea," he called after her as she disappeared up the stairs. "And I love our baby," he whispered, but only to himself.

He would be back. He would come to claim what was his, in every way, or die trying. Cursing, he began to race down the stairs.

CHAPTER TEN

PELLEA GOT BACK without anyone knowing that she'd
been gone and she covered up the escape tunnel exactly
as Monte had in the past. She didn't find out what the
alarm had been about until Kimmee came by with her
breakfast.

"I guess the old General is really sick," she said,
slightly in awe. "Can you believe it? I thought that man
would be immortal. Anyway, someone went in to give
him his morning coffee and thought he was dead. So
they set off the alarm. Leonardo is furious."

"But he's not really dead."

"Not yet. But they say he's not far from it."

Despite everything, Pellea was upset. "How sad to
come all this way home after all this time without really
having a chance to see anyone he cares for," she said.

"Maybe," Kimmee said. "Or maybe," she whispered,
leaning close, "the meanness finally caught up with
him."

"Don't speak that way of the sick," Pellea said automatically, but inside, she agreed.

Still, she had a hard time dwelling on the sad condition

of the man who had been Ambria's leader for all her life. Mostly, she was thinking about Monte and his pledge to invade very soon, and she was sick at heart. She knew what danger he would be putting himself and his men in if he invaded now. If he did this just because of her and he was hurt—if anyone was hurt—she would never forgive herself.

Leonardo came by before noon. She went to meet him at the gate with her heart in her throat, wondering what he knew and what he was going to suspect. He looked like a man seriously hung-over and rather distracted by his current situation, but other than that, he seemed calm enough.

"Hello, my dear," he said. "I'm sure you've heard about my father."

"Yes. Leonardo, I'm so sorry."

"Of course, but it's not unexpected. He's been quite ill, you know. A lot worse than we'd told the people. It's a natural decline, I suppose. But for that moron to start the alarm as though he were dead!" He shook his head. "I've dealt with him." He slapped his gloves against his pant leg and looked at her sideways. "That was quite a night we had, wasn't it? I'm afraid we never did get around to announcing our engagement, did we?"

She realized he was asking her, as though he wasn't quite sure what had happened the night before. What on earth would she tell him? Nothing. That was by far the wisest course.

"No, we didn't," she said simply.

He studied her face. "Does that mean that the wedding is off?" he asked musingly.

She hesitated, not really sure what he wanted from her. "What do you think?" she asked him.

He made a face. "I think there was someone at the ball who you would rather marry," he said bluntly.

"Oh, Leonardo," she began.

But he cut her off. "Never mind, darling. We'll have to deal with this later. Right now I've got my hands full. I've got my father's ill health to come to terms with. And then there are the plans for succession."

"Why? What's going on?"

"You haven't heard?"

"No. Tell me."

"You know that my father arrived last night. They brought him in from France. I hadn't seen him for weeks. I didn't realize…" He stopped and rubbed his eyes. "My father is a vegetable, Pellea. I'm going to have to file for full custodial rights. And every little faction in the castle is sharpening its little teeth getting ready to try to grab its own piece of power." He shook his head. "It's a nightmare."

"Oh, Leonardo, I'm so sorry."

"Yes. It's all on me now, my sweet. I don't know if I have time for a marriage. Sorry."

Leonardo shrugged and turned to leave, his mind on other things. Pellea watched him go and sighed with relief. That was one hurdle she wasn't going to have to challenge at any rate.

Not that it left her in the clear. She was still pregnant.

She was still without a husband. What would become of her and her baby? She closed her eyes, took a deep breath and forced herself to focus. She had to think. It was time to find some new answers.

Pellea went to sit with her father later that day. He was much better. She wasn't sure what the doctor had given him, but she could see that his mind was clear once again and she was grateful.

She chatted with him for a few minutes and then he surprised her with a pointed question.

"Who was that man who was here yesterday?" he asked.

"The doctor?" she tried evasively.

"No. The other man. The one I momentarily mistook for King Grandor."

She took in a deep breath. "It was his son, the crown prince. It was Monte DeAngelis."

"Monte?" He almost smiled. "Oh, yes, of course it was Monte. I remember him well. A fine, strapping lad he was, too." He shook his head. "I'm so glad to see that he survived."

She paused, then decided to let honesty rule the day. "He makes a pretty good grown man as well," she said quietly.

"Yes." His gaze flickered up to smile at her. "I saw him kissing you."

"Oh." It seemed her father hadn't been as out of it as she had supposed. Well, good. He might as well know the truth. Did she have the nerve to go on with the honesty? Why not? What did she have to lose at this point?

"I'm in love with him, Father. And I'm carrying his child."

There. What more was there to say? She waited, holding her breath.

He closed his eyes and for a moment she was afraid what she'd said was too much for him.

"I'm so sorry, Father," she said, leaning over him. "Please forgive me."

"There's nothing to forgive," he said, opening his eyes and smiling at her. "Not for you at any rate. I would assume this is going to put an end to my plans for you to marry Leonardo."

She shook her head, sorry to disappoint him. "I'm afraid so."

He frowned. "The powers that be won't like it."

"No."

For the next few minutes he was lost in thought. She tidied things in the room and got him a fresh bottle of water. And finally, he took her hand and told her what he wanted to do next.

"I'd like to see the doctor," he said, his voice weak but steady. "I think we'd better make some plans. I'm about to leave this life, but I want to do something for you before I go."

"No, Father, you don't have to do anything more for me. You've done everything for me my whole life. It's enough. Just be well and stay alive for as long as you can. I need you."

He patted her hand. "That is why I need the doctor. Please see if you can get him right away."

She drew in her breath, worried. "I'll go right now."

The doctor came readily enough. He'd always been partial to Pellea and her father. After he talked to the older man, he nodded and said, "I'll see if I can pull some strings."

"Good," her father said once he was gone. "Leonardo will have his work cut out for him fighting off all the factions that will try to topple his new rule. He doesn't have time to think about me. I'm of no use to him now anyway and in no condition to help him." He took his daughter's hand in his and smiled at her. "The doctor will get me permission to go to the continent to see a specialist. And I'll need you to go along as one of my nurses."

"What?" She could hardly believe her ears. They were going to the continent. Just like that. Could it really be this easy?

"Are you willing?" he asked her.

"Oh, Father!" Pellea's eyes filled with tears and her voice was choked. "Father, you are saving my life."

Arriving in Italy two days later, Pellea was more nervous than ever. She wanted to see Monte again, but she was afraid of what she would find when she did. After all, how many times and in how many ways had he told her that he would never marry her? She knew there wasn't much hope along those lines.

And there was more. She knew very well that the

excitement of a clandestine affair was one thing. The reality of a pregnant woman knocking on the door was another. He might very well have decided she wasn't worth the effort by the time he got home. Was that possible? She didn't like to think so, but reality could be harsh and cold.

Still, one thing was certain. She had to go to him. She had to let him know that she was not in danger any longer, that she was not marrying Leonardo, and that her well-being was not a reason to launch an invasion. She was no longer in Ambria and no longer in need of any sort of rescue. The last thing in the world she wanted was to be the catalyst for a lot of needless killing.

She'd left her father in a clinic in Rome and she'd traveled a few hours into the mountains to the little town of Piasa where she knew Ambrian ex-patriots tended to gather. She found his hotel, and with heart beating wildly, she went to the desk and asked for him.

"He's not seeing visitors, miss," the concierge told her. "Perhaps if you left your name…"

How could she leave her name? She wasn't staying anywhere he would be able to find her. She turned away from the hotel desk in despair, losing hope, wondering where she could go.

And then, there he was, coming out of an elevator with two other men, laughing at something someone had said. Joy surged in her heart, but so did fear, and when he looked up and saw her, her heart fell. He didn't look happy to see her. He seemed almost annoyed.

He excused himself from the other men and came

toward her. He didn't smile. Instead, he pressed a room key into her hand.

"Go to room twenty-five and wait for me," he told her softly. Then he turned on his heel and went back to the men, immediately cracking a joke that made them laugh uproariously, one even glancing back at where she stood. Had he told them why she was here? Was he making fun of her? Her cheeks flamed crimson and, for just a moment, she was tempted to throw the key in his face and storm out.

Luckily, she calmed down quickly. There was no way she could know what he'd said to the other men, or even what he was thinking. He might have needed some sort of ruse to maintain his situation. She had no way of knowing and it would be stupid of her to make assumptions. Taking a deep breath, she headed for the elevator.

She found her way to the room, and despite her sensible actions, she was still numb with shock at the way he'd acted. Just as she'd feared, he was another person entirely when he wasn't in the castle of Ambria. What was next? Was he going to hand her money to get lost? And if he did that, how would she respond? She was sick at heart. This wasn't what she'd hoped for.

She paced the room for a few minutes, but she was so tired. After a few longing looks at his bed, she gave in to temptation and lay down for a rest. Very quickly, she fell asleep.

But not for long. The next thing she knew, someone was lying next to her on the bed and kissing her ear.

"Oh!" she said, trying to get up.

But it was no use. Monte was raining down kisses all over her and she began to laugh.

"What are you doing?"

"Some people welcome with flowers," he told her with a sweet, slow grin. "I do it with kisses. Now lie still and take it like a woman."

She giggled as he dropped even more kisses on her. "Monte! Cut it out. I'm going to get hysterical."

"Do you promise?"

"No! I mean… Oh, you know what I mean."

He did, and he finally stopped, but his hand was covering her belly. "Boy or girl?" he asked her softly.

She smiled up at him, happiness tingling from every inch of her. "I don't know yet."

"It's hard to believe."

She nodded. "Just another miracle," she said. "Are you happy about it?"

He stared into her eyes for a long moment before answering, and she was starting to worry about just what his answer was going to be, when he spoke.

"*Happy* isn't a strong enough word," he told her simply. "I feel something so strong and new, I don't know what the word is. But there's a balloon of wonderfulness in my chest and it keeps getting bigger and bigger. It's as though a new world has opened at my feet." He shrugged. "And now that you're here, everything is good."

She sighed. "I was worried. The way you looked when you saw me…"

"In public you'll find I am one person, Pellea. In

private, quite another. It's a necessary evil that someone in my position has to be so careful all the time." He
traced her lips with his finger. "But with you, I promise
always to be genuine. You'll always know the real me,
good or bad."

She was listening, and it was all very nice, but she
still hadn't heard certain words she was waiting for. She
told him about what had happened at the castle, and
how she had accompanied her father for his visit to the
specialist.

"I hope they can do something for him," she said.

"Does he plan to go back?"

"Oh, I'm sure he does. His life is in Ambria."

He nodded thoughtfully. "You're not going back," he
said, as though he had the last word in the decision.

"Really?" She raised an eyebrow. "And just what is
going to keep me here?"

"I am."

She waited. There should be more to that statement.
But he frowned as though he was thinking about something else. She was losing her patience.

"I've got to get back to my father," she said, rising
from the bed and straightening her clothing.

Monte rose as well. "I'm going with you," he said
firmly.

She looked up at him in surprise. "But…you hate
him."

"No." He shook his head. "I hate the man he used to
be. I don't hate the man he is today."

"You think he's changed?"

"I think we all have." He pulled her close. "And anyway, there are no good jewelers here in Piasa. I need to go to Rome. I need a larger city to find a real artist."

"Why would you want a jeweler?"

"I need a good copy made."

"Of the tiara?" She scrunched up her face, trying to figure out what he would want that for.

"In a way. I'd like to find someone who could reproduce the main part of the tiara as…" He smiled at her. "…as an engagement ring."

Her eyes widened. "Oh."

He kissed her on the mouth. "Would you wear a ring like that?"

And suddenly she felt as though she were floating on a cloud of happiness. "I don't know. It would depend on who gave it to me."

"Good answer." And he kissed her again, then took her two hands in his and smiled down at her. "I love you, Pellea," he said, his feelings shining in his eyes. "My love for you is bigger than revenge, bigger than retribution, bigger than the wounds of the past. I'm going to take care of all those things in good time. I'm going to get my country back. And when I take over, I want you with me, as my queen. Will you be my wife?"

She drew in a full breath of air and laughed aloud. There they were. Those were the words she'd been waiting for.

"Yes, Monte," she said, reaching for the man she loved, joy surging in her. "With all my heart and soul."

LET'S TALK

For exclusive extracts, competitions
and special offers, find us online:

 facebook.com/millsandboon

🐦 @MillsandBoon

📷 @MillsandBoonUK

Get in touch on 01413 063232

For all the latest titles coming soon, visit
millsandboon.co.uk/nextmonth

MILLS & BOON
A ROMANCE FOR EVERY READER

- **FREE** delivery direct to your door

- **EXCLUSIVE** offers every month

- **SAVE** up to 25% on pre-paid subscriptions

SUBSCRIBE AND SAVE

millsandboon.co.uk/Subscribe

WANT EVEN MORE
ROMANCE?
SUBSCRIBE AND SAVE TODAY!

'Mills & Boon books, the perfect way to escape for an hour or so.'

MISS W. DYER

'Excellent service, promptly delivered and very good subscription choices.'

MISS A. PEARSON

'You get fantastic special offers and the chance to get books before they hit the shops.'

MRS V. HALL

Visit millsandboon.co.uk/Subscribe
and save on brand new books.

JOIN THE
MILLS & BOON
BOOKCLUB

* **FREE** delivery direct to your door

* **EXCLUSIVE** offers every month

* **EXCITING** rewards programme

50% OFF
YOUR FIRST
PARCEL

Join today at
Millsandboon.co.uk/Bookclub

MILLS & BOON

THE HEART OF ROMANCE

A ROMANCE FOR EVERY KIND OF READER

MODERN

Prepare to be swept off your feet by sophisticated, sexy and seductive heroes, in some of the world's most glamourous and romantic locations, where power and passion collide.
8 stories per month.

HISTORICAL

Escape with historical heroes from time gone by. Whether your passion is for wicked Regency Rakes, muscled Vikings or rugged Highlanders, awaken the romance of the past.
6 stories per month.

MEDICAL

Set your pulse racing with dedicated, delectable doctors in the high-pressure world of medicine, where emotions run high and passion, comfort and love are the best medicine.
6 stories per month.

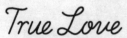

Celebrate true love with tender stories of heartfelt romance, from the rush of falling in love to the joy a new baby can bring, and a focus on the emotional heart of a relationship.
8 stories per month.

Indulge in secrets and scandal, intense drama and plenty of sizzling hot action with powerful and passionate heroes who have it all: wealth, status, good looks…everything but the right woman.
6 stories per month.

HEROES

Experience all the excitement of a gripping thriller, with an intense romance at its heart. Resourceful, true-to-life women and strong, fearless men face danger and desire - a killer combination!
8 stories per month.

DARE

Sensual love stories featuring smart, sassy heroines you'd want as a best friend, and compelling intense heroes who are worthy of the
4 stories per month.

To see which titles are coming soon, please visit

millsandboon.co.uk/nextmonth